The Enchanted Life of
ADAM HOPE

RHONDA RILEY

The Enchanted Life

of

ADAM HOPE

ecco

An Imprint of HarperCollinsPublishers

HarperCollins books may be purchased for educational, business, or sales promotional use. For information please write: Special Markets Department, HarperCollins Publishers, 10 East 53rd Street, New York, NY 10022.

FIRST EDITION

Designed by Janet M. Evans
Title page photograph © Lightscribe/Dreamstime.com

Library of Congress Cataloging-in-Publication Data has been applied for.

ISBN 978-0-06-209944-0

13 14 15 16 17   OV/RRD   10 9 8 7 6 5 4 3 2 1

For my mother, Sarah Louise Riley Auten Thomas, who was an exquisite and fortunate fit for me. I offer this as repayment for the stories she told on the front porch during countless summer evenings. She left too early. I am still listening.

This story is for her—a fiction, because, like her, I could not tell the whole truth or a single truth whole.

CONTENTS

ONE

THE LAND

My husband was not one of us. He remains, after decades, a mystery to me. Inexplicable. Yet, in many ways, and on most days, he was an ordinary man.

With him I learned that, before all mysteries, surrender is inevitable. We all give way to our true natures. This is his story. It is, of course, also my story, for I am the one left to do the telling.

Now finally, after decades, I am writing this down for my daughters, for their children and the children after them, the act of writing my atonement for all I have not told them. Until now. For now I have proof. Sweet, indisputable proof.

Sarah, our youngest daughter, sent me a photograph weeks ago, a full year since she moved to China with her husband, Jian, and their son, Michael. In it, her hair is glossy dark brown and straight. Her eyes are a deep brown as well, and the folds of her eyelids now suggest Asian ancestry. Her curly red hair and gold-flecked green Irish eyes are gone; in her new skin, she is her father's daughter. Lil, my daughter who lives with me now, insists that Sarah must have had plastic surgery and dyed her hair. She's puzzled and disappointed that her sister would take such measures to fit in where she now lives. But I know the truth.

❦

THIS TRUTH BEGINS ON a Saturday in 1944. I was fresh out of high school and already tired of working at the cotton mill when I heard our car pull up in the backyard. Then Momma trudged through the door, hard news on her face.

Without taking her coat off, she slumped down into one of the dining chairs. She stared at the table, then opened her mouth as if to speak. I propped the iron up.

Every day brought news of boys missing or dead in the war. Momma and Daddy had been visiting my widowed aunt Eva. Two of Eva's three sons were already dead. The third, Ricky, was overseas after lying about his age to sign up with the army. I braced myself, expecting Momma to announce Eva's remaining child among them. Instead, she closed her mouth, hung her head, and covered her eyes as Daddy paused on the back porch to wipe his feet.

"It's your aunt Eva, Evelyn. She's gone," he said.

Then Momma began to cry in earnest. Aunt Eva, the baby sister of my grandmother, was in spirit, if not in fact, the matriarch of our family. Closer to Momma than her own mother had been.

I unplugged the iron as Daddy went to find my sisters, Rita and Bertie.

"It's okay, Momma. It'll be okay." I rubbed her back. I loved my stern and demanding aunt Eva. I could not imagine her energy stilled by death and the farm left empty. But I sensed, even then, that this change was larger than a single death, that it would radiate out from this single point.

Daddy returned, shepherding my sisters into the kitchen. Bertie held out a handkerchief for Momma. Rita blinked nervously. Tears were rare for our mother.

Momma wiped her face and sighed a deep, shuddering sigh. "I knew something must have been wrong. She hadn't been into town in over a week. She always . . ."

I started to sit down again and reached for Momma's hand.

Daddy stopped me. "You're going to the farm with me. Eva's cows haven't been milked."

I didn't want to leave Momma, but he was right. I was the one who should go with him. My brother, Joe, had no interest in the farm. Bertie had never deigned to touch a cow's teat, and any animal larger than a house cat intimidated Rita. I knew Aunt Eva's farm better than I knew my own bedroom. I followed Daddy to the car and slid in beside him.

"Probably a heart attack," he said. "I don't think she suffered. Your momma found her on the parlor couch, pictures of her boys next to her."

He offered no more and I didn't ask. We had never been much for words, the two of us. I looked out at the houses we passed. Eva was gone. A wave of anger surged through me. I tried to console myself with the hard practical thought that the natural death of an old woman was better than one more boy dead.

Daddy muttered, cursing the roughness of the steep driveway and downshifting the old Ford.

"The coroner's here," Daddy announced as we pulled around behind the house. Eva's dog, Hobo, barked a welcome then retreated. Two men slid Eva's sheet-covered body, strapped down as if she might get away, into the back of an open ambulance. Daddy got out of the car and greeted a man in a suit, who approached us holding some papers. I walked away from their voices, turning my back on the face of Eva's house and its door propped open like a gaping mouth.

The plow horse, Becky, whinnied and pawed as soon as I opened the barn door. Eva's three cows bellowed. Their bags hung heavily, enormous and painfully pink. Manure soured by too much urine lay over the normal sweet barn smell. I started first with Maybell, the cantankerous one, working my hands gently along her bag, checking for lumps. For once, she seemed grateful for the milking.

Only then, leaning against her warm, firm side, listening to the rhythm of milk hit the tin bucket, breathing the sweetness of it rising, did I begin to cry for the woman who had taught me to milk. I cried for her and for what the war had taken. All those boys dead, a new one in the newspaper every day. Now the war was taking my refuge, the farm. It had fallen into such neglect. That would not have happened just with the death of Uncle Lester. It took the war biting off one son at a time until there were none.

Since I'd been old enough to carry a bucket or wield a hoe, I had done my best to help Eva. But blinded by grief, she had let the place go. A dull darkness slipped over me as if, in her death, Eva's sorrows had shifted to my shoulders.

After a few minutes, Daddy joined me. He snorted in disgust and stomped the manure off his shoes, then set to work on Beulah next to me. He offered nothing more about Eva's death. He hated the farm. He had grown up poor on a farm and had vowed never to go back to one. I couldn't see that we were any better off, the six of us living paycheck to paycheck crowded into the tiny mill-village house, but Daddy trusted the steady income of the textile mills. To him, farmers were a lot to be pitied. "Farmers are at the mercy of nature's whims," he liked to say. We finished the milking and started the feeding. While Daddy watered the hogs and chickens, I went into the house, drawn to it now that the coroner was gone. I pulled the screen door closed. Eva hated flies getting in the house. The stove was cold and held the same stillness that permeated the house. A saucer sat on the table, a half-eaten square of corn bread on it, a cup of coffee next to it, a spoon left in the cup. Such a puny breakfast—nothing like the ham, eggs, and biscuits she had always made for Uncle Lester, her boys, and me. I took the dishes to the sink and put them down soundlessly, not wanting to disturb the silence. I lay my hand on the pump handle, letting the cool of it into my palm. Through the window over the sink, I saw Daddy, bent at the hog pen, emptying a bucket of water into the trough. I imagined Aunt Eva behind me at the table, overwhelmed by a sudden urge to see her boys and, taking uncharacteristic leave of her breakfast and chores, going to look at their pictures in the parlor. Or had she known what was coming and decided to die there with them?

I followed her path down the dark-wood hall past the bedrooms. A stench surprised me before I got to the parlor. I sucked in my breath and I turned my head, but kept going. Her bedroom door stood open, the bed neatly made. She'd gotten that far. On the front porch, the rocking chairs sat motionless. I stood out at the edge of the yard where the land dropped to the railroad tracks. The air was calm and empty.

Then I felt the train, first in my feet—that faint, familiar vibration. The 5:40 out of Charlotte heading for the mill. I leapt and waved as the engine chugged rhythmically into sight, bursting into the air. I gave the engineer the bent-armed sign and pumped my elbow up and down. He saluted and obliged: two sharp blasts. The force reverberated in my breastbone, and I was a little girl for a moment, laughing and bouncing on my feet. The roar of the train swelled into a moving wall of sound as the long line of freight cars passed below. The ground shook.

The roar diminished as the train disappeared toward the mill and the quiet returned.

When Daddy called, I followed his voice to the parlor. He had maneuvered the sofa to the door and waited for my help. "It's ruined. She must have lost control in the end."

I held my hand up to shush him, a gesture my father normally would not have accepted from one of his children. I picked up my end and we worked the sofa down the hall. The smell was awful. Even in the dim light, the dark stain that ran half the length of the sofa was visible.

I kept my eyes on Daddy. Moving furniture was something he would normally do with my brother. Outside of his work at the mill, he was sedentary with his pipe and his rocking chair, already middle-aged, though still in his thirties. His strength and competence as we carried the big sofa through the kitchen surprised and pleased me. Sweat stuck my dress to my back by the time we got the heavy old sofa outside and, turning from the sight and smell of it, dropped it on the hard, bare clay beside the back porch.

A few minutes later, we drove away in the glow of the dashboard light. The dark shapes of trees slipped by in the dusk. I glanced at my father. His hands were on the wheel. Immutable and endlessly taciturn, he peered at the road ahead.

All my life, I had heard stories about my mother, both from her and her family. Illustrations of her stellar memory for numbers, her sly stubbornness, or her random gullibility. My youngest sister, Rita, pale and skittish as a feral cat, had always been transparent to me. Bertie, three years younger, was more complex but guileless and always willing to announce what was on her mind. My brother, Joe, born only eleven months after me and resembling Daddy as much as I resembled Momma, I knew in the thoughtless, unconscious way one knows a close sibling.

My father was a different story. I sometimes saw him laughing with other men, but at home he sat detached, his face vague behind the smoke of his pipe. Only blatant insubordination or dangerous stupidity on the part of us kids could animate him into flashes of authority. I never heard him tell a story.

Riding home from Eva's, I glanced at him again. I wanted something from him, some sign of being touched by the same loss, a token of kinship. But we did not even look like kin. I had red, wavy hair and freckles. Like all the women of my mother's family, I was tall. He was clear-skinned and compact, his dark hair straight.

We drove home in silence.

AFTER THE FUNERAL, Momma and I crowded into the small basement of the farmhouse, pulling dusty jars of Eva's beans, jams, and relishes off the shelves, sniffing and checking them to make sure they were still good. The small room smelled of mold and dust. Shelves of jars lined each wall.

"This farm kept us alive during the Depression," Momma said. From her tone, I knew this was not idle chatter.

For me, the Depression was the dim past of my early childhood. I thought instead of how the war—which, at first, had seemed like a big, bright party—was taking everything. I had done my share for the war effort: helped neighbors in their victory gardens, donated my pennies, and collected cans, newspaper, toothpaste tubes, and grease. But these seemed like such small things. In the year before her death, when I should have been helping Eva, I'd worked the mill instead, standing in deafening noise, watching the birth of thread for the war effort. At night, I'd pulled cotton from my hair and the creases of my neck. In the mornings, I pinned my underwear to my skirts because all the rubber for elastic went to the war.

Momma raised her voice to get my attention. "Careful, Evelyn. We don't have rations for more jars." She motioned for me to remove the jars from the next shelf. "During the Depression everybody helped everybody else. And we traded what we could. But it was Eva and Lester who gave us the most, and they could afford to only because they had the farm. You kids didn't get so skinny or quiet as some did."

She stopped dusting, as if expecting an answer, then continued, "Land's a terrible thing to waste, Evelyn. We've felt the lack of Eva's work this year. Your brother and sisters are still growing. The government didn't have growing kids in mind when it started the rationing."

I understood then where she was going.

"We need at least a good garden crop this coming spring. Somebody needs to tend the house and barn, slop the hogs, and milk the cows.

This war will be over one day and we don't know how things will be then. Jobs can be lost. Wages can go down. But land will keep giving, if you work it. We may need every ounce this farm can give."

Through the small, cobwebbed basement window, I saw the apple tree and the wild brown tangle of the roses Eva had abandoned in her grief.

"We'll all come up to help. Until your cousin Ricky gets back—if he gets back—it's this or the mill, Evelyn."

We looked at each other. I was seventeen. It was 1944. I was a farmer.

We went outside to watch Joe and Daddy burn the stuffing and upholstery they had pulled off the sofa Eva died on. Momma held her hand up to shade her eyes, as if the fire was the sun, as if restricting her vision would diminish the stench of burning horse hair, the loss of her aunt.

"I know we are all flesh—as much as the hogs and chickens we eat. And we go to dust. But it was hard finding her that way. A hard reminder," Momma said softly as she stepped sideways to loop her arm through Daddy's.

Though I wasn't cold, I stood near the fire and held my hands out to its heat. The smoke wafted up. Parts of Eva were in that fire and smoke—probably a hair or two from her head, a sliver of fingernail, a thread from one of her dresses, along with what had drained out of her while she lay dead on the sofa. All of that rose above us, spread out, and joined the sky.

The next day was a Sunday. After supper, I carefully packed my clothes, my Bible, and the few possessions that I did not share with my siblings. Everything I owned fit into a bushel basket and two small suitcases.

Momma walked me to the car, carrying the last suitcase. Daddy waited, the motor running. She took my arm as she slid the suitcase into the backseat. "You'll be fine, Evelyn. The land on Eva's farm is tough, but better than most of the farms around here, and you know that farm better than you know your own bedroom. Eva always told me how hard you worked. Your daddy or I will come up with your brother and sisters every Saturday to help you. Sundays you'll be at church and then have supper here." She kissed my cheek.

I hated the monotony of the mill work and was happy to leave it, but the farm was now the means to fulfill a responsibility, not the solace it had once been. Later that evening, I folded my clothes and put them away in the newly emptied wardrobe Aunt Eva and Uncle Lester had shared for decades.

Soon, it became clear to me how much of Eva's work I had taken for granted. The stove was cold when I got up in the mornings, the kitchen pump stiff or frozen. I had to do the milking and feeding both morning and night. The garden needed to be revived. The dead were a heavy absence.

Not long after I moved onto the farm, a man in uniform showed up at the back door, his hand raised, ready to knock when I spotted him. Before he spoke, I knew the news. Ricky wasn't coming back; my laughing blond cousin was gone. There was no son to take over the farm.

The farm had always been *the farm* to my family. It lay an hour's walk outside of Clarion, and about twenty-five miles from Charlotte, North Carolina, where the rest of my family, the Roes and the McMurroughs, lived. If you took Clear Lake Road from the mill and, when it veered west, continued up the narrow dirt road ahead, you crossed a creek. Then the simple clapboard house appeared perched on a small cliff formed by the railroad cutaway. At the end of the steep driveway, between the well-kept, generous barn and the creek, were Aunt Eva's three-acre kitchen garden of table vegetables, herbs, and her one frivolity—tea roses. East of the barn were the smokehouse and the outhouse. A lone tart apple tree graced the barnyard. Just past it, the land took one more short step on its rise toward the Appalachians and then settled into 150 acres of blessedly flat fields. It was open land, seemingly without mystery, clad in the same hard, demanding red clay found throughout the Southeast. If you squatted to take a handful of that soil, you would feel its strength, smell its clean sweetness, and know that it would give back if given to.

Clarion, where I was born and lived with my parents, Robert and Lily Roe, was a one-business town. Narrow streets hugged the Lenford cotton mill, and the identical, mill-owned houses of the neighborhood everyone called the mill-village stood in curved rows. Not long out of the Appalachian hills, the mill workers who lived there were a rough, hardworking people, mostly Protestant and Sunday-school literate. They had lost their Celtic accents and immigrant hope for prosperity long before they came to the cotton mill-village for the luxury of electricity, indoor plumbing, and a weekly paycheck. During World War II, they bent to the rhythm of their work, seven days a week, in shifts that spanned the clock.

Clarion was not a tolerant community. Racism was the most glaring intolerance, but even small differences were noted. My father was known for his unusual habit of smoking a pipe as he pushed the dope wagon through the mill, selling the candies, colas, and tobaccos that helped the mill hands keep the stupor of their work at bay. What set my mother, my sisters, and me apart from everyone else was our height—even the women in the family were near six feet—and our copper-red hair from the McMurroughs, my mother's side of the family. I was teased without mercy for what I could not control. The public library and the farm were my escapes.

I had hardly been more than a toddler when I first wandered away from our mill-village home. Dual lines of flapping sheets hid me from Momma's sight while I made my getaway, past the streets and the other houses, across a meadow and through woods to a creek. Nothing beyond the meadow was familiar. The rapid purl of creek water made a comforting sound, sweeter than the noise of the mill and the chattering voices. Ferns lined the narrow bank of the creek, some open-handed, others still furled tight. Overhead, in the cathedral of the bright spring canopy, a woodpecker rapped. I sat on a tree root and watched pale butterflies siphon water from the sand. An owl's bell-shaped call rose, then fell. I was happy. I was at the center of the universe, certain I had found the place where everything began.

A low branch lifted nearby, and my mother, stooping to go under it, emerged. She stepped out, scanning the underbrush and the creek, her face knotted in concern. A lock of her red hair caught on the branch behind her. I followed her glance down the creek but saw nothing unusual. Then she screamed my name and ran toward me.

I bolted, slid across a flat rock, and plunged neck-deep into icy water. Scrambling to the opposite bank, I choked on a mouthful. Momma scooped me up and turned me toward her, shaking me. Instead of scolding, she stared at me as I dangled, dripping in her extended arms. Wordlessly, she looked me over as if I was an unexpected stranger, a child she had never seen before. For one terrible moment, my mother did not know me.

Then she clutched me to her chest, her face inches from mine, fear in her eyes, an old, large fear. Her whole face opened into a wail and she crushed my head against her breasts. Her hand covered my ear, pressing me into the cacophony of her sobs and heartbeat, inside her sweet, milky odors. She stumbled back through the woods, clutching me. I could not have been more than three years old.

After that, the world began its split into twos: the spoken and unspoken, the known and unknown, home and not home, my mother and myself. Curiosity locked into my soul and put me at the edge of my tribe, an observer more than a participant, scouring the land for words and clues.

I was still very young, not in school yet, the first time I made my way to the farm by myself. Unsure of the route that appeared different, more spacious, without my family, I hiked from familiar point to familiar point. Then, there it was: the house on top of the hill. Following the narrow road up and around to the barn, I presented myself to Eva, who stood at a chest-high trellis of roses.

"I was wondering when you'd make it up here on your own. Figured you'd show up one day," she said. Then she did something she had never done before. She knelt and took my hand.

I was a well-cared-for child, and so took those who cared for me for granted. Adults were simply part of a world that moved to rhythms and needs invisible to me. Large boots or full skirts to stay out of the way of.

As Eva knelt in front of me, sunlight glinting in her clear green eyes, she took me in with a long, assessing gaze. It was as if she had stepped out of the vague ether of the adult world into a full and separate being before me. The sweetness of her tea roses surrounded us. For the first time in my life, I was conscious of loving another person.

So it was I who became compensation for Eva's lack of a daughter and my labor on the farm payment for the cans, baskets, and sacks full of food that Eva and Lester brought down the hill to my family.

On the farm, my three older cousins called me Little Sis. There, I could forget the children in the mill-village who teased me about my height and my bright red hair. I slept on a cot in the corner of the parlor. With no little sisters to complain about the lantern's glare, I could read as late as I wanted. I learned to chop wood, sew, milk cows, cure hams, make butter, sauerkraut, and biscuits, bleach apples, store or preserve almost anything, and to make a toothbrush out of a hickory stick. Eva combed out my hair in the evenings and told me I should be proud of its new-penny brilliance.

Each time I came up the hill and saw the house, its front half shaded by the chinaberry tree, the farm seemed full of possibilities and far from the drab mill-village. My love for the farm set me further apart from my peers. While other children were fascinated with everything modern and aware of the deprivations of the Depression, I collected eggs and churned butter by hand and thought myself privileged, wealthy. It was a good place to be a child, the best place to be a child during the Depression.

During my first months alone on the farm after Eva's death, I thought of these two events frequently—my mother's pained gaze in the woods and my first solo trek to visit Aunt Eva. They seemed the first points in a line that led me to where I now was as the farm's caretaker. Gradually, I also came to realize how much freedom and trust my parents had always given me. A kind of special dispensation. While other girls my age, particularly those with younger siblings, had been kept home with chores, I had been allowed to wander.

At times, I felt guilty about the pleasures I took on the farm while the suffering of war persisted. But I relished the luxury of my solitude. I worked hard. I ate when I was hungry. I took naps in the barn and, on one particularly cold night, made myself a pallet on the kitchen table and slept there to soak in the dying warmth of the stove. Whole days passed in which I saw only my neighbors, Mildred or one of the McAverys, when I took the eggs down the hill to them. Some days, I saw no one at all.

Having never had so much as a closet of my own, I now had a whole house, a whole quiet house. At night, cranky Bertie wasn't there pulling quilts off me as I slept. Rita didn't kick me in her sleep or wake me up because she heard some little noise. No radio blaring, no doors slamming. No neighbors arguing.

Privacy also had its smaller, vulgar privileges. Alone, I cursed out loud. I checked my armpits and crotch to find out if it was time for the trouble of drawing a bath in a house without indoor plumbing. Momma never would have tolerated such. On the first warm night of 1945, I slept naked, something I'd never done before. Moonlight spread across the sheets and over my bare belly, a thing not possible in a Baptist house with sisters crowded in a bed.

Later that year, when the Germans surrendered, the whole mill fell silent. Then a cheer burst from the office and rolled through the workers who ran outside, whooping and hollering, kissing and hugging each other. Kids poured out of the schools. I wasn't there. Everyone told me about it later.

But up on the farm, I heard the car horns blasting. Church bells clanged. The mill horn blew as if calling God Himself to the cotton. I stopped mucking the barn stalls and dashed outside to the road. Louellen McAvery, who lived down the hill, knelt in the middle of Clear Lake Road, praying. Her boy, Tom, was still overseas. When she finished with God, she jumped up, danced a little jig, and waved to me, shouting. The war was over!

I jumped and ran back to the barn to tell—tell who? The chickens? The cows? The chickens, the sky, the barn were all the same, as indifferent to the end of the war as they had been to the war itself. I stopped halfway across the yard. The land I had worked stretched out before me and the blind sky above.

The horns and bells continued. The people celebrating below were people I knew. I knew their sons far away at war or fresh in their graves. They'd eaten the beans and corn my family grew and brought them back to us in heaped bowls when someone got sick, or died. The boy who would dig my grave was probably out there among those cheering.

We were under the same sky, breathing the same air. All of us. And not just us. The Germans and the Japanese, too.

In the months after the victory of war, a stunned quiet followed, then the town leapt into optimistic giddiness. Everyone everywhere seemed relieved, fatigued, excited. The world seemed wide-open. At church, at the feed store, in the shops downtown, and on the streets of the mill-village, expectation and relief blossomed into robust intent. Any moment things could burst out of themselves. I felt it in the long bones and muscles of my arms and legs.

Even in the quiet of Sunday morning, returned to us now that the war was over and the mill no longer ran seven days a week, I woke aware of the people down the hill, my family still warm in their beds, sleeping the sound sleep of victors.

Downtown one Saturday, I saw a woman open a newspaper. The headline declared the liberation of the death camps. The photograph showed gaunt, skeletal Jews. She studied the front page and crossed herself.

A violent scorn rose up in me. "Fool," I thought. "You have the same God as the Germans." I imagined a Nazi crossing himself before he turned on the gas.

I stood outside Bun's Café, about to cross the street. Then, like a slap, the thought came: I, too, had the same God as the Nazis. I stepped away and turned my back to the busy street. I saw my face mirrored in the window of the café. The reflection of a passing car slid over the backs of the men eating inside at the counter. They were—we all were—Christians. Good Christian people.

A door shut in my mind. My heart tilted.

I kept that moment, running my hands over the worry stone of it. Church was not the same after that. I sat at the same pew every Sunday. My family expected me to be there and I did not want to disappoint my mother, but my throat could not be open as it had once been to those old familiar hymns.

A few weeks later, one rare day when I had finished my morning chores early, I took my lunch and walked down to Clear Lake. A snake the color of the water undulated near the shore, barely disturbing the reflection of clouds on the water's surface. Trying to move with the same deftness, I followed on the lake's bank as the snake paralleled the shore. After a few minutes, the snake turned toward the deeper waters of the lake. I watched its silent swiftness until it was lost in the glare of the sun. I longed to move through the world like that, deliberate and certain, the waters folding around me, wakeless.

I felt I could wander, seduced, into the woods and forget myself, leave my hair uncombed and let my name fall away. I wanted to lie down where I was with only the sky above me. I recognized this desire as the feral love of an animal for its place of being. It seemed most akin to the awe and holiness I knew I should feel in church. I also sensed in that impulse a kind of danger, a dissolution that could lead me from my own kind.

I was grateful, then, for the farm and the animals that demanded my attention. They tethered me, protecting me from the impulses that the land engendered.

Everything on the farm seemed purposeful: the bird calls; the thickness of the morning dew; light moving across the kitchen floor; the barn's musk of hay, fresh manure, and dust. Even the sow's prissy, mud-caked haunches were imbued with grace.

I settled in, grew lean and muscular. I ripened, ready for whatever came next, certain it would be good and new. I'd slept through the war, but now I was waking up. At night, I tossed and turned in my bed. In the house of my refuge, I set aside the God I was raised on and woke each morning, tenderized by light, bird song, and hard labor.

The farm was once again the solace it had been. It knew me and I knew it. On the hottest night in the summer, when I could not sleep for the heat and my sister Rita snorting through her dreams beside me, I made myself a solitary pallet outside under the stars. But the bugs kept me awake. Finally, with only the full moon for light, I got up and, in boots and nightgown, walked the creek and cut through the fields. A breeze stirred the corn, whispering, "Yes. Yes. Yes." Everywhere my foot pressed the land I heard, "Home. Home. Home." I was in love.

But love of land is not enough for a young body. I had put on weight and curves. I was stronger than I had ever been. At the feed store, at church, anywhere I went, I could feel as much as see how men were looking at me. Their gazes, like hands, cupped my hip or shoulder.

Some of the men were the same boys who had called me "carrot top" when I was a young girl, sneering as if red hair was an aberration worthy of hell. Many of them, fresh from combat, were broken-faced. Around them, I felt the burden of my innocence. I told myself that their attention was just the war's end, just men lusting, as I did, for the land and smelling it on me. If one of them showed up at the farm, I did not stop my work to chat and flirt. I put him to work.

∽

SOMETHING HAD BEEN IN THE CORN, so I rode the plow horse, Becky, out to check the fence between the Starneses' pasture and our cornfield. I reined to a halt deep in the shade of a broad, low oak near the border of the Starneses' land. One of their stallions was after a mare. I had seen horses mate before, but this time I went closer, right up to the fence, and watched. The receptive mare danced before the stallion and then stood still, her tail swished to the side. Becky snuffled and took a little two-step under me. Despite the cool of the shade, heat rose up from my belly.

I did not hear or see Cole Starnes ride up. But suddenly he was there in the shade, taking off his hat and wiping his face. I startled. Becky shinnied sideways again.

"We weren't planning on breeding her this season," he said, as if we had been discussing the situation for a while. "She came on earlier than we thought. Caught us off guard." He was a good-looking boy, tall and thin, with a broad, friendly face and cowlick above his forehead.

I could feel the red in my ears. I kept my eyes on the horses.

Cole kept talking. "We were working on the tractor. Didn't know she was coming on. I don't like that tractor much." He glanced back toward his house as if he expected to see the tractor coming his way. His horse stomped and pulled.

I turned without a word and left just as the stallion dismounted.

After that, Cole gave me a little nod and a comment every time we ran into each other, which began to happen more often. Every Sunday after church he was there, not saying much, talking about fences, tractors, and the foal that was coming. He never mentioned seeing me in the pasture that day. The swirl of his dark brown hair above his forehead made him appear continually windblown and slightly surprised, qualities that I began to find endearing. He'd never teased me about my hair or my freckles. I found myself thinking of him.

Then one night, he showed up at my back door with a bouquet of cornflowers and lilies, and a little Mason jar of moonshine. The day's chores were done; there was no work for him to do, so I fed him supper. We drank the moonshine for dessert. I cut mine with cider, but he drank his down manly, grimacing. Outside of family, it was the first time I'd had company for supper on the farm. I felt like a grown woman, entertaining in her own home.

I was fine until he slid his hand over mine as I passed the jar of shine back to him. Once he touched me, it was all over. I lost my virginity that night and so did Cole, the two of us fumbling at each other until we got the job done. I don't think either of us was very impressed. I had brought myself more satisfactory pleasure alone at night—a pleasure I'd never associated with boys. But the intensity and how badly I had wanted it stunned me. We were suddenly shy and sober afterward, the booze sponged up by our amazement at what we had done.

The next day, I waited for God to strike me down. I thought I would feel bad, but I didn't. I felt relieved that the first time was over. I was curious to try it again, to get a better look at Cole. The barnyard can take some of the mystery out of the mechanics of the act, but a man is not a hog, a bull, or a stallion, though some do aspire to be one of the three.

A week later, Cole was back at my door. He had flowers again, but no shine, and asked in a shy, sweet whisper if we could try "it" again.

There had been no punishment from God, so, being curious about both God and Cole, I said yes.

After that, he would wait until dark fell and cut across the pasture instead of coming up the road. For the first time in my life, I made a conscious decision to sin and continue sinning. I braced myself for God's retribution. I was careful though, making Cole withdraw. I didn't want a baby to be the payment for my sin. Cole would have married me. He was that kind of boy, but I didn't want that either. We were just very young and doing what nature told us to do.

Still, I was doing something I had been warned against all my life. A terrible sin. I continued listening, expecting some punishment from God. But there was none. In that silence, I kept remembering something I'd once heard that contradicted all else I'd heard about sex and sin.

When I was about twelve years old, Grandpa Mac, Momma's grand-father, came to Sunday dinners at our house. Rail-thin and nearly blind, he sat on the front porch one evening with Momma. He rocked in the cane chair and she shelled peas beside him. I stood just inside the screen door behind them, bored until I realized they were discuss-ing the mother of a boy I knew and a man she snuck around to see. I got very still, wishing Grandpa would stop creaking in the rocker so I wouldn't miss a word. As if he had heard my wish, he paused. I thought he stopped to listen better to Momma, but he looked off toward the mill and said, "I don't understand how something that beautiful be-tween a man and a woman could ever be so wrong as people make it out to be."

To my amazement, Momma nodded, smiled, and kept shelling as if he was discussing the beauty of sunshine, not sin. Grandpa spit off the side of the porch and went back to rocking.

Being quiet around adults, I was often rewarded with gossip or bawdy jokes. But suddenly, I realized that there were other worlds and ways of thinking, secret agreements and understandings among adults.

After I had been with Cole, I thought about what Grandpa had said. "Something that beautiful between a man and a woman" didn't seem to describe what I did with Cole. But what we did didn't seem to be an awful sin like stealing or hurting someone, either.

Momma and Daddy didn't mind Cole courting me. He was a good, respectful boy. They were fine with him walking me to church and Momma welcomed his help on the weekends when my family came up to the farm, but they would not have tolerated his night visits. So Cole and I had to be discreet.

Still, Momma seemed to know somehow. Frank Roe, a cousin on my father's side, had been discharged and would be coming back from Japan, she told me. He'd need a place to stay. With him at the farm, I would not be alone and I would have live-in help with the harvest every day.

"It's not good, you staying up there by yourself. What if something happened to you? We might not know about it for days," she said.

My being on the farm alone had never bothered her before.

Frank was not one of my favorite cousins, and I did not want my solitude broken, but how could I protest? The farm was not mine, I was just the caretaker until it was decided who would inherit it. But I told myself, if I had less work to do, I might be able to meet Cole more often.

As soon as Frank jumped off the back of Daddy's truck and I saw his swagger, the way he wore his uniform and threw his duffel bag down, I knew that seeing Cole would be more, not less, difficult. Frank always had an edgy side to him, like a strange dog, alert and ready to lick you or rip into you. You could never tell which, and you didn't want him to do either. His eyes seemed smaller now, more doglike, his body harder and more compact. The war had concentrated what he had been as a boy. He was not a man you would want to give the advantage of your secrets.

He moved into Ricky's old room at the far end of the hall from me, and the house immediately took on the smell of his cigarette smoke and shoe polish.

"Looks like my little cousin is all growed up and got herself a farm," he announced after he had given himself a tour. Then he looked me up and down in a way I did not like, sucked on his cigarette, and flicked the butt down onto the barn floor. I stared at the smoldering stub and he stomped it, twisting his heel into it. "I got it, I got it. I'm not going to let your precious barn burn," he said.

As we walked out of the barn, Cole came up from across the field. Frank saw Cole's face change as he realized I was not alone.

"I guess you are all grown up," Frank leered.

Frank was a hard worker, but he was also a man. He expected me to fix all of his meals. The first night, I did make him a nice ham supper as a welcome. But on the second day, when he came to me at noon, I returned his dog-stare and told him, "You are not my husband and you are not my daddy. For the work you do around here, I'll get our supper in the evening and if I make biscuits in the morning, I'll leave you some. Otherwise, you take care of yourself."

He ate heartily each evening, but never cooked. His eyes followed me. But he seldom spoke. Only at night did I hear much from him. I shut my bedroom door, but I could still hear him turn and shout in his sleep. His bed lurched and squeaked when the ghost of the war visited his dreams.

At the end of the first week, he went into town, bought a battery radio, and put it in his bedroom. Then there was smoke and music every night. Sometimes I could smell the booze on his breath by mid-afternoon.

He had been at the house a few weeks when I walked by the half-open door of his room one night. He sat on his bed, his back to me, staring at some pictures spread out before him. A man and a woman whispered to each other from the radio. I opened my mouth to speak, then realized that he had his hand down his pants. He may have just been scratching himself. As I stepped back, he turned, grabbed the pictures with both hands, and laid them over his lap. He shot me a look of pure disdain and said "war pictures" over the cigarette smoke that curled up his jaw.

Frank began drinking more and going into town during the week. One of the nights he was gone, I went into his room to see the pictures. I expected they would be images of naked girls. I couldn't tell what the first one was. In the middle of a gray, textured background was a black spot, like a hole or a rip in the negative.

The next few photos, all black-and-white, showed the rubble of bombed-out buildings, like the photos I'd seen of London but flatter, ashen to the horizon. Japan after the bomb. In one picture, an American soldier stood in the field of trash under a low, dark sky. Nothing stood higher than his knee. He grinned, holding up a bottle in a congratulatory toast, his left foot propped on a half-crumbled block of stone. What I first thought was a flutter of torn, singed paper sticking out from under the block was, when I examined them closer, two arms. One stuck straight up from the elbow, and the blackened hand at the end of it had only a thumb and two fingers. The other, much smaller arm, ended with a splay of bone at the wrist joint, no fingers. Bile stirred in my stomach, water in my mouth. I looked back up at the soldier's smile. There was no way to be sure if he knew about the arms. But how could he have missed them?

The next one was similar, the same dark sky, the same lifelessness to the horizon. In the foreground, the GI from the other photo had been joined by four American GIs, all with their shirts open or off. They smiled triumphant and happy. Not a line on their faces. Their bare, hairless chests pallid against the background of sky. The next photograph showed more GIs, more smiles, and ashy lumps on the ground. The GIs were smaller, the sky lower and darker with each photograph as if the photographer had moved farther away with each shot.

The last photograph was a close-up of a Japanese woman, her eyes closed. Shown from the waist up, she lay on her side. From her temple down her jaw, her neck, and over one breast, the skin puckered in a strange way, halfway between the crispness of a burn and the swirled, glossy scarring that comes months later. Her other breast, the one she lay on, was smooth, the cylindrical nipple only slightly darker than her pale skin.

I thumbed back to the first picture. The gray textures resembled the delicate ash left when we burned garbage. The hole in the middle was shaped like a baby, a baby curled on its side—a baby-shaped hole with no light in it, no reflection, no texture. Nauseated, I put the pictures back. My hands trembled.

All night I saw those pictures, the baby, the woman, and the GIs. Such wholesome smiles amid the hell of destruction; they seemed like some new kind of evil. Yet their faces looked like mine, like the faces of my people.

Not long after I found the photographs, Frank came home late one night, cussing, stumbling drunk at the back door, and woke me. I went to help him, but when I got close, he grabbed me and pressed me up against the door frame.

"Betcha give it to that Cole boy. Gimme some," he hissed, as he tried to find my mouth with his. My arm hurt where he gripped it, but he was very drunk. I got my knee up between us, pushed him backward down the steps, and bolted the door.

I found him on the steps in the morning. Stinking, muddy, and bloody from a scrape on his cheek, but sleeping like a baby. I kicked him to wake him up.

That afternoon I left my work early, walked down to the mill-village, and told Momma what had happened, showed her the bruise on my arm.

"His daddy was bad to drink. But I was—we all were—hoping the war would make a difference in him. Grow him up," she told me.

I shook my head, remembering the photographs. "I think the war made it worse, Momma."

"I reckon you could be right about that. Made things worse for a lot of people. Go get your daddy and have him drive you back. Tell him we need Frank down here in the mill-village more than you need him up there. He can come up with the rest of us to help on Saturdays. Meanwhile, we can knock some sense into him if he goes after any of his own family again. If your daddy has questions, he can come see me."

Daddy talked to Momma and then drove me back to the farm. It took Frank about five minutes to pack up the duffel bag and they were gone.

Later, when I was putting clean sheets on the bed in his room, I found one of Frank's photographs under the bed—the one with the burned girl in it. I kept it.

I hadn't liked what Frank said about Cole. I didn't know what else he might say. Since Frank had arrived, Cole had visited only a few times and then we just sat on the porch talking, the tension of what we wanted sparking around us. If we got caught, both our daddies would have shotguns after us, baby or no baby coming. I wasn't particularly romantic, but I wanted to choose my husband rather than have my daddy decide for me. Though I wanted to be near Cole, I wasn't sure I loved him, and he was still more boy than man. Not ready to be a husband.

The next time I saw Cole at church, I told him he couldn't be coming over anymore, that I was afraid of getting into trouble. He thought I was talking about getting pregnant. He'd be careful, he assured me.

"I mean getting caught by my daddy," I said. "Momma seems to know something. And if she knows anything, he'll know it soon enough." At the mention of my daddy, Cole took a step back and looked so sad and defeated that I found myself adding, "Not forever, just a few months—until after Christmas."

"So you gonna wait until after Christmas to give me my present?" He trotted off to join his family, but I heard the grin in his voice.

That was late October. The cold nights were already coming on, and the trees had turned. Christmas seemed a long time to wait.

But those weeks alone again gave me time to think. Becoming Cole's wife—or any man's, for that matter—would mean leaving the farm. A wife was expected to follow her husband.

By then, I'd been on the farm over two years. I'd managed to keep a good-size kitchen garden, most of the livestock, and a few acres of hay, corn, and alfalfa. Even with the help of my family, it had not been easy. I was proud of my work. I wanted to stay where I was. Alone in my bed at night, I wanted Cole, but I didn't want anything else to change.

But things did change.

For Christmas, Momma got one of her wishes. By virtue of her interest in the farm and the small sum she paid her siblings, the deed to the farm was hers. None of my aunts and uncles wanted to live in a house without an indoor toilet or electric lights. If it had been up to Momma, she and Daddy would have moved to the farm, but he wouldn't have it. Momma made it clear to me that the farm was mine to live on as long as I kept the family in vegetables, eggs, milk, and meat. I knew I could keep my part of that bargain.

As everyone returned to their post-holiday work routines and Cole, who still had not received his "present," was laid up with the flu, an early January snow fell. The house ticked and sighed around me with the change of temperature. Outside, an expectant hush of white enveloped the land. The contours of the world changed, angles softened to clean abstractions of themselves. The blank expanse of the fields seemed new, brilliant, and beguiling.

A week later, as the snow melted, receding to expose the rust-red clay again, the farm seemed reborn. A hard, steady rain followed. Lightning winked on the horizon and thunder muttered, still distant. Within hours, water rose between the house and the slight elevation of the fields. From the parlor window, I looked down at a narrow rush of water, roiling against the foundation of the house like a trapped animal seeking escape. The fields usually drained east behind the barn, then on to the creek or south to the tracks. But now they sent their runoff straight at the house as if the land had, indeed, undergone some subtle shift. In all my time at the farm, including the times with Eva when I was a little girl, I'd never seen that happen. But I'd also never seen rain like this, either. Lightning was unusual for a winter storm.

At dusk, as Eva's dog, Hobo, and I stood on the back porch watching the storm, the blown mist swirling around us, I was glad for all the canned vegetables in the pantry and for the cords of firewood split, stacked, and dry. Beside me, Hobo whimpered and nudged my hand with his damp nose. Rain undulated across the fields like a living thing, in wild, flapping rows.

TWO

THE YIELD

The next morning, well before dawn, a flash of lightning woke me.
Immediately, darkness returned and thunder vibrated the windowpane.
The drumming of rain followed as I rolled away from the bed's warmth
and groped for the lantern and a match.

After I dressed, I put on my uncle's oilcloth coat and a leather hat,
then went out to the barn. Lester had been dead for years now, but the
recent dampness brightened all odors. As I went about my morning
chores, the smell of his sweat and tobacco lingered around his clothes.

By the time I'd finished my work in the barn, the rain had slowed
to a steady soft sprinkle, giving me an opportunity to check the drainage outside the house. That odd gathering of runoff I'd seen the day
before made me uneasy. It was too close to the house. I couldn't risk a
flooded basement or a compromised foundation.

I stoked the stove, draped a fresh set of clothes and a quilt over the
dining chairs nearby, then headed for the front yard. The storm had
uprooted a small tree, washing it against a clot of dead leaves and blackberry bramble. Overflow from the field backed up the shallow ditch
that normally drained down to the railroad tracks.

When I'd finally extracted the last branches, the plug of debris broke. The freed water plunged twenty feet to the tracks below. Not convinced that the tree, hardly more than a sapling, and a bunch of dead leaves and vine could account for such a backup, I shoveled the newly drained trench. The exertion warmed me, but my hands were wet and cold. I looked forward to the warm stove and my dry clothes as I slogged around the house toward the back porch. Hobo barked a greeting from the steps.

But something caught my eye. The ridge where the land rose a foot before plateauing into the fields had collapsed in one spot. Red lumps of clay lay tumbled down onto the roots of the apple tree below. I walked along the edge of the rise. The ground felt solid and gave no more when I pressed my foot at the edge. But it needed support. There were old fence posts and some planking in the barn. Daddy or Joe would have to help me, or maybe even Cole. He was probably over the flu by now.

Despite the rain's pause, the horizon remained dark and mobile in all directions. There would be more rain very soon. Beyond the fresh-washed barnyard stretched the unbroken brown of bare trees and the rust of the earth. The air felt clear and cold, as if it had never been breathed.

Leaning slightly forward, I listened. Hobo leapt to the ground and took a quick trot around the yard. He bounded around the barn, then skidded to a stop a few yards away, his nose to the ground. His tail uncurled and he sniffed and whined.

I stepped toward him. He jumped back, barked at me, and then circled as if avoiding something on the ground. He pressed himself against my leg and whined again. I reached down to pat him. The ground was slightly depressed before us. I'd never noticed rain puddling there before.

"It's just a puddle, boy. Just water."

Hobo danced beside me, bumping my leg, not taking his eyes off the ground.

I squatted and skimmed my hand over the water. Fat, sparse raindrops spattered the ground.

Hobo barked sharply, then muttered a low, startled growl. I petted him with one hand and fanned my other hand through the puddle. The water was not more than an inch deep, opaque and rust-red. I meant only to reassure the dog, but saw that something was down there. Something round stuck up out of the puddle, solid like a rock, but the texture of it was unusual.

For balance, I kept my hand on Hobo as I stretched farther; the thing in the puddle gave when I pressed it. Instantly, Hobo leapt back from my hand with a full-throated bark. What was in the water? Wet fur? Skin? I thought I saw a bubble of air rise through the puddle, but it was difficult to tell as the rain pocked its surface harder now. Hobo ignored my commands to quiet.

I pulled my hat down more firmly against a gust of wind and pushed my sleeves up. Kneeling, I used the flat of my arm to rake the water away, clearing the odd lump. Hobo barked and whined, pacing. I pushed more mud away. For a second, I didn't recognize what I was looking at: a shoulder and the slope of an arm. I jerked my hand away and tried to scramble sideways, but my knee, sunken in the mud, hit something—a hip. I'd been straddling it.

"Oh, God! Oh, God!" I scooted back farther. I glanced over my shoulder down the hill. No one would hear me shout from there. I motioned violently for Hobo to shut up. He dropped to a loud whimper.

What was a dead man doing here?

I forced myself to look again. Judging from the hip-to-shoulder distance, he was about my height. I followed the line of his shoulder down to the muck. Stretching forward, my belly almost touching the ground, I pressed my fingers into the mud where his hand would be. There it was, solid. I felt it twitch and saw my own fingertip rise with it. I lurched back and set Hobo barking again. The rain picked up.

I took a deep breath and reached forward again. The wet clay gave easily. I held the arm aloft by the wrist. The mud-caked mitt of a hand hung limp. Then it flexed, turning in my clay-slick grip.

I froze. Blood rushed to my head.

He was alive!

I dug into the slurry, following shoulder and neck to the roundness of his head. I scooped him up, straining to gain leverage on the wet ground. There was a loud sucking sound as the soil released him from its grip. Mud encased him completely, obscuring his features. I tried to hold him with one arm and wipe his face, but he slipped, tilting in my arms, his face turned away.

Rain spat down harder. I jerked off my hat and used it to shield the head I cradled. The rain battered my bared head. "Can you hear me? Are you okay?" I shouted. A low mutter of thunder erupted behind me. The wind flared, whipping my hair across my face.

He hung limp, heavy in my arms, entirely covered in clay. No sign of clothes. I twisted out of my coat and threw it over him, tucking it quickly across his chest and over his body. I tried to hold the hat with one hand and use the other to wipe his face, but that only seemed to make things worse.

I hunkered over with his head against my waist and glanced under the hat, my wet face inches from his. Under the shadow of the hat, he seemed to have no face and no hair, just a muddy round head. I drew back, slung my hair out of my eyes, and tried to blink away the gray-white curtain of rain.

"Are you okay?" I yelled, my voice drowned by Hobo's barks and the deafening rain. I tried to focus, squinting at the form slumped against me. The pelting rain exposed the lower half of his mud-caked head. I touched his jaw. His warm skin felt gritty, not the stubble of beard. His face cracked, and a small, lipless mouth opened. His chest expanded, a long, ragged breath. Then expanded again. He was breathing!

A strange sensation rose again from my belly to my chest. Hobo went silent. Under the white noise of rain pounding my head, I heard a tone like a large bell. It rushed up, sweet and soothing, through the bones of my chest. Rising and rising until it came out the top of me, clearing my head—through me or from me, I could not tell. Hobo leapt into the puddle, wagging his tail, licking at me and the man in the mud. The man's hand flexed again. His arm jerked.

Suddenly, I felt the frigid water soaking my clothes. I had to get him inside. I grabbed him under the arms, dragged him out of the puddle to firmer ground. I could barely see for the blowing rain and my drenched hair, but he seemed caked with mud. Every inch of him covered. I tried hoisting him up, but we were too slippery. "Stay, Hobo, stay. I'll be back."

I ran inside to get the quilt I'd left warming at the stove. I grabbed the oiled tablecloth, too. Outside again, I struggled against the wind-driven downpour. Blinded by pounding gusts, I threw the quilt over him, then jerked the coat out from under it. I felt my way around him. Tucking the quilt under, I worked quickly down from his head to his feet. Then I spread the oilcloth over him. I shoved my arms into the coat and pressed the hat down onto my head.

Wrestling his bundled weight up into my arms, I managed to stand. Inside the quilt, he moved in small, spasmodic jerks, like someone doped or on the edge of sleep. Wind gusted at my back. Staggering, I once went down on my knees with him. His weight and size were at the edge of my strength. Hobo nudged me, whimpering inquisitively.

"It'll be all right. You'll be all right. I can get you there. It's warm inside. You'll be warm and dry soon," I shouted. Easing him on the porch floor, I wrapped the quilt and tablecloth tighter around him, keeping him completely covered, and half-carried, half-dragged him across the porch into the kitchen. I shoved the chairs aside and pulled him up close to the warm stove.

The relative warmth and quiet of the house stunned me. My arms ached from carrying him. I peeled the oilcloth away. Mud streaked the sides of the wet quilt beneath, but it was surprisingly warm from his body heat. "Are you warm enough? Are you okay?" I asked softly near his covered head. He didn't respond. I went for more quilts. I debated unwrapping him completely. But I was reluctant to expose him, even for a few seconds, to the cold bare floor. Instead, I left the wet quilt on him and pressed another quilt around him firmly for a moment to wick some moisture away, set it aside, and then swaddled him in a couple more dry quilts, head to toe like a mummy. He didn't move as I tucked the quilts around him.

I knelt beside him, my hair and clothes dripping. In the dim kitchen light, I could barely discern the subtle rise and fall of his breathing. My teeth chattered. But I continued staring at the wad of blankets not knowing what to do next when I felt that sensation again. A strange, uncoiling calm hummed through me. This time I was sure I heard something below the drumming of the rain, a chime, sweet and soft, then it vanished. I wiped my chest, smearing more dirt on myself. I was freezing, suddenly aware of my heavy, drenched clothes.

"I'll be back," I said and grabbed the fresh clothes I'd left warming by the stove.

In the bedroom, I stripped and changed as quickly as my shaking hands would allow.

He lay still and bundled on the floor when I returned with the rest of the blankets and quilts. I took two warming bricks from the stove and folded them in flannel. After I eased a pillow under his head, I lined the bricks up at his feet, then wrapped myself in a blanket, lay down behind him, and pulled the remaining quilts over both of us. I had no idea how long he had been out in that cold storm; I needed to keep him warm. I shivered and pressed up close.

Who was this strange man? How had he come to be buried on the edge of my field? What was wrong with him? With his face? I decided I should give him a few more minutes, to make sure he was warm. I should be as warm as possible, too, before starting down the hill to Mildred's to call Momma and Daddy. They would know what to do. I'd have to go soon. The steady applause of rain continued on the metal roof. The expansion of his ribs as he breathed reminded me of sleeping with my sisters. I felt that odd hum in my chest again and, despite my plans to go for help, I fell asleep.

I WOKE SUDDENLY. We were still spooned up tight, my arm around him. We hadn't slept very long. The stove still radiated heat. Early evening light shone through the windows. Rain pounded hard on the roof and windowpane, drowning the sound of the strange man's breath, but I felt his chest rise under my arm.

Curious, I lifted a corner of the blanket from his face. He was grotesquely, vividly ugly. His skin was lumpy, rough whorls like burn scars. Worse than the woman in the photograph Frank had left. I'd never seen such jaundice, an unnatural dark yellow. Only his cheek and part of his nose were visible, a flat nose, small like a baby's, with no bridge. How could I have missed that? The memory itself seemed dreamlike. I lay the blanket back across his scarred, bare shoulder and let it fall forward to cover the side of his face again.

I got up. Outside the dining room window, the sky was a solid iron-gray. I had no telephone and the road was out. There was no way to get this poor man to anyone who could help him. I didn't want to leave him alone.

He must be a soldier, I realized, horribly disfigured from the war. But how had he stumbled naked onto my land and ended up nearly buried in the mud? What was wrong with him?

An unfamiliar scratching sound came from the porch, followed by a sharp bark. I opened the back door and Hobo darted in. He went immediately to the man on the floor, sniffing voraciously and wagging his tail. The barn cat followed, her fur as damp as Hobo's. Rain blew in with them.

Farm dogs and cats are not let in the house; their jobs are outside. I'd occasionally tried to bring Hobo or the cat in just for the company and to have a pair of eyes to look at while I talked to myself. But Hobo, out of his usual territory, would be shy inside and usually stayed near the door. The cat, an opportunist, always curled up close to the stove or the pantry. Now both circled the man, sniffing him vigorously, and then lay down, Hobo at his feet and the cat near his chest.

I let them stay. The kitchen was more companionable with them there, the man somehow less exceptional. The rush of cold air that had surged in with them dissipated.

Rain drummed, shooting off the roof and hitting the ground in a solid sheet. Dusk fell, but no houses were lit down the hill. The electric poles were down. The only illumination was farther away, the faint light of the mill's generator.

I knew I should check outside to make sure the drainage was still good beside the house. But first we needed food.

I lit a couple of lanterns, loaded the stove, and, stepping around the man, the cat, and the dog, I began to make some biscuits. While the biscuits baked, I went out to the front porch. Wind whipped the trees near the bank and slanted the rain nearly horizontal. But the runoff sluiced efficiently away from the house. A thin film of ice slicked the floorboards. Carefully, I hurried back inside, feeling oddly calm, aware of the man and how his position in relation to me changed as I moved through the house—behind me as I walked to the front door, ahead of me as I came back down the hall toward the warmth of the kitchen.

The man sighed as I took the biscuits out of the oven. A long, sweet-sounding sigh, but nothing else. He shifted inside the quilts and rolled onto his back. I was relieved to see that the blanket remained across his face.

He had to be hungry. I dragged the cat and the dog outside so I could feed the man in peace. Then I warmed some milk, and set it, the fresh biscuits, some jam, a thick slice of ham, and a bowl of canned peaches on a plate beside him and got down on the floor. I lifted the blanket away from his face again to see if he was awake.

It was hard to look at his face and hard to look away. The whorled scarring covered him—his scalp, temples, face, eyelids, and neck—as if his skin had recently been liquid, stirred by some cruel hand. His lips, though, were normal. Just thin. He had very small ears. All of his features were small and faint, his cheekbones wide, and his whole face flat the way some babies' are. The way some Chinese and Japanese faces are. I had only seen black-and-white photographs, but the Japanese were called yellow. Were they really this strange a color? Was he a Japanese prisoner brought over after the bomb? I thought again of the woman in Frank's photograph.

Then his odd, flat eyelids opened. His eyes were not brown, not Asian, but light, like my family's. He was not an escaped Japanese prisoner. The pupils were strange, though—very large—and the line between them and the iris was vague, his gaze unfocused. Was he blind?

"Hello," I said, keeping my eyes on his so I would not have to see his skin.

He blinked slowly. His eyes focused, the pupil coming into definition, and he opened his mouth. "'Ello" came out. An old, heavy door opening, a cat being choked.

"You hungry?" I held up the plate.

"Hungry," he stated, his voice a little less rough. He took a quick breath, opening his mouth slightly, the way a tomcat does when it's getting a scent.

I shifted him up, putting my leg under his shoulders to prop him up and support his back. I offered him a slice of peach. He did not take his eyes off mine, nor did he open his mouth any wider.

"They're good. I canned them myself." I popped the peach into my mouth, then forked another slice and offered it to him. He stared at it and slowly opened his mouth. His teeth were small and round, like a child's baby teeth. Chewing slowly, he locked his eyes on mine and swallowed. A sigh of pure joy came out of him and he shuddered. I heard and felt that sweet chime I'd heard outside, felt it in my belly and chest and head, nearer now, softer than before. It came from the man!

Resistance, a snake of fear convulsed along my spine, then lay still and vanished under his gaze. Looking into those eyes, which were now a pure, lucid blue, I saw no harm or malice. Only strange, expansive otherness. Sitting on the floor, cradling his head in the bend of my knee as his odd voice hummed through me, I fell not so much in love but into fascination, into a deep and tender accord.

I smiled and he smiled back, his face creasing, his damaged skin surprisingly supple. I fed him a few more bites. Then his hand emerged from the blankets—the same horrible skin as on his face. His hand swerved twice before he took the biscuit I held. He brought it slowly to his mouth. The scarring covered his palms and fingertips, too. Miraculously, he seemed to be in no pain.

With every bite, he beamed. I'd never seen anyone take such unabashed pleasure in simple food, at least not an adult. He almost swooned.

"What's your name?" I asked.

He stopped chewing and swallowed.

I pointed at myself. "I am Evelyn, Evelyn Roe. What's your name?"

The smile left his face. He stared expectantly as if he had asked the questions.

"Where are your clothes?"

Nothing, no reply. Just his open face, waiting.

I stammered on, "Why were you in the dirt like that? You could have drowned in that puddle."

Still, just that steady, bright gaze.

I could not tell if he understood what I was saying, but he listened very closely, reluctantly taking his attention from the food each time I spoke. The way he watched me reminded me of the deaf girl who lived down in the mill-village. She had the same intense way of taking everything in through her eyes, drinking in the world. But when I laughed at his ecstatic expression after he took his first bite of the blackberry jam, he stopped his chewing to watch me and listen. He was not deaf.

Maybe he had amnesia. Maybe if I told him about my family and where I came from, he would be reminded of who he was. So I talked, telling him my name and where we were and everything we were eating, as though he were from another country.

We ate and ate. Three plates of food and two glasses of milk, him watching me each time I got up to get more.

When he finally seemed to be full, he sighed deeply. The room went oddly quiet and still.

I laid my hand on my chest and opened my mouth to ask about that sound, but he stopped me with that gaze. Then he placed his hand carefully over mine. The roughness of his palm against the back of my hand was both pleasant and repulsive. Slowly, his eyes closed, but his hand did not move from mine. After a long, quiet while, I laid his hand down, gently lowered his head from my leg to the pillow, and covered him again.

I thought I should offer him a bath and some clothes, but when I finished cleaning our supper dishes, he still slept, breathing deeply.

As I slipped into Lester's coat, I wondered about the stranger's people. Were they somewhere, not far from us, slipping into dank coats and going out into the same rain? Sick with worry about him? He did not look at me like any of the local boys, but something was familiar about him. I was certain he was a good man. His people would be searching for him.

When I stepped off the porch, the rain on my hat overwhelmed every other sound. I stopped in the middle of the barnyard and surveyed the horizon. Where could he have come from so naked and scarred? I went to the place where I had found him. The depression in the soil still held his general shape, but it was already beginning to vanish, its sides collapsing. I put my hands into the cold, opaque water and felt the round spot where his head had been, the deeper indentation his shoulder had made, then down toward his hips. Just clay slick and grit. Not a clue, not a hint of clothes or identity. There had to be something. I pushed my coat sleeves up higher and dug into the harder clay below. Nothing. I remembered that strange sound surging through me when I found him, and I stopped digging. Whoever he might be, he was a naked, hungry man out in the cold. A close flash of lightning followed by an instant boulder of thunder sent me scurrying for the barn.

Becky snorted a welcome and one of the cows belched a soft moo. They shifted in their stalls when I lit a lantern. I spread fresh hay and felt a surge of tenderness for the animals' familiar bodily warmth. They needed only dry, secure shelter and food.

What would the near-mute, ugly man inside my house need? As I lifted the full, covered buckets of milk, I felt the fatigue in my shoulders from carrying him.

Back in the kitchen, I dried myself again and got things ready for when he woke. I pulled out some of Uncle Lester's old clothes—overalls, wool socks, underwear, and a flannel shirt. They smelled musty, so I laid them over the dining chairs to air. I got out the tub, towels, and a washcloth, then checked the temperature of the water in the stove tank. I tried to read while I waited for him to wake up, but my eyes kept leaving the page for the long bundle of quilts on the floor.

He did not wake. It was late and I began to feel sleepy. I didn't want to wake him to move him again, certainly not to a cold bedroom. I couldn't bear the thought that he might wake in the middle of the night alone in a strange place. All that scarring; he'd already been through so much. What if he needed something?

So I brought out the rest of the pillows and quilts. I lined his cold side with the down pillows, then made myself a bed on the floor so we could sleep head to head, forming a semicircle near the stove.

For a long time, I did not sleep. An alertness filled me, but I also felt a peculiar calm. I thought again of the awful picture of the Japanese woman, how the skin on my strange-looking guest was so similar to hers. I was pleased that he was alive, however he had come to be half-buried on my land. There must be a secret military hospital nearby, I reasoned, a place for specially damaged soldiers. I tried to imagine such a place, and how he might have managed to leave naked. Lightning snapped, brightening the room. Rain on the tin roof drowned the sounds of his breathing. Then, despite my nap earlier that day, exhaustion overcame me and I drifted into sleep.

※

BEFORE DAWN, I woke with a start. In the dimness of the clouded moonlight coming through the window, I could sense more than see him looking at me.

I rose, stumbled blindly against the table, and then lit a lantern. He had turned in his sleep, his back to the stove. He stared up at me from his bed on the floor, that bright gaze drinking me in. He seemed familiar in a way I could not place. His skin appeared much better. The swirling and roughness remained, but less severe, like very old burn scars.

He pulled himself awkwardly up on his elbows, as if about to speak, and I knelt beside him. Reaching up, he touched my face and ran his fingertips lightly over my cheeks, lips, and eyelids. His hand had become smoother. His color was better, too, sallow rather than rusty, his head not nearly so spherical. His nose and eyes were more normal. Short, barely visible reddish hairs sprouted from his scalp. His ears were normal in size. The room fell away. Fascinated, I touched his cheek and forehead. He was not healing. This was too fast for healing. He was changing. Small sparks of alarm caught my breath. His hand on my jaw stopped, a question on his face.

"Who are you?" I whispered. "Where are you from?"

"From?" He pulled his hand slowly away, and his face went blank and still. I could almost hear him thinking. His gaze left my face and lost its focus. I leaned closer to him, touched his bare shoulder. I wanted his focus back. Fear surrendered to tenderness, a shift deep in my chest. "Are you feeling better?"

"Better." A statement, not a question. Even his voice, far less coarse than the day before, sounded familiar. Maybe he was a local boy, his war scars making him unrecognizable.

The blanket slid farther off his shoulder. I remembered the clothes. "You should have a bath first, to get the dirt off, but these are for you." I laid them on the blankets next to him.

He rubbed his hand along the pant leg of the overalls.

"Rest until I get the water and breakfast ready."

I dressed, stoked up the stove, and fed the animals while he seemed to be sleeping again. I pulled the tub as close to the stove as I dared. After I filled it with warm water, I touched him on the shoulder to wake him. "Does this hurt?" I massaged his shoulder lightly.

"No."

"You can take a bath now."

He held my hands and pulled himself up into a sitting position. His grip was strong.

"You okay sitting up?"

"Okay." He nodded back at me.

He didn't seem to understand what to do next. Helping him stand was like pulling a very large, drunk child out of a low bed. He kept his eyes on me and I kept my eyes on his face so I wouldn't have to see his naked body.

As soon as I got him standing, I let go and grabbed a towel. He swayed a little, but caught himself and planted his feet firmly apart while I reached behind him and wrapped the towel around his waist. I pulled his arm over my shoulder. We were the same height. He teetered awkwardly.

"You must have been on a real bender before you got here." His hapless nakedness made me giddy.

He turned his head, so close now I could smell the clean, sweet odor of his breath, and gave me a blank, patient look.

"Just joking," I said. The second step, which got him to the edge of the tub, was smoother.

"Get in," I told him. "It's warm, it'll feel good." But he only turned his head and regarded me with that pale-eyed gaze again. I reached down and lifted one of his legs, easing it slowly into the warm water. He let out a sharp "ahhh" of surprise as soon as his foot touched the water. I startled, afraid it might be too warm. But then he beamed a sweet, wide smile as if I'd just given him a whole tub of blackberry jam.

Once he got both feet in, he just stood there. I had to help him sit. In what I took for modesty, he left the towel on when he went down into the water. He sat in the tub smiling, waving his hands in the water, but not making any effort to bathe himself or take the cloth I held out. So I began to bathe his arms and shoulders very gently. He watched my face and hands, all the while smiling at me. A sweet odor rose from the water. He smelled like a newly mowed summer lawn. He sighed and shut his eyes. I sensed that odd sound again, the soothing resonant chime. I touched his chest. He opened his eyes wide, and the sound changed timbre and pitch. I could feel its vibration through my hand.

I took my hand away from his chest and forced myself to move around behind him to wash his back. The scarring was there, too. My throat clenched. I needed words to counter what I saw, to soften the horrors I imagined had caused such damage. "Are you from around here? Where are you from?"

He said nothing. I couldn't see his face, but imagined his blank then confused expression. After a moment, he spoke. "I don't know where I am from." Each word stood carefully by itself, his first full sentence.

The bath water began to cool. I held his hands again and he stood with more confidence. But the towel stayed in the water. He did not seem to notice and just held the dry towel when I handed it to him.

"Dry yourself. Here. Like this." I rubbed his shoulder with the towel, careful not to look down. "You can get dressed. Hurry before you get cold." I dried him off and he helped in his awkward way.

He just stood there when he was dry. Clearly, he needed my help getting dressed. I knelt in front of him holding his underwear open and, averting my eyes, I motioned that he should lift his leg. He got the idea and, steadying himself by holding on to my shoulders, stepped with his other leg into the shorts. I bent forward, holding them open. As I rose to pull them up around his hips, I had to see what was right in front of my face. There was an awful protruding mangle of flesh, neither man nor woman, and a fuzz of red pubic hair.

"Who did this to you? Who hurt you like this?" I held his rough face in my hands. "What happened to you?"

His face contorted, alarmed and puzzled. He put his hand up and touched a tear on my face. "Hurt?" he said. "Who did this?"

"Were you in Japan?"

"Japan?"

I was upsetting him. He didn't seem to know how to answer. He stared at me, waiting to find out about Japan.

"Let's finish putting your clothes on and then I'll show you something," I said. I helped him put on the rest of his clothes. They were too big, even the shoes. He was not as tall as Uncle Lester. I slipped Uncle Lester's socks on over his scarred foot. Like the bath, socks seemed new and unexpected to him, but after the struggle of the first one, he held his foot firm so the second one slipped on easily.

"Wait," I said when he was dressed. I brought the picture of the Japanese woman back to him and held it out. He took it carefully, holding it by the corner, and studied the woman. A ragged sigh rose from him.

"This is hurt?" He held the photograph out for me to take.

I touched his hand, feeling the strangeness of his skin, and turned it over next to my hand, comparing. "I know who did this to her, but who did this to you?"

He seemed to struggle for words and then announced, "I am not like her. I am not hurt. I do not hurt." I took the photograph back.

"You don't hurt anywhere?" I rubbed his shoulder. He leaned into my touch like a purring cat.

He shook his head, then turned his attention back to our hands. Taking my hand in both of his, he held it, touching me lightly at first, then searching the bones and tendons of my wrist as if memorizing them.

I did not bathe after him, as I normally would have, to take advantage of the labor of getting up a hot bath. I let the water go cold. When I went to throw it out, it was not muddy as I had expected it to be, but almost clear, with just a bit of grit in the bottom. There was not much dirt on the quilts, either, not nearly what there should have been given the conditions I'd found him in.

The rain continued that day, the waterfall of it crashed off the roof, keeping me housebound with my odd stranger. I had begun to think of him as mine. Mine to protect and teach. Mine to bring back to what he had been before. I tried not to think of the unnatural speed of his recovery, or the faint vibrating drone that sometimes emanated from him. I still thought of him as a damaged soldier.

Except for my brief trips to the barn, I spent that day holding him by the hand, guiding his clumsy steps around the house, and talking to him.

Again and again, I asked him about his family and where he was from. Did he remember anyone or anything? The answer remained the same, "I don't know." The only thing he seemed to be certain of was his lack of pain.

In the hope of triggering some memories, I told him stories of my family. Stories about my momma's family, poor Appalachian hill farmers coming down to work in the cotton mills. About her crazy cousin who robbed post offices and the federal agents who came looking for him. I told the story of my father's half-sister, the only relation I had never met, who ran off with a boy from Chicago named Hardin.

Of all things, I thought my talk of the war would make him remember something, but even that seemed news to him. He could not remember anything from his past. Reluctantly, I concluded that he must be brain-damaged. But he was so lucid. He filled the room.

Something in his manner and bearing seemed so familiar. I was certain that he was a local boy. I covered the local geography, naming towns, counties, hills, rivers, and creeks nearby, hoping to jog some uninjured part of his brain. None of what I said helped him remember his people, but he turned that deaf-man gaze on me, and I felt like I was reciting Holy Scripture to a drowning sinner.

I saw no judgment, no appraisal in his eyes. He wasn't like the boys in the mill-village. He reminded me of Cole. I was not too tall, red-haired, or freckled when I talked to him. I was unaccustomed to the intensity of his attention, and at times it made me shy, but I wanted to meet his gaze. I wanted to tell this man everything, to give him the world he seemed to have lost.

By the end of the day, his gait was almost normal and the questions were coming from him. He followed me, watching everything I did. He wanted to know the name of everything—a knife, the stove, the buckle on his overalls.

That afternoon, I discovered that he had even forgotten what a chamber pot was for. The outhouse was not close, so I had taken to using a chamber pot sometimes even during the day, and I certainly wasn't going out in the continuing downpour just to pee. Since I had been living alone so much, I'd taken to leaving the pot on the back porch. In bad weather, I used it in a corner, behind the tool shelves. He found me there just before sunset that day. I was squatting over the pot, doing my business, when he appeared. I startled, but there wasn't much to be done except finish peeing. He watched me with the same intense interest he had in everything. Beside him, Hobo peered at me, sniffing the air. Then the cat stuck her head around the corner.

"I guess this means we're pretty good friends, but even my family doesn't find this so interesting they have to watch."

My comment seemed to please him.

"Oh!" he said when I finished and he saw the pot behind me. He stood very close to me. I smelled his faint green odor. He sniffed, too. I offered him the pot and walked away until I heard the metallic clink of the fasteners on his overalls. I couldn't help myself, I peered back over my shoulder. When I didn't see him standing over the pot, I took a couple of quiet steps backward and peeked over the shelves. He squatted like a woman, staring down between his legs like a child. I blushed, remembering what I had seen there when I helped him dress. After he finished, he beamed up at me, happy, completely unself-conscious.

Later, when we ate dinner, I noticed his skin was much better. Not quite normal, but in the lamplight, I could see that it had lost its odd yellow hue. Only traces of the burn-like scarring remained. His skin was smoother. The roughness now seemed just below the surface, like the dimpling and slight lumpiness of fat. His hair formed a short copper halo. He reminded me of the children in my family when they were younger. His emerging familiarity kept my mind off of how he had looked when I found him. I no longer felt the urgent need to call Momma and Daddy for help. This strange man had begun to feel like a gift instead of an emergency. A curious gift.

It wouldn't have been right to have him sleep on the floor again for his second night. At bedtime, I put him in the room closest to mine, not the one Frank had slept in. Getting him into long johns was easier than dressing him after his bath. He did most of the work himself, but I had to remind him to keep his socks on for warmth. His bed squeaked when he sat on it. He echoed with his own squeak of surprise and leapt up. I laughed. He grinned before gazing warily at the bed.

"It's just the springs." I lifted the mattress to show him and then I sat down bouncing and patting the bed beside me. I left him squeaking and grinning.

In my room, the sound of the rain drowned any noise he might have made on the squeaking bed, but I was aware of the wall between us as I changed into sleeping clothes and got into bed. I had been in bed only a few minutes when I heard him at my bedroom door. Then he was a darker lump in the darkness beside my bed.

"I want to be in here with you," he announced with such simplicity that I opened the covers. Given what I had seen bathing him, he was in no shape to take advantage of me.

We slept that night spooning together for warmth as we had the afternoon I found him. All night, I dreamed of hands and eyes and tongues, of an indistinct jumble of flesh and skin sliding by and around and then into me. Boundaries disappearing and reappearing. My own hands cupping a kneecap or a shoulder blade, or tracing the rippled expanse of ribs. They were liquid dreams, familiar and unfamiliar. Disturbing.

Waking in the morning, I was conscious first of something good and new. Then I remembered. Yes, him. That was how I thought of him— just Him. He needed a name. I wanted to find out what his name was rather than give him one. His lack of knowledge about himself was, otherwise, becoming peculiarly undisturbing to me.

He turned in the bed beside me, a column of warmth. I lay there a moment, not moving as I listened to his breathing and the rain. Beyond the rain there was silence. Even the trains were flooded out now. It would be days before the road would be clear again. I would have my stranger to myself. We were alone in a house of present tense; for now, he did not need a name or history. The extreme weather fit him. Something equally extraordinary and extreme had happened to him.

When I got out of bed, he moaned sweetly. Before I got the stove warm, he walked into the kitchen looking even better than the day before. His hair, about an inch long, was red—bright red like mine and my mother's. A carrot top like me. His skin was more natural, all the yellow gone out of it, though it did not appear quite normal in its smoothness. He moved well, too, lowering himself gracefully to sit cross-legged on the floor where he watched me make our breakfast. His eyes never left me, going from my face to my hands and back again. I did not ask myself how he could heal so quickly. My mind went around that question like creek water around a stone. I thought, instead, of a cicada I'd once watched emerge from its chrysalis. The short, nubby wings, clearly not large enough for its bulk, had expanded as if converting the air itself into more wingspan, the delicate veins growing as I watched.

All day, he shadowed me, watching and listening while I did my chores. We went to the coop first. The chickens murmured as I unlocked the door. They fluffed themselves and strutted to the feeding pans. He laughed when he saw them, a bubbly, metallic laugh. I measured their feed at the first pan and he copied me with precision at the second feeding pan.

We were a parade of three, me doing my routine chores, jabbering away. Him big-eyed, one step behind me. And Hobo was at the man's side at every opportunity. While we were in the barn, the cat joined us. I explained everything—chickens, the sow, bridles, the pump, the water coming up from underground. Everything seemed new to him.

Becky nickered softly and one of the cows lowed deep and long when I opened the barn door. Behind me, he exclaimed, "Ooooh!" and stopped on the threshold. I pulled him out of the rain into the barn. I lit the lantern. He stood beside one of the cows. Becky turned in her stall to face him.

For the first time, he seemed oblivious to my presence. Solemnly, he studied the cow, running his hands along her back and shoulders. Then he went to her ears and face. The cows, particularly, were not patient when waiting to be fed, but they were quiet as he went to them one by one. Without complaint, they let him touch them—hooves, tail, ears, and muzzle. I moved closer with the lantern. The planes of his face reminded me of my mother's family.

An expression of complete absorption and concentration filled his face. The sound of rain pelting the roof dominated, but I felt a steady, barely audible drone beneath it. Becky snorted softly, straining toward him, and he went to her. He lifted his face and shut his eyes. She rubbed her head against his, sniffing him loudly.

He moved into shadows as he circled Becky. Then he reappeared and gently combed his hands through her mane. He sighed deeply, then stepped back, smiled at me, and opened his hands. The barn fell completely still and I realized that the humming drone had ceased. "Show me how," he said.

I did. We fed, watered, shoveled, and combed. His study of the cows and Becky seemed to have sobered him, but when we got to the milking, he grew more excited. He squatted beside me, so close he could have suckled the cow. When the first squirt of milk hit the bucket, he squawked and rolled back onto his heels.

"It's just milk," I said.

"Milk!" His mouth hung open in surprise. He leaned back and eyed the cow respectfully. Just then one of the other cows farted loudly. Still open-mouthed, he swirled toward the second cow, then glanced quizzically at me. I started laughing and could not stop. I giggled and guffawed in waves until I cried. All the strangeness of the last days uncoiled from my diaphragm.

He just watched me, a patient smile on his face. Clearly, I was a benign, interesting idiot.

When I finally stopped laughing and wiped my eyes, he sat up straight, cocked his head, and said, "You okay?" He touched a tear on my cheek.

"Great," I said.

He held his hands out as if ready to take over the milking. I showed him how to hold the udders. I wrapped my hands around his so he could feel the pressure as I pulled and squeezed. His hands were warm and the same size as mine. When I let go, he continued the milking. He was a quick study.

On the way back from the barn, the downpour soaked us. Lester's old clothes hung bedraggled on him. I offered him a shirt of mine. As he changed, I saw that he had a heaviness in his hairless chest, his nipples were puffy, the way some boys are as they change into men. Maybe I had overestimated his age. He did not need any help with the shirt. I scooted out the door when he started taking his pants off, which he did without bothering to turn from me.

In the evening, the rain continued washing over the house. I taught him how to make corn bread. While it baked, I prepared the beans and ham. He stood at the big kitchen window, peering out one side and then the other, taking in as much of the view as he could and giving me a rare chance to watch him unobserved. Beyond him, the horizon was dark and cloud-banked. The way he lifted his chin and swiveled his head—I'd seen my mother do that, her hand on the sill like that as she surveyed her backyard.

He looked healthy and good. He could have been one of the boys from town, his facial features still a little fuzzy in some way I couldn't put my finger on, but very normal. A little feminine. His skin was now as smooth as mine. No sign of a beard. No sign at all that he had ever looked so strange.

He was like the cicada expanding into itself—a normal face and skin emerging from his muddy, ugly surface. My anxiety about his unnatural transformation still rested under my diaphragm. But I felt the same sense of privilege studying him as I had when I watched the cicada.

At the dinner table, he saw me observing him and put his fork down to look back at me. I had no doubt anymore: he was not foreign at all. He smiled. Lord, he had a smile.

He reminded me of my momma and my brother, Joe.

When we were going to bed that night, he asked if he could sleep in my bed for the whole night. I thought of Cole, then set that thought aside. This was not the same. This strange man was different and, I reminded myself, not quite a man anymore. I pushed the blanket aside to make way for him as I had the night before.

He laughed a soft belly laugh, clear and pretty as springwater, and climbed in beside me.

Though we slept fully clothed for warmth as we had the night before, I was very conscious of him next to me under the covers. He went to sleep almost immediately. Then there was just the warmth of his breath on my neck, the sound of the rain, and, harmless on the other side of the walls, the night.

What he was doing was impossible: no one healed or changed so fast. It was impossible and unnatural, but I had watched it happen. Tentatively, I touched his hand and found it as warm and smooth as my own.

What he had done could not be done; it could not *be*. But it was. A dizzying panic filled me. I took my hand away from him. I wanted light. I focused on the gray rectangle of window in the darkness, forced myself to listen to the rain. Rain was still just rain. It sounded on the tin roof as it always had. I calmed myself by listing the other things that were also the same: Hobo sleeping on the porch, the chickens in their coop, and the cows making milk, my family sleeping down the hill, the houses of the mill-village spread out on either side of my family's house. In each of those houses slept the people I had known all my life. Nothing else had changed. And no one else knew about him. I was the only one who had seen him change. The experience was mine. Only mine. How could I possibly explain what he had done? I pictured myself trying to tell my momma, and my mind froze. How would anyone believe me? Eventually, I slept, dreaming the same dreams as the night before— disturbing, beautiful dreams of touch and taste.

For two more days I explained the farm and its various chores to the strange man who shadowed me, ever more agile and confident, recalling nothing of who he was or where he came from. The rain abated for hours at a time, then swept through with renewed fury.

Sunday morning arrived. I got up in the darkness, stoked the stove, set the coffee on it, and then went back to bed. On Sundays, I allowed myself the luxury of snuggling warm in bed for the time it took the kitchen to warm up and the coffee to begin percolating. Aunt Eva would have considered it a sinful self-indulgence not to begin the chores immediately upon waking, which I did every other morning. But I was queen of the farm now, and the animals were no worse for the half-hour Sunday delay, and the Lord, I was certain, had better things to judge.

I returned to the bedroom with the lantern, and, as I slipped back between the covers and settled on the pillow, he turned, his face inches from mine. His eyes were green now, flecked with gold. Like Momma's eyes and Eva's, the eyes I'd looked into all my life. We lay there for a long time, absorbing each other. No one had ever regarded me like that, not even Cole when he lay with me. We touched each other's faces— lips, eyelids, cheeks. A single reverberation of thunder broke our reverie. The rain began its pounding anew. We got out of bed.

I heard a voice call my name as if from far away. I turned him to face me, to see if this was one more strange thing he could do.

His shirt had come unbuttoned in the night, and I saw them— breasts. Not the fatty chest muscles of a boy, but a woman's small, fully formed breasts. I stepped back, alarmed.

"I have to see!" With my hands shaking, I fumbled the lantern and pulled him toward the light.

I opened his shirt. His nipples puckered in the cold. "You're a girl!"

He peered down at his breasts, too. "I'm like you." He smiled, as if his breasts were gifts for me. Behind his voice was another, fainter, more familiar call: "Evelyn!" He had breasts, and he called my name without opening his mouth. Blood banged in my chest and ears.

I pulled the long johns away from his stomach. He was a woman for sure: small breasts, curve of hips, and nothing at all coming out from the patch of light red pubic hair.

Blood rose to my face, a flush of embarrassment, not for his naked- ness but for my own. I was in deep waters, drowning in innocence, be- trayed in some new way I had no name for.

"Don't," he said softly. "It's okay." He wiped a tear from my chin, and I realized that I still held his pants open, still stared down.

Again, I heard my name as I turned to the mirror on the wardrobe. Just for a second, I saw the two of us, facing the mirror, identical. He had my face. I took a deep breath. My diaphragm locked. Then he turned from me, toward the voice that I suddenly understood was com- ing from outdoors. My name again, small under the pelting rain, "Ev- elyn! Help, Evelyn!"

It took great effort to breathe, to pull myself away from him, from the reflection of us in the mirror. A voice outside called and the stranger was a woman now and looked just like me. Anything was possible. Anything, anyone could have been outside calling my name. I had to go and be ready. I wanted, suddenly, to get away from him. I stopped only to put my boots and coat on, and I ran to the voice that continued to call to me.

Sharp, icy rain slashed at me. I clenched my jaw and willed myself not to shiver. Cold was easier to take than what I had just seen. Rain pecked my face, so I could barely see. There was no ground, not a surface to step on, just an expanse of moving, shallow, clay-red water. I waded toward my name. "Help! Evelyn!" It was Cole's voice.

I staggered down the driveway until the ground dropped away suddenly. Cole sprawled on the ground four feet below me. He lay in the mud, facing up, his hat had tumbled away from him and his left leg stuck out beside him, the angle of it so wrong it seemed to belong to someone else. His horse, a young gray mare his daddy had just bought, stood a few yards off, tensed as if to bolt. There were deep gouges where the stone and clay of the driveway had given way.

Cole held his hand up to his eyes, shielding his face from the rain, and struggled to get up on one elbow when he saw me. I glanced back at the house. My stranger was in there, warm, dry, and calm where we had been alone for five days—a place like a dream of comfort. I was the link between Cole and the cold and her—*her*—in the house.

I could barely see. My skin prickled with the heat of alarm. None of this was a dream.

I turned back to Cole below me, shouting over the rain, "Cole, I'm here. Don't move! I'll get help."

I felt a warm hand on my arm. She was there beside me, a jacket and Uncle Lester's hat on. I allowed myself one short glance. "Stay here with him. I'll be back."

Below us, Cole grimaced with pain, his face ash-white against the mud. The rusty rainwater eddied around him.

"Cole, we're going to pull you up. I'm going to get some rope."

When I returned with rope, a wide plank, and an old sled, she stood where I'd left her, looking down at Cole, who squinted up. His face was all pain, but his eyes held a question. I gave her one end of the rope and had her back up a little while I went down for Cole.

His voice was hoarse. "I was worried 'bout you."

"Hush," I told him, and tied the rope around his chest. The fabric of his pant leg was blessedly coarse, easy to grip. I straightened his leg. He made a high, whimpering sound, shuddered, then passed out. While I strapped his legs to the plank, his horse came over and pulled at my coat. With Cole so slick and wet, dragging him up onto the sled took several tries. Unconscious, he was heavy, dead weight. We would need the horse.

I glanced up, but the mare was gone. Then I heard a sharp whinny behind me. Further down, past the driveway where the rise was less steep and covered with grass and rock, she stood above the horse, her hands open, encouraging. Under the drone of rain and the horse's sharp cries, I first felt, then heard a tone expand, sweet and imploring. The horse struggled, muscles straining at the collapsing mud. Crouching, she opened her arms. Her strange voice soared, split through the drumming of rain. Brilliant. The horse reared and beat the ground below her. She straightened, her arms open wider. The mare gained purchase, heaving up, then pranced straight toward her, neighing triumphantly. She tilted her face up and closed her eyes. The mare nosed under her hat, mouthing her short red hair intimately. She held the horse's head, laughing as her hands trailed the wet mane. Turning, they encircled each other.

I had to look away. Take a deep breath.

The two of them walked side by side, both seemingly oblivious to the rain and cold, to where she had dropped the rope. She picked it up and tied it to the saddle horn in a knot, her movements swift and sure.

I checked the line that bound Cole to the sled, then dragged him to a spot close to where the horse went up. She led the mare pulling the sled, and, with me guiding and pushing, we made it up over the rocks.

Cole came to, shouting a curse of pain just as we reached the top. Raising his head enough to see her and the horse ahead of us, he grunted, "Who is she?"

She. I glanced at her. Uncle Lester's big hat covered most of her face. She was drenched to the skin. *She.*

"I don't know," I mumbled, unable to form an explanation.

In the white noise of the rain, he heard a name. "Addie Nell? Addie Nell," he said. He grasped the sides of the sled as it lurched forward. "That's a nice name." Then he cursed God and passed out again.

She put Cole's horse in the barn and came back to help me. She was strong and well-coordinated, taking his whole weight from the bottom as we pushed him up the steps. I fought to keep my concentration, to not stare at her.

We set Cole up by the stove, on the spot where I had slept beside her a few days before. He shivered and then opened his eyes. He inspected her as she wiped mud off his face. "Evelyn?"

"Yes?" I replied.

He peered down at me as I cut his pants away from his swelling leg. His eyes went from me to her and then back and forth between us. "Addie Nell, right?" It seemed to please him that he remembered the name.

She turned to me. I shrugged.

"Yes," I told him.

Cole opened his mouth as if to say more, but a wave of pain hit him as I pulled the boot off of his bad leg. He closed his eyes and trembled silently. The bone had not come through, but it was a bad break. Except for a few moans, he lay quietly while we finished covering and cleaning him the best we could without moving him anymore.

We stood, dripping on the floor. My momma's eyes—my eyes—staring back at me. She left, came back with another towel, and began to dry my hair.

"No." I pushed the towel away. "I have to go get help. He needs help now. I'll just get wet again. We have to keep him warm or he'll go into shock. You get some dry clothes on."

She nodded and disappeared down the hall. I went for more blankets. I moved mechanically and did not allow myself to think.

She returned quickly and began wrapping warming bricks in towels. I froze, unable to take my eyes off her face. She laid the bricks at his feet then stretched on the floor next to him. She motioned for me to tuck the blankets around them. "Like you did for me."

I touched her arm as I pulled more blankets over them. She held my gaze a moment, then smiled. One thought came to me, overriding everything: I don't know who she is, but I trust her.

Then I had to go.

I shut the door behind me and stepped into the familiarity of the cold, stinging rain. In the barn, Cole's horse startled and backed away, head high, and rolled her eyes while I saddled Becky. I fumbled the bridle. Cold and shock numbed me.

The ride to Cole's house seemed endless. Twice I had to get off and walk for fear that my own horse would slip. My mind was as blurred by her, by Addie Nell, as my sight was by the veil of driving rain. I worried about Cole, but I knew what a broken leg was. Broken legs could be set and healed. Addie Nell—who had been neither woman nor man and now seemed to be my twin—I did not know.

What I had seen in the mirror just before I ran out to Cole rang like a deep blow to my chest. I had to catch my breath, to let my internal organs slip back where they should be. There was no logical, no reasonable explanation for her to look like me, no natural explanation for her transformation. My mind kept going back and forth from the seemingly faceless person I'd found in the mud to the face I'd seen next to mine in the mirror. My panic rose again. I dismounted, fell to my knees, and retched. I stayed there kneeling on the ground until long after I had stopped gagging. I was dumb, senseless as the water that streamed down my shoulders and back.

I wanted to go on past Cole's and into town and tell Momma. I wanted the dry comfort of my mother's kitchen. But she—Addie Nell—appeared so normal now. Would anyone, even Momma, believe me? It was unbelievable. But I had seen it with my own eyes.

I thought of her bright gaze and smile, of the sorrow on her face as she handed the photograph of the Japanese woman back to me. Another kind of panic filled me. I knew then, instinctively and with certainty, that I would not be able to tell anyone the truth. I sensed, just beyond my attempts to imagine telling anyone, a darkness and confusion, an amalgam of all the people around me—those smiling GIs in Frank's pictures, the Thompson family sneering when the Catholic family moved in next door to them, the eyes of the white men at the gas station and the feed store as they followed the colored people walking by, the strained face of the Murray girl as she hurried her bastard kid down the street. I remembered the faces of the boys who had teased me voraciously, sometimes cruelly, simply for the color of my hair or my height.

Soon she would be among Cole's family, then my family, then the town of Clarion.

For the first time in my life, I feared and distrusted my own kind. I saw them for a moment as an outsider might. If I told them and they believed me, how would they view her? A circus freak to stare at? Someone unnatural to be avoided? And if I told exactly what had happened and I was *not* believed, would I be pitied and tolerated or would they think I was crazy enough to be locked away? Away from her? I could not imagine her among the people in Clarion, the people I had known all my life. Folks who got up every morning and walked to the mill, the other kids I had gone to school with, or the congregation of the church. My head throbbed and my stomach churned violently. I fought the wave of nausea that swept through me as I lurched into the saddle.

She waited for me on the farm. I had to say something. I needed a plausible explanation for her presence and our resemblance. I needed to protect her and myself.

For a crazy moment, I imagined us boarding the train, heading for a new life in Chicago. Maybe we could find my aunt there, my father's long-lost sister, Doris, who had run away so many years before. No explanations would be necessary where no one knew us, and surely she would take us both in as family.

Immediately, I abandoned that idea. I knew I could not run away. I could not leave the farm and my mother. I could not leave the people I loved.

Then it hit me and I stopped, stunned.

Ignorance ran both ways. If my aunt in Chicago knew nothing about us, then it was also true that no one in Clarion knew anything about her. Rather than explain Addie Nell to my estranged aunt, I could use my estranged aunt to explain Addie Nell to my family. She could be the daughter of Doris Roe and the Hardin boy Doris had run off after. Addie Nell could be my cousin, come to find her mother's family. That would explain her resemblance to me. The thought seemed as wild as running off to Chicago, but it was the only thing I could think of. Within minutes I'd concocted a story: I'd ridden Becky into town for bag balm. The cows' udders were often chapped in winter. I'd taken Becky instead of walking, hoping to beat the approaching storm. Addie Nell, arriving in town to find her mother's relations, had immediately spotted me as family when I passed the train depot. Then the rain hit and we headed straight back to the farm to stable Becky and pick up fresh dry clothes for Addie Nell. It was plausible. I'd taken Becky on mid-week errands a couple of times.

Addie Nell Hardin. It could work. No one had heard from Doris since she left when my father was a teenage boy.

Giddy with relief, I laughed into the cold rain and urged Becky toward the Starneses' land.

All my life, I'd been a good daughter. Except for my nights with Cole, I'd never lied to Momma and Daddy, never done anything of importance that I knew they really didn't want me to do. But the lie would, I thought then, be easier than the truth. For everyone. Especially me.

I worked the details of my story, clinging to it like a drowning woman, while I made my way to Cole's family. I imagined Addie Nell at the train station and how I would phrase my story. I repeated the story of Addie Nell to myself as I crossed the Starneses' pasture. Wild fear pressed into the core of me, guarded by my desire to keep that bright gaze safe. By the time I got to Cole's house and saw his mother's worried face at the door, my teeth chattered violently. But internally, I was iron-calm, steady as a rock. As Mrs. Starnes opened the door and the warmth of her kitchen embraced me, I remembered her first name—Nell—and realized that Cole had heard the name Nell because he was familiar with it. We hear what we expect to hear. We accept things in the terms we can understand. That's what I was hoping for—that everyone would, like Cole, see what they expected to see and believe me.

From that point on, Addie Nell was just Addie to me.

WE RODE BACK TO MY HOUSE. Cole's father, his two brothers, and me. We squeezed into the front of their truck, with me sitting on the younger brother's, Reese's, lap bunched up against the door. We drove as far up the road as we could, then walked and slipped the rest of the way. The sky had grown even lower and darker, a hand slipped between us and the sun. Mr. Starnes fell coming up the bank and muttered something about his son being a fool. Otherwise, we were silent and hunched against the thick, cold rain. I feared this first meeting: my strange new twin and these quiet men who smelled of tobacco and cold leather.

Inside, Addie rose from the floor where she had been lying next to Cole. I was the first in the door and heard that soothing faint bell tone withdraw like a wave back toward the two of them. The skin along my forearms tingled. Cole did not move; he seemed to be asleep or unconscious.

The men filled the room awkwardly, watching Addie get up and then glancing at me for an explanation. "This is my cousin, Addie Hardin."

Without question, they nodded politely at her, then turned their attention to Cole, who had begun to moan as soon as they touched him. Only Reese looked back, his eyes going from her back to me, as they began to lift Cole.

His face blanched again and he twisted his neck to see me. "I just wanted to know if you were all right. You have wood and food?" The men stopped.

"I'm okay. We've got plenty of both."

"She's got better sense than you, Cole, going out in this weather," Mr. Starnes said, then they continued maneuvering him toward the back door.

"Bye," I told him and pulled the oilcloth over his face to keep the rain off. "I'll come see you as soon as I can."

Addie and I went to the front of the house, returning to the bedroom window to watch them ease down toward the road with Cole, and then reappear at the truck. Covered like that with his brother crouched beside him in the rusted truck bed, Cole resembled a dead man.

Alone again, Addie and I turned to each other. She was flesh and blood. Undeniable, impossible flesh and blood. I felt the startle of her presence in my chest, deep in my gut, but made myself look at her and breathe normally. She still had Uncle Lester's hat on. She'd had it on the whole time. Maybe the men hadn't seen her face very well. I felt the pressure of her unformed questions, but I held my hand up before she could speak and pulled her back over to the mirror.

"Take your clothes off," I told her. And she did, just like that. The hat, too.

"You?" She pointed to my clothes. And I took them off, everything. The air was cold, but the cold stayed outside us. I turned to her, staring. We were exactly alike. The only difference I could see was her straight left collarbone. Mine had a lump in it where I'd broken it as a baby. Her hair, much shorter than mine, was the same copper color and just as coarse and curly. We were the same height. Her toes were long, like mine. The veins branching across the backs of our hands were not identical. I turned her and saw, for the first time, my own back. "Is my behind that broad?" I asked. I didn't expect an answer, but she backed up against me and ran her hands from her hipbones back to mine.

"We're the same," she announced.

"How did you do this? What did you do?"

She stared down at her own hands, then her breasts. "I don't know. You were next to me." She shrugged.

"Why do you look like me? How?"

"I am like you. I don't know why. I opened my eyes and you were there. If I knew why, I would tell you. I would give you that. I am sorry. I don't know."

Her hands were warm. Her breath, as she turned to me, a thin vapor. We were inches apart. I saw nothing but her face and those familiar eyes, green flecked with gold. I felt nausea of fear and confusion, then a wave of calm. Under her gaze, the panic in me dwindled down to quiet the way a child's cries fall away under the rhythm and melody of a lullaby.

Suddenly we were both cold, and I remembered the animals unfed and unmilked in the barn. We dressed quickly, laughing when we stumbled in our rush.

We did chores, made coffee, and ate breakfast. I did the things I had done on countless ordinary days. Habit carried me through the job of slopping the hog, feeding the chickens, and milking the cows. But my skin was on fire, my nerves ping-ponging from "it cannot be" to "it is."

While we ate breakfast, I told her the story of my father's sister. I explained that she would be the daughter of my long-lost aunt, come to Clarion looking for her mother's relations. We had met at the train stop. As the train pulled up to the station, she'd seen me across the street at the feed store, and was so taken by our resemblance that, in her haste to get off the train, she forgot her suitcase. That's why she had nothing. As I finished my story, she took the dirty dishes from me, carried them to the sink, and began washing up as if she had been doing it for a lifetime.

"We have to say those things?" she asked.

I nodded.

"You think people will not like me if we don't tell them your story?"

I winced to hear it put so bluntly. "Mostly I think they wouldn't believe me if I told them the truth. But I have to tell them something. There has to be a reason for you to look like me."

She peered down at her body and her dripping hands. "Okay." She smiled. "But you are not afraid of me? And you like me?"

"Yes," I said. "I do like you and I'm not afraid."

She laughed. "You don't scare me either, and I like you, too." She turned that gaze on me while she dried her hands. "A train stop? Tell me about the train stop." She put her arm through mine and led me out of the kitchen, and I realized, with a shock, that she was comforting me.

The sun shone for the first time in days when we stepped outside late that afternoon. Everything glistened, new and distinct. For a moment I saw everything—the pump, the house, the barn, the apple tree, the fields—through her eyes, through the eyes of someone new. Every run-down, beautiful, waterlogged bit of my world. I was happy.

That night the lights came back on down the hill and the trains ran again. I took Addie outside when I heard the 8:10 coming. We stood in the thin light of the moon, our breath fogged around us and the train gleaming as it cleared the curve. It was deafening, but I could feel her beside me, the low, vibrant hum of her expanding under the sound of the train. When the conductor blew the horn, she laughed and, letting go of my hand, she held her arms out as she had earlier for the mare.

ON THE FIRST NIGHT after Cole broke his leg, I dreamed that she and I were Siamese twins, joined belly to belly, and I woke in the middle of the night to find that we, in a sense, had merged. Only years later would I have the words "lover" or "sex" to describe what we began that night.

The next evening, we began to touch each other as soon as we got into bed. In the darkness, she seemed to make of her body a room that we entered. And there was nothing but that room and her presence. She left no part of me untouched.

The moment I touched the warm, moist folds of her, she ceased moving. She sighed deeply then; an audible chime tingled up my arm and chest and into my head. Her strange, unnatural voice expanded, rising, then soaring past hearing as she shuddered and convulsed.

For a second, she was silent. "Are you okay?" I touched her face.

"Yes." Then she laughed, deep and sweet, as she would each night.

I did not know then that there was a vocabulary for what we did, or that other women had done the same before us. So, for me, there were no words for what we did, just as there was no word for how she had changed, emerging from the dirt and transforming into someone so like me. How we touched each other at night in bed seemed a small thing next to that. But I knew, without doubt, that it was good, as good and pure as the eyes she turned to me each morning. Good, but one more thing I could not speak of.

THREE

ADDIE

I've never been able to say with any precision why I responded to finding Addie as I did. I was very young, often alone, and without self-consciousness on the farm, a girl raised among people who did their jobs, seldom questioning what fate, commonly called the Lord, gave them. Then she arrived, inexplicable as the Lord. Undeniable, intelligent, and strange. To have her come up literally from the land I loved seemed natural, a fit to my heart's logic. The land's response to my love. So when fate gave me Addie, I let her be given.

HOW OTHERS WOULD ACCEPT HER remained a question that January as the sky finally began to clear, the mud dried, and the place I'd found her became only a slight depression in the soil. My thoughts were on my family and Addie's first meeting with them. But there were others closer at hand.

The Lay family—Mildred, Ralph, and their son, Crandall, who was a few years younger than me—lived west of the farm. Their house was downhill from us and there was a narrow field where they kept a couple hogs and a small garden.

Crandall was peculiar. "Not quite right in the head" was the way most people put it. He never learned to read and, by fourth grade, had been allowed to drop out of school. He did not like to be touched, and I'd heard that he once had some kind of fit in church. He rarely spoke and spent most of his time outside, rocking side to side and playing scales on his harmonica. Never a melody, always scales. Tow-headed and scarecrow-thin, he'd stand in the sun, out by his momma's vegetable garden, and play like there was nothing else in the world but a harmonica. Certainly, people were not in his world. He looked right through everybody.

The day before the roads cleared up and anyone else could make it up to the farm, something brought Crandall Lay close to our land. He stood down by the creek, next to the barbed-wire fence that separated our farm from the Lays'. I watched him from the back porch, listening to the monotonous drone he made of note after note when Addie appeared at the barn door, bucket in hand. She put the bucket down and strolled toward Crandall, who swayed side to side with the precision of a metronome.

It was a relief and a pleasure to see her from a distance, to take her likeness to me in a smaller dose. Her back and shoulders seemed straighter, more graceful than I felt myself to be when I walked. She stopped at the fence and held her hand out as I had instructed her to when meeting someone for the first time. From where I stood on the porch, I saw her in profile. Her mouth moved, but I was too far away to hear what she said.

He didn't break rhythm of his scale or acknowledge her. Her hand remained in the air, innocent. Suddenly, I realized that I needed to explain his odd behavior to her. I jumped off the porch and jogged toward them, focused on her hand, motionless above the fence. As I came near, she tilted her head and, bending over, peered up at his face. For that second, they seemed similar, twin oddities. I had my hand out to touch her shoulder. As Crandall paused to inhale, a crisp, loud tone pealed through the air one perfect octave above his last note, like nothing I had heard from her so far. A short, clear pop of a question like a single sharp rap on a triangle.

Crandall froze. Addie's hand shot out and caught the falling harmonica. His eyes focused, shifted rapidly from her to me then back to her, his expression dead calm, open, as her nonverbal question fell into silence. I could not see her face, but as his gaze returned to it, she held the harmonica out to him, touching his hand. For a second, he looked at her. Then his features contorted and he exploded in a guttural scream. He spun, snatching the harmonica from her and ran, stumbling back toward his home.

Suddenly, I could not breathe. I was sure he recognized her unnatural nature. My next thought was that we were safe: whatever he'd seen or heard, he would not be able to report, no one would believe him.

She whirled around to face me, wide-eyed. "What happened? I was asking him to say hello."

I opened my mouth, mirroring her.

Then she answered her own question. "He is not like us," she announced.

"Like 'us'?" I thought. Like us? I giggled.

She frowned and glanced toward the Lay home. "Why is he afraid of me?"

The question sobered me. "No one can do what you just did. None of us make those sounds." I touched my own throat and asked, "Can all your people do that?"

She waved the question away. "I don't know who or where my people are or what any other people can do." She spread her fingers on her chest. And I heard a drone, the timbre of a large bell, a pure tone without question or inflection, a simple demonstration that blossomed through my head and chest then vanished into the air between us. "No one can do that?" she asked.

I hesitated. Perhaps others could. Maybe I was the innocent one, the ignorant one. But I shook my head and took her arm to lead her back toward the house. "No. No one here can." Suddenly, it seemed best if we were out of sight. "He's in his own world, Addie. He usually doesn't notice anyone. I've never seen him look anyone in the eye, not even his own momma. He's not hurt. He's just different. It was a kind of compliment that he reacted to you at all."

She tapped herself on her breastbone and then waved her hand in a graceful arc. "If no one else can do that, then I won't do it out here. But I won't be able to stop it at night with you. Then I forget everything. Everything. For a moment."

"Then is okay." I remembered the night before, the moan of her into my mouth, flushing through me. For a second, I could barely walk. Then I ran ahead of her up the steps of the house and held the door open for her. She entered, grinning like an ordinary woman.

❧

WHEN IT COMES TO PERSONAL THINGS, affairs of the family or the heart, there seem to be two kinds of men. There are men who ask questions and may even pry. These men may be tender in their solicitations or simply authoritarian, but they are present to their families. The second kind of man never asks questions and certainly never pries, particularly about emotional situations or conflicts. These men give an angry or sad woman a wide berth, and they will leave a hapless child to wander into trouble. At times these unquestioning men may seem wise and patient. Other times, they don't seem to be there at all. They can have an air of absence about them that leaves their women and children lonely.

Daddy was the second kind of man. He rarely asked me about anything except money, food, and the farm. The only subjects of conversation for him were the concrete, daily arrangements of things. He did not seem to want to know what was in our hearts. Whether it was shyness, lack of curiosity, or indifference, I never knew. Once, when he had come to the farm to bring me some flour and feed, Cole's cap lay on the sofa where he had left it the night before. Daddy glanced at it without a word.

Perhaps Daddy was like that because he had too much of his own burden to keep hidden and quiet. It made sense that he would not want to speak of his half-sister who, without benefit of marriage, ran off with a strange man, but he seldom mentioned anyone else in his family either. They were all poor farmers. Most of them drunks, I heard, his father the worst of them. His mother had died when he was a boy and his father married again. With his new wife, he had had Doris, Addie's "mother." When other men told their stories, Daddy would laugh with them, but he told none of his own.

He was not a bad father, not much of a disciplinarian, and never cruel. Yet his love was like light to me. I could see it and I knew intellectually that it touched me, but I could not touch it back. And like the sun's light on an overcast winter day, it did not warm me, just reminded me of warmth and made me hunger for it.

With Daddy, Addie and I were safe from scrutiny. But Momma was a curious woman, one who liked to know the end of stories. Out of respect, she would leave Addie alone, for a while, at least. But over time, I was sure, she would give voice to her curiosity.

They would, I knew, be coming to check on me as soon as they could, and so I did my best to make Addie look less like me. I curled her hair on Eva's bobby pins. That made one small difference—she had short, very curly hair. Mine was long and hung in waves. Aside from her hair, there wasn't much I could do. I went over her story several times. But my knowledge was limited. All I could tell her was the names of her momma and daddy and where she was from. I hoped no one else knew more than I did and that my father's half-sister had truly vanished.

I coached her to shake hands with my parents when she first met them and to call them ma'am and sir till they told her not to. They would, I assured her, be like Cole's family and nothing like Crandall Lay.

So when we heard the truck shut off down the road, we were ready. They came walking up the driveway, just Momma and Daddy. They had left my brother and sisters at home. Daddy had on a good shirt, and Momma had on one of her shopping dresses. Not Sunday stuff, just better than their everyday clothes. Clearly, they had heard about Addie.

She emerged from the chicken coop with the eggs. They hollered a hello to her, and she raised a hand hesitantly. Momma started over to her, reaching out to touch what she thought was my newly shorn hair. She turned to me when I called.

"Good Lord," she said and shut her mouth on whatever else she had been about to say. We all stood there a minute—Momma and Daddy looking back and forth at me and Addie.

Momma glanced back over her shoulder to Daddy. "No doubt about it, she's kin." Then she took the hand Addie offered. By the time we all got inside, I had told them most of Addie's story, being careful to meet Momma's gaze once or twice. The discomfort of lying to my parents fluttered through my chest. Then I felt the very faint, now familiar humming of Addie next to me. Momma and Daddy did not seem to notice anything at first, but their faces softened. In the kitchen, Daddy cocked his head, a look of concentration on his face, and Momma rubbed her breastbone. I touched Addie's hand and in that split second of contact the humming sensation vanished, lifting from the room. Momma's hand dropped to her side.

Addie left us to put the eggs away in the pantry. While Daddy stopped at the stove to pour himself a cup of coffee, Momma pulled me down the hall and into Ricky's old bedroom, squeezing my arm. "It sure is strange how much she looks like you. She ought to look like that Hardin boy and your daddy's side of the family. But she sure resembles you and my side of the family. Looks like her momma ran into one of my brothers on her way out of town. What will everybody think?"

What could Momma's brothers have to do with Addie? Then I realized how utterly stupid I'd been. I looked like my mother's side of the family. I had big hands like Daddy and thought my chin looked like his as much as Momma's. But the McMurrough red hair, height, and freckles from Momma's family trumped everything. How could Addie have gotten those through my daddy's side of the family? My mind went blank.

She gave me a glance I couldn't read, then turned her attention to the kitchen where Daddy and Addie were.

I heard him ask how the patch on the porch roof had held up through the storms. Would she know what a patch was? She replied softly, barely audible.

Momma pulled me close. "She even sounds like you," she hissed. Panic rippled through my belly and I thought I would be sick. I opened my mouth to respond but Daddy called out for Momma then, and her face returned to its normal expression. "Come on," she said. "Let's go see what your daddy wants. She's family. We can figure the rest out later."

They were cordial but they did not sit down, and stayed only long enough to make a list of the things I needed from town. Addie was quiet, big-eyed, and shy. They were leaving when Daddy stopped at the door and turned to Addie. He held his hat in his hands, turning the brim slowly. "Your family, how are they?"

Momma raised her eyebrows at me in surprise. Daddy inclined his head listening for her answer, his gaze drifting to the floor.

Addie glanced at me. "Her momma died not long ago," I told them.

Momma touched Addie's arm, muttering, "Oh. I'm so sorry."

Daddy just nodded, his eyes still on the floor. He put his hat on and looked directly at Addie. "It's Uncle, Uncle Robert. Welcome to North Carolina, Addie." That was the last and only time he ever asked Addie anything about her family.

Momma and Daddy came back soon, of course, and they brought the rest of the family with them. Joe, Bertie, and Rita piled out of the back of the truck and stood in a line, their eyes darting from Addie to me and then back again in that ping-pong of glances that would become so familiar in the next weeks and months. Surprise showed on their faces, but they were meeting Addie with an explanation in hand, and I'm sure Momma and Daddy had prepared them.

For a long moment, we all just stared at each other, and then Addie laughed, sweet and pure.

Joe held out his hand. "Welcome, Addie Hardin. You are definitely among family." I thought he might be making a veiled reference to her questionable paternity. But the wide grin on his face was a guileless match to Addie's. He winked at me. "Next long-lost relation you bring home has to be a boy like me, okay?"

Bertie crossed her arms on her chest. Her mouth turned down at the corners and the tendons in her neck twitched. She didn't like change or things that took her by surprise. "You came all the way from Chicago to work on this farm?"

Addie shrugged. "I like it here."

Rita erupted in a shy giggle and touched my arm briefly as if checking the reality of what she saw, then she dashed past us into the house.

That was it: they accepted her. My story about her origins may have had its flaws, but she was clearly one of us.

❧

I BRACED MYSELF for Addie's introduction to the rest of Clarion, certain someone would see her as an imposter or find a hole in my story. Someone who would claim they had not seen me on Clear Lake Road just before the storm. Or someone who had been on the train and knew she had not. Suddenly, my home and community did not seem so transparent. My heart pounded every time she held out her hand to a new person and announced herself: "Addie Hardin." I followed with the announcement that she was the daughter of my daddy's half-sister, Doris. There was the moment of hesitation while everyone took in the similarity between us. I am sure that there must have been some speculation about our situation and who Addie's father might be, but I heard none of it. In fact, the only person, besides Momma, to bring up Addie's mother was Miss Biddy.

Addie's first time off the farm was the Sunday after she met Momma and Daddy. She and I finished the morning chores, dressed in our Sunday clothes, and walked down to the mill-village church. It was a cold, bright morning, the ground still soggy from the days of rain. Addie beamed—at the trees and the houses, at each person we passed on the way to church, then, at church, the whole congregation. Every set of eyes we met bounced swiftly back and forth between us. But I'm sure the differences were apparent immediately that day. She was the quiet one with the smile and the ready handshake. I was the anxious, chatty one. I was sweating under my coat by the time we sat down on our pew in the sanctuary. I kept thinking of the day she met Crandall Lay and wondering what sound might burst out of her, but she produced only words, handshakes, and her infectious smile.

For the sermon, she sat between me and Rita. She gave the preacher her full attention, looking at me occasionally, her eyes wide with questions. When we opened the hymnal and began to sing, she did not join us until the repeat of the chorus. Her voice was strong and, to my ears, richer than my own. She glanced at me between verses, a question on her face. I did not understand, at first. I ran my finger along the hymnal words, but she shook her head. That's when I realized she couldn't read. She had picked up some of the books on the farm. I had assumed she could read them. But my assumption suddenly seemed foolish. She had arrived knowing nothing, why should she know how to read?

Outside, after the sermon, Rita gazed up and asked her, "How come you didn't sing all the songs, Addie?"

Addie took her hand and gave her that smile. "I couldn't. I don't know all the words yet."

"Why not, you ain't been to church?" Rita smiled back. "Or they didn't sing in your church?" Normally very reserved, Rita swung Addie's hand now, and peered up at her almost flirtatiously.

I didn't wait for Addie's truthful answer. Instead, I took Rita's other arm and turned her toward Momma. "Scoot," I told her and turned my attention to the gauntlet of introductions as everyone filed out of the church. There was a ripple of attention from the older women. The younger men eyed us from across the churchyard. Addie took the attention well.

She and I lingered longer than usual outside the church. My family had gone on ahead. I was trying to explain the sermon to Addie as we walked toward Momma's house when Miss Biddy stopped us.

Miss Biddy wasn't her real name, but that's what half the town called her. She had a long, unpronounceable Polish name that started with a B. She was a tiny woman and had a birdlike way of tilting her head side-to-side. Something of the Pole remained in her speech and made a peculiar blend with her Southern accent. She and her husband had a laundry and, later, a dry-cleaning service downtown.

She plucked at my elbow, and, squinting up at us, waited for her introduction to Addie. "I just wanted to tell you girls how happy I am to see you in church. Especially you." She tilted her chin at Addie. "I knew your mother. She was a sweet girl, quiet and a little sad sometimes. But good. A good girl regardless of what anyone says. She ironed for me. She was always neat, a good worker. I was sorry when she left."

"Thank you," Addie replied and held out her hand. "Thank you for telling me that about her."

Miss Biddy opened her mouth, as if to say more, but Addie clasped Miss Biddy's slender, freckled hand and smiled. "We have to go now.

Aunt Lily is expecting us for dinner." She tilted her head, mirroring Miss Biddy, and they beamed at each other.

I was calmer by the time we got to Momma's. At the dinner table, she was just another family member, passing a plate of ham down the table. Momma was the only one who treated her like company, offering then reoffering second helpings.

That night, when we were alone, Addie began the practice of repeating the names of people she had met, asking me about them and mapping out the social relations of the town. I found an old reading primer in the parlor bookcase, dated, worn, and childish. She sniffed its pages as she spread it open on the dining table.

"We start here." I flipped to the first page. I felt my tension release as I recited the alphabet to her and pointed to each letter. She had made it through her initial introduction to Clarion without incident. No one knew our secret. No one but me.

Addie ran her finger over the faded illustrations and short sentences, her voice rising and falling as she read aloud, sounding out the simple nouns and verbs. I stood behind her and brushed her short hair, as Eva had done countless times for me. In that moment, I had no questions for her: it did not matter where she came from or what strange things she could do.

She learned quickly, finishing the primer before we went to bed.

What I saw at church that day was repeated over the weeks of introductions everywhere we went—the mill-village, Rhyne's store, downtown, the feed store—people stopping to fuss over us and exclaim about our similarity. Addie was attentive and calmly gracious, speaking very little and volunteering nothing of herself in terms of facts. Smoothly deflecting questions with her warm smile and gentle touch.

❧

FROM THE MOMENT I found Addie in the mud, my fears calmed by her unique voice, I felt myself bent to a new form. Part lullaby, part plea, and part question, the sound she made was a peculiar combination of elements. It had the metallic droning vibrato of a bell and the hummed warmth of the human voice. I felt its sweet harmonics in my bones as I heard them with my ears. Deep in me, something cracked open and unfurled, a giving way that would neither need, nor brook repair.

For months after I found her, I was in a heightened state, my nerves on a slow, white-hot burn. I could not sleep for more than five or six hours at a stretch, often getting only four hours in a night. I could not eat much at a sitting. Food, even plain biscuits with syrup or jam, turned heavy and too rich after a few bites. I lost weight and clothes hung on me, yet I was not tired.

For all of this, I did not feel upset. An odd calm lay over me, like the calm that comes in the middle of some great disaster, when things must be done quickly, yet the world seems to move slowly and with more light and precision. Everything was sharper and more defined, brighter, as if my pupils were open more than normal. The sky's light, the patterns in cloth, the minute convolutions of a tree's bark, the speckling of rust on a car fender—all these I looked not at but *into*. When I spoke to people, I looked directly into their faces, and there was more there in each of them than I'd previously seen. Not different things—just more of who they were—as if their souls were coming to the surface of their skin, giving themselves to me.

Addie's arrival was a baptism by adrenaline, yet my body's fight-or-flee response left me, and I could do neither. All I could do was surrender. Allow the seemingly inevitable, the fantastic, to come in and eat at my table like a long-known neighbor.

But I did not surrender passively. I wanted the slight metallic taste of her, the grassy odor of her sweat. Her sweet, strange voice at night. I wanted all that she contained that was *not* like me. Each time I touched her, I bonded my longing for her otherness to the nerves and fibers of my body.

Sometimes she would sit on the bed in the dark next to me with her legs crossed and lightly touch me everywhere—from the crown of my head to my heels and toes. Again and again her hands would roam over me, as if she were a blind woman trying to memorize my contours. She was always silent when she did this and, if there was moonlight enough, I could see that her eyes were half-open, her face calm and slack, as if all of her being had gone into her hands. Her touch buoyed me. When she was done, she leaned over and pressed her chest against mine, her hands on my face. Her body became a room we entered. Everything else fell away and I forgot myself. Her strange voice rose around us, the harmonics of it on my skin, then ringing like light in my breastbone up to my skull and down through my hips. She found the core and pressed in.

I was nearly undone, as if the literal fibers of my being were unwinding themselves—dissipating. Her touch and her laughter would carry through into the day, sticking like fine powder on my skin.

One night I lay stunned, limp, and humbled next to her. "Does it bother you that I can't do everything you can do? That I can't do with my voice what you do with yours?"

"It doesn't come from here." She touched me lightly on my throat. "But here." She tapped between my breasts. "Would it still be called a voice?"

"It's like a voice. But it is not a voice. How do you do it?"

She pressed her lips together and closed her eyes. A short, declarative tremolo radiated from her. She opened her eyes. "I don't know how I do it. Most of the time, it just happens. I'm not trying to do anything."

"At night, here with me, you always sigh 'Aaahh' first, then you start to . . . to resonate."

"I resonate?" She laughed. "It doesn't matter that you can't give me the same kind of 'voice' I can give you. You gave me all this." She skimmed her hand lightly over my face and down my body.

I did not know what to say. I had given nothing. She had taken her identity from me, yet left it with me and given me every reason to see how vastly different we were from one another. She pulled me closer and, pressing her mouth to mine, gently exhaled into me.

No name for what she was or what she did. No name for the place she had come from.

But each night there was her sweet voice.

On my moonlit, sleepless nights, she lay beside me, sleeping. Everyone, everything else slumbered, and the world was quiet. In the surreal silence of midnight, I watched her, studying a face more like my own than a mirror. I lay close enough that I breathed her exhalations and she mine, the air going in and out of us in matched rhythm. Watching her eyes move over the dream world under her closed lids, I could not imagine what she saw. A world peopled with others like her? I saw the face my mother must have seen when she watched me sleeping, the face I would see later when my own daughters, so like me, slept. I was inside and outside my own skin, both the mother and the daughter, the other and myself.

Other nights, I would have to rise from our bed and walk the house, touching the walls and the furniture until the ordinary proportions and places of things returned.

Once, while pacing the bedroom, I saw a fox cross the bright, night-gray yard, trotting purposefully, confidently on small, delicate paws. I wanted to touch those paws, to feel the press of them on the ground and know the texture of her coat. To be outside in the cool darkness, my nose in the air.

Sometimes, without moving, Addie would open her eyes and look at me from a seemingly deep sleep. I would see, then, who I was not. The distinctness of myself lurched within me, the tender presentness coming over me as she opened her arms and pulled me into them again.

FREDDIE AND MARGE RUMFORD WERE A YOUNG COUPLE, just married. I had known Freddie all my life, but Marge, whom he married shortly after coming back from the war, was from Cramerton. Freddie, a thin man with a dry sense of humor, had returned from the war almost mute until he met Marge, a big, friendly girl, her body seeming to move in loose, relaxed circles. After they married, local musicians gathered every Sunday evening for picking parties at their home.

One Sunday, Addie and I passed Freddie and Marge's on our walk back to the farm from dinner at Momma's. The early spring air was warm enough that they had left the door open. Music tumbled out onto the street—banjo, guitar, fiddle, and mandolin. Addie stopped dead in the street, her head cocked to one side. She followed the music into their house. Just opened the screen door and strode in. I was right behind her.

Freddie sat on a tall stool in the kitchen. One of the Wilkes girls and a few of the old fellows who used to play with my uncle Lester crowded the room, not skipping a beat of their waltz as Addie barged in.

I couldn't see Addie's face, but I saw Marge's when she turned from cleaning up at the sink and realized we were in her kitchen. There was the little flash of surprise that crossed people's faces when they met Addie. I waved so Marge would know which one of us was me.

Addie stood motionless, transfixed by the music, then cackled with delight as the tune ended. Amid the noise of everyone shifting around to pull in some more chairs, I introduced her. No one blinked or asked a question as we settled in our seats.

"I've heard about you," Marge said. "Glad to meet you, Addie."

The musicians picked up their instruments again and started playing "Haste to the Wedding." Marge pulled me to my feet. We turned in the middle of the kitchen and danced out to the porch and back. Addie stood up with her hands held out expectantly. Marge took her for a spin, the two of them laughing. Addie followed surprisingly well.

When they danced back into the kitchen and Marge released her, Addie sat and stared at the musicians, enthralled. During their next break, Freddie leaned across the kitchen and said to Addie, "Here, you look like you want this in your hands. Try it."

Addie took the banjo and ran her hands over its strings, "ahhing" like a child, and everyone laughed at what they took to be comic exaggeration. She bent over it in precise imitation of Freddie's shoulder-hunched way of playing and grinned up at me as she plucked.

After Addie returned the banjo, the musicians resumed playing. She closed her eyes as she listened, tilting her head as if zeroing in on one instrument then another. We stayed until milking time.

Days later, she found Uncle Lester's old fiddle at the bottom of the wardrobe. It made an awful squawk when she first touched bow to string. She winced and echoed with her own surprised cry. Holding the fiddle out away from her shoulder, she glared at it.

I'd been around enough fiddle players to show her some basics—the tuning pegs, the bow, the rosin. The next time we went into town, we bought strings. She worked on her fiddle-playing every spare moment, her face screwed up in concentration. She paced the house, the yard, and the barn, fiddle to her chin. Soon she had notes and had taught herself a simple song. In the next few days, she pulled me from my chores and asked me to sing for her. I'd sing a song and then she'd work at it and work at it until she got it right.

Once, after I sang "The Old Rugged Cross" for her, she spent every spare moment of her day working on it. She showed up at the barn while I finished the evening milking, fiddle and bow in hand, her brow furrowed. "Once again? I almost have it," she said. I sang it again, leaning my head on old Lilac's warm side. She listened intently, staring up into the rafters of the barn, the way I'd seen Daddy stare as he listened to the radio. Then she played it again, swaying in the lantern light, her eyes closed.

Not long afterward, she carried the fiddle down to Momma's for Sunday supper and we stopped by Freddie and Marge's. They recognized Lester's fiddle in her hands and playfully asked her what she planned on doing with it. Without a word, she stepped into the center of them, put it under her chin, and started on a slow version of "The Old Rugged Cross," a little rough but all there. Rusty, an old man well known in the area for his fiddling, picked up on the chorus with her. When they were done, he put his old, mottled hand on her shoulder and said, "That was real sweet, darling."

After that, we spent our Sunday evenings at Freddie and Marge's. She preferred to play standing. Among the mostly middle-aged, meaty men who met at Freddie's, she was a bright contrast, swaying pale and slender. Sometimes she set the fiddle aside and we sang, harmonizing like sisters. Her skin seemed to shine then, and when she turned that gaze on me, she was brilliant. Absorbing. She filled the room.

COLE WAS CONFINED while his leg mended. The thought of the two of them meeting again made me nervous. Addie had told me that, while I'd gone for help, Cole had mostly been unconscious, moaning and cursing some. Still, I wasn't certain what he might think about me and her. When I visited him during his recovery, I went alone. I brought him magazines and a pie. He spent his days in his family's parlor, his broken leg encased in a thick white cast, stretched out the length of the couch, the rest of him covered with blankets. I told him about Addie, reminding him of how she favored me.

He nodded. "I don't remember much but the pain and cold. She held my hand and hummed to me. That helped. She reminded me of you." He rubbed his chest thoughtfully.

I distracted him with a question about my plans to get his daddy to loan us the tractor in the spring.

He would have to come with the tractor, he told me. His daddy wouldn't want a girl driving it by herself. Beyond that, we spoke of nothing important. We had no privacy sitting there in the parlor, awkward with his family around, coming and going. I stayed only a few minutes each time.

By late March, Cole's leg had healed well enough for him to get up on a horse. I was sweeping the back porch when he trotted up on his old chestnut. He dismounted slowly, easing his bad leg down, then walked up to the house with a limp that made me wince. He had a bouquet of dried mistletoe tied with a red ribbon. "This is the best I can do this time of year." He grinned. "I was hoping to remind you of my Christmas present."

He meant my Christmas promise to him. I had expected he would want to be back in my bed. But too much had changed. He and I had not so much as kissed since early December. I could not be with him like that, not while I was with Addie. For the first time, I had to admit to myself that what I did with her was what I had done with him. That admission stunned me speechless. He laughed, misunderstanding my stammering blush. Waving the mistletoe over my head, he leaned forward for a kiss.

Just then Addie and Hobo came around the corner of the house. She stopped, smiled at him, and held out her hand. His mouth hung open. He looked from me to her and then whistled. "Geez, I'd heard you looked alike, but I really didn't remember. I didn't see that well when my leg . . . Geez." He shook her hand. "Thank you, Miss . . . Addie, for . . ." He pointed toward the road. ". . . When I . . . umm." It was his turn to go red-faced.

"Just Addie. Where's the horse you rode before—the gray one? I liked her." She walked over to his horse and stroked her neck. The mare sidestepped closer to Addie, nudging her shoulder.

"She's too lively for me now with my leg. Too spooky to begin with. That's why we got her so cheap. Though I reckon I have paid a price for her. She's worse now. Daddy's thinking of selling her. She's still trouble." He rubbed his leg and moved to sit on the edge of the porch.

"I've seen her out in your pasture and talked to her. I'll take this one to the barn for you," she said and turned. The horse followed, its reins dangling. Cole watched them walk away.

"God, she looks like you." Then he turned to face me. "Can I come see you some evening?"

"Just me?"

"Well, yes, just you. Like before." He moved closer but I continued to sweep the steps. A subtle move, but it registered in his face.

"I can't. Cole, I can't, not with her here."

"We can be quiet."

"No, we sleep in the same bed. She's scared of the dark. She doesn't like being alone at night since her momma died." I talked too fast, made new lies without thinking.

He sighed. "Okay, okay." Then he glanced toward the barn. "If you want to, you can sneak out when she's sleeping. We could meet in the barn."

I imagined disentangling myself from her arms to go to him. I didn't want to leave her at night. "I'll see . . ." I couldn't think. I knew he could see the answer on my face.

"You blush too much," he said, his grin gone. He hobbled off, following Addie into the barn. A few minutes later, he rode away. I tried to read his back as he disappeared, but his posture told me nothing of what he knew or sensed between me and Addie.

〜

MY SILENCE ABOUT THE JOY Addie gave me pulled me away from the people I loved, particularly my mother. All the things I couldn't explain about Addie created a void that wanted filling.

The Depression and the war were right behind us, thick in everyone's past. But Addie was a clean slate. When anyone asked about her past, she was vague. An outright lie seemed an impossible act for her. But she was deft with a turn of phrase.

I took on the task of storytelling and lying, volunteering when I was alone with the curious questioner that Addie was shy about things, embarrassed by her momma's past. I felt oddly compelled to make her imaginary life as extraordinary as she herself was. By the time she'd been with me a few months, I'd told quite a bit about her. Not much to one person, but everything together would have amounted to a life—a life that to my small-town eyes was exotic. Addie had one brother, a blessedly small family. They lived in an apartment in Chicago. They went to live plays on Saturday nights, a Lutheran Church on Sunday.

For the first time in my life, I had the pleasure of telling a complete anecdote. No one tried to finish sentences for me, correcting or adding to what I said. No one knew her story but me.

One night, before we fell asleep, I asked her if it bothered her not having a past, a family, or a place she came from. "I come from here," she whispered close. "Just like you." She spoke again in a slow, deliberate voice. "I don't like lying. I can't do it without laughing."

"I know, and you laugh when you hear someone else lying, too. But nobody gets upset with you. They just laugh along."

She rolled over on her back. In the dimness, she stared up at the ceiling. "It's funny when people lie. They know they're lying and they think they're getting away with it. But they're like a naked man trying to straighten his tie." She paused and sighed. "Other times, it is not a lie, but something else. I've heard others tell about something that happened when I was there, but they tell it differently than I would."

My eyes had adjusted to the faint moonlight through the windows. I studied her profile, conscious of how others must see me.

"They do it without thinking," she added. "To keep other stories going. Their own stories, or the things their mothers or cousins or the preacher have told them. They're also telling about themselves. You hear two things at once—the facts and the storyteller's heart." She rolled onto her side, facing me, and laid her hand on my chest. "I know you're helping me fit into your family's story. They need the stories. And so do you. But I don't."

"So what do you tell yourself?"

"That I am here. That I am. And I am."

I suddenly felt naked. Naked and so unlike her.

She turned toward me again and touched my face. "So go ahead. Tell any stories you need to."

ᕂ

HOW COULD THEY NOT HAVE KNOWN about Addie then? Not sensed on her skin or seen in her eyes the deep, strange difference of her? I kept expecting someone to pull me aside and say they knew she wasn't one of us. Once I dreamed that Momma, Daddy, and Joe buried her—put her back in the dirt where she came from—her eyes, open, calm, and beseeching as they shoveled dirt on top of her.

But no one ever accused her. No one stopped us. No one tried to take her away.

Gradually, I saw that everyone would treat Addie as people have always treated their relatives and neighbors with embarrassing but essentially harmless traits. They would ignore the trait. Or, in Addie's case, the question of her father.

My mother was the only rupture in the acceptance of my lies about

Addie. Momma was rarely on the farm alone with me and Addie. She didn't drive. Usually, Daddy or Joe stayed after they drove her to the farm. Bertie was in high school by then and was too busy with her hair and her schoolmates for anything but the most necessary farm chores. Rita often tagged along, happy to shadow the "big girls," as she referred to me and Addie.

But on this day it was only the three of us—Momma, Addie, and me. Daddy dropped Momma off at Mildred's down the road and she had walked from there. She planned to stop on her way back and pick up some quilting scraps Mildred had prepared for her.

Momma and I were in the kitchen doing dishes. In the yard, Addie groomed Cole's gray mare. The horse had somehow gotten loose, shown up that morning, and followed Addie in from the field. We could see them out the window over the sink.

Momma nodded her head. "She has a way with that horse." She studied Addie a little longer. "I like Addie, but I can't figure her. There's something unusual about her," Momma said, handing me a pot to dry.

I felt a jolt in my chest and belly and almost dropped the heavy pot.

She hadn't taken her eyes off Addie since she first spoke. Outside, Addie mounted the mare bareback. "Her momma never told her who her real daddy is?"

I shook my head.

"Well, somebody in the McMurrough family was involved, from the looks of her. Doris might not have known she was already pregnant when she left with that Hardin boy."

I didn't speak. I didn't breathe. She passed me another pot and the milk pitcher, washing the dishes by touch, keeping her eyes on Addie.

"Momma, she's a good girl. A good person."

She turned to me then, the same eyes Addie had. "I know, Evelyn. She's got a good heart and a good head. She's a good worker for you, too.

I'm glad she's here on the farm with you. And, in the long run, that's all that matters."

The tightness in my chest eased. I wanted to tell her the truth, to confess my lie. I wanted company.

Momma glanced out the window again. Addie headed for the porch, the mare followed. Momma turned back to me, her eyes moving over my face, judging me, weighing something. "I guess we all have our secrets."

Hot, bright fear surged up my chest again, higher. My neck and ears burned. "Momma . . . Momma?" was all I could get out.

"Oh, Evelyn, don't cry now." She put her arm around me and kissed my temple. "I didn't mean anything. It's okay. You and Addie are both good girls. Everything's fine."

Addie opened the door and stomped the dirt off her shoes. She looked at us and I felt a very faint hum as she bent to brush the clay dust off her pant leg.

"I was just telling Evelyn what a fine job you girls are doing on the farm." Momma took me by the shoulders and turned me toward Addie and the door. "Now, walk me down the hill to Mildred's before it gets dark."

The three of us strolled down the road in silence. The sky flushed velvet-pink above us as dusk settled. Birds called from the spring bud of the trees. I wanted Momma to say more but feared what she might say or know. Addie was quiet. I thought she sensed something and listened, too. I felt a twinge of guilt at my relief a few moments later when Momma latched Mildred's wire gate behind her and waved good-bye.

Momma never said another thing like that about Addie. She was always good to Addie and comfortable enough around her, but I sometimes would catch her watching us, comparing. Addie had become a wedge between me and Momma. Not Addie herself, but the lies I told about her. I'd always been able to tell Momma everything. Not quite everything. Not Cole. But even that I felt I would have eventually told her—maybe years later, after I was married, with my own kids, and it would be something she would understand, maybe laugh about. She was a forgiving, understanding woman. To have to keep something so strange and so important from her seemed an affront to those cherished qualities. Not being able to confide in her made a difference between us, more of a difference because I feared what she might already know about Addie. Maybe she had seen something, more than just the resemblance between me and Addie. I wanted to know what she knew, but we kept our silence—both of us.

After Addie and I returned from walking Momma down to Mildred's that evening, she returned Cole's mare to the Starneses. She rode her bareback—the high-strung, mean horse that none of the Starnes men could handle. To hear Cole tell about it at church the next Sunday, Mr. Starnes had been more than impressed. Addie continued visiting the mare at the fence, and the horse galloped to Addie whenever she saw her.

A couple of weeks after the mare's first visit, we were out in the field hoeing the corn. The mare spotted Addie when we were a good ways from the Starneses' pasture. The work was hot and tiresome. We pushed ourselves. Every time Addie glanced up, that mare paced the fence and called to her.

By the time we got within thirty feet of the fence, the mare was farther off in the pasture. "Looks like she's finally tired of you," I said.

"I don't think so." Addie peered across the field, shading her eyes.

Then I heard the mare coming, a full, hard run.

She cleared the fence in a leap that seemed to stop for a second in midair, all grace. It was a beautiful thing to see, the kind of thing that stays with you. The mare, which she renamed Darling on the spot, followed Addie up and down the rows of corn, docile as a dog, oblivious to the four-foot corn tight against her flanks. I'd never seen anything like it.

Dark had fallen by the time we finished our work, so we stabled the mare overnight.

A few days later, Cole came by. From the garden, I saw him stroll confidently up to the back porch where Addie was bent over the wash-tub, singing. Her hair, now as long as mine, hung down her shoulders. He reached out to touch it. But when she glanced up and smiled that smile at him, he jumped back awkwardly.

As I joined them, Addie was telling him when she could be at his house to meet with him and his daddy. Cole jumped again when he realized I stood next to him. His eyes darted toward me, then quickly away.

I understood his confusion, the strangeness of seeing her face, so similar to mine. It was still a small shock to me if I saw us in a mirror. I longed to smooth things for him, put him at ease, but I didn't want to lead him on. My offer of tea sounded lame, almost formal, and I felt a twinge of relief when he refused. His eyes flitted awkwardly back and forth between me and Addie as if he couldn't decide where to look. With a tight, cordial smile, he muttered something about needing to get back home, then he left.

Addie studied his back as he limped away. "He'll be okay, Evelyn."

After supper, she saddled our Becky and left for the Starneses, an extra bridle in hand.

When she returned, Darling belonged to her, and Mr. Starnes was entitled to a quarter of our hay plus the hay for his livestock that he'd been promised in exchange for the use of his tractor. Addie had her first horse.

Her ease around animals, especially large animals, amazed me. I managed Becky and the cows well enough. But I could never shake my awareness of their size and power or my assumption that they longed for the herd, the open plain, and an undomesticated sky above them. A part of me always braced for their revolt.

Now there were two things—ordinary things—that we did not

share: the fiddle and Darling. It felt right to have our vast, less obvious difference reflected in such public talents.

❧

AFTER SEVERAL MONTHS with Addie, I calmed down a bit. I had no choice. I forced myself to eat more and eventually I put some weight back on. I was able to sleep a full night. My monthly cycle returned. Gradually, the world lost some of its bright hues and became more ordinary. But I often felt as if I lived in dual worlds. One eye saw everything and everyone as they had always been and the other eye perceived a world in which anything might suddenly, impossibly give forth, transforming itself as Addie had. Some days, I felt crazy and alarmingly innocent.

Addie, in contrast, retained her own unique take on things. After I showed her how to fold the soft cotton rags and safety-pin them to the inside of her underwear for her first period, she pulled her pants up, pressed her hand over her womb, then gave her hips a little shake. "It feels different. The emptying of it. Too bad we can't stop and start it, like peeing or spitting."

I laughed. I'd never thought of it that way. I dreaded my monthly. The rags we used were washed and hung out on the line to dry and be ignored along with all the other "unmentionables," then reused the next month. But Addie took it all in with her normal aplomb.

There were, of course, other facts of life. I did my best to explain the biology of boys and babies. I thought I'd completed the job, but one day Addie came striding out of the field with my little sister close behind. Rita, a long, knobby twelve-year-old by then, adored Addie, following her around like a chick does a mother hen when she came to the farm. They both had a look of concern on their faces.

"We saw a stallion in the Starneses' pasture," Addie announced. Then she put her arm protectively around Rita and nodded. "Go ahead, ask her."

Red-faced, Rita whispered, "How big does a man's thing get?"

I held my hands out about a foot and a half apart.

Rita gasped, covering her mouth. Her eyes widened and she blanched.

Amazement flashed across Addie's face, then her eyes traveled from my hands up to my face. "Evelyn!"

I bit my lip to keep from laughing. They scowled. I brought my hands closer, to about six inches apart.

Addie glanced at Rita then back at me. "Does your momma really call it a doolywhacker?"

"Yes!" Rita and I crowed. Then we all exploded, laughing till we cried.

Later, I watered the horses as Addie and Rita finished the evening milking. Addie, squatting at Maybell's side, muttered, "Doolywhacker!"

From the side of the other cow, Rita giggled.

From then on, if Rita was in one of her glum moods, Addie could make her smile by simply mouthing the word "Doolywhacker."

❧

ADDIE EVENTUALLY HAD MORE PERSONAL QUESTIONS about sex. When I first told her I had slept with Cole, she'd simply shrugged and raised her eyebrows as if to say "of course." But weeks later, as we pumped water for the livestock, she asked, "What was it like with Cole? What was different from being with me?"

I waddled to the hog's trough, the bucket of water sloshing at my side. Addie followed with a second bucket. The morning was crisp with the first hint of fall, but sunny as midsummer.

Talking about sex so directly made me uncomfortable. I laughed. "I can't slop a hog while I think about doing that. With you. Or Cole."

She waited patiently, her face serious.

"Well, you and Cole are very different from one another . . . I don't know, Addie. Other than the different body parts, everything else is sort of the same. Kissing. Touching. But all I know is him and you. With Cole, it was always over pretty fast. You and I have so much more time together. You smell different. You touch me differently. You fill up the whole room. And when I touch you, I know what it feels like to you. We're alike."

She had been tapping her chest lightly as she listened to my answer. I stopped her hand. "Except for that. No one else has a voice like yours."

She glanced down at my hand on her breastbone. "I can see how I'm different from Cole. And you're right. I don't think anyone else can do this." She covered my hand with hers. "You inspire me." She smiled as she drew me close, but I thought I saw a spark of sadness in her eyes.

I didn't pursue that spark. But I wondered how she bore her gifts, her differences. What costs there might have been for her. I had no means to measure my choice in turning Cole from my bed, from a possible future. I had no scale, no map for the territory I found myself in.

It was Addie's gift—not the private gift of her voice or her origins, but her gift with horses—that brought Cole back to our door with his own question. A few days after his daddy gave Darling to Addie, he rode up into the yard on his daddy's mild old gelding. I waved him down from the garden before he got to the house.

"I came to find out how Addie got the mean out of that horse. I can't figure it," he called as he rode up.

"She's in the barn. Ask her."

He glanced at the barn, but did not leave. His hat shaded his face.

I squinted up and shielded my eyes against the sun. "How're you doing, Cole. How's your leg?"

He dismounted, smoother, more confidently. "Anything changed?"

"No."

"She still sleeps in the same bed as you?"

I nodded.

"Just checking." He gave me a long look, his mouth in a grim line. "My leg still gives me some trouble, but it's healed." He squared his shoulders and strolled away, his leg stiff as he tried to hide his limp.

When I finished cutting the okra, I joined them in the barnyard.

Addie had led Darling out to him. "She handles real smooth now. Be firm and gentle with her and she'll do what you want. She's like new now. Don't think about what she was." Addie handed him Darling's reins.

"I'm ready," he said softly, his face still and determined, the same expression I'd seen when he showed up at my door months before. He vaulted into the saddle and walked her in a slow, broad circle.

"Take her out," Addie called. "She's easy now. Talk sweet to her. Stay loose. Don't clinch. Don't pull."

Cole waved his hat and urged Darling up to a trot along the field.

Addie smiled at me. "He'll be okay. I talked to her."

"Talked?"

"Like I do with you only . . ." her lips parted. "Hear anything?"

I heard Becky paw in the barn. Hobo barked a single sharp response from somewhere behind me.

"No. But the horse does. Hobo, too."

"Feel anything?"

I closed my eyes. The basket of okra I held dug into my hip.

"No."

"Keep your eyes closed. Now?"

I felt a faint hum in my chest and face. Becky nickered loudly from the barn. I opened my eyes.

Addie winked at me and took my hand, pressing my palm to her sternum. Warmth shimmered up my arm, a barely perceptible tingle. "That's what I did with Darling before I led her out. So, he'll be fine." She nodded toward Cole, who galloped back to us, a wide grin on his face.

I felt a twinge. Would she, like me, find him attractive?

Cole dismounted smoothly. "You musta found some Goody headache powders for horses. She was some kind of headache before. She's smooth as silk now."

"Did you talk to her?"

"Addie, I wasn't talking, I was praying. If I hurt my leg again on the same damn horse and couldn't work, my daddy would shoot the horse and me. You've got to show me what you did to get her this way." It was good to hear him laugh again.

◈

COLE'S QUESTIONS ABOUT OUR SLEEPING ARRANGEMENT bothered me. Although people did not make the assumptions they do today about two women sleeping in the same bed—it truly was the love that dared not speak its name—it seemed logical that he would know, that his intimacy with me, however brief, would make him privy to my desires. We needed his good will, his friendship.

The next time Cole dropped by, I invited him to supper. He sat stiffly at the table, like a boy in church, while I set out the dishes. Addie watched us a moment, then said to Cole, "I've got a question for you." She pointed at the barn. "About Darling. Can I show you? She doesn't like the bridle we have."

His posture softened immediately and he turned to her with genuine interest when he heard Darling's name. She led him out to the barn, both of them talking excitedly about bridles and horses.

After that, they talked horses and went riding whenever they had a chance. At first, I thought he might have been making a play for her, perhaps some ploy to make me jealous, but I soon realized they simply shared a philosophy and an ability to talk nonstop about horses. Gradually, I saw that Cole treated her like she was one of the boys. For him, her skills seemed to override any sexual tensions. Through Cole, others began to hear about Addie's touch with horses.

The day she went to watch his father break a new horse she came home at dusk, riding Darling. She slammed the door on her way into the house. "I never want to see that again!" she announced, her face dark with outrage, and she marched out again.

She paced the hall until she was calmer, her gait normal. Then she came back into the kitchen, where I sat reattaching a shirt button. She picked up the lantern that sat next to me and held it out at arm's length. "If I drop this and break it, I don't have a lantern anymore. It is broken. I'll have light, but not the kind of light I want. Just fire. When they break a horse, they *break* it. The horse is gone. Gone."

She was magnificent, her face flushed, her arm steady. Gently, she lowered the lantern back to the table. "They go around on horseback, but they are not *with* the horse. The horse is gone. Conquered, not led." Her voice was low, normal now.

That was the beginning for her. She read everything she could find on horses. She rode every chance she had. For weeks, she carried around a book, old and yellowed even then, written by an Englishwoman, on gentle methods of "sweetening" horses. She and Cole spent hours that fall discussing the best ways to train a horse. They went to horse shows and auctions, much to the chagrin of his new girlfriend, Eloise, who tagged along with them.

They talked long and hard to convince me to move the kitchen garden and make way for a new corral adjacent to the barn. As soon as they finished building the corral, Cole brought a colt over to sweeten, away from his father's watchfulness. Within a day, they were on its back.

One Sunday, an old farmer from Stanley showed up with a tall, lean white mare. "Some damn geese landed last spring when I was turning the field. Whole cloud of 'em landing all of a sudden. Not more than twenty feet away." The old man swept his hat through the air. "She nearly dragged me to my death getting away. Now she won't go near fowl of any kind and I got forty laying hens. When the rooster starts in the morning, no one can get near this one." He stroked the horse's mane. "The coop is near the barn. She won't go near the barn or take the harness now." His shoulder was bandaged and the horse had fresh whip marks. His wife wanted the horse shot, but he couldn't bear to do it, he admitted.

The mare became the first test of Cole's and Addie's new methods—their first job, though there had been no discussion of payment. They agreed that the horse would stable with us and Addie would do the initial daily work with the mare, "sweetening" her to the chickens. Cole would advise and cheerlead until the horse was ready for a test rider. I knew Cole needed to be careful with his bad leg, and it made sense that he be the second rider. But I knew plenty of young men who would not have been so comfortable letting a girl take the lead, regardless of their admiration of her skills.

Addie did not force the mare into the barn or near the chickens, but rose earlier every morning to turn Becky and Darling out into the corral with her so she would have some calm company when the rooster crowed. During the day, Cole and Addie groomed and rode her as much as they could.

The third morning, Addie saddled the mare for the big dawn event and leaned over the mare's neck, soothing her in the predawn darkness. They were barely visible in the middle of corral. I heard, then very faintly felt, that familiar low drone vibrate from Addie. My part was to rouse the chickens and get the rooster going. He was on his third morning chorus when I made it back to the corral. The mare flinched and tossed her head, but did not buck or pull back.

"Cock-a-doodle-do!" Addie crowed and laughed.

After that, Addie wore one of Eva's big aprons when she was in the barn or the corral, a couple of chirping biddies in each pocket as she combed the mare down.

By the end of the week, it was Cole's job to hold one of the chickens as Addie rode the horse around the corral, passing within a few feet of him. I contributed by providing Cole with hot coffee.

"I sure feel stupid being the chicken-holder," Cole said. "But it's working. Look at her." Addie and the mare trotted, steady and calm, bright in the first of the day's light.

When she reached the opposite side of the corral, Addie gave a signal and Cole held the hen up and shook her so she squawked and flapped. The horse's hide went tight and she complained, but kept moving very slowly toward the hen. Addie leaned low, whispering. I knew what the horse felt, that sweet harmonic blossoming through her bones.

If Cole sensed anything unusual beyond the ruckus of the chicken, he gave no sign. He held the angry hen at arm's length. His eyes followed Addie intently, ignoring me, ignoring the chicken shit on his sleeve. I saw the admiration on his face and wanted to say, "She's cheating, she has something you don't know about." But all I got out was his name.

He turned, the excitement still on his face, then it changed. It wasn't the usual guarded expression he'd had since I'd stopped sleeping with him, but there was still a small hesitancy. Part of me wanted him to look at me with the same admiration. But I was happy to see them working together, excited about what they were doing. He tucked the chicken back up under his arm, held his hand out for the coffee, and mouthed the words "thank you" with such a broad smile that I felt forgiven for whatever potential future I might have taken from us. He raised the cup high in a toast.

Within a couple of days, the horse could pass the chicken without hesitation even as it bobbed furiously in Cole's hands. Getting the mare to take the plow harness went easily after that.

When the old farmer returned, Addie asked him to wait in the yard. She rode the horse out of the barn and Cole brought out a hen, which he handed to her. She rode the horse around the barn, past the chicken coop to the corral, holding the clucking hen in her arms. The farmer jogged behind them, shaking his head.

When they got to the corral, Addie signaled the old man to follow them in as she dismounted. "She's going to have to trust you as much as she trusts me. Last she knew, you were the one who whipped her. You can't whip her again. Ever again. Now she needs to know something of you that is not the whipping."

The old man nodded and wiped his eyes. "That chicken next to her. Good Lord, that was a beautiful thing."

Addie led him to the mare. She reached for his hands. The old man obviously wasn't used to young women holding his hands. His arms stiffened and he stepped back.

I couldn't hear what she said to him, but he let Addie take his hands again and they slowly circled the horse, touching her all over. Then they walked away together, letting the horse follow them to the chicken coop. The farmer spit his tobacco juice and cackled.

Addie and the farmer took short turns plowing. The mare pulled steady and straight. The poor hens released in her path fluttered to the ground and strutted in confused circles.

The old farmer bought his feed at Rayburn's feed store downtown, and the story of his ornery, chicken-scared mare and Addie's "cure" spread fast.

A few weeks later, a bright new truck pulled up, hauling one of the fanciest horse trailers I'd ever seen. A big girl wearing an English riding outfit that probably cost more than a year's groceries for us tumbled out of the driver's seat and told us she was from Charlotte. I don't know how she'd heard of us or found us.

"My daddy gave me this horse, but I can't ride him. He won't let me," she announced. "I'll pay you. A hundred if you can get him so I can ride him and show my daddy when he gets back."

I sucked in my breath. A hundred dollars was an enormous sum then.

Addie went to the horse and stroked his neck. She let him mouth her hand inquisitively as the girl watched, keeping her distance. "Two." Addie held up two fingers. "I have a partner and I'll need his help on this. One hundred dollars now and one hundred when you can ride out of that corral, happy and easy, on this fellow." The girl nodded and took out her wallet.

I was in shock. We were in business.

It turned out that the problem was the girl, not the horse. Her father loved horses. She wanted to please him, but she was terrified of them. We boarded the horse while the girl's father was out of town. Cole and Addie required that she come several times a week to feed and groom the horses. And they took turns riding with her on her horse, a gentle, jet-black gelding. The girl's face would go soft when she rode double with Addie. I knew what she felt, Addie's arms around her, that glow at her back.

But Addie talked, too. She honed her philosophy and developed the vocabulary she would take into decades of working with horses and people. "Make it true. True yourself and the horse will go with you," she urged the rich girl. "Willingness, calm, and balance." Addie waved her hand across the horse's shoulders and down his spine. "For both of you." She tapped the girl on the chest, then lightly pulled her shoulders back.

Gradually, the girl's spine became more supple and she began to look like she belonged on a horse. The day before the girl's father came back to Charlotte, Addie slid into the saddle behind her and tied a blindfold around the girl's face. The girl dropped the reins in protest, and a shiver ran down her legs and into the horse, who whinnied and shook himself. Addie reached behind with one hand and touched the horse. With her other hand, she gently returned the girl's hands to the reins. After a long moment, the horse and the girl were calm and waiting.

"Your final test. You know this farm well enough. Think of where you want to go and tell him from here." She patted the girl's thighs. "No words. I'm here with you."

The girl's brow furrowed, but she nodded, took a deep breath, and they took off. Later, I found the girl in the stable, brushing her horse down, singing softly to herself. I'm sure she got her money's worth. Addie and Cole got that second hundred dollars.

I NEVER FULLY UNDERSTOOD what Addie did with the horses. She just seemed to be with them, to sweeten and socialize them with patience, contact, and good grooming. She never used any force. She just glanced at them and talked to them and soon they followed her like lovesick pups, nosing her shoulder. I know, when no one else was around, she soothed them with that strange voice of hers.

I watched Addie and Cole working together with an odd combination of emotions. I was glad that Cole was comfortable coming to our house. Though some awkwardness remained between us, he was a kind man. I regretted having hurt or disappointed him, and wanted him to understand that I hadn't left him on a whim. I longed to tell him who and what she really was, to have him see what I saw, to know what I knew. I was also a little jealous of the attention they gave each other. He was, in his own way, as seduced by Addie as I was. But I could also see that he was smitten not by her touch or her voice, as I had been, but by her skill. He flat-out bragged about her horsemanship to anyone who would listen.

They both had an easy, apparently effortless grace on horseback, but my eyes always returned to Addie. On horseback, she was part of the horse. I'd never been interested in horses, but I began to admire them. I loved seeing her so engrossed in her work with Cole and the horses. I followed her hands as she groomed the horses, humming to them, her hands sliding over their shoulders and down their legs.

I loved how she took things into her hands, holding and touching everything—food, Hobo, horses, the stove handle, the ax, me—in a way that seemed more than mere contact or simple utility. There was gusto, intent, knowledge. At night, when she touched me, I felt the difference between her and others. The horses felt it, too. They turned toward her, sniffing her, licking her.

Addie's hands made me look at the world anew, to study surfaces and textures I might otherwise have ignored. This was not simply a lover's envy of objects touched by the loved one. My eyes lingered on after her touch, curious as to what she had just understood. I saw in her a lack of inhibition, a possible way of being that I could never have learned in my Baptist family. As she touched the world, her hands seemed to be inviting me to do the same. She, who had so recently needed my help crossing the floor, now gave the world back to me in subtle and profound ways.

A Russian philosopher, Mikhail Bakhtin said that "the self is the gift of the other." It seems to me most true now. The genes I carry, the clothes I wear, the food I eat all have come through the hands of others. Even these words I write now, my vocabulary, are not only mine. They are an agreement, a social contract between the two of us.

I did not see this when I was a young woman. I was so sure, even as I held my hands out to Addie and took all she gave, that I was self-made, an individual before all else. And there she was, so unlike any of us, the only truly unique person I have known, pulling her identity straight from the flesh of others.

She seemed eager to absorb everything around her. She read voraciously, her arms loaded with books when we came back from the library. I preferred stories, my favorite that year was *A Tree Grows in Brooklyn*. We read it out loud to each other at night. But her curiosity roamed beyond novels: biographies, science, history, even fairy tales. Her focus settled for a while on religion. She worked her way through the Clarion library's slender religion section.

I'd made her promise not to ask anyone else about church or Jesus, so she leveled all of her Sunday questions at me: If God is omnipotent and good, why is there suffering? If there is only one God, why did we worship the Holy Trinity?

I gave her everything I had, repeating what the preachers had told me about life and sin until everything I'd been taught sounded strange even to me. More and more, I saw my people as an outsider would. Church was becoming an obligation, something I did only to belong, which, of course, was exactly what it had been for her all along. I'd never truly believed, but I'd always felt that one day I might. Addie's questions seemed to preclude that possibility for me. I wasn't going to see the light or be saved.

Her questions often popped up on Sunday walks from the farm to join my family in church. One Sunday, during our trek into Clarion, her questions about God were particularly exasperating. I literally threw my hands up in the air. "Addie, I don't know where God came from. Or if He really exists. But evil people exist. And we all die. We need some way to explain. Otherwise, it makes no sense. And some people would go crazy if they didn't have God or Jesus. Or, for that matter, sin." The next question crossed her face and I added, "No, I won't go crazy. But this is where I live. This is what people think."

The church bulletin that day requested our dimes and dollars for a new campaign to save the poor souls of New Guinea. Addie tapped the photo of smiling native children, then whispered, "If they're already good, happy people when the missionaries get there, how do the missionaries convince them that they're sinful and need Jesus to save them?"

I had no response.

Addie leaned her head toward me as we slipped into our pew. "Do you think I need to be saved?"

"No!" I whispered and grasped her arm. "No." A hot anger bolted up my chest.

A bitter sadness gnawed at me all through the sermon. The preacher's focus was original sin and God cursing Eve with the sorrow of childbearing. Each time I glanced at Addie, I remembered her arrival. No hair, no breasts. Not like me. Not like us. Just that gaze. Wide-open, intelligent, and curious. Unsullied by guilt or sin.

On our walk home, she issued a declaration rather than a query. "They're wrong. Childbearing is not a sorrow like the Bible says or a curse like the preacher claims. I've seen how your momma looks at you sometimes—how other mothers look at their children. It's not a curse. Not a sorrow."

I nodded my agreement and began to cry. I don't know who I cried for—the cursed mothers or all the innocent children taught they are sinful wretches.

That evening, Addie took my hand and led me outside. She made me lie down at the edge of the fields recently shorn of their hay and alfalfa. A single oak branch stretched out over us. Beyond it, the sky was clear deep cobalt and spread with endless points of light. Hobo lay down at our feet.

Addie stretched out beside me. "Nobody agrees or really knows. The Catholics and Jews believe, just like the Baptists and the Methodists, but they don't know anything for sure, either. They all—you all—seem to need to believe in something. You have to have a story."

I didn't like it when she talked like that, setting herself apart. I thought of how tenuous her presence was and how she might slip away as inexplicably as she had appeared.

"I've been reading about the Milky Way, too." She swept her arm in an arc over our heads, then patted the ground between us. "This is all we really know." Her voice resonated with urgency and calm. "It is a mystery, but it's beautiful, Evelyn. And it is all we need. All we are." She held up a fistful of dirt and let it fall between her fingers.

A breeze passed over, filled with the cool promise of rain.

I knew she spoke the truth. She brushed her dirty fingers over my lips, transferring the primal grit to my tongue.

She may have become like me physically, but I was, in my own curious way, becoming like her.

∽

THERE WAS ONE OTHER THING I couldn't begin to explain to Addie: "Whites only." Clarion was completely segregated in 1948. Except for the women who came into town to work as maids and the men who picked up the mill workers' kitchen slops for hog feed, the only time Addie and I were around black people was at Pearl Freedman's barbeque shack. Hers was the only business in town that served both black and white people. Her barbeque ribs and pulled pork were the best in the county. Her place near downtown, corrugated tin on top and three sides, was dark and hot year round and filled with a distinct blend of sweat, spices, and wood smoke. If the wind blew right, folks would be salivating in the post office as they bought stamps.

When Joe and I were kids, Momma often sent us over to Pearl's to pick up dinner. I loved the tart, hot ribs, but Pearl scared me. She stood over six feet tall with arms like hams and breasts larger than my head. Pearl was very dark-skinned, and in the dimness of her shack, her features were difficult to pin down.

She'd flash a big smile at us as she handed over the warm ribs wrapped in wax paper and then folded into sheets of newspaper, and boom, "You enjoy, now. I hope Lily Mae sends you back real soon." Her accent wasn't the same as the other black people. Some said she was Gullah and a "conjure" woman. She'd take our money and retrieve the change from a cloth bag stored deep in her cleavage, dropping the warm, moist coins into our small, open palms.

Pearl's only child, Peg, was close to my age, a tall girl but, unlike her momma, slender in the waist and hips. She hunched her shoulders forward and slunk everywhere, like a cat that had been kicked and was trying to avoid the next foot.

One Saturday, Addie and I were downtown, a quiet still time in the middle of a hot summer afternoon. We'd picked out a yellow gingham at Ina's shop for kitchen curtains. While Addie paid, I stepped outside. Peg walked by, clutching a shopping bag to her chest.

"Good morning," I said.

Peg smiled, almost too fast to see, and then returned her gaze to the sidewalk. I remembered her grin from when we were little girls, each peeking out from behind our momma's skirts. She had not been shy then. Her gaze was direct, her smile quick and wide.

Addie joined me and we headed toward home. The street was empty except for us and Peg about half a block ahead. Addie watched her carefully.

"If she had been the one to find me, I would look like her," she said.

My skin prickled in the heat, and a wave of dizziness rolled over me. What would it be like to be able to say that about anyone you passed on the street? I looked at Addie and tried to imagine her different, my features gone from her and Peg's emerging from the muddy new surface of her.

A car pulled up suddenly at the next intersection, John Thompson at the wheel. John's family lived outside of town in a little house surrounded by bored hound dogs and dying cars. He hated "Yankees and niggers," as though it was the only occupation a man needed, the kind of vehement racism that allowed the rest of us to feel noble in our more genteel and subtle racism.

The hood of his car stopped directly in front of Peg, cutting off her path. His hand darted out, grabbing at Peg, who flinched, wrenching her arm out of his grasp, then scurried around the back of his car and continued rapidly down the street.

John turned right, following her. "I'm gonna come get me some more of that dark meat, girl. You watch out," he called. He sped up to the red light and braked with a short screech. She sidled on, her shoulders bunched forward, her head low.

"Hold this." Addie handed me the bag of curtain cloth, then jogged ahead to John's car. She slapped the top of it to get his attention. Before John could turn to her, she bent over and whispered something in his ear. Just as the light changed to green, his head jerked to the side and his shoulder came up as if he had been tickled. He floored it then, and his daddy's old Ford sped across the intersection and straight into a telephone pole in the middle of the next block.

Ahead of us, Peg looked from Addie to the car, her eyes wide. Addie and I rushed to the car. His hand dangled out the window. His head hung over the steering wheel and rested against the bloody, smashed windshield. A single line of blood rolled out of his left ear and down his neck. Then the streets filled with people.

After the ambulance had taken John away, I asked Addie what she had said to him. "I told him I didn't like what he said."

Later, at home, as we chopped cabbage to make sauerkraut, I asked, "Did you know that he would do that?"

"No. I just wanted him to leave her alone." She shook her head. "I wasn't trying to make him do anything. I didn't mean for him to get hurt, but I don't regret trying to keep him from her. He's not a decent man."

"Did you use your other voice when you spoke to him?"

"Not the way I do with you at night. Not the lower voice I use to calm Darling. But what I said to him came from the same place." She pressed her fist to her breastbone. Then she scooped the cabbage shreds up and dropped them into the wide measuring bowl.

The next time we went to Pearl's for barbeque, she waved our money away. "My Peg says you were a help to her. Today, your ribs are on the house—Pearl's house." Peg stepped out from a dark corner of the shack and smiled shyly.

Addie's hand disappeared in Pearl's grip. "Thank you, ma'am. We'll relish our supper." Then Peg delicately shook her hand.

After that, when we passed Peg on the street, she would say, "Hey, Miss Addie."

"Hey, Miss Peg," Addie would respond.

From the day of his accident, John Thompson was deaf in his left ear, and never again held a job. He spent the rest of his life harmlessly wandering around town collecting bottles for the penny deposit. I never heard of him harming or insulting anyone after his accident. The old men who hung around downtown, outside the drugstore, let him sit in on their conversations and laugh at their jokes.

Because everyone knows everyone else in a small town, there can be an appreciable acceptance for human idiosyncrasies, for the accidents of the body and heart. Privacy was limited in Clarion and most of us assumed we would live and die close to where we were born. By our mid-twenties, we knew a great deal about each other. Knowledge accumulated over decades of church bulletins, brief exchanges on the street, and casual observation. Faces filled with health and hope or fell into the stupor of love or work or misfortune. We watched each other grow older, our gaits and wardrobes reflecting both age and fortune. And we knew that we were known by others as we knew them. All of this made for a kind of quiet personal tolerance—but only for the accidents and stupidities that we or our children might fall prey to. Acceptance of those who were clearly different was another thing entirely. Race mattered more than anything. Racism is the laziest hatred. The quickest, most peripheral glance is all it takes to categorize.

༄

OTHER THAN WHAT HAPPENED with John Thompson, Addie and I lived on the farm without incident. By the end of our second harvest together, I had been on the farm over four years. She quieted my restlessness. I no longer imagined myself wandering off into the woods. She drew me into the world of Clarion. Certainly, I would not have gone to Freddie and Marge's on Sunday evenings without her.

So we lived our daily lives, each being who we were, identical and vastly different. Working together during the day and tangled in each other at night. I felt sinful, but uncertain which was the greater of my sins—lying about Addie or lying with her.

Secrecy might seem to be the ultimate privacy, but in truth it is the antithesis of privacy. A social solitude. Secrets are only necessary when others are present. I was more alone in my secrecy than I had ever been in my actual solitude.

Despite the tensions of secrecy, the time with Addie had a kind of peace to it, an exciting tranquility, like stillness of the first snow—clear, fresh, and new. Only later would I realize how fortunate I was to have that time between being the daughter of my parents and becoming the parent of my daughters.

Still, from the moment I bundled the seemingly formless Addie and carried her in from the cold, I had sensed a tidal wave in the distance, something large approaching, just outside my peripheral vision, impossible to really see but coming nonetheless, large and unstoppable. All I could do was wait, hoping I would hear the far-off rumble of it as it came into sight, hoping that, by then, I would know how to swim or surrender.

〜

MY BROTHER, JOE, MARRIED his sweetheart, Mary, in the spring of 1949. They had known each other most of their lives—probably knew each other a little too well late that winter of '48–'49. Their engagement was suspiciously short. At the wedding, Mary cradled a large bouquet of yellow roses at her waist. Joe seemed stunned and not nearly old enough to be doing what he was doing, but happy.

Everyone teased me for letting my little brother beat me to the altar. I reminded folks that he was barely a younger brother, more like a delayed twin, the two of us being born in the same year, me in the first weeks of it, him in the last. That was one race I didn't mind losing.

Yet the boys were interested—in both of us—and most often approached us in pairs, walking us home from Momma's or church or inviting us on double dates. But there was no one in particular that either one of us wanted to keep seeing. The men who fought in the war were either shell-shocked or they had an unsettling urgency about them. The boys who had been too young to go to war or had not made it to the action, seemed naive, more boy than man.

All of them took Addie's direct gaze as an invitation. But they were like house cats stalking a wild turkey, confident and focused at first, then shying away as they got closer and saw that she was not the jay or wren their instincts and abilities were prepared for.

Once some mill-village boys borrowed an old car and drove me and Addie west for a picnic, a rare midday Sunday excursion outside the county and Addie's first time in the mountains. I saw one of the boys kiss Addie. The heat of jealousy bolted up my gut through my chest and coiled there painfully for the day. That was all that happened, as far as I knew, and Addie seemed no different. New mountain landscape seemed to impress her much more than the kiss did.

❧

MONTHS LATER, BABY BUD, the first grandchild in the family, arrived only seven months after Joe and Mary's wedding. Babies often came early then and were, without the benefit of medical intervention, miraculously healthy and well-formed in their premature state.

Thanksgiving dinner at Momma's house was Baby Bud's big debut. When I passed through on my way to the bathroom, I found Mary sitting on the bed, her back to the door as she nursed Bud.

"Come here, Evelyn." She patted the bed. Little Bud had just finished feeding, his eyes rolled back, and his full lips parted, showing the small nursing blister. Mary was still exposed, her big pink nipple flattened and wet.

"Look at him. It's like there's a sleeping potion in my milk," she whispered. "He does this every time, passes right out. Here, hold him. You're the only one who hasn't yet. Go on, he won't bite."

He felt surprisingly light and warm in my hands. He sighed and squirmed. I felt the strength of his tiny body and, when he yawned, smelled his milky breath. Mary got herself back into her blouse. I stared at Bud, lifting his little fist with my finger, when I felt a hand on my shoulder.

"You want one," Addie whispered so close I could feel her breath on my cheek.

She was right. I did want one. Like all girls then, I assumed I would have children one day. I naturally imagined myself married and with kids. It was not something I'd ever questioned. I had never felt the physical urge to have a baby, the way I had felt an urge toward Cole, toward the land I lived on, or toward Addie herself. But I felt it then, holding Bud, touching that perfect soft skin and breathing in the moist sweetness of him.

"You'll need a man first," Mary said. "Both of you."

"We'll get one then," Addie whispered back, sitting down beside us.

Mary pulled Bud's little sprouts of hair up into a peak with her fingers. "Better get two. You two can't share everything."

Little Bud wiggled again, pulled himself into a ball, turned red, and audibly shit. I felt the force of it in my hand and half-expected that he had gone through his diaper, the gown, and the blankets. Mary looked at my face and laughed. Bud woke. Calm and wide-eyed, he stared up at us.

For days after, Addie was quiet and subdued, often taking long rides alone. She spent a Sunday afternoon at Cole's house learning how to drive. Then she somehow talked his momma into letting her borrow the family's old Ford truck the next weekend. She told me she was going "up into the mountains" as if she was doing more than changing geography. And she was going alone. She packed an old pup tent borrowed from Joe and two days' worth of food. When I saw her fold the tent and put it in the back of the truck, anxiety snaked through my gut. I waited until she came back outside with blankets, the same ones I had first wrapped her in two years before.

"Don't go." I took her arm. "Why are you going? What are you going to do up there?"

She rubbed her forehead. "I don't know what I'll do. But I need to go."

Her eyes had the focused, faraway look of someone already on her way. She caught me staring at her, worried, and snapped back into the present.

"Don't worry. It'll be okay, Evelyn. I'm coming back. Just tell everyone I've gone hunting." Then she laughed that staccato laugh that reminded me of Joe.

I did not want to, but I let her go.

Two days later, she came back as she had left, without explanation, herself again.

❦

I FELT THE PRESSURE to marry and have a family—that was the expectation of my community, my family, and my body. I was content with Addie. But the ripeness of my body was not something I could resist or suppress.

After I held little Bud, I thought of these things more often. I couldn't see how I would fit a man into the house Addie and I lived in. We would each have to find someone at the same time or share a single man. The former was unlikely, the latter seemed impossible. But that is just how it happened. We found a man.

FOUR

ADAM

The morning sun shone bright and unseasonably warm, though it was still winter, with no sign of buds on the trees yet. Addie and I had just come from Sunday dinner at Momma's. Logy from overeating, I chose an easy but prickly task for the afternoon—pruning dead stems off the blackberries. I perched high up on the bank where it began its drop from the road to the railroad track, my clippers in hand, when I heard whistling and then the crunch of shoes on the gravel skirting of the tracks below.

A man's voice called out, "Hello! There a place around here I could get a drink of water?"

I glanced down, expecting to see one of the local boys, but a stranger peered up at me. The brim of his hat shaded his eyes. Too nicely dressed to be a hobo, he held a small, battered suitcase and a wrinkled, grease-stained brown paper sack in one hand. He needed a shave. His jacket was slung over one shoulder and his sleeves rolled up.

"Ma'am is there a place nearby where I could get a drink of water?" he repeated. "That's all I want is a drink of water."

He pushed his hat back farther on his forehead, exposing his face. He was not much older than I. A lock of dark hair fell forward over his brown eyes.

"If you go down the track about another fifty feet there's a path up the bank. Be careful you don't get scratched by the blackberry briars. There's a pump in the back of the house." I pivoted and swept my hand toward the house.

"Thank you very much."

Out of the corner of my eye, I watched him climb the bank. His shoulders and head were visible above the brambles. I judged him to be six foot two, maybe three. He reached the crest and paused. Silently, I pointed toward the house. He grinned, the grin of a man used to smiling at women, and continued. I followed, watching his shoulders move under his cotton shirt.

He set his suitcase down immediately and took a long drink from the ladle at the pump. After a second deep drink, he bent lower, scooping up the cold water with his hands, and rubbed it on his face and into his hair. Addie leaned out the back door, her arms folded across her chest.

The stranger pulled a white handkerchief out of his pocket and slowly dried his face, letting us watch him. He carefully folded his handkerchief and put it back in his pocket before regarding us.

"You two must be twins?" he said after he had taken us both in.

I shook my head.

"Sisters then?"

We both shook our heads. "Cousins." I said.

He glanced quickly from me to her. Addie nodded.

"Must surely be more to it than that," he said, grinning again and combing his wet fingers through his hair. A current went through me; I wanted to have my hand in his hair. Then he held out his hand and announced, "Roy Hope from Kentucky. On my way home from Jacksonville, Florida."

Addie and I introduced ourselves.

He leaned back against the watering trough, resting his hips on the lip of it. "I should be sitting in a train on my way to Kentucky instead of walking the tracks. But some lucky bum is sitting in my place."

We nodded our interest and he launched into his story. "I'm not a mining man and where my people come from in Kentucky is nothing but mining. I was gonna make something of myself. Jacksonville, Florida, seemed to be the place for that, but it didn't work out that way. So I'm heading back home for a while. Then I think I'll go out West."

I studied him—the width of his wrists, the span of his neck where it joined his shoulder. He turned his hat in his hands, smoothing the brim as he told us about his brother in Jacksonville, who fought with his wife, and their baby, who woke up at all hours of the night. His opportunities and savings that had dwindled.

"The Florida beaches, though." He whistled his amazement. "Clean white sand, fine as powder." He rubbed his fingers and thumb together and laughed. "And on Saturday afternoons, girls. Girls everywhere in bathing suits."

He was even younger than I had first thought—early twenties, maybe his late teens. He had not been in the war.

I watched his beautiful mouth and straight white teeth while he relayed the details of being robbed of a suitcase and train ticket when he napped in the Charlotte depot. "So, I'm broke now, with nothing left but this." His foot nudged the little suitcase at his side. "Nothing to do but hoof it home." He glanced at the chopping block. "If you ladies could use some help around here, I'd be happy to split some wood for my supper . . ." He paused and pulled a pack of cigarettes out of his breast pocket.

Addie looked at me and raised an eyebrow as he bent his head to light his cigarette. I smiled at her and she offered him some supper. I handed him the splitting maul and a wedge.

While Addie cooked, I stood at the kitchen door watching Roy split wood. She came and stood behind me. "You just gonna stand around and watch him?"

"There are worse things a girl could do," I said.

"And I imagine you are thinking of at least one of them."

"I don't think he's real smart," I answered, then pitched my voice up into that high scratchiness of Granny Lou's and quoted what she had said that day at church when she saw the Clemson boy making eyes at me and Addie. "He's a fine example of a man. A woman could get good, healthy children off of him." I giggled.

Addie snorted back at me and I repeated the phrase, pointing at him. I pulled her closer so she could get a better view. He put the maul down and headed toward the outhouse.

"Look at him, Addie. He is well-built: good shoulders, strong arms. Good-looking, too. For once, Granny would be right."

Addie watched him till he disappeared behind the outhouse door. "Yep, she would be right about this one."

Later, when we sat down to dinner, he ate quietly, all of his attention on his food. The lamplight made the slight cleft in his chin more apparent. He wiped his plate clean with the last of the corn bread as Addie and I cleared the serving bowls off the table.

Roy pulled a flask out of his back pocket. "You ladies mind?"

We shook our heads. He unscrewed the cap and took a long swallow, tilting his head back, exposing the movements of his throat.

When I came near the table where he sat smoking and drinking, I could smell the warm liquor on his breath and feel the heat of him. His situation grew darker and more dramatic the more he drank. By the time he finished the whiskey, he was railing against the mines, the unfriendliness of Jacksonville, and his sister-in-law. Even through my stupor of attraction, I could hear the bitterness in his voice. He caught my eye, tilted his shoulder my way when I passed by.

We let Roy sleep on the couch in the parlor. In the morning, he did not seem to be in much of a rush to leave. Addie and I discussed things and decided to offer him some money for his labor—not much, just two dollars, but it would have taken him pretty far back then. We worked him hard, dragging in some fresh-fall logs for firewood and replacing some boards on the back porch. In the afternoon, the three of us mucked the barn. All day I was aware of where he was and what he was doing.

After supper, when I returned from the outhouse, he stood on the back porch, his cigarette glowing in the dark. I passed him as I went up the steps and he pulled me toward him. His breath smelled of moonshine.

"Evelyn is a pretty name," he said. "I've never known a girl named Evelyn." He traced the line of my lower lip with his index finger, and I felt it all the way down my body. My hips curled involuntarily up and toward him.

"I can see it's just the two of you out here all alone," he whispered close to my face. Then he took my lower lip between his teeth and bit very gently, pressing his hips tight against me. I shuddered, and then pushed him away. It was too much, too fast.

Roy stumbled backward a step. "Go on then," he said and patted me on the rear as I walked away from him. "I don't need it no how."

I rushed inside, trembling. Not from fear or anger, but from what I wanted to do.

"You all right?" Addie asked and took me by the wrist.

"I'm all right, but he's getting pretty drunk. Did you show him where the whiskey was, the pints of shine Uncle Otis left us?"

"No, he must have found that on his own. I guess he figured we weren't paying him enough. I'll make sure he doesn't get more than one."

"Good. I'm going to bed," I told her.

From where I lay trying to calm myself and sleep, I heard them—at first very faintly, then louder when they came inside into the parlor. The trace of his touch lingered on my lips.

I must have fallen asleep. I woke sometime later and reached across Addie's side of the bed. My hand slid over cool, empty sheets. I heard some noises, faint voices, but no recognizable words. I tiptoed softly down the hall. The noises from the parlor became rhythmic as Addie's voice rose in excitement. My heart jolted, then clattered in my chest till I could hardly hear. Numbly, I took the last steps up to the parlor door. Through a crack of the door, I saw the middle of Addie's bare back, the curve of her behind, and, below her, the tops of Roy's thick, open thighs. She moved up and down on him. I watched, my fist jammed into my mouth, the burn from my belly to my crotch doubling me over. Then they slid from the couch to the floor. He shifted to the top. I could see only his feet sticking out past the couch. Their rhythm increased until he sputtered and groaned to a stop.

I crept backward down the hall as quietly as I could, crawled into bed, and curled up under the covers.

A few minutes later, Roy began to snore and I felt Addie slipping into the bed behind me. I pretended to be asleep, but Addie snuggled up and laid her arm across my waist. "I know you're awake," she said.

She smelled of his sweat, of whiskey, and of sex.

"Why did you do it?"

"Because I never had. It's good. It's different, too. Is it something you thought I would never do?"

"I just never thought of you with a man."

"You just thought of yourself with a man? I saw how you watched him. He's not as nice—not as good a person—as you."

"He smells like whiskey."

"I know." She pulled me closer. "You want to marry and have children, right?"

"Yes, but not with someone like him."

"I know." She kissed me until the tightness in my belly eased, then reached around my waist, touching the sweet center of me until I cli-

maxed and slept, dreaming she was in and around me, her voice humming through my bones.

⸎

I WOKE BEFORE DAWN to find the bed empty again. The first thing one
of us usually did when we woke was light a lantern. But I didn't stop
for that. I searched the house. Moonlight through windows was enough
to tell me: Roy, his suitcase, his hat, jacket, and shoes were gone. Bare-
foot and still in my nightgown, I lit a lantern and ran to the outhouse,
then the barn. Nothing but surprised livestock. Becky and Darling
neighed when I climbed up to the hay loft.

Outside, I scanned the horizon, hoping for any sign of them. I called
Addie's name into the cold predawn air.

They were gone.

Mechanically, I dressed and forced myself to eat. I listened for their
return as I finished the morning feeding and milking. Mid-morning, I
found myself sitting at the kitchen table, hollow and stupid as I waited
for them to return. Then I saw that the big peach-shaped cookie jar
where we kept our egg-and-butter money had been moved. The money
was gone, all fifty-three dollars.

I threw the jar against the kitchen wall, shattering it into a spray of
pink and green shards. I regretted it immediately. The jar had been
Aunt Eva's. I cried as I picked up the pieces. Twice, I cut myself.

I checked the closet and the bureau drawers. Some of our clothes
were missing, too. I flung everything off the bureau, stripped the closet,
and emptied every drawer. I collapsed on the heap of clothes and wept.
I kept going over everything that happened since Roy Hope had walked
up and asked for a drink of water, but I couldn't imagine why she'd gone
with him.

Eventually, I unfolded myself from the mess of clothes and got up to
finish my work for the day. Stunned and puzzled, I tried to think of

anything I'd ever seen in her that would lead her to disappear, abandoning me. That was what her fictional mother had done, just disappeared after a boy. That was all I could think of. Was she doing what her "mother" had done, following a fictional lead? Why had I lied? I banged my head against the barn wall.

The house and barn seemed too quiet without her. I consoled myself by giving Darling a long combing. Then I moved on to Becky and the cows. Numb, I watched my hands move over their haunches and withers. Hands identical to hers.

No, hers were identical to mine.

I went outside to the place past the apple tree where I had found her, knelt there, and pressed my hands to the ground. Nothing. No depression, no puddle, no warmth. The red earth was its simple mysterious self, fertile and relentlessly dumb. My innocence shamed me.

That evening, as I picked up the clothes I had hurled around the bedroom earlier, I felt the crumple of paper. On a small brown bag torn open and flat was a note in Addie's handwriting, sloppily written, but clear: "Back as soon as I can. 2 weeks? I love you. —Addie."

I headed straight back outside and lay down on the same spot. The sky stretched endless and blue above me. Peripherally, I saw the fields, the apple tree, and the barn. This had been Addie's view when I pulled her out of the ground. She was coming back! But what was she doing? Why leave me for two weeks? How was that love? Still, she was coming back. I spread my arms and moved my legs, making an angel in the dirt.

Kept busy with chores, both hers and mine, I managed to pass the rest of the week. I checked the road and the tracks every chance I got, hoping Addie would appear. Her absence loomed everywhere. I'd lost my talent for being alone. I was unmoored, awash in recollections of Addie's first days with me. In her absence, her extraordinary qualities seemed even more present.

That time of year my family did not come up to help unless they heard from me. But Addie and I often went into town to run errands on Saturday. On Sundays we met them for church. They would be expecting us. Saturday morning, I walked down to Mildred's to call Momma. Rita answered and I told her that I wasn't feeling well, and we wouldn't be coming to town. No, we weren't that sick, just that time of the month. We'd be okay. We had everything we needed.

Sunday evening I heard steps on the back porch and ran to the door, flinging it open. Cole, his hand raised to knock, laughed in surprise. Then, quickly, his face dropped, mirroring my disappointment. I stood speechless in the open door, trying to recover.

"I'm sorry . . ." Cole stuttered. "You and Addie . . . your momma said you weren't at church."

"Everything's okay. I'm not feeling well . . . Can you come back later?" I pulled the door nearly shut.

"You don't look so good. Is there anything I can do? Where's Addie?"

"She went away on a trip, Cole."

"A trip? Where?" He stepped up closer to the door.

"I can't talk now. You need to go. Please." I didn't want him to see me cry.

"Wait, Evelyn." He slipped his hand around the door frame. "Is Addie okay?"

"There was this boy. She left with him. There was a note. That's all I know."

He shook his head in disbelief, his face screwed up in concern. "Evelyn, let me . . ."

I waved him away and bit my lip to keep from crying. "It'll be okay, Cole. She said she would be back. I know she will. I'll let you know if I need anything. Okay?"

He nodded and took a step back, but didn't seem convinced.

"Thanks for coming by."

He nodded again and walked away, his shoulders hunched and his hands jammed down in his pockets.

The next weekend, I didn't bother calling Momma's. Suppertime Saturday, Momma showed up. She held a plate of scones wrapped in wax paper when she got out of the truck. Immediately, she knew something was wrong. "Evelyn?" she called as she came into the kitchen.

I had prepared answers to the questions about Addie if anyone else came by. Addie was on another mountain trip. Or she was out on a long horseback ride. But as soon as Momma set the scones down on the kitchen table and turned to me, I started to cry.

Weeping into her shoulder, I told her everything about Roy, except, of course, how he had touched me, what I had seen through the parlor door, and the missing money. She held me and did not scold or tell me that we should not have let a strange man stay in the house.

She took my face in her hands and made me look at her. "If she said she will come back, then she will, Evelyn." She wiped my tears. "Now, you quit this crying."

She stayed the afternoon, helping me press butter and cheese.

Her conviction reassured me. Still, I kept seeing Addie on top of him. I gagged on my own confusion and sickening jealousy. I wanted each of them and wanted to be each of them.

What had felt like blessed solitude and privacy before Addie came into my life now felt jagged and harsh. Admitting her absence to Cole and then to Momma made it more real. Equally real was the fact that if she did not come back, I would never know who or what she was. With each day that passed, those unanswered questions seemed a greater and greater injury. It seemed incomprehensible that I could have held her so intimately and not known. Inwardly, I railed against my imposed innocence. I grew lighter and more delicate, frayed by the air I leaned into as I listened for her return. I stayed close to the house and hung on every little sound.

Exactly two weeks from the day Addie and Roy left, when I had lost almost all hope, I heard footsteps coming up the drive.

I ran toward the back door, hoping for Addie, but Roy stepped into the kitchen. He stood there alone, expectant, wider and taller than I remembered him.

"Where's Addie?" I craned my neck, peering past him for Addie.

He said nothing and opened his arms as if I would step into them.

I tried to shove him out of the way to see if she was outside. "Where's Addie? Is she okay? Did you do something to her?"

He refused to move. "I am Addie."

"No. Where's Addie? Tell me!" I screamed in his face.

He held his hands out, calmly offering himself. I stared up at him, at Roy's brown eyes, at Roy's face and lips, his neck, shoulders, waist and hips, at his feet planted on the floor.

I backed up into the kitchen. "No. Where is she?" I went cool and hard.

"I am Addie." He stepped toward me. There was something familiar in how he looked at me, nothing like the swaggering Roy.

"No!" I shook my head. "No!" My voice thin as a whip.

"You said that he was a fine example of a man, one a woman could get healthy children off of. And you want children," he said.

I stared at him. Addie must have told him what I'd said.

"I did this for you, Evelyn."

His voice did not fit. It was still Roy's voice, but the phrasing was different. And it was deeper, more resonant. He stepped closer and reached out as if to catch me. I smelled the familiar chlorophyll odor of Addie as I collapsed onto the chair he held for me.

The room dimmed and turned grainy. I grabbed his arm instead of the hand he offered, and dug my fingers in. "Don't do this to me," I snapped. "I want Addie back. I want you to look like . . . like me?" My words faded to a whimper and I sat down.

He touched my face gently. "Evelyn, it will be all right."

I leapt up. "Who are you? Not my skin, not his skin, but *you*! I have to know! What are you! Show me what you look like! Let me hear your voice! Yours."

He gave me a long, intent look that made me step back and sit again.

"Okay," he said.

He planted his feet. His opened his mouth slightly and sighed. His fingertips spread across his chest. Had Roy ever seen Addie do that? Then a sweet chime rang out from him, followed by a slow deep chime that settled into a steady drone. Then the sweetness segued to raw sound. Pure harmonics. A hard wail. He was aiming at me! Wave followed wave, higher, larger. His pupils dilated. The floor resonated. The arms of the chair hummed. My head filled. Louder and brighter, filling me, pulling me out of myself. Overwhelming. I wanted to cover my ears, my chest, my belly, but I didn't move. Then something in me rose to meet that sound that was now no longer sound. Beautiful and horrible. Not color, not light, nor odor, taste, or touch, but some distillation of all. Buoying me, holding me, pressing. Beyond him, I sensed other harmonics. And it seemed to me I heard the voices of children—our children, I was sure.

Blindly, I put my hand out and touched his chest, and his voice receded, pulling back into him, rippling into questions as it withdrew. We breathed hard. Outside, a bird called. A train whistled far away. The 10:10. The world continued to turn. Morning light shone in across his shoe and up his leg. His hand at his side was large, a meaty man's hand. The hair on his arm, dark. His face red from effort. Sweat, beading at his temple, ran down past his ear and onto his throat. His hair a deep brown. His eyes the golden brown of burnished oak.

Keeping his eyes on mine, he took my hand from his chest and cupped it in his hand, then moved it down between his legs.

I felt him growing in my hand, pushing against the fabric of his pants. I closed my eyes as he led me down the hall to the bedroom.

He lay down on the bed and opened his arms. I lay down beside him and pressed my face into his neck. I wept.

He held me tightly, his voice emanating sweet and light from his chest. But, for once, it had no effect on me. The tidal wave heaved itself up from the distance and hurtled toward my shore, its beautiful, obscene curve come at last to wash me, to drown me. I cried, trembling and clutching him to me, then beating him away.

Eventually, I sobbed myself to sleep inside his arms and the purr of his voice. I woke alone in the slant-light of late afternoon, the ends of all of my nerve cells swept clean. I heard him humming down the hall—a normal man humming a hymn. The sound of frying eggs interrupted a deep male voice singing Addie's odd, jazzy version of "Onward Christian Soldiers."

Wobbly on my legs, I walked down the hall and stopped in the kitchen doorway to watch him. He turned from the stove with a question on his face.

"I'm okay," I told him and eased myself into a chair.

He pulled some perfect biscuits out of the oven. God, he was beautiful.

I motioned toward the bedroom. "I'm sorry."

"It's okay. I should have realized what a shock it would be for you. Should have planned it with you. But I saw the opportunity." He set a plate of scrambled eggs in front of me. A slice of ham beside it. Addie and I had done that—made breakfast for supper, when we were tired or hadn't gotten around to making anything else.

"Tell me," I said. "How did Roy like having a twin?"

He filled his plate and sat down across the table from me.

"I don't know," he said. "I didn't ask and he didn't say. He'll drink as much as you give him. I kept him drunk, very drunk, and the shades drawn. Not long after you fell asleep that night, I heard him creeping around in the kitchen. Then the back door squeaked. I checked the cookie jar and figured out what he was up to. My first thought was to get the money back, then I realized what else I could do. Or at least try. I wrote you the note and ran after him. He hadn't gotten far. We hopped the midnight freight out of the mill and got as far as a Forest City motel. I was sure I needed to be isolated with him, like I was with you."

The two of us ate hungrily, me looking at him and him gazing back at me. Incomprehensible. Yet he sat like any man, eating eggs, chewing, lifting his coffee cup to his lips. I could hardly breathe. But I, too, sat like any woman and ate my supper.

He ate with the same concentration and gusto as Addie. When he had sopped the last smear of egg yellow with his biscuit, he wiped his hands, then took a small wad of money out of his pocket. He laid it on the table and pushed it toward me. "That's what's left. I wish it was more. But there was food, the motel, and the booze. I had to buy some clothes, too. I left him enough money for the train back to Kentucky. He looked up at me early one morning before I handed him the bottle and said, 'I never knew you were such an ugly, goddamned ugly woman. How'd you get here?' I was starting to get a beard by then."

He tipped forward, slurring and jerking his shoulders the way Roy had when he was drunk. I laughed then and Addie laughed, too. "Ugly, goddamned ugly woman," he repeated and we could not stop laughing. Every time we glanced at each other, we giggled and he mimicked Roy again. My face locked into a laugh, I felt hysteria rising.

Finally, I choked on some biscuit and had to stop myself.

"Do you like this?" I asked when I had calmed down. "Being a man?"

The question sobered him. He sighed and answered, "Yes, I do. But I don't like it more than being you." My skin prickled when he said "being you."

"I wasn't sure if I could even make it happen. It took longer than I thought it would. I had to concentrate everything I had on him. With you, it just happened. I went out only for food, booze, and clothes—and a haircut. When I saw I was finished, I came straight back here."

"Did it hurt? Will you stay like this? Will you need to be around him?"

He sat very still for a moment, rubbing his chest. "No, it didn't hurt. But I could feel things coming apart and reassembling." His hands rocked up and down over our empty plates. I felt my own wrenching internal realignment.

He smiled and shrugged. "I feel okay. I feel . . . stable. Fixed again." He put his hand over mine. "And you?"

"I am not stable yet," I whispered and began clearing the table.

We washed the dishes, side by side, not touching, though I felt his warmth next to me, waiting, available.

Near sunset, he went out into the barn. Quietly, I followed to watch. Hobo stood alert at the barn door, barked once, then wagged his tail. Addie stopped and knelt. Hobo approached her with familiarity but no affection. Addie took Hobo's muzzle in her hands—in his hands. Suddenly, Hobo leapt up, licking Addie and running excitedly around him, barking.

In the barn, the livestock rustled—a muted snort, a whinny of interest. I walked down the porch steps to get a better view. Addie went first to Darling's stall. I heard that faint hum. Darling nosed him and nickered in recognition. He ran his hand down her neck, Addie's touch. But a man's deep, full laugh accompanied it. When he opened the stall gate, she pressed into him. Hobo circled them, yapping. The cows bellowed at the excitement, the chickens clattered in the coop.

Addie bridled Darling, mounted bareback. With a wave, he cantered off, disappearing into the pasture. I could see them for a long time, then, at the far end of the pasture, dusk snuffed them out of sight.

By the time I heard him shutting up the barn for the night, I'd made his bed—the same bed I tried to get him to sleep in after I found him in the mud. I laid out some of Lester's clothes for him, certain this time they would fit, at least in length. The shoulders might be too narrow.

That was all I could do. To do more, to have him in my bed then, on that first night, felt like it would be the undoing of me. Too much for one day. I was numb.

He did not comment when he saw the bedroom door open and the bed turned down, but stopped and, taking my head in his hands, kissed me gently, squarely on the forehead and said good night.

"Good night, Addie," I replied. But I could not walk away from him. "You need a man's name. I can't call you Addie. And I can't call you Roy. He knows where we live. What if he shows up again? You need a name, one that sounds like Addie." Then I said the first name I could think of, "Adam. You can be Adam."

"Adam? Yeah, I like that. Adam." He sat on the bed and took his shoes off. "I don't think Roy will be back this way to raise questions. But I might run into someone who sees a resemblance. It would make sense for us to be from the same clan. And I owe him for this." He swept his hand across his lap. "My last name should be Hope. Roy can be a middle name."

"You need a story, too. Where do you come from? And why are you here?"

My questions filled the room for a minute.

Adam took a deep breath. "From here. For you. As always. Though I forgot to think up a name, on the way back, I decided that I'm from Kentucky, like Roy. The other side of the mountains. I came here because I heard about how good Addie was with horses. I'm good with horses, too. So I came to see if you two could give me a job. And now it looks like you will really need a new hand. So do I get the job?" He smiled an invitation.

I let it pass. "Adam Roy Hope," I pronounced him. He gave me Addie's smile, her gaze through his new face.

We went to our separate beds.

I could sense him through the walls. Then the fatigue of my confusion and desire came down like a hammer and knocked me into a sleep in which there was no skin, no voice, no entangled limbs.

The next morning, I woke to the sound of footsteps in the hall, the floorboards telegraphing the new weight of Addie—of Adam. Everything else remained the same, the squeak of the oven door as he opened it, the groan and sputter of the pump as he drew water for coffee.

I dressed slowly and went into the kitchen, into the welcome of his wide grin, into a normal day. We did the same chores in the same order. Same cows to milk, same chickens to feed, same pitchfork for the manure. Same red dirt underfoot. But she was now he. The world seemed surreal in its placid continuity while, in me, tectonic, dizzying shifts took place.

I could almost taste the strange irony of my desire. For her. For him.

After the morning milking, we finished sawing the fall logs, a job that we had started with Roy. Sawing the thicker log was a two-person job. We didn't talk much. All I had were questions. The same questions I had had all along. There were, I was sure, no more answers now than there had been when I found him. I felt drained, stunned, my skin stretched over nerves held together only by routine. The noise and effort of sawing offered a small antidote.

He took over the splitting and stacking when we finished the sawing. Through the open barn doors, I watched him while I cleared the manure and lay down fresh hay. He circled the stump we used as a chopping block, then swung the maul in a practice swing. He shook his head, then stepped back farther from the stump and swung again. Rocking back on his heels slightly, then forward, just as Addie used to do, he swung again. The maul landed dead-center and he laughed.

In the afternoon we stopped for lunch. Adam noticed the healed cut, a thin red line at the base of my thumb as I handed him a sandwich. He touched my wrist. "What happened?"

I pointed to the shelf, "The cookie jar, I smashed it against the wall when I found it empty. I hadn't found your note yet. I cut myself cleaning it up."

I smelled the grassy, fresh-mown odor of his sweat. The warmth of his touch lingered on my hand. "I need to take you down to meet Momma and Daddy. I want to let them know you're here. The sooner they meet the new hired help, the better, I think."

We walked to the mill-village, cutting through the woods where I had played as a child. To cross the creek, we walked single-file over a narrow fallen tree. Halfway across, I heard, above the soft burble of the creek, a single, crisp chime, clear as the water behind me. I turned to look, almost slipping on the slick log. Adam grabbed my elbow, to steady me, and grinned sheepishly at me.

"I know it's you." I continued across the creek and down the path.

Otherwise, we were quiet. The sun shone through the sparse canopy of late winter. With him behind me on the narrow path, I could imagine that nothing had changed, that I would see Addie if I glanced over my shoulder.

We reached the edge of the mill-village and my self-consciousness immediately returned. I felt naked, aware of him by my side. We waved to the old lady who lived in the first house. Her little granddaughter, sitting in the porch swing, waved back, but the old woman continued her sweeping without noticing us.

Momma and Daddy were alone at the table when we arrived, a pot of pinto beans and a plate of corn bread between them. They stood when they saw Adam.

"Momma, Daddy, this is . . ."

"Adam. I'm Adam Hope. Pleased to meet you, Mr. and Mrs. Roe." He held his hand out. Daddy shook his hand and nodded.

Momma's eyes were wide with surprise. "My, it is nice to meet you,

Adam. Sorry, y'all are missing Evelyn's sister, Rita, she's off with some friends," she said as she took Adam's hand. She motioned for me to get more plates and forks and returned her attention to Adam.

"Y'all are just in time for supper! Sit down."

"Thank you, ma'am. Sorry to barge in like this. I'm from Kentucky. I came to Clarion looking for work."

"Are you a good mechanic?" Daddy asked. "One of our machine boys left for the Radley mill about a week ago."

"Thank you, sir. I'll keep that in mind, but I'm not much of a mechanic. I'm a trained groom and stable hand. Too many of us already in Kentucky. I came here because I heard about Addie Hardin and Cole Starnes's work with horses, so I—"

I interrupted, "I'm pretty sure the Starneses aren't looking for any help. But I have really been missing Addie's help. If she doesn't come back . . ."

Daddy's interest had lagged as soon as he saw Adam wasn't looking for a mill job, but now he pulled out a chair for Adam and sat down opposite him. "That's something to consider. Her momma never came back."

Momma touched my arm and sighed sympathetically. She ladled ham and beans onto our plates and pushed the skillet of corn bread closer to Adam.

I shook my head. "I could use the help."

Adam took a piece of the corn bread. "It's a small place, but more than one person can do. I'd be happy to work for room and board for the time being. Until you know what the situation is. I've done farming, too."

There was a beat of silence, then Daddy turned to Momma. "Lily Mae, why don't you offer the boy some of your sweet pickles?"

Momma got the pickles and some of her corn relish, opening a fresh jar of each and presenting them on the little flowered dish she reserved for company.

Adam added a generous portion of each to his plate and moaned appreciatively when he had a mouthful of pickles. "These are great, Mrs. Roe. Did you can them yourself?"

"I did," she beamed. "With Evelyn and Addie. They grow the best pickling cucumbers. That land is good for corn and peppers, too. Call me Lily Mae."

Adam spooned the relish onto his corn bread and took a big bite. "Mmm . . . this is really good!"

"So, Adam. Horses? I wouldn't think there would be much call for horses now with everybody in cars and filling stations on every corner." Daddy searched his pants pocket and pulled out his pipe in preparation for his after-dinner smoke.

"Rich people will always have horses. Keep them as pets and investments," Adam replied.

"Investments. I imagine that's so." Daddy tapped his pipe on the edge of his plate.

"Some people just like them." Momma nodded her head.

The porch door slammed and Joe walked in. I introduced them. While they shook hands, Adam pointed to Joe's newly purchased truck parked in the yard and asked, "How's that one running for you?"

Joe's face lit up. He'd saved for months for that old Ford. He launched into a story about it as the men went out to the porch. I realized, with a shock, that Adam was courting my family. And succeeding.

Momma and I cleaned the table. Over the noise of the running water and the dish-washing, all I could hear of the men were indistinct words, punctuated by occasional laughter.

"Evelyn, honey, you haven't heard anything from her?"

I shook my head and turned away to slip a stack of dried plates into the pantry.

"That is peculiar," Momma said.

I nodded, but did not offer anything.

"She can take care of herself, Evelyn. Don't worry about her."

I didn't want to make Momma complicit in my lies. But I didn't know what to say.

"Adam seems like a nice fellow." She stopped wiping the counter and looked at me quizzically.

"He would be a big help, Momma. Now that Joe has a family. And Bertie never helps anymore, even Rita wants to stay in town with her friends. And Cole is full-time at the mill. Now with Addie gone . . ." I shrugged and tried to look convincingly sad and tired. "All he's asked for is food. He can't eat much more than Addie."

Momma smiled at my reference. Addie was known for her appetite at family dinners. "I know you miss her. And it looks like you've been eating less up there by yourself." She pulled at the waist of my dress. "I don't see how it could hurt for you to have some help. He'd eventually want to find a paying job, so don't get too used to it."

Before I could think of anything to say, Daddy, Joe, and Adam came in from the porch. Momma squeezed my arm and asked them if they wanted coffee.

"I can't, Momma," Joe said. "I gotta get back to the house soon. Mary'll be looking for me." He turned to Adam. "So what were you, army, navy? Not air corps. You haven't said a thing about flying."

I felt a surge of panic.

But Adam just sighed and said, "I didn't serve, Joe, sorry to say. Maybe if the war had lasted a little longer . . ."

"I didn't quite make it either, buddy," Joe commiserated. "Momma made me finish high school, and by the time I was ready to sign up, they were starting to turn 'em loose. Some say I'm lucky, but I don't know." He looked at both of us. "Can I give you a ride on my way home? It's getting dark."

"You were lucky, son," Momma said. Then she turned to Adam. "Now, about that room and board. We'll need to decide where that room will be."

Adam glanced at me quickly. Neither of us had thought of that.

A half hour later, Joe dropped me off at the farm. As they pulled away, Adam turned to wave at me through the truck's back window. He would be staying at Joe's and coming to help me during the day.

Over the next few days, we worked together as Addie and I had. I made him leave before sunset each day and walk back down to Joe's. I did not let him have me or come to me at night. I was not being coy. I wanted him, terribly, powerfully. I wanted that encompassing touch and the ring of that unique voice, but I was caught in the whiplash of change. Addie was now wholly different from me, and, in Adam, both absent and present. I needed those evenings alone to let what I'd seen of him during the day seep into my skin and muscle, to register on my nerves.

In my struggle to make sense of Addie becoming Adam, I needed a way to think of them as the single being I knew them to be, a term that bridged their obvious differences. Without any conscious decision to do so, I began to think of *them* simply as A. From that point on, A. became the private name that, in my mind, encompassed both of them as well as the person I had pulled from the land, who was neither man nor woman. A. was their totality.

While I was alone at night, my family slept down the hill, innocent and distant. Momma in her nightgown, her hair loose on the pillow, oblivious. Bertie and Rita dreamed in their beds. Freddie and Marge slept down the street from them. From my bedroom window, the street-lights of Clarion seemed smaller and farther away. Even the mill lights seemed dimmer now.

I imagined myself squatting by Momma's bed in the dark or bent over Rita's sleeping face, whispering the truth to them, my words set-tling onto their shoulders and slipping into their ears. They would wake to carry into their days a few ounces of what I knew.

To all of them, Adam was a large, well-mannered, good-looking per-son, clearly and solely a man. They would wonder, as Momma had, about

Addie's disappearance and my sudden bond with Adam, but in the end they would, I knew, accept what they saw before them. Still, I could not fully quell my fear that their credulity would be exhausted, that they would somehow recognize him as the violation of nature that he was. Of the two, Adam did seem the greater violation. He was not the innocent, earth-sprung being of Addie, but a consequence of will and desire.

With Addie's arrival, I had been in an adrenaline-soaked haze, amazed at what I had seen, certain I would be thought crazy if I told the truth, and, if I was believed, that she would be thought a freak. These things seemed equally true for Adam, perhaps more so. Lying about him seemed more calculated.

I kept my own introductions of Adam to a minimum—he was simply a horseman from Kentucky looking for a job—and refused to embellish. The lack of detail would work itself out. Meanwhile, it may have lent him a greater air of mystery. The next Sunday, when he came into the church with Joe and Mary, Uncle Lester's old suit tight across the shoulders, a brief pause of attention in the preservice whispers followed him. I'm sure the young women were taking his measure and, when I moved over on the pew to be closer to the three of them, calculating my relation to him.

As we filed out of the church, I lost sight of Adam in the crush of Sunday suits and hats. I caught up with him as Momma introduced him to some of the church ladies. Adam, of course, had to act as if he had never met any of them. He graciously shook hands and repeated his name. Old Mrs. Bailey stood next to him, scrutinizing him from under her hat brim, then casually brushed a bit of lint from his shoulder.

The ghost of Addie seemed to linger with us as we all filed out of the church. Everyone mentioned her absence as they welcomed Adam. After Grandma Lou surveyed Adam up and down, she patted me on the arm. "Blood will out. She ran off with some strange boy just like her momma."

I glanced around for Cole, then remembered that his Eloise was Methodist and he attended her church most Sundays now.

As I fielded questions about Addie's absence that afternoon, I realized how much I heard that was not questions but statements. Others were taking up the story, giving me the missing pieces. Cole had heard Addie's name before she had one. Momma had come to her own conclusions about why Addie looked like me. Joe concluded that Adam must have, like him, been too young to serve during the war. And now it seemed that everyone would treat Addie's flight as a continuation of her "mother's" story. Addie had been right: we needed our stories. All of them had seen what they expected to see or hear. They had found what their stories told them would be there.

Except for me. What I had found was completely unexpected.

❧

LATER THAT DAY, Adam and I stopped by Freddie and Marge's. I introduced him. The circle of musicians welcomed him with little nods. Freddie shook Adam's hand and offered him a seat. Marge nudged me after giving Adam a complete, swift look-over. I laughed and shook my head at her suggestion. But she didn't believe me. She winked at me and nodded. The vague unhappiness of her childless marriage seemed to inspire in her a radiant enthusiasm for others' romances.

Adam walked me home afterward. We were quiet in the darkness. He kissed me chastely on the forehead and left me at the back door.

❧

MOMMA AND DADDY CAME to help with the farm work the next Saturday and brought Rita. As they were saying their good-byes, Adam waved from the barn and continued brushing down Darling. Joe was coming by later, and Adam would get a ride back to town with him.

Daddy and Rita waited in the truck, but Momma stopped on her way out the door.

"See you later." She waved to Adam, and then turned to me. "I'm proud of you, Evelyn. You've done good here." She nodded her head toward the barn and fields and gave me a slight tilt of her head, her eyebrows raised, her don't-screw-up gaze.

"Momma, it's all right. He's just going to help me some." I pretended to wipe something from my skirt. She squeezed my arm till I looked up and held her gaze. She could smell intention on her children. She did not need the sin itself to start sniffing around like an old hound dog.

"I'm all right, Momma. I'll be careful." I saw it on her face, as she registered that there was need for care. Daddy honked the horn.

"Do be careful," she whispered and let me go.

Adam waved again as they drove off, and then locked eyes with me across the backyard. My veiled admission to Momma was still fresh. Something in me gave, shifting into a new place. Before the truck disappeared down Clear Lake Road, Adam leapt onto the back steps as if I had called him.

I motioned for him to follow and led him down the hall. He hesitated, and then stepped into the bedroom he had slept in the first night.

"Take your clothes off," I told him.

He obliged. Everything came off, even his socks. I looked at him, taking in every part—toes, ankles, knees, the thighs I had last seen under Addie, the pale planes of his hip joint, genitals, belly, breastbone, hands, arms, neck, ears, eyelids, lips, teeth, cheekbones. I had never studied a man that way before. Silently, he let me. This was Addie, whom I had loved. I turned him around and looked at his backside. I traced his spine with my fingertip and was done. "Thank you."

"You are welcome." He turned to face me again, not acknowledging or attempting to hide his erection. I glanced away. He moved as if to reach for me. I took his hand but placed it back down at his side.

"Will it be like this from now on?" he asked.

"I don't know." Tension leaked out of me. Suddenly, I felt exhausted. He took my hand and pressed it to his chest. I braced myself against the start-up of that gentle vibration, but there was only his heartbeat, warm bone, and muscle under my palm.

"You wanted a husband, a family?" he asked.

I nodded, my chest tight.

"Would you rather have Addie back?" he asked.

"You can do that? You could be Addie again?"

"I don't know if I can do it again, I'm not even sure how I do it. But I would try if you want me to. Then you could have a family with someone else. I could, too. Or I could stay as I am and father children with someone else."

Another thing I had not thought of.

"We could," he continued, "each find someone else. Is that what you want?"

I thought again of Addie with Roy, and flushed with jealousy and confusion. "No, no, no. Not that." I began to cry, and backed out the bedroom door. He grabbed my wrist. I stood there, covering my face with one hand, the other arm held awkwardly out toward him.

"I don't know what you are. What if our babies? What if they are? What if they are like mules and can't . . . ? What if we can't?"

He waited until I caught my breath and said in a measured voice, "Do you know who you are, Evelyn? Who all of you are? Where do *you* come from? You don't know any more than I do."

He dropped my hand and began to pace. His erection had fallen. "I listen in church, Evelyn. No one knows, no one truly knows. There is faith, but not true knowledge. All we know is how we are supposed to act to keep living and to get along." He gripped the footboard of the bed and peered at me. "But I have to know? I have to be able to say who and what I am? Or you won't accept me now?"

He opened his arms and looked at me until I felt as naked as he was. "Here I am. This is all I can offer you." He was exquisite, beautiful.

Suddenly quiet, he sat on the edge of the bed, his head in his hands. "I will not be alone because I cannot say what I am. I want children, too. I want them very much. And, no, I cannot tell you how normal they will be." There were drops on the floor between his feet. I stared at them as if I had never seen tears. I had never seen him cry before.

He shook his head. "I know it, as certain as I know that I have lungs though I do not see them. I know it, Evelyn. I can give you children."

He got up and slowly dressed. "Marry me, Evelyn."

I sat, still staring at the floor when Joe's truck pulled up. Adam shut the door as he left.

Heartsick with confusion, I saw myself in the mirror. I stayed in that room until Adam's tears dried on the floor and the room darkened down. Something in the core of me went quiet. I listened and listened until I could hear no more, until I knew. There was really only one answer I was capable of giving him.

I made an admission to myself then locked it away in my heart as if it were a treasure: he is not one of us. To have him and to bear his children was to depart from not only my family and my people, but from my kind, from my—the word rose up unbidden, startling—*species*.

☙

EARLY THE NEXT MORNING I heard Joe's car in the driveway and then Adam thanking him for the ride. I walked around the table to see out the kitchen window. Clouds, orange-gold and clipped with silver, fanned out from dawn's blood-red sun. Joe's truck disappeared down the road.

Adam walked in the back door behind me and stopped.

"I missed her," I said, keeping my eyes on the sky. "I missed her so much."

He came up close. "Ooh," he said when he saw the sky. I leaned my head back against his chest. "I missed *you*." He put his arms around me.

We stayed like that a long time, watching the dawn diffuse into day, then I took him by the hand and led him to the bedroom.

We began slowly, tentative as if we had never done it before. The weight and press of him was not like Addie. He was flat and hard and boney where she had been soft and curved. He had hair where she had been naked smoothness. But the odor of him was familiar, and Addie was in his touch. He moved over me like silken water, encompassing me, making a room of his body, as she had. That familiar hum rose in him. Our rhythm changed, quickening, and he arched. I jumped back from him. "Come out. I don't want babies now."

He smiled down, amazed at the mess he'd made on my belly. "There's so much," he muttered apologetically. "I . . ."

I laughed. "I had me a virgin." I wiped my fingers across my belly, touched my lips and then his. He tasted the bitter saltiness of himself and laughed. A big, deep, beautiful belly laugh. We smeared ourselves, laughing the relief of sin after drought.

We lay still for a long time in the echo of what we had just done. Then we turned toward each other again.

"Yes," I told him.

"Yes?"

"Yes," I said. "Yes. I will marry you."

❧

WE DECIDED TO WAIT a few weeks before telling anyone about our plans to marry. A nine-day courtship would be short by anyone's standards.

Soon, Adam had met everyone but Cole. Mr. Starnes had been sick lately. Also, with full-time work, and his girlfriend, I knew Cole had little extra time. He'd been coming around less even before Addie left, but still I was surprised that I hadn't seen him yet. Adam and I planned to go see him and Mr. Starnes the next Sunday.

I stood in the kitchen Friday afternoon, dressed but still vague and soft from making love with Adam, when a sharp knock broke my reverie. Cole smiled at me through the door pane. His smile turned to concern as I smoothed my hair. I opened the door and let him in.

"Evelyn," he said. "Are you . . ."

We both turned to the sound of footsteps in the hall. Adam appeared. Looking down as he zipped up his pants, he didn't notice us. His boots were tucked under his arm, his hair messed up.

Cole shot me a glance of surprised disappointment and turned to leave.

"Cole!" Adam boomed, dropping his boots. "Good to see you!" He beamed, caught off guard, his arm out as if to hug Cole, who leapt back, knocking over one of the kitchen chairs.

I held my hand out to slow his retreat. "Cole, this is Adam Hope."

Cole righted the chair. A short, awkward silence followed. Adam looked at me helplessly. Cole stared at the floor.

"Is Addie back? You heard anything?" Cole directed the question at me with a quick glance.

I shook my head. I wanted to say, "It is not what you think, Cole! I've known him for years. You know him." Instead, I asked Cole, "Can you help me with something out by the barn? Can I show you?" Cole held his hand out stiffly. "Nice to meet you." They shook hands briefly.

"Sure. Let's go." He stepped aside and I led him outside.

We squatted to inspect a split in one of the corral posts.

"Cole, it's not what you think."

"I think you hardly know this guy."

"And how well did I know you before?"

"You knew stuff about me. I lived in the same town. Who is he?"

"This is different from . . ." I admitted, then added, "And now you're with Eloise. Right?"

He examined the post, ignoring my question. "We can just bind this. Don't have to pull it. With a two-by-four and a few long screws it should last a couple more years at least." He stood up and brushed the dust off his hands and narrowed his eyes as he glanced toward the house.

I straightened up and moved into his line of sight. "Cole, I miss Addie something terrible. I'm alone here now, and I want something like what you have with Eloise. And he reminds me of Addie."

Surprise flashed across his face. He glanced away at her name.

I continued, "Trust me, Cole. I was right about you. I'm right about him. He's a good man. And I'm alone now."

His face softened. He nodded, conceding. "The house still smells like Addie. It's so strange, her going off like that and not even saying good-bye. Like her momma, I guess. But if she found a fella, I guess you should have one too. It's just that it's all so fast." He scuffed his boot in the clay and studied the ground. When he looked up again, a slow smile crept across his lips. "Yeah, it's been a year for me and Eloise. I'm going to ask her to marry me soon."

"Cole! You're getting married?"

"Shh! I haven't officially asked her. Don't tell anyone." He nodded, suddenly as bashful as the boy I'd met in the cornfield a couple years before. He brushed away my surprise. Then his face was serious again. "You've got to be more careful, okay? What if it'd been your daddy or momma at the back door instead of me? I'll be back tomorrow to help you with this post." Then he mounted and rode off.

I called after him, "Good luck! I hope the answer's yes!"

He laughed and waved as he trotted off.

He did come back. Adam deferred to him in the corral repair. Cole was brusque and to the point while they worked. But as soon as they were done, Adam leaned on the fence, then asked about the white chicken-scared mare Cole and Addie had cured. Cole started slow, but warmed each time we laughed at his flapping imitation of Addie's apron full of biddies and his chicken-holding duties.

I fried us some corn bread and sausage for lunch. While I washed up, Cole joined me at the sink. "I see what you mean. He is like her. He's got the gift with horses. Darling follows him like a puppy. Just like with Addie. Spooky." He gave me a friendly, quizzical glance, then grinned. "Maybe it's you. Maybe a body has to be good with horses to hang around with you."

"You have no idea." I laughed.

❧

ADAM WAS DEFT AT COURTSHIP of every kind, and within a short time had won Cole's respect and friendship. Having been Addie was good preparation for befriending Cole. But there were other times, when our combined experience as women left us unprepared. Neither of us had been a man. I couldn't offer Adam tutorials, as I had with Addie. A few weeks after Adam's arrival, Joe and Daddy showed up to help rehinge and rehang one of the barn doors.

Adam and I were hanging up laundry when they pulled up in the driveway. They got out of the truck and walked up to the flapping laundry.

I was farther down the clothesline and couldn't see them but I heard Joe snicker and Daddy make his funny huffing noise of disgust. I peeked over the lines of damp clothes just as Daddy turned away and started for the barn.

Joe leaned close to Adam. "Look, buddy, you may have it real bad for her, you may be so sweet on her you just gotta help in every way. But you just gotta let her take care of those things." I dipped under a wet shirt to see what the fuss was. For a heartbeat, Adam stood there looking puzzled, and then he handed me a bundle of my damp, clean panties he'd been hanging up. Joe rolled his eyes at me and dope-slapped Adam as they left the clothesline to join Daddy, who squatted by the barn studying the derelict hinge.

I asked Adam about it later.

"There's a lot of subtle stuff to this manhood," he said and spread the fingers of one hand over his breastbone—Addie's gesture. Suddenly, it seemed effeminate. I straightened his wrist and lifted his elbow a little.

He thumped himself on the chest. "Better?" he asked.

"Yep."

"So no more hanging up panties for me—at least when anyone else is around," he continued. "Some other lessons I've learned." He held up his fingers, counting them off. "Limit questions to those about cars, engines, and sports. Do not look another man in the eye for more than a second when you pass on the street, one quick glance and a nod will do. Most men want you to stand beside them and look at something else with them, not face them when you're talking. Don't spend much time in the kitchen with the women. Arrange yourself before you leave the bathroom." He glanced down at his new body. I laughed, remembering Addie's puzzled survey of her crotch when I had told her about menstruation. I felt his strangeness viscerally, a stirring in my solar plexus.

AFTER A COUPLE OF MONTHS we were ready to announce our engagement. We decided against him formally asking my daddy for my hand; Adam did not want to leave Momma out. But he did give Daddy a pouch of his favorite pipe tobacco after we finished dinner that Sunday. Momma and I joined Daddy and Adam on the porch after we finished the dishes. Daddy was lighting his pipe when Adam and I announced that we wanted their permission to marry. He dropped the match, stomped it, and took his pipe out of his mouth. They both stopped their rocking and stared at us. Adam had been successful in his courtship of them. They liked him, I was sure of that.

Momma searched my face and her expression of amazement burst into a smile of satisfaction. I felt a twinge of anxiety when I saw Daddy's surprised face. He'd never liked surprises and tended to foist them on Momma whenever possible.

"It's . . . Uhm, it's awfully soon, isn't it?" Daddy directed the question at Momma, not us.

"It is soon, Robert. But that's not the question. They're asking for our approval. If we approve, what does it matter if we approve now or in six months? They're not asking to get married today."

Daddy listened. A second match flared and he sucked on the pipe.

Momma glared playfully at him, but her voice held serious undertones. "Nobody's rushing you. We can take our time with the answer. But, Robert Roe, do you remember how many times you had dinner at my daddy's house before you asked for my hand?"

Daddy rose to his feet. "As long as I am not being rushed . . ." He held a congratulatory hand out to Adam and nodded to me as he excused himself to go inside. A second later, we heard the bathroom door shut. He hadn't agreed, but he was letting us have our way.

Momma sighed. "Mark my word, he'll soon be saying it was all his idea. Welcome to the family, son." She beamed up at Adam.

Adam and I grinned at each other. We were home free.

∽

THAT NIGHT ADAM SNUCK BACK OUT to the farm from Joe's and woke me in the middle of the night. We went outside and made love near the apple tree. He lay under me on the very spot where I had found him, the smooth undersides of his open arms pale against the dark, red clay. A cloud passed over, dimming the moonlight for a moment, and I had a sudden fear that he might go back into the mud he had come from, that he could vanish, dissolving beneath me as I pressed onto him. But he did not. He pulled me down to his perfect mouth and remained as he was, a man.

Everyone seemed surprised at the speed of our engagement, but not the engagement itself. After everybody knew about it, Momma and Daddy paid less attention to Adam's comings and goings on the farm.

We went at each other like drunken rabbits. Everywhere, anytime we could, working late into the night to make up for chores we had missed during the day. I was as crazy in love with him in his new body as I had been before. Everything I had done with Addie could now spill over into the world. In the fields, in the barn, in the daylight, in every room of the house. What I did with Adam had a name and required simple privacy, not secrecy. I put my fears about children behind me, but they followed me, mobile and unobtrusive as shadows.

༄

ON THE MONDAY AFTER OUR ENGAGEMENT had been announced, we were making love when Adam surprised me with a question. "I don't want to pull out. Do you want me? Do you want this?"

I could not look away from that bright gaze. His whole body was so warm, almost hot. The last of my resistance uncoiled. "Yes," I said.

What rose from him was not his normal sound of pleasure. Stronger, his cry swept past sweetness into a joy intense and sharp as sorrow or rage. It rose and passed not through, but into. *Into* me.

That was it. When my monthly time should have come, four weeks before the wedding, I knew. He was right about his fertility. We'd gotten on the train there is no getting off. Too late for more questions. Only time would bring the answers.

We had stepped into the public whirlpool of events that comes with a wedding and having a child.

I was in a state of bliss. Sweet, wide-open joy.

༄

WOMEN USUALLY TALKED ABOUT sex back then only as something to put up with. The physical details were left unstated. If a girl was lucky, her mother might give her a frank private talk about the specifics of what parts were going to go where the night before she married. But most mothers skirted the issue, assuming the barnyard to be education enough. There were no women's magazines in the grocery store checkout aisle, proclaiming the joys of multiple orgasms. No books or charts for us.

With A., I never needed a chart or a manual. The act itself could vary so. Some nights I felt myself unfurl. Other nights our lovemaking tightened down as if to single points of skin and nerve. At times, all the energy came from me, other times it came at me, A. all heat and need in my arms. Our simple, closed-mouthed good-night kiss might erupt into passion, leaving us exhausted and wet. There were nights of skin, surfaces rubbing and rolling into each other. Or we were just our mouths, drinking each other in. Frenzied nights when I wanted to devour him. Nights when our lovemaking was a single breath on an ordinary day: short, barely noticeable, and completely necessary. Complex or simple and common as pounding rain, the texture of it could be anywhere. Tender, sweet, hard, predatory, silly, muddy, clear, cathartic— whatever a face or a glance or a word could be the whole act could be—in a single night. Adam was like Addie in one other way: the same exquisite sound burst from him when he climaxed and then immediately afterward, a beautiful, contagious belly laugh.

Usually, we went straight from climax into the state that precedes dreams, when thoughts are unmoored and drift heedlessly on their own. Other times, it was as if we had been revived and we'd have to read to calm ourselves before we could sleep. There were times when gratitude, awe, or tenderness would take me so that afterward, when we lay beside each other, I would reach for him again. Later, I would bring one of the children back into the bed with us, and we would sleep all a tangle of arms and legs, of sweet, young breath and thicker, older breath. And each of our daughters at one point as infants interrupted our lovemaking with her cries and I brought her to our bed, where she suckled and slept again while I lay on my side, Adam, spooned behind me, entered me again, and we continued gently, slowly, bodily bridging the child and the act that made the child. We called it "rocking the baby."

I have often thought of what my old grandfather said about the beauty of sex. I think not just of what he said, but why he needed to say it. The act is a vessel that can hold a continuum of human intentions—a sweet, holy song of flesh and love, the simple, mindless rut of youth, or the darkest violation. It encompasses what we bring to it. Too often people fill it with shame.

The association of shame with sex was alien to A. Sex with him seemed a thing unto itself, neither wholly *of* nor *from* either of us, but some perfect distillation of the two of us. Making love to him felt like a form of worship. Not a worship of him or of me, but Life worshiping Itself through our bodies. Life praying to Itself and to all that is not Life, asking for more Life and thanking Itself. The holy stuff of life springing through us as it springs through every living thing.

It lasted decades with A. I never got over it.

Never.

❧

THE WEDDING WAS NOT GOING TO BE very fancy. Momma would make my wedding dress. We went together to pick out the cloth. She led me toward the whites at the back of Ina's shop, but I wasn't sure. I showed her a pale blue. She rubbed it between her fingers and said, "So, you, of all brides, should not wear white?".

"Someone might step on this." I bent over and picked a straight pin up off the wood floor.

"Only one reason I can think of for a girl not to wear white at her wedding," she continued. I walked away to consider a bolt of rosy-pink satin.

Momma brought over a bolt of white she favored and plopped it down on top of the cloth I looked at. She lowered her voice. "Evelyn Roe, if every woman who had been with her man before she married him wore a colored wedding dress, white wedding dresses would be as rare as a milk bag on a bull. If I wore white, you can, too."

"Momma? You . . . ?"

She nodded.

"But I always thought you were . . . I . . ." I couldn't have been more surprised.

"Everybody thinks that of their momma. And everyone is human, even mothers. No need to proclaim in public what's done in private. You pick the white you want. I'll do the stitching."

"It won't be so private soon, Momma," I whispered.

She glanced up quickly, the shock and disappointment I had expected in her eyes. Then she searched my face, wide-eyed, as she had the day I wandered away when I was a little girl, but she did not seem to see me. Suddenly, her whole face broke into a smile and she said, "Well, I'll be goddamned." She never cursed, but she said it again. For a second, her mouth hung open in shock, then her eyes brightened.

She looked around the store. I thought she was checking to see if anyone had heard her curse, but she seemed to be seeing something else. She pushed out a sigh. "Evelyn, I don't think I can make it home without a cold, sweet drink."

I giggled with puzzled relief as we walked down the street to the soda fountain.

We each had a float—an unusual extravagance for my mother. She sat opposite me in the booth, sipping from a straw like a girl while I tried to imagine her so in love with my daddy that she, like me, could not wait. High school girls tittered and whispered behind me in the next booth.

"Are you happy, Evelyn?" Her voice was low and serious.

"Yes, Momma. He makes me very happy."

"And you're sure about this. All of it?" She waved her hand at my waist. "This is what you wanted?"

I could only nod and blink my tears away.

"Well, that's all I need to know." She patted my hand.

I had stepped over into motherhood. I had joined the club.

We bought the white cloth, a cotton eyelet. For that afternoon it did not matter that there were other things I could not tell my mother. At last, there was one important thing I could tell her. Standing in line at the cash register, waiting for Ina to ring us up, we were like all the other women, ready to make out of patterns and whole cloth something new.

Days later, I stood on a footstool in Momma's bedroom, turning slowly while she pinned the hem of my dress. Rita and Bertie joined us. My life had suddenly become interesting to them. They both had a crush on Adam, particularly Rita. Bertie would finish high school soon and had a beau who, though steady, did not seem like the marrying kind. My dress was too simple to truly sustain their interest, but they seemed reluctant to leave, as if afraid they might miss some secret bridal ritual. They began a primping marathon, brushing and grooming each other, considering their profiles and the fashion magazines they had bought for me.

Rita and Bertie wanted me to wear my hair in a style they had seen in a movie and were determined to demonstrate. Rita sat on the low bench of Momma's dressing table while Bertie fumed at her fine, light hair. She winced each time Bertie swept her hair up. The more Rita whined, the harder Bertie brushed and pinned. I'd seen their tiffs countless times and knew the progress of them as if they were scripted.

I'd never been as close to them as they were to each other, but suddenly I realized that I never would be. My inner life had spun away from their world. I looked down at the top of Momma's head. The three of them thought they knew what this marriage was to me, but they did not. They thought they knew Adam, but they did not.

"Hold your head still," Bertie admonished.

Rita pressed her lips together, tears of frustration in her eyes.

I gazed at my flushed face in the mirror. Momma knelt before me, pulling the hem of my dress even on both sides and sliding the last straight pin through the cloth. I caught Rita's reflection and tried to smile my encouragement, but she saw the tears in my eyes and took them as confirmation of the outrage she suffered at Bertie's hands. Her face crumpled. Crying, she shoved Bertie away and dashed out of the room.

Momma glanced up at my face.

I blinked and tried not to cry.

Momma glared at Bertie. "You, too. Out and take those magazines with you. Apologize to your sister."

"What'd I do?" Bertie sulked.

Momma shut the door behind her, then turned to me and smoothed my dress sleeves down over my arms. She handed me a handkerchief. "Evelyn, this is a big step, a big change. It's normal to be a little rocky. But Adam has a good heart. I think you're doing the right thing."

In a gush of gratitude, I tried to laugh, but managed only a strangled snicker.

"Are you feeling bad in your stomach? You might try some soda crackers if you are."

I wanted to tell her so badly, but how could I explain that I was afraid to have the babies of such an obviously robust and normal man? The truth seemed like a heavy weight then, and the lies were a gulf between Momma and me. Instead, I blew my nose, wiped my eyes, and took the dress off.

"Evelyn, it's just the baby coming making you feel this way. Everything'll be fine." I laid my head on her shoulder and cried.

❧

EVEN BEFORE WE WERE ACTUALLY MARRIED, the benefits of marriage were evident: gifts and help. Once we announced we were getting married and were going to live on the farm, everybody—particularly the men—began to take the farm seriously as a place to live.

First, Daddy had to be convinced that Adam really wanted to live on the farm. Daddy saw the mill as security, a place where a man could work his way up and get a good retirement, a life less dependent on local rainfall.

Adam pointed out that if Addie and I had been able to run the farm, surely he and I could do better. "Robert," I overheard him say one day when they were out on the porch, "I promise you, if your daughter is ever close to going without anything, I'll be down at the mill the next day looking for a steady income. I expect most of our money to come from the horses. Addie made some money with them, and I'll do the same. Better, I hope. Evelyn and our children will not do without."

"I'm glad to hear that, son. That's good to know. You'll have a family to support."

They went straight into a discussion of how the farmhouse should be wired for electricity. An ice-box and indoor plumbing were also in the plans. Suddenly, everyone thought it was a pity that I had to go outside to relieve myself, that I washed my clothes in a tub, or lit a lantern at night. Before Adam, it seemed to everyone that we had just been two girls keeping house, waiting for a man to come along. If we had known he'd come with an ice-box and a washing machine, I'm sure we would have found one sooner.

❧

THE WEDDING WAS SIMPLE: the preacher at Momma's house, the new white dress for me, and a borrowed suit for Adam. Then, after the ceremony, plenty of food set up on sawhorses and boards in Momma's front yard under the oak tree. Mostly family and a few friends. Cole came with Eloise, now officially his fiancée. Freddie, Marge, and the Sunday-evening picking folks provided the music. Even my strange, aloof cousin Frank contributed by photographing the wedding. Everyone got fed, the men drank, and some of us danced.

Our honeymoon was as simple as our wedding. We got married on Saturday, left right after the wedding, and drove to my cousin Pauline's place in Florida. Momma took a rare day off on Monday to take care of the chores and Joe took Tuesday.

Pauline had moved to Florida only months before and rented a cottage on Lake Swan, a large, spring-fed pond. The cottage was tiny, only two rooms and a porch.

When we arrived, Pauline announced that she would not interfere with our wedded bliss. She winked and was gone, off to stay with a friend. We were out in the middle of nowhere, miles from Gainesville where she worked. The lake, shallow with a pale, sandy bottom, was clear as drinking water.

We made love that night in the water under a gibbous moon, quietly, with as little motion as possible. "I think I can feel the baby in you. Our tadpole daughter." He pulled me under as he climaxed, his sweet voice suddenly muffled and shimmering the water above us in the bright distortion of moon. We tumbled through the water, my hair floating around us, his face inches from mine, laughing bubbles.

Later, I stood shoulder-deep in the crystal water as he floated beside me, pale belly, rope of penis, long legs, and, below him, his shadow like an angel on the sand as he waved his arms. I put my hand on my belly, which was still flat, and asked myself the question every expectant mother asks: "Who is this child?" Then there was the other question that I dared not ask out loud: "*What* is this child?"

FIVE

ORDINARY LIFE

Being pregnant bonded me to Adam, as it can bond any woman to the father of her child. I wanted to give him a child. I wanted to have a part of him inside me in every sense. But my pregnancy also put us firmly on opposite sides of an experience. Addie and I had been the same. While I could commiserate with Joe's wife, Mary, and with any other woman who had had a baby, for the first time what was happening to me could not be shared with A. in the same way

That Adam could exist the way he did was, for him, as it is for all of us, the first given, the absolute. He took his own existence for granted. But the impossibility of his existence, the guilt and isolation I felt in choosing him over my own kind and bearing his children, these were things I wanted to share with him but did not. What good could come from telling him I had these conflicts?

But in my sleep, I gave myself away.

During the fourth month of my pregnancy, the nightmares began. In each dream, I was with the baby in public. Happily, I showed off my new child and everyone admired her. But then I looked down and I saw that she was shapeless and faceless. In some dreams, I tried to hide her face from everyone and get away. Other nights, her shapelessness seemed to be my own craziness and no one else saw it. I tried to keep the night-mares to myself. But I would wake from them with Adam holding me, rocking and humming.

Once when Momma and I were alone in her kitchen, cleaning up after Sunday supper, I asked, "Did you have bad dreams when you were pregnant?"

"Most women do. Don't let it worry you."

"But these are real bad—really bad. They wake me up." Then I told her one of the dreams.

"Everybody's scared when a baby's coming, Evelyn. That's normal. But all you can do is take it easy and let Nature do the rest."

Suddenly, her ignorance irritated me. I shook my head. "You can't understand. You can't!"

I saw the hurt in her face as she paused before starting to speak. I held up my hand to interrupt her, but my own words backed up in my throat. Nothing came out of my open mouth. The puzzled expression on her face as I left the room reminded me of the faces in my dreams.

The week after I told Momma my bad dreams, she insisted on taking me to Dr. Hanks, who delivered most of the babies in Clarion then. I knew she was trying to reassure me, but it didn't help. He talked about what I should eat, what work I should do. Everybody assumed that I'd be having the baby at the hospital, of course. Only backwoods or desperately poor women still had their babies at home. To have sought any alternative then would have been seen as a kind of insanity. But in a hospital, I would be asleep and alone when the baby came out, as helpless as I was in my dreams. I didn't want others to be the first to see her. I was afraid of what they might do if she looked like her daddy had when I first saw him.

By the time I neared my seventh month, I was irrational with worry. Women then referred to the deep anesthesia of hospital labor as the "twi-light sleep." The phrase seemed ominous to me and I became convinced they would kill my baby or spirit her away before I woke, then tell me she had been born dead in order to spare me having to see her or raise a deformed child.

I woke in a sweat one night with Adam holding me. "Tell me about it," he whispered. And, finally, I told him about the dreams and my fears.

"I'm sorry," he said. "I'm so sorry."

"I chose. I chose to do this."

Then I realized he might not remember much of those first few days. I turned on the light and got out the picture that Frank had left, the one of the Japanese girl burned in the bombing. I had put it away, deep in the small drawers of the wardrobe.

"Do you remember this?" I asked. "Do you remember your skin being a different color and looking like this?" I traced my finger along the burnt shoulder of the woman.

Adam moaned, low and awful. "I remember this picture. I know I was different from you, but I don't remember being like this. I never saw myself. I only saw you. Even when I looked in a mirror, I saw you." He drew me to him and pressed his face against my big belly.

After a while, he got up and pulled the covers up tight around me. "Go back to sleep. No more nightmares. Let me think about this." Despite the chilly night, he went outside and sat in one of the front-porch rockers. I listened to its rhythmic squeaking as I fell back asleep.

Hours later, I woke to the sound of the truck pulling away. I leapt up out of bed. My first thought was that he had left me because I was so afraid of having his baby. But the bedroom remained undisturbed. He hadn't taken any clothes. The photograph still lay on the bed where we had left it. I found a note on the kitchen table: "I'll be back in an hour, two at the most.—Love, Adam." The morning's milk sat in the ice-box. Outside, the chickens were happy, scratching in the coop.

Soon, he returned with a solution. I wouldn't need to go to the hospital, he told me. A week later, we went to Pearl's barbeque shack. He waited outside while Pearl took me into the back room to meet the midwife Adam had arranged the morning he went off alone. "This is Granny Paynes," Pearl introduced us. "P-a-y-n-e-s," she spelled it out after a quick glimpse at me, then left the two of us alone.

Granny Paynes was a thin, very old black woman, but she rose quickly and stood erect. She shooed two little boys out into the backyard and turned on a bare-bulb light that hung in the middle of the room. She sat down on the only chair, next to a gigantic old wood stove. She observed me a moment, expressionless. The room smelled of sweat, hickory, and sorghum syrup. The warmth and sweetness made me drowsy.

"Take off your coat and come over here." She motioned and spat tobacco juice into a cup, then sat the cup back down next to the stove. Her deep voice sounded much younger than she appeared. "Stand up straight and lift up your shirt," she said.

I complied.

"Now"—she looked up at me as her strong hands worked around my belly—"why you want a colored granny woman to help get your baby into this world instead of going to the hospital in Charlotte like all the other white women?"

I'd never had a colored person touch me that intimately, but her hands felt strong, sure, and, like her voice, young. "I'm scared of hospitals," I told her. She had turned her head sideways, as if listening to my belly, as she studied my face. Her brown irises had a faint ring of pale blue around them.

"I'm scared of not waking up when they put me out. I don't like hospitals," I added.

"I hear you on that one." She nodded. "It ain't natural for a thing like that to happen and a body feel nothing a'tall. Your people know you here? Would your momma want you here?"

"No, ma'am. Nobody knows about this but my husband." I stared straight ahead at the wall of the shed. Her hands were low on my belly, pressing up.

She stopped then, pulled my shirt down over my skirt, and straightened herself to eye level. One quick glance down at my wedding band. "I do not get rid of babies for people. Have you got yourself into trouble with a colored man?"

"No, oh, no," I stammered. "I'm just scared, that's all. I'm so scared. And they would make me go to the hospital. I know they would." She studied my face again. She must have heard the truth of the fear in my voice. She patted my arm.

"Well." She took a snuff tin out of her dress pocket and put a pinch in her cheek. "I have only brought along a few white babies—only when necessity made it so."

"I've heard of you, Granny Paynes. Pearl tells us you . . ."

She raised a hand to shush me. "They was poor white women. You don't look rich exactly, but your people could afford to take you to a white doctor, I know. My Rankin has done some work on your farm, years ago before you was living up there. I'll come to you when your time has come, but, like I told your man, I want twice my normal birthing fee. If anything happens to you or your baby, your people will be after me. You understand?"

"I do, I do," I told her. I had not considered what a risk she might be taking. "Thank you, Granny Paynes, thank you."

She inspected me again, her eyes scanning me head to toe, and then smiled so broadly her whole face erupted into fine lines. "By my reckoning you have yourself a Christmas baby, most likely a daughter. Between now and then you eat as well as your purse and land will allow. Take a sip of wine or beer—nothing harder—after supper if you can't sleep and stewed prunes if you can't relieve yourself. After December first, don't eat garlic, chocolate, or tomatoes. And no tobacca. They go into your womb. They'll spoil your milk and make your baby fussy. The baby needs your milk."

She walked me toward a side door of the shed. "Now, if you pass blood without any pain, you let me know. When your child is coming, the pain will be like your monthly, only stronger. Your man should come for me when you cannot finish singing through all the verses of 'Amazing Grace' twice between the pains."

I laughed. "'Amazing Grace'?"

She smiled again. "You do that, child. And you come see me one more time beforehand—come the Saturday after Thanksgiving. This is your first, right? Maybe three times through all the verses then. Then Granny Paynes will be happy to come help your baby get here." She held on to my arm as if she needed help walking, but I could feel her fingers working through my coat sleeve as if she was checking my strength as she returned me to my husband.

Outside again, Granny Paynes and I squinted at the brilliant morning sun. Adam waited, a slab of wrapped ribs in his hands. He had that tentativeness men have around birth, and his eyebrows shot up in a question. For the first time, he seemed wholly a man. A pang of grief for Addie surged through me. Granny Paynes winked at him and handed me off like a bride.

I felt how young we were, how new the world was in that cool autumn light. I rode home in the truck with the warm ribs on my lap, one hand on Adam's leg and the other on my belly.

❧

PREGNANCY CHANGED THINGS between us. Adam became my protector. Not that I was in any danger. But I felt my primal vulnerability. My belly stuck out between me and the world. Any danger coming at me would come through our child. I was an animal then, more than at any other time in my life.

Adam probably felt more like my servant than my protector. In the last month, he took over most of the milking and all of the heavy work while keeping the horses, too. Protector or servant, things were very different from how Addie and I had been. Like so much with A., the new arrangement felt both strange and natural.

He was not squeamish or disgusted as some men are by periods, pregnancy, birthing, or breast-feeding. Of course, for a man, he possessed a unique perspective in these matters. His passion became gentler, sweeter. At night in bed, he knelt before my belly, stroking it, singing to the child until the vibrato of his unique voice made me ache with tenderness. At the sound of his voice, the baby turned inside me, wriggling.

Momma had told me not to let Adam make love to me in the last month. She said it was not good for the baby. But we did. I did not feel very erotic, but I craved the sound and odors of him, his hands on me, and his body surrounding me. When my own pleasure increased, my womb tightened and that satisfied the way a good scratch does an itch. I thought the contraction of sexual climaxes would make my womb stronger.

I spent the last weeks at home, not even wanting to go to Momma's. In the evenings, I walked through the house, touching everything and thinking of how my baby would soon be in those rooms seeing the same things I saw. We packed away everything in the parlor—everything but the photographs. I put up new curtains, too. The jars of food Momma and I had canned the previous summer overflowed the basement shelves. The new electric refrigerator hummed in the dining room. Over and over, I sang "Amazing Grace," as if it would charm our child into the world.

I was ready, past ripe.

The heaviness and the waiting did not sit well with me. On some of the last nights, I tossed and turned around my big belly. In my misery, I kicked Adam out of the bed. He tried to comfort or distract me, singing or reading, sometimes bringing up his beautiful harmonics. But even that worked only for a few hours—until the next time I woke up to pee. I sometimes used a chamber pot again, even though we had indoor plumbing. The bathroom seemed so cold and so far down the hall in the middle of the night.

On the morning of December 22, I woke with a start in the darkness. Adam took a sharp breath behind me, his arm around me, his hand cupping my belly. "This contraction woke you up." My womb clenched hard as a rock and painful down through my legs.

"Yes. It hurts."

Softly, he sang "Amazing Grace," all verses once, then went through them a second time. Silence followed and no more pain. We listened, the two of us in the dark. Another five minutes passed before the next contraction.

All day long, painful, but erratic—twenty, maybe ten, sometimes five minutes apart—the contractions came. I boiled towels, sheets, and a single white shoelace as Granny Paynes had instructed, grateful for the automatic washer and wringer. Before dinner, Adam drove into town to warn her that my time approached. Otherwise, he stayed close by. We went through our normal routines. I ate well. Then, about nine o'clock, the pains came on hard and always right at the end of the second round of the song.

Suddenly, I was afraid to be alone. I didn't want Adam to leave to fetch Granny Paynes. He dragged in Hobo, who seemed puzzled but stood patiently by the bed, his snout on the pillow next to me. I moaned my way through contractions, clutched handfuls of his hide, and curled up fetal around my own womb.

With each contraction, everything broke into a grainy blueness, then returned to its natural color and density when the pain released me. Then Adam was back with Granny Paynes and Hobo was gone.

Granny Paynes and Adam coaxed me out of bed. "Walk the baby out. You keep moving and it'll come out easier. Walk it out. Sing it out," she urged.

Into the kitchen, then into the parlor and back to the bedroom over and over we walked, with her and Adam singing "Amazing Grace." His strong, soft baritone on one side and her rich, old alto on the other. "Sing through the pain, li'l momma. Sing."

I tried, but my voice evaporated into a tuneless hiss. I wanted to tell them to shut up, but words were too much. Movement and even breath seemed too much. Pain obliterated everything.

At last, they led me back to the bedroom. Granny Paynes smoothed a clean oilcloth and a layer of towels across the bed. They helped me lie down. The pain grew until it overcame everything. The visual world narrowed to a single crack and everything else disappeared into the pain. I began to disappear, too. There was only pain.

Then, it felt like the hand of God reached inside me and pulled down. Abruptly, the pain changed direction. I was pushing. The pain gathered in the diffuse, overwhelming blueness and shot down to one sharp, blind-white spot between my legs. I screamed high and scared, grabbed Adam by his shirt, and pulled his face up to mine until there was nothing but his brown eyes. I thought I was dying.

Granny Paynes pushed herself between us and took my face in her hands, forcing me to look at her. "Stop that screaming up in your nose. You are working now. Grunt. Low, low down in your throat." She growled at me and patted my collarbone.

I growled back, low. The next wave of pain began, but I rode it, pushed behind it, not at its mercy, not drowning anymore. Again and again. I pushed and growled and grunted and pushed and growled. Granny Paynes knelt on the bed down between my legs. I felt her rubbing me, massaging my perineum between the pains. Then she held up three fingers. "Three more times," she said. "Maybe two."

I took "two" as a challenge and began pushing before the next contraction. After the second one, both she and Adam hunched between my legs, staring. I pushed again. I felt the slither of shoulders, hips, and feet. Then the first newborn bleat.

Silence followed. Everything stopped. Adam and Granny Paynes peered down at the baby. I closed my eyes and saw a featureless face in the mud.

When I opened my eyes, Adam smiled at me. Tears ran down his face and he nodded. All I could see of the baby was the top of her wrinkled head and her waving arms as Granny Paynes held her between my legs. The skin on her scalp appeared strange.

"Tell me," I said.

"The Lord have mercy." Each word out of Granny Paynes's mouth rang separate.

Suddenly, I felt very cold and dizzy. I held my voice as steady as I could. "Boy or girl?" I pulled myself up against the headboard to see. Adam looked to her and she shook her head.

Granny Paynes cut and tied the cord. They quickly dried the baby, wrapped her, and slipped a knit cap over her head. Adam brought her up to me. He gazed at our child enraptured. Everything still seemed fuzzy in the dim light, but I could see that the baby's facial features were oddly flat. Still, all the parts were there—ears, nose, mouth, and, when she opened them, clear blue eyes. I counted fingers. Ten. I began singing "Amazing Grace," but my voice cracked out from under me.

I lifted the blanket and tried, through the fog of exhaustion, to focus. "A girl?" I blinked. She looked like a girl, but in the shadowed lamplight, there seemed to be too much there between her legs.

"More girl than boy, I'd say," Granny Paynes agreed. "We need to keep her wrapped against the cold." She pressed on my belly for the afterbirth. "This is not a birthing problem. Nothing could have been done. You gonna have to let a doctor look at her. Maybe they can do something."

"She's beautiful. Our Grace." The certainty and resonance in Adam's voice calmed me.

My fear subsided as I surrendered to my fatigue. My child was whole and well. I touched his jaw, but he did not take his eyes off our baby. A strong final contraction hit me. The dense, thick odor of blood filled the room.

"A big, healthy afterbirth and all there." Granny Paynes dropped it into a basin and turned her attention to the baby. She laid the baby on the bed beside me, unwrapped the blankets, and took a long look. "I have to tell you, I ain't never seen nothing like this," she said.

She lifted Grace up by her little fists, then turned her and looked at her back, her neck, and skull. Grace's arms shot out when Granny Paynes laid her back down and she began a full-throated wail, her face flushing dark pink. Granny Paynes worked the baby's arms and legs, looked in her mouth, and then announced, over Grace's diminishing cries, "She might not be quite right when it comes to learning—only time will tell you that. But everything else seems to be working fine. Specially her lungs. She's not at all early and she's strong. Born so close to Christ's day, she'll be a good one."

She diapered and swaddled Grace then pressed her against my breast. "We need to see how she sucks," she said.

Grace latched on immediately. A visceral, sharp tenderness radiated up my body into my breasts. The three of us watched as she sucked and grunted, her fists working under her chin. I was happy. She looked better than I had feared, but I wanted to see more. I motioned for Adam to turn on the overhead light.

I fought an impulse to flinch and cover my eyes as the harsh yellow light flooded the room. Her slightly jaundiced skin did not have the rough swirled texture of her father's when I first pulled him from the clay. Rather she resembled Addie on the second or third day. Every surface of her was oddly dimpled, like fat under the skin on a woman's thighs. Her neck, face, shoulders. Individually, her features were normal. Tiny reddish brows, puffy newborn eyelids and lips. Bridgeless button nose. Toothless, shallow jaw. But the total effect was off. Was that my imagination? I held her close. Everything was there!

"She'll be okay, Granny Paynes. I know she will," I mumbled. Then, to Adam, "And, yes, she is beautiful."

To him, she may have been pretty. The texture of her skin might have been deeply familiar to him. He now had someone who was truly his own flesh and blood, however much his flesh might now resemble another man's.

For what seemed like hours, Granny Paynes cleaned me and the bed up—though there was far less mess than I had expected. She sent Adam into the kitchen to make a tea from some herbs she pulled out of her bag.

"It's got catnip and some other good stuff in it. Good for your blood and the baby's." She spooned warm drops of it onto Gracie's lips.

She announced that she would be at my side until I could relieve myself. The four of us sat in silence, one new life among us and the odor of blood iron in the air. Granny Paynes eyed us as we gazed at the baby. She must have been surprised at our peculiar relief at having had such an ugly, sexually ambiguous child.

After she sent Adam out of the room and helped me with the chamber pot, she gathered her things and gave me instructions. She made me promise that I would drink more of her tea, take the baby to a doctor as soon as I could, and not let my man at me for six weeks. Then she gave me some homemade salve for the baby's cord, lit a pipe of something foul-smelling, and walked out the door.

She and Adam talked softly in the kitchen. The tea tin where we kept the money since I'd broken the cookie jar clattered gently when Adam opened it to pay her. It was four in the morning on December 23, 1950. Almost four years since I'd found Addie.

"Merry Christmas! Jesus be with you," Granny Paynes called down the hall to me before she left with Adam.

The next thing I knew, winter sun blazed through the bedroom window. I studied the baby's sleeping face in the bright morning light. Already, she looked smoother. I remembered the shadowy, profuse genitals I'd seen earlier. I wanted to take her diaper off but the room was colder now, she was sleeping, and I wanted Adam with me when I looked. I ran my finger gently over her cheek, which felt smooth and soft as any baby's. She grunted and turned instinctively toward my finger, her mouth open. Her eyes opened a slit, then wider. She focused.

In that simple, clear moment of focus, I saw Addie's first glance.

I got out of bed stiffly and went looking for Adam, first thinking I would leave the baby asleep on the bed and then finding that the cord, though cut, remained strong. I turned, halfway down the hall, and shuffled back for her.

The clock chimed nine times. Everything had changed for me and Adam. Our child had arrived. I held my daughter up so she could get her first look at her home. I tried to imagine all that would occur in those rooms—the parlor, the kitchen, the hall. She would do and say and think things in those rooms that I could not imagine. She was the first daughter of Adam, who was not a man.

At the back door, I called Adam out of the barn. Our baby stared up blinking, undisturbed by the cold or my shouts to her father.

Adam came and stood on the step below me and I handed him his daughter. They were beautiful.

"Let's do name her Grace," he said. For weeks we had tossed names around. Grace had been his favorite.

"Let's take a close look at how things are going first. Make sure that we don't have a Gary," I said. Adam took her inside and I followed, waddling down the hall, anxiety rising in my chest.

He laid her on the bed and unwrapped her, ceremoniously letting the diaper fall away. She kicked her spread legs and muttered at the cool air. We peered. Definitely a vulva, protruding and very ornate, swollen, open. At its peak, a mushroom nub of pink, covered in foreskin, too large to be a clitoris. Bulging skin, unmistakably scrotal, framed the outer labia. She was both.

I sunk down onto the bed.

"Give her time. Hold her close to you. She's our daughter, I'm sure." Adam took my arm to help me sit. "She's perfect." He beamed at me. Then he pulled his waistband out and looked down at himself. He lifted my nightgown and made a show of examining me. "Yep, I'm pretty sure we don't have a doolywhacker here. She's Grace. Our Gracie."

I laughed and swatted his hand away, pretending that I shared his confidence.

We re-pinned Gracie's diaper, then lay down, one of us on each side of her. After a moment, Adam pressed our daughter against me as he slipped out of the bed. "I think she needs to be next to you now. That will help her be more girl. It worked with you and me, with Roy and me."

I held my ambiguous daughter closer and, despite my anxiety about what I had just seen, I slept. I dreamed that I woke and found them both looking at me, one set of brown eyes, one of blue eyes regarding me with equal knowledge and wisdom.

I woke again with Adam offering me a cup of Granny Paynes's tea. Gracie's face seemed better. Her features were knitting themselves, her face seemed less flat, her skin smoother. Good enough to be just an ordinary ugly baby, I thought. I hoped the same was happening between her legs.

"Go get Momma. It's time she knows Santa has arrived," I told Adam. "Just Momma," I thought to add before he got out the door. "Tell them just Momma tonight. We'll all be down for Christmas."

It felt wonderful to be moving, to have a much smaller belly, and be light on my feet again, but I moved slowly to keep from getting dizzy. I sat at the kitchen table, holding the baby and sipping a cup of Granny Paynes's tea when Adam and Momma arrived. I handed my mother her new grandchild. "Grace Adele Hope," I announced.

"Oh, my Lord," she said, clutching at our arms. "You delivered her yourself, Adam?" she kept asking as if she could not believe a man could do such a thing. She fussed and went on about the fast birth and how good I looked and how pretty the baby would be as soon as she got a little older and "lost the newborn look," as she kindly put it. I don't know what shocked her most, Adam delivering Gracie or how Gracie looked, but she, uncharacteristically, did not seem to know what to do with herself.

Finally, she settled on making us a meal and starting on laundry. Soon the house filled with the smell of her corn bread and chicken soup. I napped again, curled up with my new baby in a warm bed, lulled by the voices of my mother and husband talking in the kitchen. There could not have been a better way to have a baby.

Christmas Day, Momma urged me to stay in bed and rest. Everyone could come see me, she insisted. But I didn't want to miss Christmas dinner. I was tired, but not nearly as tired as I thought I would be. Finally, I convinced Momma that it would be easier on us and the baby if we did the visiting and came to Christmas dinner rather than everyone coming to see us.

By the time she met the rest of my family, Gracie looked normal. Only from certain angles did her skin have an unusual texture. Her genitals were more normal, less swollen. What had looked like a small penis had receded. The scrotal creases on the sides of her vulva had relaxed into a normal smoothness. She had a steady gaze, as intelligent as her father's. Her fine down of hair glowed a faint copper in sunlight. We, of course, thought she was gorgeous. Still, I was gratified when Momma held her again and exclaimed, "Oh, her color's better already. And she doesn't look so newborn!" Gracie stared up at her grandmother. A calm, but very alert baby, she closed her eyes only to nurse and sleep. She went through all of the bustle and noise of Christmas dinner with those blue eyes wide-open, never complaining.

Again and again, I told the story of how fast she had come—told it at the supper table and then to everyone who came by from around the mill-village to see the baby and exchange Christmas visits. I didn't like leaving Granny Paynes out of the story. She'd been good and patient with me. But I did, disloyal as it may have felt. It bothered me most to lie to Momma.

I did the majority of the talking. Adam basked quietly in the praise as he held the small bundle of Gracie upright against his chest.

"Why didn't you just pick her up and cart her off to the doctor?" Uncle Otis asked Adam. "That's what I'd've done. Just picked her up." Being a bachelor, Otis was both squeamish and inexplicably knowledgeable about such situations. "Just hauled her out that door," he added, "before she knew what was happening and got her to a doctor. A man shouldn't deliver his own children."

Adam leaned across the table toward Otis, but winked at me. "Otis, you and I both know nobody makes a McMurrough woman do something she does not want to do. Especially if she is hurting and feeling mean about it."

Daddy agreed. "Lily Mae was mean then, too. If she had taken a notion to, I'd have had to let her have her babies in the middle of the railroad tracks."

"I was not about to get in that old truck and go bumping down the road. It was too late for that," I cut in.

"Does it really hurt that bad?" Rita asked, looking worried and tearful. That year everything made her giggle or weep. Nothing was neutral. Bertie leaned down the table, eyeing me and Mary skeptically as she listened for my reply.

Momma patted Rita's hand and shot a look down the table at me and Mary to let us know we were not invited to share our pain. "Look around you. How bad can it be if everybody keeps having babies? And besides, Adam is right. We McMurrough women only do what we want to do."

"I've heard you forget about the pain real fast," Mary added and rolled her eyes at me.

Later, as we passed the first pie around, Uncle Grady's sister, Lou, dropped in from down the street. Cole arrived with Eloise, now his wife and herself a few months pregnant. Cole gave Adam a bear hug of congratulations and kissed my cheek. He and Eloise were a sweet, warm contrast to Frank, who appeared soon after them, edgy and brusque as usual, his camera ready. We all crowded around the table, eating our slices of pie from little saucers, smiling for Frank's snapshots.

Lou stood in the kitchen door, swaying back and forth with Gracie spread over her big bosom, ignoring the streak of spit-up on her blouse. "That's how my second and third ones got here, just popped out before I could hardly get out of the bed. Getting them out doesn't have to take much longer than it takes to get them started in there in the first place. I was lucky, I guess. Some have a lot of trouble on both ends of that one. But my last two boys turned out fine without a doctor."

Silence rippled across the room as we suppressed our laughter and tried not to think of both ends of that one.

Even Frank smiled, his normal brooding stare gone for a moment.

Momma waved a warning at Joe, who gazed intently at the crumbs on his plate, his lips pressed shut. Rita looked puzzled, opened her mouth, but never asked whatever question Lou's comments had brought to mind.

"Fine Christmas supper as usual, Lily. Fine pie," Daddy announced, pretending to laugh at the pleasure of mincemeat and pumpkin.

I loved them all. My child was normal and whole. We were a family among family. I was a lucky, lucky woman.

By the time Christmas visits were over, everyone had made their comments and told us their stories of babies being born. Depending on the point of view and the sex of the friend or relation, Adam was foolish and henpecked for not having made me go to a hospital for decent care. Or he was a hero, a man able and unafraid to do what needed to be done. The women in the family liked him better for calmly delivering his own child. That, and the way he cradled her so comfortably in his arms. He got almost as much attention as Gracie. I, on the other hand, became the butt of jokes about my exaggerated meanness and ability to intimidate. I felt sore and I tired quickly, but I would not have missed Christmas dinner in the mill-village for anything. I had just given birth to the world's most beautiful child. How could I have kept her at home?

Within two days, she appeared completely normal. Beautiful. Her skin as smooth as any baby's and her genitals, though still puffy, had taken on the normal cleft of a female.

∽

GRACIE WAS A GOOD BABY, calm and watchful, always moving but never frantic. To my relief, she walked and talked very early. When Adam came in from the stables or home from a job, she would roll back her head, stretch out her arms, and give a gleeful screech of welcome. He called her "my girl" so often that when she began to speak, she introduced herself as My-Girl-Gracie. We did not spoil her. She, in her good-natured and cooperative way, spoiled us.

From the time of Gracie's birth, we were an ordinary family. Like most ordinary families in the 1950s, we were making a living and making babies, not much else. I spent more time in the house and Adam spent more time in the stables. He had made a solid business of training, boarding, rehabilitating, and sweetening horses. We were down to one cow, but even then there was not room for all the horses. Building the new stable was our first major change at the farm, outside of plumbing and wiring for the house. Adam and I owned the farm free and clear by then. Momma had signed the deed over to us on our first wedding anniversary. The stable was our only debt.

Gracie was almost two years old when she had her first cold. Normally an easygoing child, she became demanding and whiny. I'd been up with her the night before and was happy to have Rita come help. Late in the morning, I found them both asleep on Gracie's narrow bed.

I went looking for Adam. Between family and carpenters working on the new stable and Gracie being sick, the only time Adam and I had alone was at night, when we were both exhausted. We had not made love for days.

For the first time that week, there were no cars or trucks in the driveway. All the workmen were gone. I found Adam in the clean, virgin stable, spreading sawdust and hay in the empty stalls. The odors of fresh wood filled the stable—no scent of sweat, manure, or leather yet. I came up quietly behind him, pulled his shirt out of his pants, and slipped my hands across his bare belly, then down to that flat, smooth spot I loved so much where his legs joined his hips. That was all it took—for either of us. Moments later, I conceived Rosie in the third stall on the left, on a bed of sweet, fresh hay.

We went through the same process, meeting with Granny Paynes at Pearl's for the preliminary examination. Adam waited outside, holding a slab of wrapped ribs with Gracie perched on his shoulders. He handed Gracie over to Granny Paynes. "See what you started?"

"Don't go blaming me for this here," she chuckled and held Gracie up to get a better look at her. "You sure this is the same baby? You didn't switch her for a pretty one?"

Adam ran his hand through Gracie's bright red curls. "Where would we have found another one like this?"

Gracie smiled and patted Granny Paynes on the cheek.

❧

LIKE GRACIE, Rosie was big, healthy, and delivered by Granny Paynes. An easy, fast delivery that Adam once again got credit for. She came into the world faster and with more bustle than her sister. Granny Paynes barely got there in time. Gracie woke midway through the delivery. Adam dashed out of the room to get her and returned with her in his arms. "She won't go back to sleep," he apologized. Solemn and sleepy, she witnessed her sister's birth. Rosie emerged with a full head of deep auburn hair and blinking, bright blue eyes.

As ugly and unformed as Gracie had been at birth, Rosie took her first good look at the world and began a scream that lasted for months. Granny Paynes looked at Rosie and then nodded toward Gracie, who had fallen asleep, again, in Adam's arms as soon as her sister began to wail. "This one's a girl, too, I reckon, and as ugly as her sister was, only she's mad about it."

Adam and I laughed.

She was a cute, normal-looking baby girl within a couple days of birth. Fair-skinned redhead, with blue eyes that shaded toward green after a few weeks.

But Rosie was also colicky. She woke every two hours and suckled as if there was a time limit and a long line of other babies waiting for my breast, then she screamed till sleep took her, then woke again to feed and restart the cycle. In the evenings, I passed her off to Adam. He adapted a blanket into a sling and, with Rosie secured to his chest, he rode Becky the old plow horse around the corral. She plodded slowly along, while he sang in his normal voice, below the lyrics, a low, steady hum. Gradually, Rosie's crying would stop. Her father's voice and the motion of the horse were more effective than me in a rocking chair. After Adam brought her in, she would sleep for hours. Soon she outgrew the sling.

When she woke in the night, he would bring her to me, then take her again when she had fed and we knew the screams would begin. Often I rose from sleep to find them in the parlor, him rocking her across his knee or high on his chest. But always he motioned me back to bed and held up whatever book he was reading to show me he had entertainment. There were many mornings when I woke to find him slumped in the rocking chair or sprawled across the couch, his book on the floor and his daughter bundled on his chest, the glow of her hair brighter in the light of his reading lamp.

Rosie's first word was "horse." As soon as she mastered walking, she learned to scoot one of the dining chairs up to the back door and pull herself up to stand on it. "Hoss, hoss!" she demanded, pointing toward the stable, one hand on her hip. For what seemed like years, this was our morning ritual. She ate her breakfast in tears and red-faced frustration, inconsolable.

One day, her cries for "hoss" lasted through breakfast and into the afternoon. After lunch, I thought I had finally gotten her down for a nap, and I went out to clean the back porch and steps. A set of small footprints in the remains of the morning's snowfall led down the steps, across the yard, and straight to the barn. Too small to be Gracie. Adam had stabled a new boarder horse, an aggressive sorrel, in the barn to separate him from the other horses in the stable. I ran to the barn. As I opened the door, the door on the other side opened, too. Adam led Darling in.

"You seen Rosie?" I asked.

Before he could answer, we spotted her.

She crouched on the top rail of the back stall, facing the sorrel, her arms spread gleefully above her head. Adam shoved Darling aside. He jerked the sorrel's stall open and slid in as Rosie whooped joyfully and leapt toward the horse.

The sorrel screamed.

Adam shouted as he threw himself between the horse and Rosie. Not his regular voice but a deep, percussive blast of alarm.

He caught Rosie midway between the horse's flank and the floor. The horse pivoted, blocking them into the corner of the stall.

Rosie wailed.

The horse erupted, neighing violently. Ears back, eyes rolling, he reared. Hooves smacked the stall wall. Adam clutched Rosie to his chest. He spun to keep his back to the horse.

In the adjoining stall, I pulled myself up to stand on the bottom slat so Adam could pass Rosie over the wall to me. I held my arms out to take her.

But Adam did not seem to see me. He pulled Rosie tighter and took a deep breath. His face changed from alarm to concentration.

A sweet, pure tone undulated through the barn. Then the timbre of his voice shifted through the warm tones into a firm command. Calm and powerful. Solid as flesh.

I clutched the rail to keep from falling. Inches from me, Rosie closed her eyes. Her grip on Adam's shirt relaxed.

Then silence. The quiet of alert, listening animals followed. One motionless second passed, then the cow muttered. Darling, still standing where Adam left her, whickered. The sorrel lowered his head. His tail swished gently.

Adam handed Rosie up and over to me. She burrowed her face into my shoulder, her weight soft in my arms.

"Shit, that was close," Adam whispered. He slouched, his head against the top rail as he reached over and touched my head, then Rosie's.

"You okay?" I asked. He looked up, nodded, and motioned for me to take Rosie in. Then he turned and spread his hands on the sorrel, who now regarded us complacently as he chewed.

Rosie took a long nap and was quieter than usual for the rest of the day.

After that, she shifted from demanding a ride to asking for permission to ride, and though she was still several days from her third birthday, Adam began brief, well-supervised lessons to teach her riding, grooming, and better barn etiquette. I thought she was too young, but Adam insisted, "If we can't keep her away from the horses, then we need to make sure she knows how to be around them."

A ride became part of her bedtime ritual. While Gracie bathed, Adam and Rosie rode double. Becky, the mildest of our horses, walked a slow, stately pace. Around and around the corral they went, Rosie leaning back against Adam's chest, her face solemn and attentive.

The time with Rosie and the sorrel was the first time I heard that sudden percussion and command in Adam's voice. Except for our pleasure in bed, I'd seldom heard his unique voice. Sometimes, usually during a rare, unexpected moment of quiet at the table or when we tucked the girls in for the night, I felt rather than heard a low hum in the room, warm, content, and seemingly without source, like the vibrations of a motor running in another part of the house. Occasionally, at Marge and Freddie's, Momma's, or the church, I sensed a subtle shift in the room. I would look at him for confirmation, and he would simply smile back.

Whatever charms Adam had with animals, he had with people, too. Carolina blue-collar folk and farmers in the 1950s and '60s were not a people inclined to physical contact. But, as it had been with Addie, people liked to touch Adam. Children crawled into his lap.

With women, he had the advantage of an unnatural understanding. They turned toward him when he walked near. Old women smoothed his collar or plucked lint off him as if he were their son. At church suppers, women pressed their fried chicken and beans on him, gratified by his appreciation and the gusto with which he ate. He sucked the juices off the rib bones. He had delivered his own daughters and would go elbow-deep into a mare to deliver a foal, all without flinching. Nothing of the body made him turn away. Not every woman knew all of this about him, but they could all read the musk of it on him.

Most men liked him as much as the women did, slapping him on the back or shaking his hand when they met him. Younger men sparred with him, punching and jabbing in mock fights. A few of the younger husbands seemed uncomfortable near him, stiffening in resolve when he was near, but that ceased as they got to know him.

I still expected someone to sense how truly different he was, to step forward and point a finger. But no one ever seemed to suspect anything. In the crush of our family and daily life, weeks could pass without me thinking of the difference. Except at night in bed. Always then his voice filled me, reminding me of what set him apart. As I listened to the last vibration of it vanish, I did not know him as an ordinary man.

I listened to our daughters, too. At times of contentment, they made soft, purring moans that were endearing but not out of the ordinary. As babies, both had an unusually high-pitched scream that, when they were very upset, rose almost to the limits of human hearing and bounced back painfully from the corners of the room. Gracie rarely got to that point, but Rosie's tantrums rose straight to the peak volume, especially when Gracie took one of her toys. When this happened, Gracie would quickly return the toy and flee. But for both of them, the power and pitch of that scream seemed to diminish as they grew from toddlers to little girls, and I'd heard nothing that sounded like Adam's voice.

I looked for other signs, too, examining their bodies for any changes beyond normal growth, indications that their facial features or genitals were slipping out of form. I felt twinges of guilt, as if such inspections showed a lack of gratitude, an affront to Adam's and their obvious perfections.

I found nothing. They were normal, healthy girls. Beautiful and round-faced. They were slim and muscular, with masses of curly red hair. Within months of birth, their blue eyes changed to shades of green. Except for Rosie's colic, they had suffered nothing more than a few mild winter colds. They, like their sisters who followed, were preternaturally agile and fast learners, but nothing stood out beyond that. In fact, I could see little of Adam's—or Roy Hope's—features in them. They looked like my baby pictures.

One night, after I had put the girls to bed, Adam and I heard the stabled horses neighing in alarm. He ran out with a flashlight to see what had spooked them. I followed in my nightgown, holding Hobo and the new dog, Gabby, back by their collars.

An owl, luminous in the moonlight when Adam opened the stable door, turned its smooth, heart-shaped face toward us. It skipped sideways and fluttered a few feet into the air before falling back to the stable floor, its left wing dragging. The horses whinnied. The dogs pulled and barked.

Adam took off his shirt and threw it over the owl. "Get the dogs out of the stable. I'll take care of it," he told me. I shut the door on the faint, soothing rise of his voice.

As I tucked the girls in, I considered, for the first time, that his voice might have qualities beyond what I heard and felt. Could he use it to heal? Was that what I'd heard him doing with the owl?

When he came in from the stable, my question seemed to surprise him. "No. Nothing like that. It's just a different kind of voice."

"Just a different kind of voice?" I echoed.

He grinned. "I admit it's a good voice, a useful tool. A calm animal doesn't fight what you need to do. I had to strap a splint to the owl's wing." He cupped his hands as if holding the bird. "He was so strong and light, Evelyn. I think he'll be okay."

"You really don't know what you have, do you?"

"Oh, I know." He lifted my hair off my shoulder and kissed my neck. "I know."

In the morning, he fashioned a cage out of two crates and chicken wire. The girls were in charge of the mousetraps. Gracie set the traps and Rosie dropped the dead mice into the cage. On the days we caught no mice, we fed the owl meat or scraps from the table. The cats, one as pale as the owl, the other a pregnant calico, sometimes perched on top of the cage and hung their heads over the side, peering upside down at the owl that stared blankly back at them.

After a month, we freed the owl. Rosie had had her ride and both girls were ready for bed. The girls and I clustered outside in our pajamas under a bright moon. Adam held up the thick stick of the perch the owl clung to. He removed the makeshift hood. For a moment, the owl did not move. Turning its face toward Adam, it took one long, unblinking look, hopped from the stick to his gloved wrist, then, slowly lifting its wings, took silent flight. The girls oohed beside me. The white speck of the owl vanished quickly into the dark, distant bank of trees.

For once, the girls went to bed without protest. I kissed them, and Adam began singing for them—two songs, one for each girl. As I climbed into bed, I heard the familiar refrain of "Amazing Grace," which Gracie considered her song. "Silent Night," Rosie's choice, followed.

I listened as Adam came down the hall, then felt him get in bed and spoon up behind me. He held me, but we did not sleep. It seemed to me that we were listening for something. Finally, I turned to him and he lifted my nightgown. I did not reach for the rubbers. I thought of the owl, of the impossible, silent lift of it into the air, as I drew my husband to me.

The owl, in all its wisdom, did not go far from the barn and stable mice. And it did not forget the curious cats. Not long after we freed it, I saw it hunched in the stable rafters when I took coffee out to the stable for Adam.

One morning, before the milking, I stopped to say hello to Darling. The cat had had her kittens by then, a bunch of orange tabbies and calicos that flickered around the barn. I found the bloody tail and most of the spine of an orange kitten draped over the corner post of Darling's stall. I couldn't imagine how it got there. Then I looked up. Our barn owl peered down, ghostly in the rafters. I banged the milk pail against the barn wall in protest. The owl simply tilted its wide, flat face down and stared impassively.

Outside, I bent over to bury the little spine so the girls would not find it. Bile surged up my throat. I dropped to my knees to vomit and recognized the particular nausea of early pregnancy. I'd had morning sickness with the other girls, but nothing this bad. The powerful waves of nausea ripped through me, the first indication that this pregnancy was different, not one but two babies.

☙

I SAW GRANNY PAYNES once at Pearl's when I was about five months along. She nodded tersely at my swollen belly and said, "Looks like you carrying one too many. You need to go to the hospital."

Months later, deep in anesthesia and dead to the world, I was delivered of twins at Mercy Hospital in Charlotte. This time, I was not afraid. Gracie and Rosie were normal and bright. There was no need for subterfuge.

In the hospital, hours after the birth, I emerged from my twilight sleep of drugs to find Adam and Momma in the room with me. Momma dozed in a chair at the foot of the bed. A silken evening light shone through a break in the drawn curtains. From a chair next to the bed, Adam leaned into the column of light. He held up two fingers. "The doctors are not sure. But I saw them. We have two more girls. Like Gracie and Rosie, like you," he whispered.

The moldy cotton of anesthesia filled my mouth. I shook my head and croaked, "Like you. Bet they're ugly like you."

He held a cup of water to my lips and nodded. "They're healthy and all there. But, yes, they look like Gracie and Rosie did, only a little smaller and skinnier."

The tepid, chlorinated water did little to slake my thirst. "What do the doctors say?" I tried to sit up straight, but felt the soreness in my bottom and slouched back down again.

"They had to stitch you up. You tore some. You okay?"

I nodded.

"They want to keep the babies for observation," he continued. "They're puzzled, of course."

"I want to go home. I want them with me."

"You should all stay for a few days and rest. Momma and I can take care of the girls at home. Rita and Bertie are with them now."

Momma stirred, woke with a startle, then oriented herself. Adam stood up to let her sit on the bed beside me. She smoothed my hair away from my face and took my hand. "Has Adam told you?"

He cleared his throat and spoke up. "Evelyn, the doctors are very puzzled. They think something may be wrong with the girls." He spoke in a level and serious voice as he grinned over Momma's shoulder.

I hiccupped and stifled a smile.

"Oh, honey." Momma rubbed my hand. I felt terrible. The moment should have been a joy for her.

I slid back into sleep and woke later, to a darkened room. Momma was gone. Adam snored softly in a recliner next to my bed, his hat tipped over his face.

The next morning, Adam and Momma brought Gracie and Rosie to see their new sisters. The five of us stood looking in the nursery window at a row of babies sleeping in plastic bassinets. Pink, not blue, blankets swaddled Jennie and Lillian—a good sign. The doctors agreed with Adam on the sex of the babies. I pressed my face to the glass and stood on my tiptoes to get a better view. Both of them slept. Not much was visible between their blankets and the knit caps. But their cheeks had the same roughly dimpled skin I had seen on Addie and their two older sisters.

"Are they all right, Momma?" Gracie leaned against me and put her arm around my hip. Momma had pulled her hair back in a single tight braid. She looked up at me, her broad face solemn.

"Of course they are. They're fine. Perfect like you and Rosie were when you were born," I said.

"Maybe we got a bad one, so they gave us another one to make up for it," Rosie volunteered, hopping up and down beside us.

Adam and I laughed. Momma rubbed Gracie's shoulders sympathetically.

Two nurses in surgical masks came into the nursery and picked up the twins. The younger nurse gave us a brief, anxious glance.

Adam put his hand on my back. "They were early, Evelyn. It may take a day or two longer to lose the newborn look." The two nurses took the twins into an adjoining room and shut the door.

"Adam, I need to have them close to me. I need to hold them like I did Gracie and Rosie. Like I held you. I want them," I whispered.

"Wait here," Adam said.

Still a little groggy from the anesthetic, I let him go without further comment. My engorged breasts ached. I wanted to hold my babies. Momma and the girls, exclaiming over the other babies, hadn't noticed Adam leaving.

Across the nursery, another glass wall revealed a parallel hall. Adam appeared opposite us on the other side of the nursery and knocked at a glass door near the room the nurses had taken our babies into. The nurses came back out without the twins and went to the door where Adam stood. He said something. The younger nurse looked at the older one, who shook her head at Adam. The older nurse pointed back to the room where they'd left the twins; she began to shut the door. Adam put his hand out to stop her, his brow furrowed in protest. He stepped into the nursery. Both nurses stepped back.

"Back in a minute, Momma," I said.

She looked up and saw Adam, too. I waved away her question.

I waddled over to the other side of the nursery to join Adam.

An unfamiliar hardness resonated in his voice. "No blood tests. We don't want any blood tests. No tests of any kind. My daughters are fine. You can't do that to our children without our consent."

The nurses exchanged looks. The older one brushed past us as she strode out of the nursery and down the hall. The remaining nurse smiled weakly and said, "Twins."

The older nurse returned with a doctor. He held a chart and seemed surprised when Adam reached out to shake his hand and formally introduce himself. "I'm Adam Hope, father of the twins your nurses are examining. There's no need for any tests."

The doctor shook his head and raised his hand, dismissing Adam's objection.

But Adam continued. "Their reflexes are normal. Lungs and heart normal. They have taken some formula."

The doctor's face hardened with each statement as Adam's voice grew more firm. "Mr. Hope, I am not even sure your children are female. We need to discuss some options. There are procedures for children like yours."

"They are girls. They look exactly like our other two daughters did when they were born." This registered in the doctor's eyes, but his face remained set. One of the nurses shifted beside us and cleared her throat softly.

I squeezed Adam's arm to shut him up. It took effort to think through the lingering veil of anesthesia, but his tone alarmed me.

"We don't want blood tests. We're Jehovah's Witnesses," I lied.

The doctor snorted. "No tests," he said to the nurses.

"They're fine." Adam's voice dropped. "And we want to take them home."

I slipped my hand into Adam's. "As soon as possible." I stared back at the doctor, who regarded us as if we were demented.

The doctor opened his mouth, snapped it shut, then quickly scrawled something across the chart. "These babies should be examined by pediatric urology. But I'm signing for early dismissal. Tomorrow." He thrust the chart at the nurses and marched away.

I went back to my room while Adam stayed to argue the nurses into letting me keep Jennie and Lil with me for the night.

They were good babies, crying so softly and infrequently that they did not wake the newly delivered woman who shared the room with me. I ignored the bottled milk and let them relieve me. I held them close, willing them to become normal girls.

The next morning, we checked out of the hospital without blood tests and without incident. Tired, sore, and happy, I took my ugly carrot-tops home.

Then the shit hit the fan of domestic life—the shit and the laundry and the spit-up and the spills and the scraped knees and the shoes and the holidays and the biscuits and the grits and the cats and the dogs and the rain and the manure and the weeds. We had tilted toward chaos with two kids, a farm, and a stable full of horses, but the addition of twins tipped things straight into the gutter. The next years were a blur of babies and work. They were probably the happiest years of my life.

We needed more assistance on the farm than family could supply. For the first time, we hired regular help, Wallace, Granny Paynes's nephew. A natural stable hand and an otherwise quiet man, he muttered to the horses as he worked, a deep, rhythmic chatter that calmed them. His daughter, Macy, sometimes helped me in the house.

In temperament, Lil and Jennie fluctuated between Gracie's calm and Rosie's natural-born outrage. More than any of the other girls, they were left to their own devices. All energy and wide eyes, they calmed and excited each other in turns. As babies, they burbled contentedly at each other for hours until one of them bit, hit, or scratched the other and all hell broke loose. Each added to the other's wails in an endless cycle. If they were left unattended, their cries reached a crescendo at which they gagged then threw up. Together. On each other. Their mutual mess provided immediate distraction and they grew quiet again. Quite the team.

Before they were two years old, Jennie and Lil learned to pull themselves up the side of their crib, crawl over the top, and slide down the rails to the floor. Soon they began appearing everywhere—in the barn, under the house, in the chicken coop. Like me, they wandered fearlessly as toddlers, but they were doubly bold and agile. Wallace often called to me from the back door, the two bright-haired, squirming girls in his dark arms and an apology on his lips, as if he were to blame for being unable to bear them underfoot in the stable.

One day, Adam spotted them at the end of the driveway. Their bright curly mop tops disappearing as they descended, heading for the railroad tracks. He bolted after them. I found the curtains of their bedroom fluttering out the window and the screen on the ground below. Adam trudged back to the house, the girls struggling, unharmed, in his arms. That evening he and Wallace screwed all the screens into the window frames and began work on fencing. By the end of the week, the front and side of the house were fenced and the driveway gated.

In rebellion against their terrible confinement, Lil and Jennie made their own playhouse. With help from Adam, they built it out of scraps and anything they could successfully filch from the house or the barn. They were good thieves and scavengers. The playhouse held a collection of bottle caps, empty birds' nests, a stinking fox skull, and a seemingly continuous litter of kittens. A semicircle of little rocks at the entrance forbade anyone else entry. They worked out complex fantasies in their little playhouse. At the supper table, they embellished the stories in dual chattering blasts of an English patois known only to the two of them, a peculiar Southern drawl sprinkled with nasal, Asian intonations.

On our tenth wedding anniversary, Momma took care of the girls while Adam and I went to a restaurant and a movie, a rare night out for us. When we returned, rather than going inside, I waited by the car while Adam checked the stable. Lil and Jennie would be asleep, maybe Rosie, too. But Gracie's voice carried through the windows, followed by Momma's reply. A faint breeze crossed the yard. I leaned back over the hood of the car and scanned the thick field of stars vibrating above. A beautiful, clear night. Adam joined me.

I took his hand. "Let's not go in yet. We haven't been outside alone at night in years. Let's take a walk."

But when we passed the twins' house, he stooped and pulled me in after him. Some small animal scurried away. We leaned against the trunk of the oak that was a corner support and kissed. We made love there on the dirt floor. The sweet voice of his pleasure echoed against the tin walls. What should have been a safe time of the month was, instead, Sarah, our fifth child.

Her birth was uneventful. I had not even bothered consulting Granny Paynes, who had grown frail in the last few years. The hospital nurses were concerned. But the doctor, after I repeated my lie about being Jehovah's Witnesses, was nonchalant about our daughter's oddity and our confident refusal of his services.

The quietest of the girls, Sarah spent her first months content among her cavorting sisters and the daily chaos. Watchful and calm, she reminded me of Addie. She grew in leaps, seeming to develop skills overnight. Standing one day and running the next, babbling incoherently, then suddenly speaking in complete sentences. She learned to hold a crayon one day and covered the walls with smiling faces and stick-figure horses the next. Only in her quest for art supplies did she exhibit Lil and Jennie's gift for theft and deception. For her, a crayon or pen was incomparable for fixing the boo-boos and injustices of being the youngest of five daughters. Gradually rising smudges, gray fingerprints, and crayon drawings on every wall marked her growth.

With her, we were done. No more children. I felt it in my heart.

By the time Sarah learned to walk, the focus of the farm had shifted from the fields to the stable of horses. Except for a few acres of feed crops and the kitchen garden, the farm was pasture and a riding arena now. We kept a cow and the chickens, too. I became the bookkeeper and part-time secretary for the horse business, often taking calls with a baby on my hip.

Wallace was our full-time, all-the-time stable hand and groom. We sometimes hired a second part-time man to help him. In a pinch, Cole also helped us. He and Adam were not the partners he and Addie had been, but they were still a good team when occasion arose.

Cole, his wife, Eloise, and their two boys often joined us on the Fridays when Lloyd, the farrier, was on the farm and stayed for dinner. With Lloyd, Cole, and Wallace, there were enough men for post-dinner poker in the barn. Sometimes Joe or Freddie joined them. If the wives came too, we women would let the kids run amok while we retired to the front porch for iced tea. I loved those evenings on the porch with the women, especially when Eloise and my sister-in-law, Mary, both came. When the men came alone, their voices drifted out the open barn door. I loved their unhurried masculine conversation, the quiet rhythm of the game punctuated by an occasional question or a laugh.

We boarded mostly normal horses, but some that came through our stable were the fine-bred, splendid, and damaged animals of the wealthy and obsessed, brought to Adam, often as a last-ditch effort to reclaim them. People from Charlotte and Louisville with contrary horses showed up or called on a regular basis. Often, they paid Adam to come to them.

Sometimes, we organized small groups of riders for "classes." On those days, the pasture filled with horse trailers, the larger, round pen we eventually built, crowded with riders and horses come to learn good manners. Adam continued refining his philosophy of horsemanship, urging the riders to true themselves. Calm, balance, lead. Willingness, not will.

He spent a lot of time observing horses, particularly the troublesome ones. His methods with them varied. But there was a pattern to his process of sweetening a colt. Before the saddle went on, a subtle seduction began. Adam and the horse regarded each other, then turned slightly away. His gaze was expectant then but without the tensions of anticipation, his whole being a simple, upright announcement: I am here. Adam possessed a special kind of stillness then, stalwart and open. He blinked, a single, slow blink. Though I heard nothing, I could tell by the turn of the horse's ears when Adam's unique voice came into play. The young horse would sniff with added curiosity and stretch his neck. Gradually, Adam moved toward the horse, then the interaction of touch began. Within minutes, the colt would follow him around as if drawn by some invisible line. If at any point the horse balked, backing away from the blanket or saddle, Adam's stillness returned. Sometimes then, as he paused, waiting briefly for the horse to reflect his calm, I would feel a slight hum in the air, a feathery drone as if he'd changed pitch or tone.

In the early mornings, when I took coffee out to Adam, the snort and shuffle of horses and the clean odors of large animal health filled the stable. On winter mornings, when I stepped into their animal warmth from the cold yard, my head still thick with sleep, the horses seemed like an animal extension of my dreams, an animate den of horseness that I moved through. I loved them then, for that unconscious availing of themselves. I admired the sleekness of their hide, the powerful depth of their chests and legs, and the whiskery velvet of their inquisitive mouths. The rare times I had alone with them in pasture when they were at rest, I felt honored by their indifference and the glimpse they offered of the herd's solace. Their grace at play in pastures never failed to stop me and hold me for a moment.

But for all my developing appreciation, I never became a good horse-woman. I remained most content among horses rather than on them. My attempts at honing my skills had been constantly interrupted by pregnancy, and I could never quite be convinced any animal wanted me on its back, that it preferred me to the open sky above.

All the girls eventually became respectful and skilled on the back of a horse. Adam made certain of that. Gracie, like me, appreciated the horses' company but was the least interested in riding. She often carried a chair out to the stable and read, her back to the light of the open door. She'd glance occasionally from her book to the horses as she read. Jennie and Lil dressed the milder horses in scarves. They loved to steal away on Darling together, but their interest was not deep. Sarah drew them, of course, and, as soon as her vocabulary was equal to the task, began to advise Adam. He'd listen patiently to her analysis of a horse's emotional state, his head cocked to one side. She was often right, he told me. Rosie remained the most interested in the horses. She lived in the stable, apprenticing herself to her father, and became his chief riding partner. Nights when she wanted refuge from the antics of her younger sisters, she slept in the stable. More than once she missed a day of school after being up all night with Adam nursing a sick horse or a mare in foal.

Once, when Sarah was still a baby, I passed the corral on my way back from picking squash and paused to watch Adam deep in his own observation of a fearful, volatile mare that had been brought to him for social repair. He stood a few yards from the corral fence, his hands relaxed at his side, seemingly oblivious to my presence. I was thinking about what was under his clothes—his shoulders and the slope from his back to his waist. He turned, smiled, and then crooked his finger, calling me over. "What kind of horse is this?"

I gave him a blank look. The horse circled the corral, her eyes darting back and forth.

"Is she scared, content, nervous, healthy?"

I shook my head and shrugged.

He raised his eyebrows. "Look. The kind of horse she is shows right there on her skin and how she moves." Then he began a recitation, pointing at her ears, the tension in her neck, how she held her tail, the balance of her spine, and the condition of her skin. "She's been poorly groomed and someone beat her," he announced. He waved his beautiful hands, tracing the horse's back and the curve of her neck in the air. He entered the corral and raised his right arm. Immediately, the horse stopped circling the corral and began an agitated pace opposite him, neighing sharply.

Later that evening, while Adam finished in the stable, I got the girls ready for bed. I squatted by the bathtub bathing Sarah, who, completely soaped, wiggled in my hands and struggled to climb the shower curtain. Lil and Jennie perched on the sides of the sink, peering into the drain, their heated debate about toothpaste bringing them close to blows. Gracie sat on the toilet, peeing and tracing my spine with her toes. Rosie rushed in, accused Gracie of stealing her favorite stuffed horse, then bit her sister. Suddenly, the four of them were in full skirmish behind me. Sarah rubbed soap into her eyes and screamed. I calculated whether I'd be able to let go of her and have time to knock the others' heads together before she drowned. "Out!" I shouted. "Everybody out!"

Adam popped his head into the bathroom.

"What kind of girls are these?" I snapped at him over the ruckus.

"Huh?"

"What kind of children are these?" I shouted. "It's on their skin and how they move."

He grinned. "Children with a mad momma, children with a tired momma."

From then on, when Adam or I wanted the other to pay attention to someone or something, we played the question game. The girls caught on and the game expanded. What kind of blossom is that? What kind of sky is that? What kind of report card is this? The questions might be a simple invitation to curiosity, a request for praise, a lesson, or a warning.

I loved the playfulness of the question game. But there were times it seemed to be shadowed by the questions I did not ask, the questions now less urgent, subsumed by normal daily life. What kind of man is my husband? How are our daughters like him?

ADDIE'S SOLO MOUNTAIN TRIP became an annual ritual with Adam. He would leave just after morning chores on a Sunday and come back two or three days later. Many men did the same, going hunting or fishing. But Adam always went alone and brought home nothing. His trips were dependent on the seasons and our work. But they always seemed sudden, imperative. Tension built in him the weeks before he left. I felt uneasy as he packed for his trips. But each time, he returned refreshed and ready for work.

One Sunday, after church and dinner, the girls and I were still at Momma's. Daddy, Momma's brother, Otis, and another old guy from the mill sat on her back porch, smoking and spitting. I leaned on the porch rail nearby, watching the kids playing in the mill yard. I paid little attention to what the men said until Otis raised his voice to be heard over the girls. " . . . Just like a woman keening, the most gawd-awful thing a man would want to hear." I turned at the strange comment.

Otis's buddy shook his head and spat off the edge of the porch. "No, weren't no wolf. Besides, it sounded pretty sometimes. Like singing, but no words. That old hill farmer said it was a haint."

Otis nodded in agreement. "A queer sound. I couldn't figure out if I wanted to lie down and sleep to it or go out and shoot it. We didn't see sign one of deer, fowl, or squirrel out there. And it peak season."

"Not the first time you've come home empty-handed," Daddy said and they all laughed.

Cigarette smoke wafted out the back door. Frank's voice muttered behind me, "How 'bout your Adam? He hear anything up there?"

I remembered Frank's smell in the farmhouse years before and his disturbing photos. I pulled my sweater up closer around my shoulders. I herded the girls onto the porch, past Frank, and down the hall to Momma's warm kitchen, leaving the old men to their tobacco and gossip.

That night, I asked Adam what he did in the mountains. "Molt," he said simply, but with a grin. I wasn't sure I wanted to hear more, but he continued. "I go up the mountain as far as I can and just listen to whatever there is to hear—the mountain, the air, the ginseng growing."

"You don't just listen."

"Well, sometimes I talk back, too. It's like any other conversation, Evelyn. No one does all the listening. Why are you asking now?"

"Uncle Otis and one of his buddies heard you. Some people think you're a 'haint.'"

He laughed the sweet, big laugh I always found irresistible. "The deer—some of them let me touch them. They're strong as a horse but it's a different strength. Lighter, with more spring. And there are places where the mountain answers. Like an echo, but there's always something in it that didn't come from me." He pressed his fist to his chest.

"You pet deer and sing to the mountain?"

"Not to. With."

❧

THROUGH THE WINTER and spring that followed, the image of Adam's solitary howl in the mountains stayed with me. I imagined his voice filling the hollows and slopes, the deer docile and the mountain dwellers puzzled. But when the heat of summer settled over the farm, taking up residence in our un-air-conditioned house, and Adam suggested we take the girls up into the mountains, I thought only of the blessed cool relief.

The seven of us drove up out of the clotted summer heat until Adam found the special spot he wanted to show us on Mount Mitchell. We hiked down a short distance from the narrow dirt road to a creek. The girls scattered like pups as soon as they heard water. At the creek, the forest opened. An outcropping of boulders sent the water in a sharp turn and created a short waterfall. The girls stripped to their panties and plunged, screaming, into the water. They splashed and swam until they began to shiver, then leapt out of the water to make water angels on the flat, warm rocks. Once the sun warmed them, they plunged back into the water.

While I prepared our lunch, Adam found a patch of ginseng and cut us each a piece for dessert. The girls, their lips still tinted blue from the cold water, wrapped themselves in towels. Their panties and hair dripped onto the rocks as we ate our sandwiches.

When we finished eating, Adam pointed up the mountain. "There is a beautiful waterfall east of us. Not as good a swimming spot as this one, but the view is amazing."

I rolled my pedal-pushers up a little higher and waded into the icy water. Adam stripped to his boxers and the girls dragged him into the water. Gracie held back a little, shy to see her father almost naked.

She had shot up that summer. Change would come soon, but for now, she shouted and dodged with the other girls as Adam splashed them with icy water.

I climbed up the trail to put away our leftovers. On my way back, ducking the overhanging branches, my arms full of fresh, dry towels, I felt a vibration through the rocks under my feet, like an approaching train. Puzzled, I stopped and listened.

Below me, Adam lay spread on the large, flat boulder—Da Vinci's Vitruvian Man encircled by daughters. Sarah curled up on his chest, her hands tucked under her belly, her eyes shut. Gracie and Rosie lay parallel to him, their heads pillowed on his outstretched arms. Jennie and Lil draped across their father's legs. The four of them had their eyes closed, too. They appeared to be napping, but something in their posture suggested anticipation. Adam stared up at the sky.

Carefully, I made my way to the edge of the clearing a few feet above them. A pure, sweet tone lilted, threading through the sound of falling water. Adam's voice, but not the sharp crescendo of his pleasure with me at night. A broad, tender tone, undulant, almost narrative.

Everything, save the sensation of his voice, seemed to have stopped. The girls were motionless. Adam's eyes were still open, but he did not seem to be present.

The distance between me and them seemed enormous. I was outside their circle. Adam was the different one, the outsider. But here, alone with my family, I realized I was the different one.

His voice, undulating up to me, filling the air, seemed to be the manifestation of my difference from him, from them. Suddenly, I wanted to fight its seduction, to stop my ears and cover my chest. I stooped to pick up the towels I'd dropped.

My breath drew short. Then a single word flooded me: *No*. I shivered and pushed away my resistance.

Abandoning the towels, I climbed down and circled the rock they lay on. I knelt near Adam, a knee on either side of his head, my hands softly on his temples.

My legs tingled. The vibrato changed, sweeping up and down, seeming to fall into the timbre of the waterfall and reemerge over and over. Shimmering, joyful.

Gradually, his voice vanished as if withdrawing into the rocks and water. No one moved. A bird called nearby, and then a single-note retort followed down creek. Adam reached up and touched my wrist. He tilted his face up at me and we looked upside down at each other. The girls stirred. The spell broke.

Jennie looked up, drunkenly, and announced, "Momma, Daddy's right, if we get very still and listen for a long time, the rocks sing."

Sarah looked up from Adam's chest, first at her sister and then at me. I saw in her eyes, so like her father's then, that she knew it was not the rocks. I pointed out the towels for Gracie. She retrieved them and passed them out. The girls and Adam dressed. Speechless, we moved slowly. As if underwater, we gathered our things and returned to the car.

Sarah slept in the front seat with me and Adam. Gracie and Rosie stared out the windows. Lil and Jennie snored between them. Adam drove us down the winding mountain road, his face soft and relaxed.

As the road grew flat and straighter, the girls began to wake from their stupor, fidgeting and mumbling. I didn't want to think or talk. I started singing "Red River Valley." The girls picked up on the chorus, their voices harmonizing perfectly from the backseat.

Once home, they were unusually subdued. We all went to our home-work and chores. I fixed us a quick late dinner of eggs and grits.

Later that evening, Sarah, the last to bathe and the only one still young enough to need help, stood naked in the tub, her arms at her sides. I poured a final rinse over her smooth shoulders and down her back. "It was Daddy singing today. He sang with his mouth shut. Not the rocks," she said.

"I know, honey. But it was the mountains. Daddy can only do that in the mountains."

She stared at me dubiously.

"It's true, baby. Some places are special. Some things can happen one place, but not another."

More staring and silence. Then she held her arms up for me to lift her out of the bath. "I want to live in the mountains then," she declared while I toweled her back.

That night, in bed, I asked Adam if he had ever "made the rocks sing" for the girls before.

"No, not like that. But I realized we were alone and I could do it without disturbing anyone else. Besides, the mountains do echo my voice in ways that the open land here doesn't. The mountains do sing."

"What was their reaction at first, before I got there?"

"Same as when you were there: they listened. I don't know what they can do. How much like me they are."

"Sarah reminds me of you as Addie in some way. She knows things."

He sighed and pulled me toward him. "Don't worry," he whispered. "The girls will be okay."

Until then, I was the only person who had heard his other voice. I remembered the power of his voice the day he came back in the skin of Roy Hope. Anxiety thickened in my diaphragm and I took a deep breath. Adam spooned up against me, then rolled over me, as his voice had earlier.

The girls never mentioned what he did that day. Perhaps they saw Adam's explanation of singing rocks as just another adult charade, like Santa Claus or the Easter Bunny. Or maybe the relative isolation of the farm made it easier for them to assume that we were the norm, that all fathers in the privacy of their families could make the rocks sing.

Either way, I was waiting for the other shoe to drop. For them to question or to change.

As Gracie reached puberty, my fears about how normal the girls were returned. How would they cope with their changing bodies, would Adam's genes mitigate or amplify the normal or somehow pull it offtrack?

That year, Gracie had grown almost five inches. We marked the girls' growth on the door frame of Gracie's and Rosie's bedroom. Gracie's height marks were always at the top. The other girls followed in stair-step clusters of names and dates. Recently, Gracie had passed five and a half feet and was now within inches of the mark indicating my height. Her chest also popped out, first in pink, puffed buds, then small, round breasts. She began to lock the bathroom door when she bathed.

Months before her thirteenth birthday, she called me into the bathroom one afternoon to show me the bloody stain on her underwear. We were prepared. I'd shown her the sanitary pads and how to attach them to the elastic belt I bought for her. I felt the buoyancy of relief as I sent her off to her room to change while I washed her first pair of bloody panties in the bathroom sink. She was a normal woman.

A few weeks later, she passed through the kitchen as Adam helped me unpack a load of groceries. He handed Gracie the toilet paper. "Take this to the bathroom on your way." Then he held up a box of pads. "These, too." He stacked the box on top of the toilet paper in Gracie's arms. "So much better than those rags, aren't they?" he commented with the certainty of experience.

Gracie nodded enthusiastically at her father. Then frowned, puzzled, and turned abruptly, striding off to the bathroom.

SIX

THE STORM

By the spring of 1965, we were in a state of equilibrium. We were finished having babies. The girls were all healthy, all in school, and doing well—normal, sweet, and ornery as any children. No longer the main reason we needed help, they now worked in the garden and stables. Business was good. A new corral extended out from the stable and we were thinking of adding a second stable. With the new highways complete on two sides of our land, the farm was worth more than we'd ever dreamed possible.

ON THE MORNING OF SATURDAY, APRIL 10, 1965, I woke and sat up on the edge of the bed. Everything shifted sideways. But nothing in the dim bedroom had moved. Silently, I checked myself and stood up. The world seemed normal again. Just some odd quirk of the body, an unexplained dizziness that passes over and is gone. Momma would have said a possum had walked over my grave.

The girls woke and we all began our morning routines. Gracie brought in the milk while I started breakfast. Rosie fed the chickens and collected the eggs. Sarah disappeared into the barn to play with the

latest stray cat. Jennie and Lil revved up for their normal morning debate. They were arguing about *Mister Ed*, the TV show with the talking
horse.

"I *know* how they get Mr. Ed to do that!" Jennie shouted. Then she
appeared at my side. "Lil's not listening again," she fished for my support. She was still in her nightgown. Her bright hair tangled around her
shoulders.

"Get dressed. Brush your hair. Brush your teeth."

She marched away, down the hall toward their bedroom.

"Your sister, too. Breakfast in twenty minutes," I shouted after her.
"And no experimenting on the horses!"

While my hands were in the biscuit dough, Adam kissed me and
ran his hands along my sides. He poured himself a cup of coffee, refilled
my cup, and set it down next to me. A bar of morning light crossed his
cheek. His lips met the rim of the cup. He leaned back against the
kitchen counter and talked. The near field needed disking for the alfalfa
this week.

I listened to the grain and lift of his voice. How, inside those words
about the tractor, were the same familiar sounds, the breath of everything he had ever said to me, every groan, song, and whisper.

Outside the kitchen window, the sun shone in a brilliant slant. The
field waited to be turned. The fresh impatience of the morning breeze
blended with the kitchen's odors of bacon and biscuits as I opened the
window over the sink. Adam, the girls, and I were at the table passing
around the last of the scrambled eggs when my cousin Frank arrived to
help with the tractor.

I didn't like Frank any better now than I had during the brief time
he'd been my housemate, but I'd gotten used to him showing up a
couple of times a year and disappearing with Adam to work on the
truck or the pump. He was a good mechanic. Whiskey and years as a
civilian had worn his edge down to the common, guarded bitterness of

a middle-aged man who thinks life has not offered him what he deserves. He'd never married, though he was seldom without a woman at his side on a Saturday night. Some men envied him. During the week, he worked at the mill as a mechanic. On weekends, he drank hard.

A flask bulged in his back pocket when he stretched across the table for the syrup, but I didn't smell anything on his breath.

I didn't want him working on any motors if he was drinking. As I set a fresh plate of scrambled eggs in front of him, I took a sniff to assure myself that he was sober.

He and Adam finished off the rest of the breakfast, then headed outside to the tractor. Rosie and I set up the two rinse tubs next to the wringer washer on the back porch. She no longer needed a stool to stand on as she swung the heavy wringer head over the rinse tubs.

As we gathered the dirty clothes, the tractor motor sporadically caught then faltered into silences punctuated by Frank's cursing. Every time he worked on someone's car, a child acquired a more colorful vocabulary. For once, I was grateful for the noisy, rhythmic chugging of the old wringer washer.

The tractor sputtered and choked through the first load of washing. After a particularly long silence, Adam marched up to the back door. He held up a tattered length of hose. "We need a new one. I'll be back in a few minutes. Anything you need in town?" he called through the screen door.

"We're fine. Go on," I said.

Adam washed his hands at the spigot outside, then drove away in the truck. Frank paced in front of the open barn doors and sucked on his cigarettes. A strong breeze whipped the jeans and shirts on the line.

As I finished hanging up the first load, Adam returned, new hose in hand. Soon the motor came to a steady low rhythm and held. The men's whoops of congratulations followed. I hauled a basket of wet bed linens out to the line as Adam and Frank attached the disker to the tractor.

Frank climbed up and drove to the edge of the field. He turned in the seat and gave Adam a thumbs-up. Adam began picking up the tools scattered on the ground and returning them to the barn.

Then the tractor quieted to an idle. I pushed aside the pillowcase I'd just hung up.

Jennie stood at the edge of the path, shading her eyes as she looked up at Frank. She wore a light blue dress that had been worn down to softness by Gracie and Rosie. She looked tall and thin and faraway. Frank nodded and seemed to be speaking to her. She shook her head, pointing back toward the house. Then he rolled slowly away toward the field, the disker bobbing above the ground behind the broad tires.

I went back to hanging up our bedclothes and underwear.

I'd thrown the last sheet over the line and was smoothing it out when the tractor stopped again. I lifted a damp corner and peered. The tractor stood vacant in the field, the disker turned at an odd angle, one side higher than the other. Half the round blades jutted up. Frank had only gotten as far as the turn at the end of the first row.

He stood behind the disks, looking down as if he had dropped something in the darker streak of freshly turned earth. I thought of the flask in his pocket and the time he'd been alone in the barn. I opened my mouth to let Adam know Frank needed help. But all I got out of my mouth was "Adam." Something blue lay on the ground in front of Frank. Jennie's dress.

I ran.

Adam dashed past me. Shoving Frank out of the way, he fell to his knees at Jennie's side. Beyond him, two of the tilted disks gleamed red.

A broad, bright sash of blood surged across Jennie's waist toward her hip. A furrow of dirt dented her dress hem. A gash gaped at each ankle.

She blinked calmly up at the sky, freckles bright against her pallor. Her hair the same red as the dirt under her. "I can't get up."

Blood bubbled at the slice in her waist. Adam slid his hands under her, lifting. She coughed and smiled up at us. A thin line of blood ran from the corner of her mouth to her jaw and down her neck.

We ran past Frank, sprawled where Adam had knocked him, a dumb animal look of incomprehension on his face, the whiskey flask empty beside him.

Adam ran to the truck, clutching Jennie. I sprinted inside for the keys. Her head slumped against her shoulder as he laid her on the truck seat. The blood sash had expanded to a full skirt. The hem dripped. Adam dashed around the front of the truck and climbed in. With my back pressed against the dashboard, I knelt on the edge of the seat facing Jennie, as he revved the engine.

The steering wheel slipped in his bloody hands. He cursed and tried to dry them on his blood-soaked shirt. Jennie's pallor deepened. Her eyes opened, distant. The artery at her neck pulsed faintly, then flattened.

Nothing.

I touched her neck, then gripped Adam's leg. He stopped. We were still at the top of the drive. All we had done was back the truck up and turn it around.

Without looking at her, he stretched one hand out and laid it on her chest. Then his head fell forward onto the steering wheel. We broke. Silence ripped into screams. Adam heaved against the steering wheel. Light filled the closed truck cab, blood filled the air. Her lips were white and motionless.

The four girls stared in through the driver's-side window. Their faces came apart in recognition. I heard heavy footsteps, and Frank peered in my window.

Adam roared.

He leapt out of the truck. In one motion, he grabbed Frank by the throat and threw him. Frank bounced against the stable wall. Adam yanked him up again by his throat, Jennie's blood on both of them now.

Frank's feet dangled inches from the ground. Purple-faced, he clawed at Adam's hands.

"Daddy!" Sarah rushed Adam.

Adam's shoulders crumpled and he let go. Frank scrambled toward the driveway and ran as Adam sunk to his knees.

Lil stood at the open door of the truck, staring at Jennie, her face equally white. I took her head in my hands and forced her to look away. She turned to me, open-mouthed with horror. I pressed her against my chest. I could not save her from what she saw.

⁂

CHAOS ENVELOPED THE SILENCE at the center of that day. Momma and Daddy arrived as the coroner drove up. Someone—I never found out who—moved the tractor, covered the blood, and cleaned the truck.

The girls vacillated between inconsolable silence and bursts of weeping. Adam stared at the floor, looking up only when one of the girls approached him. Then, he held them, his face vacant. Through my tears, his features had that same not-quite-held-together look that the girls all had when they were born.

That night, Sarah and Lil were already in the bed with me and Adam when we heard crying. "Is that Gracie or Rose?" Adam asked.

"I don't know," I said.

He left the bed and came back with both of them. We slept, the six of us in a dense tangle, as if in the crowding we would not miss the one who was gone.

I woke more than once in the middle of that night, rising to the surface of consciousness and then falling back into oblivion. Near dawn, I surfaced a final time, forgetting for a moment and basking in the familiarity of the touch and smell of my family. Legs, elbows, breath, and hair. I reached down and touched someone's leg. Warm, youthfully smooth skin. One of the girls sighed and shifted. One by one we all moved, each reacting and adjusting to the others in a ripple across the bed.

Then I woke fully and remembered why we were all there. The questions crushed into my chest: Why hadn't I called her away from the tractor? Why had I turned back to the sheets? To the meaningless push of cloth over a wire line?

Everything broke up into pieces. The days after Jennie died were a series of faces; among them, Adam's face always dead-still and faraway or completely naked and mobile in his cries. I'd never, and have never since, seen a man weep so. It wrenched me, and all who saw him. Most men looked away or offered him whiskey. A few bear-hugged him as if to squeeze out his grief. The women touched him, offering him food and handkerchiefs. To me, his skin was hot, searing.

And the girls, their faces wide-eyed, were stricken with sorrow one minute, then lapsing into their ordinary expressions the next. Lil, particularly, seemed lost. I could not protect them, could not soften or mitigate anything. I could only hold them close.

Every time I sat down, Sarah, who was only six years old and otherwise seemed to be enjoying the attention and commotion, crawled into my lap and silently sucked her thumb, something she had not done since she was a toddler. Momma seemed to be everywhere. She answered the phone. She laid out the bowls of food brought in by neighbors.

I pressed my jaw firmly shut and did not scream or vomit. I touched my daughters and my husband when they were near.

The field waited for the alfalfa seed. The horses leaned out the open stable windows and watched with curiosity as the yard filled with cars and the house filled with the faces of Clarion.

For two days before the funeral, everyone we knew passed through our home. The faces of mothers and fathers who had lost children were the hardest and the easiest to look into.

When people gather after a death, they usually discuss the dead—youthful adventures, funny stories, the arc of an illness or a life. They may recall similar deaths. It is a macabre yet humane thing to do. We keep ourselves from drowning by offering each other small cups of water.

None of the regular condolences applied. No one could say that it was a blessing, that her pain or suffering had ended. No one could say she'd had a long, good life and it was just her time. Many did credit the Lord's will. Adam flinched every time he heard that.

The second night, I stood in front of the open refrigerator, mindless before the gleaming bowls of food wrapped in shiny aluminum foil, the butter dish in my hand. Momma took it out of my hands and wedged it into a bottom shelf.

"Momma, why do we do the things we do? Why? I could have called her when I saw her near the field. I know Frank drinks."

"It's not your fault, Evelyn. Everyone has Frank fixing their cars and everyone knows he drinks. He's dented up cars, but never anything like this. No one could have foreseen this."

"But I did see, Momma. I saw her go over and speak to Frank. I was right there. I thought she was safe. What was he thinking trying to give her a ride on the tractor? I went back to the laundry. If I had just . . ."

Momma shook me by the shoulders and made me look at her. "Evelyn, you cannot think that again. Your girls have been near the tractor, the disk, and Frank before and nothing ever happened. But sometimes terrible things occur. The Lord has mysterious ways we can't understand."

I looked away and, shaking my head, wept.

The night before the funeral, Momma stayed at the house after everyone left. She'd tucked the girls in and had, I thought, turned in for the night. But when I returned from my bath, I found her in our bedroom, kneeling in front of Adam, who sat on the edge of the bed, his elbows on his knees. She held his face in her hands, directing his gaze at her, just as Granny Paynes had held mine when I gave birth.

"We may not understand how this could be, but it did happen. It was the Lord's will and we have to accept it."

"You can have the will of your Lord then," he growled.

She let her hands fall from his face. "You have four other daughters. They will need you. Bitterness will do them no good. Frank Roe is a stupid, indecent man who drinks too much."

"I don't want Frank at the funeral. I don't want to see him, ever again." His voice fell ragged and soft.

"Ever, I can't take care of. But the funeral I can. He will not be there and none will begrudge you."

❧

AS WE DROVE TO THE CHURCH, past the familiar homes and hills, the sky hung high and clear above us. The spring-bright fields and woods seemed to mock us with their greenery. I remembered being a child under such fresh canopy, alone in the woods. I longed to be there again, feral, unaware of my solitude, untouched by grief.

We walked into the church for the funeral service, down the aisle of faces turned toward us. Hands touched us. Comforting whispers broke around us. Hours, it seemed, we sat on that hard pew with Jennie laid out in front of us. Stands of flowers were propped up on either side of the pulpit and her coffin. The odor of chrysanthemums thickened the air.

Only numbness kept me from screaming. Sorrow and confusion came off the girls like smoke, their innocence burning away. Beside me, Adam, with Sarah curled almost fetal in his lap, vibrated. I kept my hand on his leg, not to comfort him but to press down what I felt rising in him, something sharp and dense. I pressed harder and harder till finally he reached under Sarah and took my hand in his. We will make it through this day, I thought.

At last, the service ended, Reverend Paul finished up, and we stood for a final hymn. My throat closed on the notes. Beside me, Adam stood with Sarah in his arms, his lips pressed shut.

Our friends and neighbors lined up to pay their final respects. The immediate family would be last. As Momma passed by us, she reached over Sarah's head to touch my arm. For a second, I met her eyes. My family began to file slowly past the coffin. Momma paused and laid her hand over Jennie's until Daddy whispered, "Come on, Lily Mae," and steered her away. Adam, the girls, and I stepped up to the coffin.

Jennie looked the same—the same perfect child she had been alive, but so still. Completely still.

The girls clutched at me and Adam. The rest of the congregation filled the aisles. Stragglers spread out in the pews behind us. I heard the low mutter of voices, the shuffle of shoes on wood floorboards.

Wordless, beside me, Lil stared down at her sister. I took a last, wrenching glance at Jennie and pulled Adam and the girls toward the door. In the press of the girls around me, I felt Adam let go of my hand. The warmth of him gone.

He turned back to the coffin. His lips parted. I heard that familiar deep sigh and felt the vibration of him, faint and tender, wash toward me. No one else seemed to notice, but the girls exchanged looks.

Adam's suit jacket tightened across his back. He gripped the coffin's edge. The timbre of his voice flattened abruptly into a mournful resonance. Spreading, filling the room.

My throat clenched. Anchored by the girls, I could not move fast enough.

"No, Adam. No!" I shouted.

A loud, plosive sob burst from him. For a heartbeat, the church fell silent. Then, as everyone moved again, leaving Adam to mourn, he took a deep, shuddering breath.

His voice slashed through the church, all sweetness gone. A new, searing wail. Jagged and dark. A blade. Through wood and bone it cut. Then it held steady, a vise of static and pain crushing my head and chest.

The girls froze beside me. The hairs on my neck and arms stood up. I pressed my hands to Sarah's ears.

Momma squinted over her shoulder, one hand out, shielding herself, the other over her heart. Daddy drew his shoulders up. His step faltered. Glaring at Adam's back, a man wrapped a protective arm around a child who huddled against him. Beyond them, a woman bent, hugging her swollen, pregnant belly, stepped between two pews, and retched. A baby sobbed, red-faced, its cries drowned by Adam's.

Adam reached into the coffin. The instant his hand touched her, a second, harsh wave lashed the room. The floorboards vibrated under my feet.

The coffin trembled.

Sarah peeled my hands from her ears. The girls dashed to Adam, hugging his waist and legs. Immediately, his cry softened, shifting higher in tone. It rose higher still, and then, like a hand lifting from us, vanished. The pain in my chest and head released. The air suddenly vacant, benign.

Gasping coughs filled the church. Dismay rippled through the remaining congregation. A single rush of footsteps, a door shut. Through the open windows, I heard the sound of someone gagging.

Adam's hands relaxed. He turned to the girls, touching their heads. His shoulders slumped. He stared, sightless, as the girls took his hands and led him from the coffin.

I slipped my arm through his and shepherded the girls ahead of us. Everyone, even Momma and Daddy, stepped back. No one offered condolences. No one touched us as we passed. A baby cried, full-throated. Someone moaned. Fear and anger were palpable. Odors of sweat and vomit leached through the air.

My skin scorched. Sarah reached back and took my hand. Gracie glanced back over her shoulder at me and her father, her chin quivering.

I nodded for her to continue. Rosie looked straight ahead and never hesitated. Lil fumbled for her hand. Adam was solid, inert. The eyes of everyone I knew were on us.

I understood, then. This was more than the end of Jennie's life.

The graveside service was brief and very quiet. Few came with us. I didn't look at any faces other than my daughters'. Words were said, but I did not hear them. Numbly, we witnessed Jennie's coffin being lowered into the ground.

At the farm afterward, Mildred and the other churchwomen who'd left the service early to help with the meal, welcomed us somberly. They'd spread the dining table with bowls and trays of food that people had brought by earlier. The chairs had been pulled away from the table so everyone could serve themselves buffet-style. The smell of ham, sweat, and pies filled the room, which felt too quiet.

Adam sat down in a chair against the wall, his face empty, his hands hanging mute in his lap. The girls gathered around him. Gracie and Rosie seemed to be standing guard, on either side of his chair. Gracie with one hand on his back as she gazed blankly at the floor. Rosie's eyes darted around the room. Lil and Sarah bunched up between his knees. Adam patted Lil's head and stroked her long curls as he stared out the window. Her slender hands traced the buttons on his shirt. Sarah bumped against Adam's thigh and stared vacantly at the food-laden table as she sucked her thumb.

I stood stupefied in the middle of the room, paralyzed until Sarah took her thumb out of her mouth and waved to me as if I was far away. When I took the few steps that brought me to her side, she patted my hip and fingered the cloth of my skirt.

Reverend Paul, Momma, Daddy, Joe, Bertie, and Rita stood awkwardly on the far side of the dining room, as if huddled against some contagion, breaking apart only to make way for the bustling churchwomen. One of the women dropped a ladle. Rita startled and gasped,

covering her mouth. Her head swiveled in Adam's direction. Bertie patted her on the back and whispered something to Momma. I understood
then that Momma was responsible for all of them being there.

Joe pulled me into the kitchen. "Bud took his momma home. Mary
wasn't feeling up to . . ." he whispered. His eyes shifted to Adam, then
back to me.

"It's okay, Joe. I understand." I forced my voice to a normal volume.
I had no idea what to say or how to hold my face.

Cole trudged into the kitchen from the back porch, holding a huge
platter with a whole turkey. His wife, Eloise, close behind with their
little daughter, Tina. Their two boys stood patiently, each holding
folded metal chairs. Their eldest son, a little younger than Gracie, gave
me his normal, self-conscious nod.

Eloise took the turkey platter from Cole and wedged it onto the
table. Cole hugged me. "I am so sorry for your loss, Evelyn." I bit my lip
and nodded, grateful for the simple words and natural embrace. Without hesitation, Cole stepped into the moat of silence surrounding Adam
and wordlessly patted his shoulder. Then I realized that Cole and his
family must have left the service early, to pick up the food and chairs. I
ignored the question on his face as he looked around the nearly empty
room. Eloise gave all her attention to carving the turkey. A current of
envy went through me. She had a normal husband, an ordinary life.

Momma waved to the boys. "Thank you for the turkey and the folding chairs." She turned to the boys. "Y'all take those back outside. We'll
bring them in as we need them."

For a moment, the clatter of the chairs being stacked on the porch
covered the silence inside the house. The churchwomen hovered nearby,
rearranging the food, their voices dropping to puzzled murmurs as it
became clear no other people were coming.

As if on cue, the three younger girls slipped single-file around the
islands of adults and disappeared down the hall without a whisper, little

blond Tina in the lead, pulling Lil and Sarah behind her. Gracie followed them with her eyes, but did not move. Rosie raised her chin up as if against a strong wind.

The screen door bumped gently behind me and Freddie walked in. I was nearly faint with gratitude to see his face. A normally aloof man, he let me hug him. I hoped to see Marge with him. Or at least one of the gang from the Sunday picking parties. But no one followed him in.

"Reverend?" Momma said.

The room went still. Every head but Adam's bowed.

The reverend, his arms raised stiffly, asked for the blessing and forbearance of God. Then the eating began.

Everyone collected their food from the side of the table opposite Adam. Everyone, even Momma and Daddy, ate standing, holding their plates, talking in strained whispers.

Gracie filled a plate for Adam. He took it, but did not eat. After a few moments, he leaned over and set the untouched plate back on the table. He did not look up, not even when Freddie walked up to him.

"Buddy. I'm sorry," Freddie said.

All other conversation in the room ceased. Rita grimaced and scurried out of the room, her heels thumping on the wood floor. Adam turned a blank and brittle face up to Freddie. I fought the impulse to flinch.

Freddie acknowledged Adam's silence with a nod.

Rosie put her hand on Adam's shoulder. "Thanks for coming by, Freddie."

The low murmur of conversation continued around us. Everyone ate and quickly left. With each departure, I felt heavier, as if gravity pulled stronger, as there were fewer of us left in the house.

Soon, only Momma remained. Daddy had taken her big casserole dish out to the truck and stayed there, smoking. The stunned smile affixed to Momma's face since the funeral had vanished. She turned around in my empty kitchen, a puzzled, fearful expression on her face, a dishrag limp in her hand.

"It's okay, Momma. You can . . ." The word "go" cracked in my throat. I covered my mouth against what I wanted to say: "Please stay and help me." I froze, frantic to have her stay and wanting her to leave as quickly as possible.

Her glance bounced around the room, and she pressed her lips together in a shallow, tight smile. She nodded, then left.

I listened to their truck pull away. Immediately, I wanted the girls and Adam. I spun around, suddenly aware that I didn't know where they were. I ran from room to room. Panic flushed through me and I sprinted through the house again, convinced suddenly that death had taken not one but all of them. I ran to the front porch, calling their names. Nothing. Then the back porch. A flash of white among the woods that flanked the fields caught my eye.

Beyond the apple tree and the twins' playhouse, in a small clearing of the trees, Adam squatted, his back to me. The girls, quietly pressed around him, did not see me.

I passed the spot where I'd first found Adam and stopped several yards from them. To my right, the field lay still unturned. I felt, then heard, his voice radiate. Loving, sad, and exquisite. Adam extended his arm and touched his fingertips to the middle of Gracie's chest. Her eyes glistened and grew wide. A tremulous smile crossed her lips.

Adam's voice swelled, ascending, hot, sharp, sorrowful.

"Adam!" I cried.

They turned as one. Alarmed, confused.

I remembered the shocked faces in the church, the frightened faces at the graveside. "Don't . . ." I choked. "They're too . . ."

Adam's hand fell away from Gracie. He looked down.

A shudder of puzzled shame crossed Gracie's features as her eyes met mine.

"Just sing, girls! Please, just sing," I pleaded. "Open your mouths and sing. Like everybody else does."

Gracie glanced at her father, then back to me. She blinked and cut her eyes quickly again toward Adam, who glowered darkly at me.

She stepped forward. I reached for her, but she did not come into my arms. She opened her mouth and sang, "You are my sunshine, my only sunshine. You make me happy when skies are gray . . ." Jennie's bedtime song. Her voice quavered, then held fast.

Adam strode past me.

I opened my arms and the girls came to me. Sarah cried. Lil bunched silently against me.

Rosie's voice rose hysterically. "Momma?"

Gracie wiped a tear from my chin. I pulled them in and hugged them. "Just sing, girls. Only singing. Regular singing." I picked up Sarah and took Rosie's hand.

"Gracie, bring Lil."

Unhinged and transparent, I struggled to keep my voice even as I led them up to the porch and handed Sarah to Gracie. "You all go inside. I'm going to talk to Daddy. We'll be there in a minute. Everything's okay, girls."

I found Adam standing in the middle of the stable. The horses huffed, restless in their stalls. His face hardened. His hand shot up in protest, to stop me. "They are the only ones who might be able to . . ." He faltered. "They are the only other ones, Evelyn."

A dark, violent sorrow for his solitude clenched my chest. I sucked in a deep breath and forced myself to continue. "I know, Adam. But not now. They're children. How will they handle it? You didn't see the faces of everyone in the church—they were scared of you."

He squinted at me.

"People were vomiting. Babies screaming . . ." I stuttered. "It hurt." I didn't mention the odd shame I'd just seen in Gracie's eyes.

His face crumpled. "No," he whispered and shook his head slowly. "No! If I had only been there. I stopped to put the tools away. I was putting tools away while . . ."

I pressed my hand over his mouth.

He let me hold him. But he was alone within my arms, his skin hot, his sweat sour. "Hush, Adam. Hush. I saw her too, by the tractor, talking to Frank, and I went back to the laundry . . ."

His eyes sought mine and held them for a long moment.

"Hush," he said. "She is gone."

⁂

HE SLEPT THAT NIGHT for fourteen hours straight. I sat up with the girls, the four of them packed into the bed Jennie and Lily had shared. We talked about everything except Jennie and what had happened after the funeral. I longed to protect them from what I'd seen on everyone's faces. And, yes, from their father's searing voice, the same voice I cherished so intimately. How much of A. was in them? They were normal girls. How much could that change?

I was alone in my questions.

Finally, when I could hear their four steady breaths, I turned off the lamp and left.

I stood in the dark dining room for a long time, listening to the new silence of my home. I thought of the street where I grew up, of Clarion, of the people I'd known all my life. Their voices, names, and faces so familiar to me, suddenly seemed alien. The town now knew that my husband was a stranger.

I crawled into bed with Adam, spooning up behind him and wrapping my arms around him. Gutted and skinned, I lay there in the pool of Jennie's absence and tried to hear what was coming.

All night, I dreamed of Jennie's eyes, so like Lil's and Momma's, receding under ice-blue water. The mingled vibrato of all the girls engulfed me. I was helpless and drowning. Out of my element.

After that night, Gracie and Rosie came to Lil and Sarah's room at bedtime. They sang the good-night songs that Adam no longer sang to them. When I heard them sing, I was haunted by the bargain I seemed to have made with them, by the voices they might have used.

Adam never spoke of it to me again.

To this day, I question my judgment. I regret my fear. I regret my silence.

∽

THE SUNDAY AFTER THE FUNERAL, Adam appeared early in the morning at the bedroom door, smelling of horses and hay, his face sallow and motionless. I hooked my garter belt to my stockings, smoothed my slip down, and took a deep breath. He made no move to get ready for church, just shook his head. Then he turned and left.

The small wave of relief I felt shamed me. I put my hand back under my slip to unfasten the garters and begin undressing. He was right. How could we do this? We were staggering, fresh amputees.

Then I stopped myself. I could not acquiesce to the fear and anger I had seen at the funeral.

I heard the girls rustling down the hall. "Hurry, girls!" I called to them. "Or we'll be late."

Sarah, who, like her father, had never cared if any of her clothes matched, wept when she could not find two pink socks. She stood in the hall, screaming and waving a single sock. Before I could get there, Gracie and Rosie ran to her. The three of them rummaged in her bureau drawers and pulled out socks until they found two that matched.

Moments later, I discovered Lil standing next to the closet she and Jennie had shared. She tugged her blue Sunday dress down over her belly. It bunched oddly at the sleeves and in the back. The collar of one of Jennie's favorite dresses, a purple-and-white cotton, peeked out at the neck. Lil spun quickly to face me. "I can do it. I'll get it," she said. She reached back, elbows high, and kept her eyes on me while she finished buttoning her dress. Once buttoned up, she quickly straightened the two collars, tucking the collar of Jennie's dress neatly under her own. Then she turned around for me to brush her hair.

"You look pretty in that dress, Lil."

She did not smile. In the mirror, she watched me pull her bright tumble of hair up into an orderly ponytail. We contemplated each other in the same mirror Addie and I had first looked at. There were no twins now.

An hour later, we pulled away from the backyard, the girls all combed, calm, and somber in their Sunday dresses. I glanced in the rearview mirror and saw a feather of dust rise from the dry yard. At the far end of the field, Adam, straight-backed and tall, drove the tractor. The disker cut the earth in a neat line that paralleled the distant trees.

We'd missed Sunday school and were among the last to enter for the sermon. Heads turned as we filed into our pew. I felt the congregation's eyes boring into my back.

Joe turned in the pew ahead of us and smiled quickly, a flash of genuine warmth and concern in his eyes. Beside him, Mary gave the girls a quick wave. Then both of them swept their eyes past us, obviously relieved to see that Adam was not there. Mary gave a subtle nod of approval and whispered to Joe. I remembered the stricken faces and the smell of vomit the week before. Suddenly, I thought I could smell it again and instinctively looked down at the clean floor.

Sarah pressed up close to me and sucked her thumb through the sermon. Gracie sat ramrod-straight, her arm around Lil, who stared ahead. Rosie fidgeted, rearranging her skirt and scuffing her shoes against the floor. Several times, I had to reach across the other girls and quiet her. I have no idea what the minister said.

After the sermon, people stepped aside as we passed by on our way out. On the church lawn, the girls did not linger, playing with the other children, but stayed near me.

I hadn't seen any of my family since the funeral. As we went down the church steps, Momma appeared suddenly at my side and touched my arm. "Y'all coming to dinner?"

I had nothing prepared for dinner. But my shoulders burned with exhaustion, my face was a mask. "No, Momma. I need to get the girls home to Adam."

Something unfamiliar flickered across my mother's face. She glanced down to make a quick, unnecessary adjustment to her purse.

"Bring them by soon, then," she squeezed my arm.

I drove the girls home, three of them in the front with me, and Rosie sprawled across the backseat. They sat quietly. As we pulled up into the backyard, I realized that none of them had mentioned their father or asked why he hadn't come to church with us. I shut the engine off.

"Momma." Gracie leaned forward so I could see her across her sisters. "I don't want to go to church anymore." She spoke softly, her face solemn and open, waiting for my response.

The others listened.

Then, from the backseat. "I don't want to either."

The thick, sweet burden of their need lay on me like lead. I took a breath and sat up straight. I still felt the burning stares of the congregation. Unbidden, unearned, shame flushed through me, followed by a shudder of defiance. I cleared my throat. "I'll think about it," I said. In our vocabulary, that meant an eventual, qualified yes.

People whose children have died do not believe in God the same way everyone else does. The death of a child is an earthquake of the soul. The landscape changes forever. I cannot say I was a believer at that time, but I knew that the church was a link that bound us to others. Now, I felt that link breaking. Did I have to let it break in order to protect my children? To do so seemed a kind of defeat, an admission that my daughters did not—could not—belong there. If they did not belong there, where they were born, where did they belong?

I decided that Gracie and Rosie could stay home from church most Sundays with their father. Special days and holidays, they would still have to attend services. In exchange, they had to cook the Sunday dinner. It would have to be ready to go onto the table when Sarah, Lil, and I returned from church. This seemed to be a reasonable compromise.

Later that week, I stopped by Momma's near suppertime. I expected to find her alone in the kitchen, making dinner for Daddy. But when the back door slapped shut behind me, the kitchen was empty. The distinct vinegary sweetness of Pearl's takeout ribs lingered. The theme from Momma's favorite TV show, *Jeopardy,* blared from the living room.

Momma stepped into the kitchen and dropped into one of the dining chairs as she motioned for me to help myself to the coffeepot and refill her cup. I dreaded telling her that we would not be coming to Sunday dinners after church.

When I told her, her brow wrinkled with concern. "Evelyn," she began. I expected a protest of some sort and perceived its beginning in her clipped delivery of my name. But something changed her mind. Her face softened. Instead of objecting, she sighed. "You might be right. Gracie and Rosie are old enough that they should be learning to cook for the family. That's a good idea."

Her quick concession shocked me. I swallowed my rehearsed defenses and reasons. As I remembered the pained shock on her face at the funeral, I tried to keep my own expression neutral. Helpless humiliation filled my throat.

"Your brother and sisters will be fine with this," she added firmly. "You all can take turns feeding your daddy and me each Sunday after church. We'll rotate among you and y'all can come here for Christmas and Easter." She grinned. "Maybe Thanksgiving if you play your cards right."

I heard the relief in her tone and I wondered if Joe, Bertie, or Rita had already had this discussion with her, maybe all of them. "Everybody else'll be okay with this?" I asked.

"Yes." She crossed her arms over her chest. She wouldn't be telling me who objected to having dinner with us. She'd always been the kind of mother who dampened rather than inflamed our tiffs and sibling rivalries. But when she leaned toward me across the table, her voice was low, confidential. "Evelyn. I'm tired. When all of you come with all of your kids, your husbands—that's more than a couple dozen people crammed into this little house. How about your daddy and I showing up next Sunday at your house? Get those girls cooking." She did look tired. Suddenly, I was embarrassed by my lack of concern for her and what all of this must have cost her. She had lost a grandchild.

Moments later, as I drove to Rhyne's store, Momma's agreement and my certainty that Joe, Bertie, or Rita didn't want us there for dinner plagued me. Bertie's disdain alone would have been easy to take; that was her standard response to most of life. But the thought of Joe or Rita wanting to avoid us jolted me. I stopped outside the store, determined for a moment to rush back to Momma's and demand to know more. But something in me collapsed, a reluctant finality that made me queasy. Everything seemed to be changing.

Inside the grocery store, every face was familiar. I knew each aisle and where to find everything on my short list. A man knelt to squeeze a loaf of bread on one of the lower shelves. Even from behind, I recognized his narrow head and the set of his shoulders. When I was a girl, his family had lived two streets over from Momma. His daughter had a gimpy leg from a fall off the shipping deck of the mill. She was Rosie's age. Did she know my girls? Had she been at the funeral?

The floor under me seemed to dissolve. I put a loaf of bread in my basket and headed toward the cashier.

As I drove back to Adam and the girls, the pink and yellow light of the sunset shed an unnatural, deeply shadowed light on the houses and fields.

I'd never been a woman to need or keep intimates. I'd always thought of myself as something of a loner, as likely to take solace from the glissando of a mockingbird as from the laughter of friends or family. With the secrecies of being A.'s lover then wife, I'd come to understand how much I relied on the small graces of those I knew but was not intimate with. I had my place among the people of Clarion. Their familiar faces and multiple acknowledgments fed my need to belong as much as the land did. Who would we—me, Adam, and our children—be here in Clarion now, if we went everywhere surrounded by silent questions? Who was he to these people now that they carried the memory of his darker voice in their bones?

I pulled up near the back door and unloaded the groceries. A horse whinnied inquisitively from the stable. I heard Adam's faint, muttered response. The mingled sounds of the girls—a guitar, the radio, and Sarah's call to her cat—filtered down the hall as I put away the groceries.

When I'd finished, I took a small empty jar out of the pantry and a hand trowel from the barn. I knelt on the spot where I had found A. and, breaking up the packed clay, scooped a handful of it into the jar. His origin. The only certainty I had. The thing that set me apart from him and bound me to him.

I put the jar on our bedroom bureau among our combs, nail files, and pocket change, next to my bobby-pin box. At night, it was one of the last things I saw before I turned out the light.

Supper the next Sunday was just Momma, Daddy, and the six of us at our house. The meal was cordial, almost formal. No one mentioned Jennie or the funeral. The girls did not ask where their cousins, aunts, and uncles were.

◡⌢

GRIEF IS A POWERFUL RIVER in flood. It cannot be argued or reasoned or wrestled down to an insignificant trickle. You must let it take you where it is going. When it pulls you under, all you can do is keep your eyes open for rocks and fallen trees, try not to panic, and stay faceup so you will know where the sky is. You will need that information later. Eventually, its waters calm and you will be on a shore far from where you began, raw and sore, but clean and as close to whole as you will ever be again.

Adam in his grief neither struggled nor floated. He took on weight and sank like a stone. His surrender was nearly total and his eyes went dead, the brightness of his gaze extinguished. At times, though, he would suddenly flash open, struggling as if grief could be gulped down entire in a single swallow. A puzzled, naked terror would streak across his face then, far beyond any consolation I could offer; he would stop where he was and weep.

I felt myself far downstream, tumbling along trying to keep the girls in sight. I could not reach him. For the first time since I found A. lying on his side in the mud, I felt alone. I did not know what to do.

I wanted him to hold fast to what was left—our four daughters and me—and not let go. I wanted us to stay afloat together. I saw his vacancy as a kind of desertion, as a deep disregard, not just for us, not just for the love that remained, but for life itself. I was afraid for him. I didn't know what he was capable of or how we would return to each other.

During the day, I was stunned into numbness. Lying in bed at night, I thought of how I could have prevented Jennie's death, imagining what might have been if I had called her to me instead of returning to that last sheet, stretching it out on the line, smoothing those inconsequential wrinkles while she climbed up on the tractor to join her drunken cousin. Helplessly, I replayed that day. Did she smell the whiskey and his sweat in that last breath she took before she fell and the disk swept across her body? Or did she smell the spring air, the sweet, clean odors of fresh-turned earth?

I allowed myself to consider the infinity of details that might have left Jennie alive. A change of weather the day she died, rain keeping the girls inside. One of us taking longer in the bathroom that morning and delaying Jennie's walk to the field. A broken washing machine and all the girls pitching in to help do laundry by hand. Sometimes my tracing of consequence and connection went back as far as the war. If Frank had not survived, Jennie would have. The possibilities were endless. I let myself comb through them in small increments. Such thoughts were madness and futility, but they vaulted me into anger and provided a respite from the daily numbness. Sometimes, those were the only thoughts that could engage me.

I did not share these musings with Adam. To speak would have unleashed an endless wail in me as well as him, I was sure. So I shut my mouth on what my heart needed to say. Adam and I learned a new vocabulary of silence.

The girls, in their raw youth, sustained me. They carried the absence of their sister, but they glowed, vibrating with life and health, even as they grieved. I had only to touch them or look at them to be given that. They did not cease being themselves.

Lil, of course, missed Jennie the most directly and actively. Her face often had the same emptied-out look that Adam had. Frequently, I found myself, out of habit, looking past her for Jennie. At times, I could hardly bear to look at her. She was a constant reminder then, as she would be for the rest of her life, of what Jennie would have been.

The twins' names had always been a single unit: Jennie-and-Lil; Lil-and-Jennie. Now we all stumbled on the lone syllable of Lil's name. It seemed too abrupt, a fresh wound each time we called her. And every time we stuttered there or paused before her name, Lil flinched.

Soon, the other girls and I began, spontaneously, to call her Lillian, a mouthful that had always seemed too much for a small child. Sarah, particularly, seemed to savor drawing out the full three syllables. Only Adam continued, without any change of inflection or timing, to call her Lil.

I found her once looking at herself in the bedroom mirror, chirping in the secret language she and Jennie had shared. She spoke back and forth in conspiratorial whispers as herself and then as Jennie. After several exchanges, her tone changed to tearful exasperation. When I moved, she caught sight of me in the mirror, froze in embarrassment, then collapsed in tears. "Momma, Momma!" I held her for a long time.

For a while, Lil adopted Sarah as her new twin. They frequently wore identical clothes, something she and Jennie had done only for special occasions. The matched clothes hung loosely on Sarah and stretched tight on Lil, who had grown since Jennie's death. She even let Sarah into the twins' "house."

But then one day at the breakfast table Sarah answered Lil in the twins' patois and Lil flew into a rage, screaming, "Don't say that, don't say that." It took me and Rosie both to pull her off her sister. That was the end of Sarah as a twin.

During the day, Sarah seemed the least affected by her sister's death, but she soon began to have nightmares, so frightened of the dark that she stood in the middle of her bed paralyzed, crying and refusing to leave her room. Often her cries woke me and Adam, and we brought her into our room. She crawled into the middle of our bed and clung to us. After a few minutes, her small, bony grip would loosen in sleep.

After Lil beat her away, Sarah began to spend more time with Gracie. They talked about what Jennie was doing in heaven, debating the merits of celestial activities as they collected things to take to the grave—a pretty ribbon, a dead butterfly, stale cookies.

Gracie, more womanly each day, bounced back and forth between a brooding darkness that cut her off from us and a tender solicitousness toward all her sisters. Every time she was alone with me, she told me of her dreams of Jennie.

Rosie, still a stick of a tomboy at thirteen, threw herself into school and the horses. Seldom mentioning Jennie directly, she talked constantly of college, never able to make up her mind if she should become a doctor or veterinarian. In spite of her efforts and interests, her grades flagged. Lack of concentration, her teachers said.

One afternoon, as I carried a basket of folded laundry down the hall, I passed Gracie and Rosie's room and heard Gracie say, "It'll be okay. They'll never know. I can fix it. See?"

Rosie answered her, "I don't want to. I bet nobody's asking him to put makeup on."

"You want Momma and Daddy to know?"

There was a pause.

"Okay, okay. Go ahead." Rosie sighed.

I made certain to be nearby when they came out of the room. Rosie had a thick swatch of makeup above her left eye, awkwardly blended into her hairline. I pretended I hadn't seen it.

We made it through supper without comment. Adam didn't notice. The scrape across her hand wasn't worth a comment. Minor injuries were part of the stables for her.

Later that evening, when I heard Rosie get out of the shower, I went into the bathroom. She tried to turn her face away, feigning sudden interest in drying her feet. But I waited until she sighed and turned to face me. The bruise on her face was bright blue, an ugly shiner, but there wasn't much swelling, and her eyes were clear. Another bruise darkened her shoulder.

"Gracie made me put the makeup on," she said.

"Put ice on it when you go to bed. It'll keep it from swelling."

"Yes, ma'am."

"And no more fights. Ignore what people say."

"I couldn't just stand there and let him say things about Daddy."

"What did he say?"

Her eyes darted around the bathroom.

"Tell me, Rosie."

"He said that Daddy hurt his momma. He claimed Daddy had to be 'of the devil' to hurt people while they were in church. He wouldn't shut up." Tears filled her eyes.

I put my arms around her and discovered that she had to bend slightly to lay her head on my shoulder. I remembered John Thompson's car veering toward the telephone pole after Addie spoke to him. "Be careful, Rosie. We don't need anything else to deal with right now."

She stiffened in my arms, broke our embrace. "I don't like people looking at us like that." Her voice hardened.

I touched her forehead, under the bruise. I felt as lacking in explanations as A. had been when he first arrived. A tender shame filled me; I had nothing to offer her. I could see no way to translate what I knew of her father into something her young hands could hold. Solemnly, she watched me as I lifted her hand to kiss her scraped knuckles.

"And the boy, how does he look?" I asked.

"Worse." She smiled.

I couldn't help myself. I smiled back.

I heard Rosie and Gracie in the bathroom later. Every morning, until the bruise dimmed to a barely visible yellow, Gracie covered it up, saving face.

After her bruises were gone, Rosie stayed constantly by Adam's side in the stable or on horseback. I wondered how Adam's dark grief might alter her affection for him. Part of her, I'm sure, yearned to ride away from the weight of familial grief and love.

Adam, I left to himself. I had little choice. Jennie's death had sharpened something in him and, to be honest, in me, too. We did not argue or have any direct conflicts, but contact seemed to involve small, invisible cuts. Each was not too painful, but the accumulation stung.

And so we all continued. We did our work. The girls finished the school year. The alfalfa and the garden came in well.

⸻ ❧ ⸻

SEVERAL TIMES AFTER THE FUNERAL, Marge had called to see how we were doing and tell me little bits of Clarion gossip. Her voice had the slightly hushed tones of taboo violation and genuine concern, but she never mentioned the Sunday night gathering of musicians at her and Freddie's house. And she never referred directly to Adam.

He hadn't played his fiddle or his guitar since the funeral. One day Gracie brought Adam's fiddle to me and laid the battered case in my hands. She tucked her hair behind her ears, a gesture that often preceded an important announcement on her part. "I talked to Marge. They're still having their regular Sunday picking party. She said Freddie would like to see Daddy there. And Grandma says it would be nice to see us one Sunday evening before we head over to Freddie's." Gracie, the diplomat. She didn't ask and she didn't say I'd fallen down on the job. She just tried to fix things.

The next Sunday, after dinner, I slipped Adam's fiddle into the trunk when we all piled into the car for an afternoon visit with Momma. Later, as we were saying good-bye to Momma, I shooed Lil and Sarah off down the road toward Marge and Freddie's. I got the fiddle out of the trunk and strolled toward Freddie's with it under my arm, Rosie by my side. I looked back over my shoulder to see Gracie tentatively grinning up at her daddy, her arm looped through his.

Sarah and Lil raced ahead of us and clambered up the steps and into the house. Marge's voice carried past the music, "Well, look who's here!"

She held the screen door open and nodded at Adam as he passed by, her familiar smile forced wider than usual.

The pickers crowding the kitchen watched as Adam entered. No one moved to offer him space. I felt a shriveling heat in my chest. Then Freddie stood. With a grave smile, he extended his hand to Adam. "Glad to see y'all back." He stepped aside, offering his chair. I was almost faint with gratitude for his simple gesture.

Adam sat, pulled his fiddle out of the case, and began tuning up. The other musicians shifted in their seats and plucked at strings.

The next tune began, a waltz. Adam paused, his bow above the strings a beat past everyone else, a distant look of concentration on his face. Then he plunged in. The tightness in my chest uncoiled a little.

Sarah grabbed Lil's hand to pull her into the living room to dance, but Lil pressed against my leg and swatted her away. Marge led Gracie into the small space left in the center of the kitchen. They waltzed through the living room, out to the front porch and back, with Rose and Sarah following in exaggerated dips and swirls. Gracie stood taller than Marge now. Her small breasts pressed above the full shelf of Marge's.

Soon Rosie would be budding, too. My girls' bodies would ferry them away from this time. An awful joy swelled in my throat and I had no skin, no bone between world and heart.

I wiped my face and picked up Lil, a barely manageable weight for me, and waltzed her across the room.

Gripping his fiddle, Adam played with his eyes closed. The waltz ended and we clapped.

As the next tune, "Pretty Polly," began, the girls, Marge, and I wandered off to the porch. The girls immediately vanished into the darkness, headed toward the mill. Their voices carried back to us. Marge and I sat in matching rockers.

"It's good to have y'all here. To see the girls dancing," Marge said after a moment. "How are you holding up, Evelyn? All of you?" The music wafted down the hall. I strained to keep one ear on the girls and listen for any falter in Adam's playing. But in Marge's question, I heard the now-familiar lilt that was more than simple condolences. Few people spoke to me those days. Those who did always asked the same question: "How are y'all doing?" But the questions not asked seemed to resonate in their voice: "What did he do? Will he do it again?"

"Fine. Fine," I usually answered. I'd hardly done more than exchange greetings with anyone outside of family since the funeral.

I looked at Marge's plump, sweet profile and wanted to bury my face in her neck and tell her that my husband seemed to be gone, that I saw how others looked at him now, a small, hard glance before their eyes slid over and away from him. I wanted to ask her how it could be that grief gutted me every day, yet my body remained whole and normal, un-bloodied. Instead, I said, "It's not easy, but we're all doing as well as can be expected."

She rubbed my hand and I saw in her face that same small surge of relief that I'd seen on others, curiosity followed by relief that I was not going to weep, not utter something terrible.

I wiped my eyes, took a deep breath, then I called the girls onto the porch.

When we got back to the kitchen, everyone sat with their instruments in their laps, their eyes on Adam. He stood at the edge of their circle, bow poised. My pulse quickened. He gave me a glance I could not read. As his eyes skipped across the girls' faces, he played the first notes of "When Johnny Comes Marching Home Again" at a dirge-like tempo. The other musicians picked up.

Rosie was the first to begin singing. Soon Gracie joined her singing, then Sarah and Lil. They faced their father as they sang. He bent slightly at the waist, swaying. The natural harmony of the girls' voices and the mournful tempo filled the room. "Hurrah. Hurrah."

After the first verse, only Freddie continued playing with Adam; the others lowered their instruments. When the last note ended, no one moved. Adam bowed to the girls. Marge cleared her throat and said, "That was pretty, real pretty, girls. Adam."

Then someone announced "Haste to the Wedding." The lively jig sprang up and the room returned to itself. Adam nodded good-bye to Freddie and put his fiddle away. I waved to Marge and corralled the girls toward the door.

Marge followed and stopped us on the steps, her eyes shining. "That was some of the prettiest singing I've heard in a long time. Where've you been keeping those voices? Come sing something at Sunday school next week."

On the way home, the girls debated Marge's proposal. Neither Gracie nor Rosie wanted to give up their new freedom from church. Lil thought it was a good idea, but wanted to sing her favorites from *West Side Story*. Sarah, who'd been silent during her sisters' discussion, ended the debate with a single pronouncement: "If they're going to stare at us anyway, let's give 'em a good reason." She looked up at Adam. "If we're singing in church, you'll come listen to us?"

He cupped her head, smoothing her hair. "I'll always be there when y'all are singing."

The girls sang first at Sunday school services, visiting a different class in the children's group each week. Depending on what part of the church they were in, I heard them as I sat in my adult class, their close sister harmony resonating down the church halls. My heart beat faster when I heard them, even at home when they practiced.

❧

AT LEAST SUPERFICIALLY, my family ignored what they now knew about Adam, as they had ignored the obvious fact that Addie's father was not who she and I claimed him to be. Her situation had been beyond her control, an old story with easily traceable motives. She was clearly a relative and treated as such. Adam, on the other hand, had transgressed in an inexplicable, willful, and literally painful way. No one confronted him, but there was a short pause, an intake of breath, when he walked into a room.

Momma continued to welcome us with unaltered enthusiasm. On the rare occasions now when we were all at her house with my brother and sisters, Momma's presence tempered Bertie's judgmental chill. Joe retreated into a kind of jovial formality. Rita never quite lost that startled look around Adam, actually flinching if he spoke with any suddenness or volume. Only Daddy seemed completely unaffected, his smoking and rocking habits uninterrupted.

Momma was the only one to ever ask me outright about what happened at Jennie's funeral. We were on the front porch, shelling the first of the white acre peas. All of the girls were out of earshot. Momma leaned over and looked straight into my face. "Evelyn, do you understand what happened at the funeral? Has Adam ever done anything like that before?" Her hands were still as she waited for my response.

For the first time in years, I felt the urge to tell Momma the truth about Addie and Adam. But I couldn't face the possibility that she would not believe me, that she would think I was crazy. The truth seemed too fantastic for the porch we sat on, for the peas we shelled. I pushed away the urge to confide and wiped my tears. "No, Momma, I don't know what happened. Adam didn't mean to hurt anyone."

"I know that. That should be clear to anybody. He was just hurting so much himself. I swear, though, I've never felt anything like that in my life and I hope never to again. Hurt so bad I thought my chest would burst. If it had been anyone but Adam, I'd've run out of the church and never come back. I've heard of people speaking in tongues, but I've never heard of anything like that—and how it hurt! It was a peculiar thing." She pressed one hand against her ear.

I nodded my agreement.

Then she told me her news: "A doctor's appointment."

I should have paid attention to that phrase. Momma, like most in her generation, rarely went to see a doctor, only if she was very sick. But when I asked her what was wrong, she waved her hand, dismissing my concern. "I'm bleeding like it's my monthly. It doesn't come regular. You know I went through the change years ago, before Sarah was born. Now it's back. I feel fine. I just want to know if I should be keeping your father on his side of the bed."

We laughed.

Jennie's death overshadowed everything then. Grief gutted me, and I relied on Momma.

I was erratic, hugging the girls, afraid to let them out of the house one minute and oblivious to their presence the next. Adam was the same. Momma became our anchor, our consistency. She spent as much time as she could on the farm, and, when she was not there, I knew I could call her. The girls were reluctant to go home when we were at her house and to see her leave when she visited the farm.

So, that day, months after Jennie's funeral, when we sat on the porch shelling peas and Momma announced that she'd decided to see the doctor, I took little notice and felt no alarm. She'd always been there. My fears were centered on the girls and Adam and what I could not say about or to them. I didn't look further for more to fear or grieve.

I heard nothing else about her doctor's visit until the evening Daddy called to tell me that the doctor had sent Momma straight to the hospital. "Female troubles," he said. "A tumor. They're taking everything out."

During the week after her surgery, Momma spent most days in a painful stupor on the couch in front of the TV. But after her bath one day, she asked me to help her into her newly made bed.

Rita had stopped by earlier with clean bed linens and a pot roast for Momma and Daddy's dinner. Daddy's shift at the mill would not end for hours. Momma and I were alone. To pass the time and distract her from her pain, she wanted to organize an old shoe box of photos.

She studied a black-and-white photo of me and Addie, taken not long before Addie left with Roy and came back to be my husband. Joe had been the first to arrive one morning to help pull a field of corn. He'd shot the photo to finish off a roll of film he wanted to get developed. In the snapshot, Addie and I stood shoulder to shoulder, smiling into the early morning sun and leaning back against the garden fence by the barn. Addie's hat threw a shadow across her right eye. My hair hung down past my shoulders.

I'd not seen the picture in years. I remembered Joe corralling us out of the barn, the morning dew still a web of diamonds on the grass, and the press of Addie's warm arm at my side. Longing streaked through me, not so much for Addie but for that time of simplicity and innocence, a time when there was just the land, the seasons, and inexplicable Addie to reckon with—no babies, no death. Behind us in the photograph, between our two heads, the old apple tree and the place where I found her were visible.

Momma handed the picture to me. "You were like two peas in a pod. It was uncanny. I wonder if she ever found out who her daddy was. I sure couldn't figure which of my brothers or cousins your aunt Doris had been with. Never a peep out of the men. That poor Hardin boy must have been surprised when Addie popped out with all that red hair." She gave me a wry smile. "The women on both sides of the family were a little too inclined to follow their hearts instead of using common sense . . . or maybe they—we—were following some other organ." She laughed at her insinuation and patted my hand. "I'm glad I never saw any of that in you. You were always sensible. You did the right thing."

"Momma, I never wanted lying . . ." I heard the words come out of my own mouth and didn't know what I would say next. I wanted so much to tell her about Addie, to have her with me in that secret.

She grimaced in what I took to be pain but then realized was shame, a thing I'd never seen on her face. "I wanted to tell you years ago. Many a time I came near. But I didn't have the courage, Evelyn."

Apprehension blossomed in my chest. "Momma what do you know? Tell me." I took her hand.

"Forgive me, Evelyn. I would have told you, but Robert always said we should let sleeping dogs lie. So the dog just lay and the years passed." Her face twisted in genuine pain. She pointed to the bottle on her bureau. "Give me another one of those morphine pills."

After she swallowed, she eased back onto her pillows again and looked out the window. I waited, my throat tight, my heart clattering.

She slapped her palms down on the covers so hard I jumped. "There was this boy . . . a man really, but he couldn't have been much older than me—twenty-one, twenty-two at the most. They were putting in the new sidewalks and parks downtown. Building the new Piedmont Hotel. Things were hopping around here before the Crash and the Depression.

"Your daddy was courting me then. Growing up in the same town, he'd always been around. But he'd begun to be around more. Making eyes at me. Walking me home from work. Not serious courting. The Starnes boy was doing the same. But I liked your daddy best. He was sweet on me. I could see it in his eyes. I'd never seen him around any other girls, and I knew that whatever was going to happen would be slow in coming. Things weren't like they are today, but even for those times your daddy was a slow mover, a shy one.

"I was only seventeen, but I'd been a spinner at the mill since we left the farm. I earned more than my brothers and had to work, we needed the money. But I thought a hotel might be better work. So one day, I ran over to the Piedmont right after work to see if they would be hiring women help. Outside, the hotel looked finished, but inside the walls were bare, no mantels, no trim, no lights. A man stood inside the front door, holding some blueprints up to the dying sunlight. A fine-looking man. Dark hair, smoothest skin. And tall—six three, maybe six four. He looked up from those blueprints, and I felt like somebody had slapped me awake.

"I didn't get a job. But a few days later, when I walked past the Piedmont on my way to the drugstore to get headache powders for Momma, he walked partway with me and introduced himself. Ben Mullins. He talked about places I'd never been. He seemed more of a man than the teenage boys hanging around. He was a carpenter from Raleigh. After the Piedmont job, he was going to work on a big hotel in Atlanta."

She paused and took a deep breath. Fatigue filled her face, but her voice rang stronger, more determined.

"Well, Evelyn, the upshot of what you really need to know is that I slept with him." She stopped again to register my surprise.

Why, I wondered, was she telling me this? What did any of this have to do with Addie or Adam?

"We snuck into his room—the first room finished in the hotel. If you went up the back stairs his room was the first door on the second floor. Fancy pink wallpaper on the walls, a nice room.

"He smoked and talked, asking me questions and laughing at some of my answers—but not in a way that put me down. There were books in the room, some open on the bed. He didn't touch me. When I left, he kissed me on the cheek, gentlemanly. 'Come back whenever you want. It's lonely here.'

"I went back as soon as I could get away. One thing led to another and we were on his bed. Afterward, he was all apologetic. He went out and brought pie back to the room for me. I came to his room only one other time." She'd been looking out the window as if something outside drew her words out of her. But now she turned back to me with renewed urgency.

"He was not a bad man, Evelyn. He was just being a man. He was gentle with me. And I was willing though I knew he'd be moving on to another job when the hotel was finished. But I thought we had more time. Then one day, the hotel was done and he was gone. The place looked like a palace. When I went in and asked about him, a woman at the counter sneered down at my old dress and the cotton stuck to my sleeves, opened a big ledger, and said, 'There is no Mr. Mullins here.'"

I leaned back in my chair, wondering if Momma's mind was going. Why would she want me to know about her sex life? She'd already told me she was not a virgin when she married. I glanced at the photo of me and Addie.

She continued without pause. "I cried and cried. I mended my little broken heart as best I could and accepted your daddy's invitation to his family reunion. Ben and I'd been discreet. The hotel had been empty. I'm sure no one saw me coming or going when I went to his room. But someone must have seen us when he walked me to the store. Your daddy was suddenly a lot less shy. Even before Ben left town, Robert had started coming by almost every day.

"Pretty soon—just a week or two after Ben left, your daddy was already hinting about us getting serious. I didn't encourage him but I didn't discourage him either.

"One evening, he strolled up the street with a handful of flowers he'd picked. While I waited for him on the porch, it suddenly hit me that I had not had my monthly since Ben Mullins left town.

"We walked down past the grinding mill to the bridge—our usual evening stroll. I was trying not to cry and he kept asking me what was wrong. I told him about Ben and me. His face was awful—shocked, disappointed, hurt. 'I'll find the bastard!' he said. 'Find him and kill him!' Then I really started wailing, crying about how my daddy would kill me. Bastard kids just did not happen then. Women in that kind of trouble married the daddy or they got out of town." Momma stopped, smoothed the covers. When her eyes met mine, I realized with a start that she was waiting for me to say something. She wanted forgiveness.

"Momma, did you get rid of the baby?" I whispered.

"Good Lord, no! I didn't even know that was possible then. This was nineteen twenty-five, Evelyn. That was you on the way! What I'm trying to tell you is that Ben Mullins is your father, not Robert Roe."

I stared at the bedspread, feeling what she said flush through me. I couldn't move.

"Your daddy is your daddy, Evelyn. He raised you. He was back the next day asking me to marry him. I didn't have to run off like Addie's momma. You were able to grow up here and know my people. Robert never again mentioned Ben to me or to anyone else that I know of and he claimed you as his own, never treating you any different from your brother and sisters."

She took my hand in both of hers, pulling me out of my daze. "I'm so sorry, Evelyn. For years I was so ashamed, so grateful to your father." She cried, her fragile shoulders shaking, her face pale. I held her and we rocked gently.

Then she wiped her eyes. "I took your daddy for a husband though I didn't love him, not at first. But by the time you were born, I was crazy for Robert Roe. It was a fuller love, a woman's instead of a girl's love. That's why Joe came so soon after you." She stroked my hair. "Good thing you looked like me and had the McMurrough's red hair." Her hand stopped at my temple. "Evelyn? You understand what I am telling you?"

Her hair, dimmed lately to the color of pale straw, framed her face. Suddenly, I saw her face as a young woman's again, her hair a brilliant copper as when she'd once swept me up out of the creek and held me, dripping wet, in her extended arms. She'd looked at me then as if I was a stranger, unknown to her. Then the awful wailing as she held me close. For decades, I'd thought that moment was about me, but it was about *him*. I thought I was the stranger, but he was the one she did not know. She'd been looking for him in me! All my life, she'd seen the shadow of another person on me. And she'd never spoken his name to me. At that moment, I did not know her. She seemed smaller now, a frailer version of her old self, as if the surgeons had taken more than her womb and ovaries. Her skin glowed soft and translucent.

I lied: "It's okay, Momma. It doesn't change anything."

Relief brightened her eyes.

I held her face in my hands and looked straight into her eyes. "I have a good daddy. You gave me a good daddy." She relaxed back against the pillows, her face calmer.

The picture of me and Addie still rested on the pile of photos. Stunned, I put my head in Momma's lap and wept for her, for my two fathers, and for all the things that never get said or known.

SEVEN

FLOOD

Within a few weeks, Momma returned to her shift at the mill. We urged her to retire, but she insisted she wanted to go back to work. She looked smaller and older. The dark circles remained under her eyes. The differences in her appearance seemed to me to be indications, not only of the change in her health, but signs of a new momma sprung from her revelation about my father.

With self-conscious discretion, I observed the faces of my brother and sisters for similarities to Momma and Daddy. Joe looked the most like Daddy, same dark hair, brown eyes, and receding hairline. The same lumbering gait. Bertie was stocky, like Daddy and Joe, but had Momma's height and complexion. Rita was the most slender and graceful, with straight red hair and fair skin. With a hand mirror, I studied my own profile. I looked like my mother. The planes of my face from cheek to jaw might have been slightly different from hers, my face maybe longer, more oval. I had fewer freckles and my hands were bigger. Those things had always been true. Nothing had changed except what I now knew. My inspections always left me with emotional vertigo.

With the farm, four kids, and the bookkeeping for our horse business, I spent little time in Clarion, and always combined errands with visits to Momma's. Since the funeral, I was less comfortable in town. I wanted to avoid every set of eyes there. And it seemed especially important to be home each day when the girls returned from school. But after Momma's revelation, I made more frequent trips to town during the school day, looking for every opportunity to be alone with her. Always someone else seemed to be within earshot—Daddy, my brother, or one of sisters. My aunts and uncles came by more often, too.

One weekday evening, I drove into town to bring Momma some of my peach jam, her favorite. I found her alone in the kitchen washing the supper dishes. Daddy and Joe were in the yard, deep under the hood of Joe's truck.

Her back looked more delicate than I was accustomed to, and it wasn't like her to not notice when someone came into the room. She jumped in surprise, then smiled when I pulled a dish towel out of the kitchen drawer. "Sneaking up on me, huh?"

I began drying the dishes stacked in the drainer.

Before I could speak, she said, "If anything ever happens to me and your daddy, I want your sisters and Joe to have the furniture and the cars." Her voice was soft and thoughtful. I'd obviously interrupted her reverie about these things.

"What?" I didn't want our conversation to go there. I didn't want to think about anything more happening to her.

"We gave you and Adam the farm. We don't have anything comparable for them. It would only be fair."

"And we're very, very grateful for the farm, Momma. Because of the farm, we don't need another car or more furniture." To my own ears, my voice sounded stilted and thick.

She heard the change of direction in my tone. The platter she was handing me stopped above my hand.

I took the platter and continued, "Why didn't you ever tell me before?"

Momma's hands dropped into the soapy water. She shook her head. "I know I should have told you sooner. First, you were just too young. And there were times when you were a little girl, you already seemed to know. You were always wandering off by yourself as if you were looking for something or somebody. For years, I convinced myself you already did, somehow, know. Your daddy didn't think it would do any good to tell you."

"Daddy didn't want me to know?" I fought the impulse to take her by the shoulders and shout, "How could you have kept it from me for so many years? How?" But something in her posture stopped me.

"Evelyn, I didn't want you to feel you were different from Joe, Bertie, and Rita. I wanted you to feel you belonged to both of us—I owed that to him, if he was willing to take on the responsibility of raising you. Then you got older, I was afraid of what you would think of me." I heard both a mild challenge and a plea in the firmness of her voice.

As I held her gaze, I heard Daddy and Joe laughing as their footsteps approached.

"You'll have to forgive me," Momma whispered. As they walked into the kitchen, she turned back to the dishes, tears in her eyes.

DAYS LATER, I WENT INTO TOWN with Adam one day and asked him to drive by Momma's house on the way to the feed store. I knew Momma would be home from the mill by then and when I saw that Daddy's car was gone and the back door open, I had Adam drop me off. I gave him the grocery list. "After the feed store, pick up these things, then come back for me," I said as I slipped out of the truck.

I usually did the grocery shopping, but Adam took the list and nodded without comment.

I hoped to find Momma alone. The house was so quiet and still, for a moment I thought no one was home. Then I saw Bertie sitting at the kitchen table sipping coffee. She'd recently dyed her auburn hair blond and the new color unsettled me. A magazine lay open in front of her, and her daughter, Susie, slept sprawled in her lap, legs and arms dangling.

Nothing in the house moved except her hand flipping the magazine pages and then stopping to bring the cup up to her lips.

Her head jerked up when I stepped from the back porch into the kitchen. I saw the pinched look on her face as she took in the surprise of me being there.

"What is it?" I asked. "Where's Momma?"

Bertie nodded her head in the direction of the bedroom. "I checked on her a few minutes ago. She was still sleeping." She went back to her magazine. The pages made a soft, rasping sound as she flicked through them. Otherwise, the room was so quiet I could hear myself swallow. The afternoon air brimmed, still and humid.

I tiptoed into Momma's room. She lay on her side of the bed, facing the window. I walked around the bed. Her face hung slack and gray. A bucket sat on the floor next to her. I touched her forehead; it was cool and moist. I went back to the kitchen.

"How long has this been going on? I thought she was getting better." I stood behind Bertie as I poured myself a cup of coffee.

She twisted around in her chair, scowling. Susie stirred on her lap. Despite the pleasure Bertie took in delivering news, she always seemed annoyed at others' complementary ignorance. "At least a week. If you were around more, you'd know. Daddy says she didn't want to worry us. I've been coming by every day this week and checking on her after her shift is over. She's always lying down. She must come straight home from work and go to bed. Every day. Daddy's been getting supper for them at Bun's Café."

I went back in and checked on Momma again. Her skin didn't look right. Adam's truck pulled up, and then the screen door squeaked.

"She's in there," I heard Bertie say. She'd hardly said a word to him since the funeral.

He appeared beside me, studied Momma's face, and glanced at the bucket. Then he touched her forehead just as I had. Momma had always been a light sleeper, but she did not stir.

Adam looked at me then, ran his eyes over my features the way he used to, but his face was sad. "I'm sorry, Evelyn," he whispered.

We walked arm in arm back into the kitchen. Susie was awake now, her head still hanging over her momma's arm, and she grinned upside down at Adam and waved. "Hey, Uncle Adam." She hadn't been at the funeral.

Bertie pulled out a pack of Pall Malls and lit one. "I'll bring a meat loaf and some potatoes over tonight and some of the field peas you canned for us."

She looked at me expectantly while Susie climbed down from her lap. But I just stood there stupidly. I shivered with the sudden under-standing that I'd been so wrapped up in my own problems that I hadn't seen the obvious: the surgeons hadn't gotten all the cancer.

Bertie got up, tapped her cigarette ash into the sink, and stared at me.

Adam rubbed Susie's back as she hugged his leg. "We'll bring some-thing by tomorrow for their dinner. Anything in particular bothering her stomach?" he asked.

Bertie directed her answer at me as she beckoned Susie. "Not that I've heard. Maybe if she has some decent food, she'll be able to keep it down. She needed more time to rest after the surgery. Y'all can go on. I'll stay with her till Daddy gets back." Her voice was thick and soft as she began braiding her daughter's hair.

Somehow, I got out to the car. We rode home in silence.

It had begun.

Momma seemed to give up once we started taking care of her every day. A few days later, Daddy rushed her to the emergency room. The word "cancer" invaded our vocabulary. "Inoperable" remained the whispered obscenity. Each day, one of us went by to stay with her and make dinner for them.

I went to Momma's almost every day. But we were never alone. Once the neighbors heard she was sick again, they began bringing dishes of food.

Finally, one sunny afternoon, she and I were alone. Daddy was at work. I didn't expect Adam to pick me up for another hour. Rita would be by then to bathe Momma and make dinner.

Rail-thin now, Momma chilled easily and preferred hot tea instead of iced tea. I heard her restless moans as I waited in the kitchen for her tea to steep. I set a glass and fresh pitcher of water on the tray with her cup of tea and carried it to her room. The doctors had recently upped the dosage on her pain medication and she asked for it every four hours on the dot.

Swallowing pills had become difficult for her; she was on liquid morphine. She opened her mouth like a child as I held the full table-spoon out and she took it hungrily. She scowled patiently, waiting for the morphine's effects. The unhealthy prominence of her cheekbones seemed like a rebuke to my list of questions about my father.

I waited for the drug's effects. Lately, it seemed to make her less drowsy, as if the pain now sopped up the morphine's peripheral effects. After a few moments, her body relaxed, but her eyes retained a vigilant brightness, as if she anticipated the pain's immediate return.

For weeks, I had questions ready for her, polished and clear, but suddenly they seemed a jumble caught between two simple sentiments: How could she have kept my father's name from me for so long? What else had she not told me?

I settled the blanket up around her chest and startled at the sound of footsteps on the back porch.

Momma turned her head slowly and smiled weakly at Adam as he paused in the bedroom doorway. I stifled a disappointed moan. My opportunity was gone. I had not told Adam Momma's news.

"I'm early, but I thought I'd . . ." he apologized.

Momma patted the bedspread beside her and Adam sat on Daddy's side of the bed.

My thwarted questions filled my throat. Everything I did not understand about both Momma and Adam seemed to congeal into one spot in my chest.

I fought my tears and swallowed. Then my frustration gave way, surrendering to his presence. "Adam, go back out and check to make sure no one else is in the house. Check the driveway. The front door, too. Make sure there's no one on the way."

He glanced quickly at Momma. Her shoulder moved slightly, suggesting a shrug.

"Go on," I said. "Then come back in here with us."

Momma held my gaze while we listened to Adam's footsteps echo the length of the silent house.

When he came back into the bedroom, I offered him my chair next to Momma's side of the bed. Still puzzled, he sat and looked up at me.

I leaned over Adam's shoulder, picked up Momma's hand, and put it in his. "Go ahead." I tapped him on the chest. "Show her."

His eyes searched my face, not understanding.

"All she's known is the pain of your voice. And she's in pain now."

"Evelyn I can't change that."

"I know. But she should know you. Let her hear who you are. And it will soothe her."

His face softened.

Momma frowned at me, confused, then looked to Adam as he placed her hand on his breastbone and covered it with both of his. His lips parted in a gentle "ahh."

As I closed the bedroom door behind me, the first wave resonated sweetly across the room.

In the kitchen, I poured myself a cup of coffee. My hands shook slightly.

The distinct, sweet tonal waves of Adam's voice rose and fell in the rhythms of a long, slow heartbeat. More complex than what he had done with the girls in the mountains, this song swelled with an optimistic sadness and receded in tender resignation.

Outside, early afternoon brilliance filled the empty streets and yards of the mill-village. All the children were in school, the same schools I had gone to. The mill hummed. All the night-shift mill workers were home sleeping. Beyond the mill lay downtown Clarion and the farm, more land, hills, then the mountains. So many different voices.

I paced the house with deliberate quietness, looking out the front door and then the back door, stopping once outside of Momma's bedroom to place my hand on the door and feel the vibration of his voice through the wood.

Slowly, Adam's song receded, as if gradually absorbed by the air. Stillness filled the house.

When I returned to the bedroom, Momma sat upright and they embraced chest to chest. Her arms circled Adam loosely. He supported Momma's back and cupped her head as he lay her back down on the pillows. She seemed to fall asleep immediately, a small, relaxed smile on her lips. Tears streaked down Adam's face. We tiptoed out.

Back in the kitchen, Adam wiped his eyes and took a deep breath. "She is leaving soon." A hard sorrow deepened his voice.

"Did she say anything?"

"Not a word. Neither of us."

Rita's car appeared in the driveway, sunlight flashing off the windshield.

"I'll wait for you in the truck," he said.

Rita shot a wary glance at Adam as they passed each other on the porch. Neither spoke.

"She's had a good day," I told Rita as I gathered up my purse.

༄

MOMMA DIED QUIETLY in her sleep five days later. She and I never had another moment alone when she was awake and coherent. We never discussed Ben Mullins again or the time she spent alone with Adam. Once, as she drifted off into a morphine drowse, she rolled her head on the pillow and looked over at me. "You've had your secrets, too." That was the last clear statement she made to me.

What do we ever know of our mothers? I thought I knew her. But I'd seen her as a child sees a good mother—pure, transparent, incapable of deception.

She was the only person I ever really wanted to tell about Adam, the only one I felt ashamed of lying to. I never got to tell her I forgave her. I never got to ask for a map to help me through the terrain of my own secrets, my own marital bargains.

❧

I TRIED TO SET ASIDE what Momma had told me while we prepared for her funeral. But I felt the current of it run through me when I was near my father, brother, and sisters. My eyes kept wandering over their features, not just for the similarities and differences between us, but for what they knew. I gained nothing by my scrutiny. All I saw in their faces was a mirror of my own grief.

The speed of her death surprised us all. She'd never been sick before. We thought we'd have her for months longer. Rita, who had held on to the certainty that Momma would get better, collapsed in on herself, her face vague. Daddy fell into a constant stupor. Joe, Bertie, and I made arrangements for the viewing and the funeral. We kept it simple, the way Momma would have wanted it.

Then Bertie called. As I drove to Momma's house, my anxiety centered on Adam. I also wondered if Momma had said anything to them. Maybe Daddy had told them I was their half-sister. Maybe they wanted to discuss that. At best, I hoped to hear about some disagreement be-

tween them, something that didn't involve me at all. But Joe stood on
her porch and held the door open for me when I got out of the car. The
apology on his face ended my suspense. We were there to discuss Adam.

Bertie sat at the kitchen table, drinking coffee. Joe poured two more
cups and set them in the pool of yellow morning light on the checkered
tablecloth. He turned a chair around and straddled its back. Neither of
them met my eye.

When Joe took a deep breath to begin, I held up my hand to stop
him and both of them looked at me, waiting. I gripped my coffee cup.
"I think my family needs a private viewing before the funeral," I said.

Joe nodded. Bertie lit a cigarette and leaned back, her jaw flexing.

I continued, "No surprises this time." I shook my head and bit my
lip. I thought of that force in Adam, that horrible cry. I knew no way to
hold that at bay.

Joe patted my hand. "That would be good, sis."

I began to cry.

"Damn good." Bertie sucked on her cigarette and went to the stove
to fill her cup again.

I wiped my face. "But I do want us to be able to say good-bye to
Momma. All of us."

Bertie turned at the stove and gave me her hard, quizzical look.

"Don't worry," I said. "I'll take care of it. I'll talk to the funeral home
and the preacher. Arrange for us to go to the church early in the morning and view the body. It'll just be me and the girls at the funeral," I
said.

Joe rubbed my hand. "Don't worry about it. It'll be okay, Evelyn."

Bertie shook her head. "I don't want Momma's funeral ruined. I don't
want Adam——"

"Bertie! She's agreeing!" Joe shushed her.

Silence followed. Bertie stood up and cleared the table, clattering our
coffee cups into the sink.

I blew my nose. "One other thing. Something I want." I waited for Bertie to finish with the dishes. I wanted to make sure I had her attention. "I don't want to see Frank at the funeral. Just thinking about him . . ." And for a second I saw Frank, his blank animal stare as he looked down at Jennie on the ground.

Joe nodded several times. "Sure, sure."

Bertie shrugged. "Keeping Frank out of a church will not be a problem."

"Mary's never liked him. Says he gives her the willies," Joe added.

I dreaded telling Adam about my family's plans to keep him away from the funeral of the only mother he'd ever known. I did so cowardly, in bed, in the darkness.

"That's a good solution. I can't guarantee that it won't happen again," he responded.

"You don't have to go at all, if you don't want to, Adam."

He lay beside me, taut.

Since Jennie's death, he'd held himself back in everything, even with me. Days went by without intimacy. Then he would turn silently to me in the dark, not out of love but out of need, and there was a fierceness to his touch that overwhelmed me. We went at each other as if the hounds of hell were after us. Or we were the hounds themselves. The act was not lovemaking, but grief-making, a new beast manifest, without tenderness, raw and exhausting, throwing us into black, dreamless sleep. His sweet tones seemed to have died with Jennie. His climax came with a simple shuddering moan.

But that night, after I told him about the arrangements for Momma's funeral, I turned him on his back and began to touch him with our former delicacy. He took my hand and moved it off of his chest.

"No," I said, pinned his wrist to the bed, and began tracing his breastbone with my other hand. I touched every part of him, my hands open against his smoothness. He did not move again to stop me, but lay rigid before me.

I knew him well. And I took him. Eventually, he pressed up to meet me, and his voice rose as sharp and dark as it had been at Jennie's funeral, though, thankfully, far less intense and much briefer. My breastbone and temples rang painfully. Afterward, we did not sleep but lay next to each other in the sudden cool of our sweat.

❧

WE DECIDED THAT ADAM AND I would skip the wake and he would have his own private viewing of Momma's body early on the morning of the funeral.

I woke in the middle of the night before the funeral, Adam alert beside me.

"We could go now. We don't have to wait for daylight," I said.

We began to dress. I went to the closet, but Adam reached for his dungarees. "She wouldn't mind," he said. "And no one else will be there."

I hung my skirt back on the hanger and put on a pair of pants and an old sweater.

We drove to the church in silence. A train whistled in the distance. Mist slid over the fields near the church. The ground sparkled white under the streetlights with the first frost of the season.

All churches were left unlocked back then, refuges for sudden repenters. We walked in quietly, as if trying not to disturb anyone. Faint moonlight diffused through the yellow glass windows. Being in the church at such an odd hour felt both sinful and holy.

Momma's coffin sat in front of the pulpit, the lid shut. I went to turn on the lights while Adam opened the coffin. The electric light brought the room back to its ordinary self.

I'd seen her the day before at the funeral home, but this was Adam's first time seeing her. She didn't look like herself. She had lost so much weight in the last weeks. Her face had a strained, unnatural look. Only her hands were unchanged. All my life, I had seen those hands moving, giving me the world. Now they lay stilled.

"Momma," Adam said, touching her hands. "Good-bye, Momma." He leaned over and kissed her on the forehead. I was acutely aware of him beside me, his ragged breath, his sweat. I braced myself for his howl.

But he remained silent. After a while, he turned and faced the pews. He leaned over and gripped the back of the first pew. His shoulders tightened. He looked so alone, the dark rows of empty seats in front of him. I thought of the faces that would fill the church later in the day, the people we were avoiding. I pressed my hand between his shoulder blades and readied myself. He took a sharp, deep breath.

There was no horrid cry. Instead, he fell to his knees and wept like an ordinary man, his head on the hard wood of the pew. We held each other for a long time. Then we went home.

He did not go to bed, though it was still hours until dawn; instead he began to pack. "I'm going up into the mountains," he announced.

I wanted to stop him, to insist he not go, but I saw the faraway look on his face. He was already gone.

While I packed some food for him, he went to say good-bye to the girls. Rosie's voice rose in protest then fell again as he soothed her.

"Adam." I took his arm as he passed.

"It'll just be a couple of days. Call Wallace for me. Let him know he may need Cleatus's help for the next few days."

Then he left.

My anger at death splintered into a brittle rage toward those people in the congregation who had turned against Adam. I could not allow myself such brittleness. I could not afford to break: my daughters slept down the hall. I lay in bed, comforting myself with images of Adam in the forest, howling his strange songs to an audience of receptive wildlife. I remembered the radiance of his face when he'd told me about his mountain trips and how the mountain returned his calls. I hoped it did this time. I wished that solace for him.

I must have slept, for I woke to the gentle percolation of the coffee-pot. Adam sat at the kitchen table, a cup in front of him.

"You haven't left yet?"

"No, I'll go after the funeral. The truck is packed. I got a few miles down the road then turned around . . . the girls . . . She was their grand-mother. I should be there with them."

"You want to come to the funeral?" I held the coffeepot over my empty cup.

"Yes, I should sit with them. I am their father." He did not look at me. "But . . ."

He shook his head. "You told me they'll be singing at the funeral and I told them I'd always be there when they sang."

I remembered his face in the barn after Jennie's funeral, when I had silenced him with the girls. I did not press him further.

⁓

CARS PACKED THE CHURCH PARKING LOT. Momma had lived all of her life in Clarion. The bereaved family is always the focus of a funeral, but I felt the extra stir of attention as we entered the church, Adam first with Sarah holding his hand. I braced myself against the stares and kept my eyes steady on Adam's shoulders above Gracie and Rosie's. Lil clutched my hand.

The funeral home usher stopped Adam halfway down the aisle. My heart pounded so hard, I coughed. But the usher nodded and led us to the second pew. Daddy sat in the front pew between Rita and Joe. I pushed ahead to make sure I would be sitting beside Adam. Next to

Joe, Bertie turned and glared, her face reddening as we filed in behind them. She grabbed Joe, who looked up, a question on his face. I touched his shoulder in a gentle plea as I passed behind him. Rita gave us a panicked, quick smile.

Behind us, footsteps sounded on the wood floor. Then the vestibule door creaked as it swung open and shut. Someone had left the church. Reverend Paul rose. The footsteps and muttering voices halted abruptly.

I cannot remember any of what the reverend said about Momma. Once again, Sarah sat on Adam's lap and I lay my hand on his thigh, under her warm, thin leg. I concentrated on fighting the waves of nausea that kept rising to my throat.

When the reverend finished, he announced that the girls would be singing "Open My Eyes, That I May See," Momma's favorite hymn. Gracie rose first and motioned to the younger ones. They followed her to the pulpit single-file. The congregation shifted, a murmur swept through the room as Gracie pulled up a step for Sarah to stand on. Gracie and Rosie exchanged looks, squared their shoulders, and gazed out over the congregation. Lil and Sarah focused on me and Adam.

Gracie nodded to the pianist, who struck the introductory bars. Then Gracie's pure, strong alto rang out, followed by the three younger sopranos. I wanted to shut my eyes and ride that sweetness, to rest mindlessly on the resonance of their voices. But I had told them to look at me if they got shy. They did not need that crutch. They sang full and steady without hesitation.

"Open my eyes, illumine me, Spirit Divine." Each time they hit the chorus, I thought I heard a fifth singer as their voices converged on those final notes. For a few moments, my heart ceased its hammering and the nausea left me. I squeezed Adam's hand as the girls finished and returned to us.

Reverend Paul led another Scripture reading. Then it was time to view her body. Adam closed his eyes briefly as Lil scrambled past his knees. "Go on," he whispered to Sarah, who held his hand and tried to pull him to his feet.

Seeing the dead helps the body understand what the mind does not want to grasp and the heart longs to deny. But I hated the ritual of the funeral at that moment. I wanted to send my girls running down the aisle out into the sun, out beyond this sorrow, past Clarion.

But we filed up to the coffin, Gracie and Rosie stately in their new poise. Lil looked once at her grandmother and then quickly away as she hugged my hip. Sarah just stared, her eyes glued to Momma's face, as Gracie, who had been holding her up to see over the side of the coffin, lowered her back to the floor. I resisted the urge to keep looking back at Adam still seated behind us. I braced myself, but there were only the normal sounds of people moving in a quiet church.

Adam met us at the end of the pew and we walked out behind Daddy, who leaned on Rita's arm. As we passed, everyone backed up or turned suddenly to speak to a neighbor. A little girl pivoted away from us to bury her head in her mother's skirt.

We were naked. My skin was on fire.

The congregation came with us to the graveside service. I noticed a few sideways glances. Then we all gathered at Momma's for the covered-dish supper. The house swelled with people, their perfumes and sweat mingling with the odor of coffee and fried chicken. The men had their whiskey and cigarettes on the back porch. They parted to let us through, but no one spoke. Bile rose in my throat and I swallowed painfully.

Uncle Otis, already drunk, hugged everyone and told them how much he loved his big sister. I did not see Daddy. I handed Sarah to Adam. With a child in his arms, maybe someone would find him approachable.

I found Daddy in the bedroom, lifting the lid off Momma's little jewelry box and then setting it back in place. Then he rearranged her comb and brush and lifted the lid of the jewelry box again. His shoulders, suddenly frail, slumped forward. I peeled his fingers off the box lid and laid it down. I held his face, forcing him to look at me. His head felt fragile between my hands. He was not my father, but he was the man who raised me. "Daddy, we're going to go into the kitchen and you will eat your supper. You have to eat now."

His watery, bloodshot eyes focused, but he didn't see me.

He let me take his arm and lead him into the kitchen. I sat him at the head of the table, the bowls of neighbors' offerings crowded in front of him. Rita made him a plate.

"Thanks." Joe tried to smile at me. "None of us could get him to come out of the bedroom. Not even Bertie."

After Daddy began to eat, I joined Adam. Mavis Montgomery had cornered him and chatted excitedly, praising the girls' singing. She had been in the hospital during Jennie's funeral. Even in the crowded house, a small space remained around them.

I stayed by Adam's side until I thought I glimpsed Frank's face through the packed living room. All I could see was that familiar brow turning away from me, but I was certain it was him. The shock of seeing him lurched to the surface of my skin. "Let's go. Now," I whispered to Adam. In a glance, I saw that Adam had not spotted Frank yet. Quickly, I gathered up the girls and we left.

The next morning, Adam departed for his mountain trip. He returned two days later, not jovial and refreshed as he normally was after his retreats, but home and safe.

༄

THE DAYS ACHED. The sky bruised my eyes. Every minor detail of daily life—the crumpled, folded brown bags the girls carried their apples and snacks to school in; the small scar on one of the horse's flanks; Adam's muddy chaps drying on the back porch—all seemed a knot of meaning, dense and indecipherable and simultaneously devoid of meaning. I hated the sorrow that seemed to be slowly unhinging my world.

The sparse, damaged fibers still holding me together were worn thinner by Momma's revelation. In my sleep, I met her in the white space of dreams, where I asked my questions and she answered. She spoke reluctantly. Her lips moved, but there was no sound. I woke in a hot, futile rage.

My biological father's ignorance seemed unjust, unnatural. Men have an alien, physical capacity for innocence: their bodies can bring forth life that they know nothing of. Only in complete insanity or a coma could a woman do such a thing.

A week after Momma's funeral, I told Adam I was going grocery shopping, and while Daddy worked his shift at the mill, I went through Momma's things, spending hours investigating every corner of her house. I pulled out drawers and turned them upside down. Sweeping her dresses aside, I searched the closet corners. I held each book by its spine and shook it. Nothing. Thirty-nine years had wiped out any trace there might have been of him. Every trace but me.

The Sunday after my private search, Bertie, Rita, Mary, and I met at Momma's to go through her clothes and jewelry. I lingered after they left, straightening the kitchen, then followed Daddy's pipe smoke through the house to the front porch. I found him in his usual spot, sitting in his rocker, puffing on his pipe. A large oak tree spread its branches over the yard and the land sloped so that the mill was a hundred feet from the porch. All my life he had sat in that same spot on the porch, facing the mill.

Now he was my only source of information. His gaze, locked on the mill, held the vague softness of a man looking out to sea, expecting nothing. He had regained his color since the funeral, but none of the weight he had lost during the last months of Momma's life. He was suddenly an old man.

My determination to confront him wavered, and my direct, rehearsed questions vanished. "You and Momma took care of all of us kids the same. I never felt I was treated worse. But you two always let me wander off on my own. I had more freedom. Why was that, Daddy?"

His rocking continued uninterrupted for so long, I thought he might ignore my question. Then he stopped and took his pipe out of his mouth. "You didn't need any more than what you were given. You kept to yourself and took care of yourself. Even when you were a bitty little thing and kept wandering off. We didn't let you go. You went. And you found your way around. Never snake-bit. Never hurt. The others—especially Rita—needed more watching, needed more discipline. You just didn't need it—Would'a been a waste on you." He put his pipe back in his mouth and began rocking again.

"Why do you think I was different?" My heart banged in my chest.

"That's just how it was. I'm sure your girls are the same, some needing more than others. That's all there is to it."

I was not prepared for him to draw parallels between his situation and mine, but I pressed on. "That's all there is to it?"

"Yep, that's it." He returned his pipe to his lips, took a long drag. His rocking chair squeaked dismissively as he squinted at the mill.

That old longing swelled in my throat. I'd always wanted more from him. More affection, more discipline, more stories, more touch. But, lately, I also felt the press of gratitude. He'd kept Momma from the wrath of her stern father and the scorn of a whole town. He was still protecting her.

I didn't want to cry in front of him. I patted the arm of his rocker. "Well, I thank you for all of it" was the best I could do. I did not have the will or energy to goad my father for more. And what good would it have done? Long ago, he had chosen his path. I let the sleeping dog of my mother's secret lie.

I was, in my own way, a perverse echo of her.

❧

BEFORE THE DEATHS, Adam had remained, in some essential way, innocent. He had, as far as I knew, never been a child. He hadn't been bent, while very young and still supple, by the knowledge of mortality that the death of a pet or a distant relative brings.

An uncharacteristic quietness enveloped him. He'd always been capable of a kind of absorbed, open calm, especially when working with a damaged horse or trying to quiet the girls, but now his stillness seemed vacant, no longer a sign of will and effort, but an absence of both. When the girls went to him or the horses turned to Adam, he opened his hands, blind hands brushing lightly over the world, his body operating on rote memory. The only time he seemed at peace and fully present was when he listened to his daughters singing.

When Jennie died, the girls mourned, but the ostracism of their father, followed by their grandmother's death, propelled them into another level of isolation. We'd always been somewhat removed from life in Clarion and the mill-village, but now the four of them were far less interested in going into town or visiting cousins. With Momma's death, they seemed to retract into a greater reliance on each other while simultaneously surrendering to their individual passions and quirks. At some point, most evenings, they would gather at the kitchen table with their homework. On the evenings they had no homework, they would linger there after dinner.

Gracie focused on academics, particularly history. Her grades had always been high but they rose to straight As. She became the family manager, spending more time with her younger sisters, helping me get them ready for school, checking on their homework, singing them to sleep at night when they needed it. Rosie continued riding as much as possible. Formerly the most volatile of her sisters, she became the most quiet and cooperative, a change I could not read as wholly positive. Lil read voraciously, mostly fantasies in which good wizards and witches prevailed over evil. If she had no chores and nothing to read, she cleaned and cleaned the house. Each afternoon after school, she swept the front and back porches, jabbing at the boards of the floor until she banished every speck of dirt. Sarah, of course, continued to draw. Orange-haired girls, increasingly more detailed and realistically proportioned, crowded her drawings, their dresses blood-red. Their eyes wide circles. Their mouths open in an O of terror or song.

❧

I STILL HAD NOT SHARED with Adam what Momma had told me. For the first time ever, I kept something from him. But Momma's story of my father began to plague me. I grasped at it for some relief from the memories of Jennie on the ground, of Adam's bloody hands on the steering wheel, and Momma's gray face before she died. If I was imagining my biological father walking down a street, eating a sandwich, lying down next to his wife for an afternoon nap, or even buried on some faraway, strange hill, I was also less aware of Adam sleeping and unresponsive next to me.

My blood and bones, the tonality of my voice, the shape of my fingernails, my love of reading, even the roundness of my hips, might have been given to me by a man I'd never met. What else did I not know? The thought of my ignorance about my paternity made me shudder. I lived daily with the secret of having chosen a stranger to father my own children. How could I brush aside this news about my father? His blood ran in the veins of my daughters, mingling with Adam's.

By 1965, the Piedmont Hotel, where my mother and Benjamin Mullins had been lovers, reeked of poverty and full ashtrays. An old, unshaven man slumped in an overstuffed chair in the lobby. The thin-necked clerk at the counter reluctantly put down his comic book to survey my plain dress and my lack of luggage.

"Is there still a stairway in the back?" I asked. "Can I see one of the second-floor rooms?"

He hesitated, then led me down a dank, uncarpeted hall and up a flight of narrow stairs, retracing my mother's footsteps.

"Here, this one." I stopped him at the first door.

He said nothing, just shrugged and unlocked the door.

The vertically striped wallpaper had faded to yellows and grays. A dark old bureau leaned in one corner, its missing leg replaced by a brick. Morning light, stark and unkind, shone through two dirty windows, illuminating a clot-colored bedspread. The curtains, a geometric patterned fabric from the fifties, were the one attempt at new décor.

Nothing of my young mother remained in the room. Nothing to explain how she could have let me grow up without such crucial knowledge.

"You want this room, lady?"

"No!" I ran from the room and out the back door.

I'd longed for some repercussion from Momma's confession, some recognition from Daddy, some change in demeanor in Joe or my sisters. Anything that would convey that I was not alone in what I knew. But there was nothing, no difference.

What was an earthquake for me was undetectable in everyone around me. What I now knew estranged me, the very thing Momma in her secrecy had sought to protect me from. Leaning against the wall of the Piedmont Hotel, gulping the sharp, fresh air that seemed to splinter in my lungs, I saw again the anguish on her face as she'd admitted what she had kept from me. That shame, I suddenly realized, was the core of the matter for me, not the nature of the man who had fathered me, not any nuanced shifts in my relationships with my siblings.

My mother was ashamed of the circumstances of my conception. That was the stone I could not swallow or balance against all I knew of us, of what she had been to me.

And now she was gone. No longer accountable, she had surrendered me to my own resources.

❦

THAT NIGHT, I made Adam accept my touch as I had the night before Momma's funeral. Forcing intimacy on my husband was a strange cruelty on my part. A kind of fear filled his face and eyes as he lay stretched out under me. But that was the only time grief loosed its grip on him. It was exorcism, and we needed it; otherwise, we would have been lost to each other. Those were the only nights that he slept the whole night without waking. I knew I was taking unfair advantage of how well I knew his body and its responses, knowledge that he had given in trust. But I wanted the contact. I needed it. Tears—his and mine—were preferable to distance and silence.

In the months following Momma's death, I was afraid for all of us. An unraveling had begun. Even the farm, my refuge since I was a girl, seemed dissonant, indifferent. The same mute slopes, the same red earth, and the same sky above the distant tree line. The apple tree bare now as it was every winter. The place where Frank ran over Jennie was visible from the back porch. I could have walked the exact trail of her blood across the field to the driveway. That part of the field and the top of the driveway, where the truck was stopped when I saw that last pulse in her neck, were my view from the kitchen window over the sink. These had been my two favorite places to look out over the farm.

Beyond the farm were the people I had grown up with—people who now shunned my husband. My anger at them seemed to backwash, flooding the very land I had so loved, leaving me helpless and poorer.

❦

WE HAD BEEN APPROACHED several times about selling some of the land. There were no malls in Clarion then. Everyone still shopped downtown, but with the interstate on the northern boundary of the land

and the state road on the east, we were sitting on prime commercial real estate. The first offer was so high we ignored it as a mistake.

A few months after Momma died, Clyde Brewer, the oldest brother in a family of local realtors came puffing up to the front door. He spread his map out on the front-porch table, pointed to the corner acre, and quoted us a price that was twice what we had been offered before— enough to support us for two years. His client, some company from out of town, wanted to open a new kind of store—a "convenience" store.

Even then we didn't realize what the land would eventually be worth. We didn't foresee the malls, movie theaters, and restaurants that would one day crowd the highway. We had no intention of selling the farm. We didn't need the cash. We raised most of our own food, had no rent or mortgage. With that and what Adam earned, we were doing well. But Clyde Brewer wanted just an acre, as far from the house as it could be. Out of curiosity, we added ten percent to his offer and called him back. He took it in a heartbeat. Fate had taken with one hand and now gave with the other.

I was waiting. Waiting for Adam to come back to himself, for people to forget what he had done, for the land around us to take on new associations and cease being sorrow's postcards.

 ❧

LATE THAT WINTER, a light, sticking snow fell one morning after the kids had left for school. I'd baked cookies for Sarah's teacher's birthday. The scents of cinnamon and ginger permeated the house as I packed the treats. On the way to the elementary school, I dropped by to see Daddy and leave him some of the beef stew we'd had for supper the night before. After I dropped off the cookies, I headed home.

As I turned off the road and up the driveway to the farm, Wallace leapt off the front porch, waving both arms. I pulled up behind the house. The stable door stood open. Inside the door, dark red blood puddled in a small oval on the floor. Nearby, a long smear of red and two bloody footprints.

"Adam?" I called. "Adam!"

Wallace jogged up behind me. "They took him to the hospital!" He tapped himself in the middle of his sternum. "He got kicked in the chest, then fell back and banged his head. He went down and I couldn't get him to come to. He was bleeding bad. You know I don't have my car with me. I called the ambulance. They took him to Mercy Hospital." Wallace talked faster as we ran back to the truck, telling me how he'd been leading out one of the stallions when something spooked the horse. A single kick had knocked Adam up against a stall post.

I sped away. Adam had never been to a doctor or a hospital.

A pretty, stout nurse pushed a clipboard at me. "Here." She handed me a pen. "These are just standard forms. They should have been signed when he was admitted, but he was unconscious."

I stared at the forms, then signed.

She took the clipboard, then thrust another form at me. "This release, too," she said as she dove for the telephone.

I hesitated, blinking at the words, but could not focus.

The nurse muttered impatiently into the phone, then put her palm over the receiver. "Honey, could you go ahead and sign? I've got to get this one and there's a call light on."

I signed the rest of the forms and pushed them toward her, hoping she would tell me where my husband was. Instead, she asked me to sit in an ugly, blue-gray waiting room until Adam was sent up from X-ray. Finally, another nurse appeared, smiling at me as if I were a celebrity, and announced Adam's room number.

Adam slept propped up on pillows, his head back and his mouth open. A bandage circled his head above his eyebrows. Another covered him from his armpits almost down to his navel. His sickly pale color alarmed me. Was there a looseness about his features? I opened the curtains to let some natural light in. Except for a yellow tint to his color, he looked normal.

I lightly touched the bandage on his chest. A nurse charged in, jerked the curtains closed again, cranked his bed up a notch higher, and started to take his blood pressure. "Don't put any pressure there, honey." She pointed at my hand on his chest, muttered her approval at his blood pressure, and then marched out.

"Adam?" I touched his face. "Wake up. Please wake up!" Nothing. I squeezed his hand, then shook it a little. Nothing. I held his hand and watched his chest rise and fall. The walls were close. Slowly, a wave of panic rose from the base of my spine up through my stomach. What would they find out about him and what would they do with him? To him?

I could hardly breathe as I called Bertie and asked her to pick the girls up after school and take them to her house for supper.

Adam slept peacefully. I prayed, appealing to the God I doubted. Please don't take Adam, too. Outside, the afternoon sun fell. The hospital lights shimmered on the thin snow below.

About six, I left and went back to the house to pick up clothes for the girls to wear to school the next day. I ate supper with them at Bertie's. "Your dad's fine. Just a little bang on the head," I told them.

"When will he be home?" Rosie asked.

"Probably tomorrow," I lied and tried to keep my face neutral, confident.

Neither she nor Gracie seemed convinced, but the dinner table crowded with the chaos of Bertie's kids distracted them.

"Are they going to shoot the horse?" Lil asked.

"They shoot horses only when they hurt themselves, not when they hurt people," Gracie told her.

Sarah's face darkened and she began to cry. "That's not fair."

I assured her that Wallace was taking care of the horses and none of them were being shot.

After dinner, I returned to the hospital and stayed by Adam's side all night, watching his face, hoping for change, fearing for the worst. "Wake up, wake up," I prayed over and over.

Near dawn, they came in to take his blood pressure again. "Go home," one of the nurses told me. "There's nothing you can do. Go home and get breakfast. Get your mind off of it."

As I left Adam's room, the lack of sleep bitter in my mouth, a young doctor strode up to me. "Mrs. Hope, I'm glad I caught you. This accident may have been a blessing for your husband. His injuries don't seem to be severe, but he is a very sick man. There's an abnormal growth in his chest." He waved a large white envelope, "The X-rays also show abnormalities in the brain, but we can't be sure. It could be a tumor. No swelling from the head injury, but the lobe formation is unusual. Has your husband recently had problems breathing or speaking? Doing simple math? Walking or working with his hands? Has he been moody or erratic in his behavior?" He talked faster and more excitedly with each question.

I shook my head stupidly at everything he said, barely able to hear him for the pounding in my chest and ears.

"I've never seen anything like this before. No impediments at all on his part? Nothing unusual?"

Again, I shook my head.

"Dr. Rumsted will be in soon. He'll look at these immediately. I've already talked to him. Your husband is a priority for us, Mrs. Hope. A priority. The nurses need you to sign some paperwork. You need to go by the desk first." He was a little boy with a new bug for his collection. He shook my hand, then walked away, disappearing into Adam's room.

I ate breakfast alone, standing up in the kitchen, then hurried back to the hospital.

I found Adam's bed empty, the sheets stripped. I ran to the nurses' station and slapped my hand on the counter to get her attention. "Where's my husband? Where is he? What have you done to him?"

She shoved more papers across the counter. One was a map. They had transferred him. The doctor would be right out if I would just calm down. I looked at the map: Duke University Research Hospital.

"They're the best for rare cases like his. He regained consciousness for a little while, so that's a good sign. They'll be able to anesthetize him for the surgery. The surgery will be scheduled as soon as possible," she assured me. "Just have a seat, Mrs. Hope, the doctors can explain more. Just wait here."

"I have to go to the restroom," I told her.

She pointed me down the hall and smiled. I dashed around the corner and ran to the car.

On the road, every light turned red at my approach, every driver took his time. I drove back to the house, threw up my breakfast, brushed my teeth, combed my hair, tossed a set of clothes and Adam's hat into the station wagon. I had to calm myself, keep my voice even as I lied, assuring Wallace that Adam was okay.

The drive sharpened me and pulled me back into myself. The snow had melted and the day began to warm. I'd never been to Duke University. I passed farms and houses and towns. People drove to work. Children played in school yards. By the time I got to the hospital, a hard calm had come over me.

I parked the car and grabbed Adam's clothes. When I asked for his room number, a nurse handed me more papers. I pretended to read them till the nurse turned her head, then dashed for Adam's room. Two young men in hospital uniforms pushed an empty gurney out of the room as I reached the door. "My husband," I volunteered, stretching a smile across my face. "Just want to see him for a minute."

The taller one answered, "You won't have much time. They've prepped him already. They're in a hurry on this one. He's pretty dopey."

Adam slept propped up in bed, pale yellow against the white sheets. The bandages on his head were new and smaller, but no hair stuck out above them. He had been completely shaved. I took his hand, the one not attached to the IV bag, rubbed it, and called his name. His eyes half-opened. He looked drunk, drugged, his eyes bloodshot and glassy. He garbled my name.

"Ya here," he said and closed his eyes. "Th' X-ray me 'gain."

"Are you okay?"

"Thin' so. The' don't. Won't let m' sleep, eat, walk. Lots o' doctors." He stopped and looked at me, his eyes half-open. Then, slowly, his head drooped forward. He passed out again.

My heart raced. I balled my hands up and pressed them into my stomach to stop my trembling. I held Adam's chin and gave him little slaps till he opened his eyes again. "Adam, I'm taking you home."

He grinned sloppily, but did not open his eyes. "'Ood, 'm hungry."

I peeked out into the hall. Then, quickly, I untaped Adam's IV, slipped the needle out, and started dressing him. He mumbled incoherently. I got the gown off and his shirt on. Then his pants. He was almost too tall and heavy for me, a bigger, looser version of the being I'd dragged out of the mud years before.

I supported his head and shoulders as I slid him sideways into the wheelchair. Only once did he seem to be in pain—when he went down hard into the chair. The bandages would give him away. After belting him into the chair, I perched his hat gently on his head, then slipped his shoes on.

I surveyed the hall again quickly. A nurse strolled around a corner. We made it past the nurses' station and to the elevator. Two orderlies maneuvered a gurney out past us. I tried to make it look like affection as I held Adam's head up steady with one hand.

On the ground floor, I wheeled him across the lobby as fast as I could without being conspicuous. Adam slumped like a rag doll. I chattered away to him as if he could hear me.

No one grabbed my shoulder, no one shouted from behind us.

Outside, I wheeled him straight to the car. I got in the backseat and quickly, gently as I could, pulled him into the car and onto the seat. Then we took off.

As soon as we were out of sight of the hospital, I pulled over and checked Adam. He slept curled up on his side, seemingly oblivious. I stripped off my jacket and wedged it under his head.

I drove just under the speed limit all the way home with the rearview mirror angled so I could see most of Adam in the backseat. The nervous stink of my own sweat filled the front seat. The metallic taste of panic filled in my mouth. I wanted Momma. All the way home, I felt the memory of his limp weight in my arms.

The sky had dimmed to twilight by the time we pulled into the backyard. Wallace jogged out of the stable to help us. He and I carried Adam in, his feet dragging between us at each step up to the porch. Wallace glanced at me over Adam's head. I saw the question on his face. He thought I was crazy to be bringing Adam home.

"It's just the dope they gave him for the pain," I said.

Wallace was no fool. I'm sure he smelled my fear. He shook his head, then bent over, gently picked Adam up, and carried him down the hall in his arms like a child. I followed close, supporting Adam's head. Wallace paused in the kitchen. I pointed to the hall and told him which bedroom. Wallace eased sideways down the hall.

Adam came to consciousness on the way in, knew he was at home, and asked for food. But he was out again before we had him settled on the bed and rolled over on his side.

After Wallace left the bedroom, I took off Adam's pants and put some shorts on him—I had not bothered with underwear in the hospital. He looked less yellow now. Was the sleepiness from the head injury or the drugs they gave him for surgery?

I brought fresh bandages and a basin of hot water into the bedroom. Carefully holding his head, I unwrapped the swaths of gauze. A smaller, square bandage centered on the back of his head. A faint blue line started at his crown, just past his hairline, and disappeared under the bandage. Slowly, I peeled the square bandage off. Centered in a blue-green bruise the width of a tablespoon was a cut about an inch and a half, a check mark with nine crude black stitches on the long part of it, five on the short end. I picked up the bedside lamp and held it over his head. The clean edges of the cut were pink, not red, already a scar as much as a wound. Very little swelling. His head remained smooth and rounded there, no dent in the bone.

I ran my hand gently over the back of his head. He moaned softly. His baldness and the intent behind the blue line that divided the crown of his head into a neat rectangle were as disturbing as the injury. I washed his head—the blue came off with a gentle scrubbing—and re-bandaged the cut. I didn't swathe his whole head, just wrapped it once in a clean white strip of sheet and tied it at the side.

I rolled two towels up into tubes and lay them on the bed behind him. Then I carefully rolled him onto them, one to support his neck and the other for the top of his head. The cut on his shaved chest, just to the left of his breastbone, formed the wide, shallow U-curve of a horseshoe. Fifteen stitches, and the same pink scarring, but the bruising around it gleamed darker and larger. The same blue line paralleled the length of his breastbone. Two perpendicular lines crossed it just above the U.

The cleanness and size of his injuries were a relief. The blue lines unnerved me. The map of someone else's work on my husband's body. Cuts to remove the essence of him. Washing the blue lines from his chest, I knew with an iron conviction he would be gone if they had operated on him. He didn't need surgery.

But I wasn't certain what he did need.

I left him there on his back, chest unbandaged, and dashed into the kitchen. I poured myself a whiskey, straight, and took it back to the bedroom. The burn in my throat and belly helped steady my hands. I rebandaged Adam's chest, rolled him onto his side, and covered him up. He slept peacefully.

Bertie brought the girls home, sniffing on her way in so I knew she had caught the scent of the whiskey. I tried to act as if nothing was wrong, but felt completely transparent. Bertie, the girls, and I walked single-file down the hall and stood crammed in the doorway. I pressed my finger to my lips, as if it were possible to disturb him. Sarah grinned up at me, her happy-Cheshire-cat grin.

Gracie stood behind me, her chin digging into my shoulder. "He looks okay, Momma," she said softly, but her voice sounded thick.

Rosie passed her hand over her own head, as if feeling for injuries.

"He doesn't smell bad," Lil said. She must have been remembering Momma's last days.

"Oh, he's not sick." I pulled Lil farther into the room so she could see better. "They shaved his head so no hair would get in the stitches. About a dozen stitches here and fifteen here where the horse kicked him." I touched Sarah on the back of the head and Lil on her chest. I kept my hand there a second, feeling the movement of her breath.

For a moment, we all watched Adam sleep. Then one of the girls farted. They turned accusing looks on each other. Lil hissed and soft-punched Sarah. Bertie wheezed a suppressed laugh.

"Enough. Dinnertime," I whispered and shooed them out of the room.

"No beans though, Momma. Lil's already tooting," Rosie said.

"No, I'm not. That was Sarah."

It is not possible to take four daughters quietly down a hall after one of them has farted. But for a moment they did not think of their bald father.

Later, I paid Wallace for his week's work and took him down the hall to see Adam again. Looking bigger in the dimness of the bedroom,

Wallace bent silently over Adam and touched him lightly on the wrist. "He went down so hard and so fast. I couldn't bring him to. You think he's gonna be all right?"

"Yes," I replied and told him how good the wounds looked, then we tiptoed out of the room. Before that morning, Wallace had never been down the hall and into the bedrooms. He looked relieved when we were back in the kitchen. With Adam down, we would need extra help. He would work longer hours, he assured me.

Somehow I got through the evening. I prepared a light supper for the girls and checked to make sure they did their homework and chores. I held myself tight and kept myself in line. As soon as I got the girls in bed, I called old Dr. Raymond, the man who had been our family doctor when I was a girl. He had been retired for years. I called his home.

My hands shook when I dialed. He seemed surprised to hear from me at that hour but he was cordial. I told him what had happened to Adam, as if it had just occurred. I didn't mention the hospital. He asked about the bleeding. The chest injury would be sore for a while, but if Adam's pain did not increase when he took a breath, we could assume there were no broken ribs. He should be fine, Dr. Raymond said, just keep the wounds clean. He explained what to look for, the signs of concussion or brain injury—dizziness, nausea, different-size pupils. Then drowsiness. "If you can't keep him awake, take him over to the hospital, Evelyn. You don't want to mess with a head injury. I thought I'd already heard something about your Adam—that he was sent over to Duke for something pretty rare. That wasn't him, huh? Wonder who it was." I didn't correct him, just thanked him and hung up. My sides felt sticky with sweat.

I went back to Adam. Rosie sat on the side of the bed, holding his hand. She put her finger up to her lips and whispered, "He's asleep again."

"He woke up? Did he say anything?"

"He was hungry and he wanted to know how we were. I told him we were fine. Then I think he asked for some corn bread. Something about a 'damn horse,' too." She smiled and wrinkled her nose up at me. "His scalp feels weird. He's going to be okay, Momma?"

I made myself smile back and led her to the door. "Of course he will be. But we'll need your help, okay?"

She kissed me and went back to bed.

My last remnant of calm dissolved. I needed to move. I wanted to run, scream, cry, or fight. Instead, I paced the front porch outside our bedroom window. Each time I checked on Adam, he slept peacefully. Finally, I poured myself another whiskey and took it to bed. I cried, my face pressed into my pillow, until I fell asleep.

I woke in the morning still curled on my side next to him, clutching my pillow. Adam's hand cupped my head.

"Adam?" I rubbed his hand and patted his cheek. "Wake up."

He moaned and turned over on his side. "A little longer, Evelyn." His regular sweet, sleepy voice!

Almost giddy with relief, I got the girls up and off to school. They waved happily as they left. They were halfway down the road to the bus stop when I saw a sheriff's car clear the curve and start up our road. I waited on the corner of the back porch. Wallace's voice carried from the barn, accompanied by the snort and impatient paw of the horses.

The car pulled deep into the driveway, almost up to the house. The local deputy, Harley Brown, stepped out, the leather on his policeman's belt creaking loudly as he shut the car door and leaned against it. I'd gone to school with his younger brother, Clifton.

"Morning, Evelyn."

I nodded. "It is a pretty one all right."

"You don't look like a woman who is missing her husband."

"I'm not, Harley. He's right in there, in our bed." I pointed back toward the house but stepped down toward him. "They doped him up pretty good at the hospital, but he's okay. He wanted me to make him some corn bread. But he's sleeping now. It was a pretty good kick he got."

"Well"—he consulted a piece of paper he pulled out of his pocket— "it seems Duke University Hospital and the CDC down in Atlanta didn't know he was going home and they're worried about him. Wanted to make sure that at least you know where he is."

"I do, Harley. You want me to wake him up? You need to come in and see him?"

He got back in his car and shrugged. "I don't know why I'm here. I should be out catching bad guys, but they wanted me to come by, said it was important. Wanted me to come by last night after supper. But Alice heard from Bertie that he was home and safe, so I waited until now. Adam is all right, you say?"

"Tired and banged up, but already cussing the horse that got him. You sure?" I pointed back toward the house again.

He laughed, shook his head, and started backing his car up. As soon as his car rolled out of sight, I ran and checked on Adam. I shook his shoulder.

"What?" he muttered.

"How do you feel?"

"My head hurts. Let me sleep." His voice was still normal, his color good.

"Does it hurt bad?"

"No." He rolled over to face the wall and went back to sleep.

Neither Addie nor Adam had ever really been sick. They both slept a lot if they did not feel well. Remembering that made me feel better. He was healing quickly, too. The bruising visible around the bandage on his chest had lightened overnight.

I'd chosen a path. They could not be allowed to take from him what they thought to be abnormal. I could not let them have him. If they discovered how different he was, would they want to examine the girls, too?

I was sorting clothes on the back porch, preparing to wash them, when I heard another car come up the drive. I looked around the corner of the house. A big car, one I had never seen before, shiny and black, had stopped midway up the drive where people parked when they were coming to the front door. I went back inside and paused at the hall mirror to smooth down my hair. I looked tired, but not half as crazy as I felt.

The sheriff and another man knocked and called my name at the screen door. I didn't know the sheriff or any of his kin, but I recognized him from pictures I'd seen in the paper. He took his hat off but the sunglasses stayed on. The man beside him, a meat-faced older man, wore a dark suit. The one in the suit held a briefcase and a large white envelope. "Mrs. Hope?" the sheriff asked.

I nodded but did not open the screen door. Then the other man took a step closer. "I'm Dr. Crenshaw. I'm from Mercy Hospital, but I represent Duke University's research hospital." I opened the screen, put one foot out on the porch, but didn't close the door behind me. He offered his hand, a thick, dry slab. "I understand that you took your husband out of the hospital yesterday without physician's approval."

"I did bring my husband home, yes." I looked at the sheriff. He did not seem any more interested than his deputy had been earlier.

The doctor eyed me critically. "Mrs. Hope, your husband is a very sick man. He was ill before he came to the . . ."

"He was healthy and working horses before he went to the hospital."

"I have X-rays I'd like to show you. There are multiple abnormalities. We scheduled the exploratory surgery for removal and biopsy. Your husband needs surgery badly."

"I've heard about the X-rays, doctor. Something in his chest and something in his brain. The lobes are unusual."

"That's right, Mrs. Hope." He smiled as if I were a well-trained dog. "But that's not all. His blood work shows some abnormal cells. It could be a pathogen or a rare form of cancer. We need to test him further."

I turned to the sheriff. "Have we broken a law?"

He pulled at his shirt and turned his blank face to me at the mention of law. "No, ma'am, none that I know of. But if your husband is sick, maybe you should bring him back to the hospital."

The doctor pulled an X-ray out of the envelope and held it up. "You say your husband has no trouble breathing, Mrs. Hope. Well, that is miraculous. There is this region of the chest—" The X-ray showed a collarbone, rib cage, and a fainter, milky area vaguely shaped like a star in the center of his chest. A sudden desire surged through me. I wanted to touch that image. My hand shot out.

The doctor jerked the X-ray away. The sheriff shifted his weight.

I forced myself to look away from the pale, broad star to the doctor's face and stepped back inside, putting my hand up near the screen-door latch.

"Whatever this lesion is, it may have something to do with his unusual blood cells. Mrs. Hope, if I came in and took a few more blood samples, then when you brought him back to the hospital, we would know more by the time you arrive. If this is a pathogen, it could be dangerous to you or your children." Polite authority filled his voice as if he spoke to a stupid but obedient child.

"My husband is resting and should be left alone."

"Mrs. Hope, you must bring your husband back to the hospital. The sample has been sent to the Centers for Disease Control. He may need to be quarantined. If I could just take a few more blood samples now . . ." He stepped closer to the door. I did not step back. I smelled the musk of my fear and felt it solid in my chest. Suddenly, I couldn't remember what quarantine was.

"Sheriff, have I broken a law?"

A wrong move. The sheriff uncrossed his arms and took a step toward the door. "Ma'am, there is no law against leaving a hospital. But if, by refusing to return your husband to the hospital, you are endangering his life and possibly your children's, then you could be held accountable should any of them suffer harm or die. Do you understand that?"

"Yes." My face reddened. I slipped the latch down. My hand trembled and they heard the lock slide into place. "You can't cut on him. You can't take anything out. I won't let you." The doctor opened his mouth to interrupt but I kept on, lowering my voice to steady it. I didn't trust myself to look at them. "I'll have him there by noon tomorrow for your blood test, at Duke University Hospital. No sooner. You should go now."

The doctor started again, his face redder, his voice rising, "Don't be stupid! Your husband is very sick. You need to bring him in now. Today."

But the sheriff turned and walked off the porch. Sputtering, the doctor followed. Halfway down the steps, he turned to glare back at me. "Your husband needs help. He needs surgery, Mrs. Hope. We can explain everything to you."

"No, you can't. He's not like us, doctor. He's not one of us. And he doesn't need your help." I had never said those words out loud before. My whole body shook.

After a long, puzzled squint, the doctor trudged off.

From the bedroom window, I watched as they got in the car. The doctor shook his head and said something about "goddamn hillbillies."

I had a little less than twenty-four hours. I wasted the first hour pacing the house. We had to leave, that much was clear. But where could we go? Adam made frequent trips to Kentucky and Tennessee for his work. I or one of the girls had gone with him a few times. Lots of people we could stay with there, but the police would look in that direction first, where he had the most connections. The mountains were an option.

Adam knew them well and could vanish there on his own. But the six of us roughing it? And for how long? My cousin Pauline was still in Florida, my only relation living more than a hundred miles away. Adam and I hadn't been back to her house since our honeymoon, and she hadn't been to Clarion in a couple of years though we exchanged Christmas cards. Every spring, I sent her the kids' school pictures. I trusted her. She didn't live on the lake anymore. But her little town south of Gainesville—Micanopy—was easy to find on the road map.

Under the watchful eye of a bank teller, I withdrew most of our money from the savings account. I doubled Wallace's salary, paid him three weeks in advance, and threw in fifty dollars for him to hire extra help. I made him swear that he would not tell any police or doctors that we'd left, but would call Joe if there was an emergency or anyone came looking for us and would contact Cole if anything happened to the horses. He agreed, but I saw the doubt in his face. There was no time, nothing I could say to convince him, but I knew he would do as he'd promised.

With the six of us in the car, we wouldn't be able to take much more than clothes. I filled the back of the station wagon, throwing in the dirty clothes I had been sorting when the doctor showed up. I packed all the things I could think of that the girls might want—small things that might make them feel at home—favorite pictures, cups, books, pillows, my best skillet, the paint set we had given them for Christmas.

Half an hour before the girls would be home from school, I was as ready as I could be. I stopped, suddenly exhausted, and walked slowly through the house. All I knew of my strange husband, marriage, birth, and death had come to me within those walls and on that land. I listened as hard as I could, hoping for wisdom. But I heard only the urgency of adrenaline and my own conviction. What the doctors wanted to cut away was vital. Getting him safely away was the important thing; everything else had to wait.

I put on a fresh dress and set biscuits and milk out for the girls. It would be their last fresh, home-grown milk.

As soon as they strolled into the backyard, Rosie, Lil, and Sarah circled the loaded-up car. Gracie took one quick look and dashed up the porch steps. "Momma, is Daddy okay?"

"Yes, he's sleeping. Bring your sisters in. We're taking a trip. A little vacation!"

Lil and Sarah clapped and jumped up and down, chanting, "A vacation! A vacation!" Rosie went straight to Adam's side. Gracie followed me back out to the car. "Why are we going anywhere now? Daddy's hurt!" She was not a child anymore.

"Gracie, I know this seems sudden, but I want it to be a surprise for your daddy. A little trip will be good for all of us. My nerves are shot— first Jennie, then Momma, now this with your daddy. I need your help now."

Her tears started at Jennie's name, but she did not cry. I needed to keep her moving and not thinking. I sent her in to collect the food I'd packed while Wallace and I checked the ropes holding the boxes and luggage on top of the car.

I went inside for more boxes and found Gracie dialing the phone. I took the receiver from her. "I don't want anyone else to know for now. You can call your friends after we get there."

She looked at me in amazement, then her face changed to confusion. "Momma, you're scaring me." Her chin quivered.

My own smile of reassurance felt like it would crack my face.

Rosie elbowed up beside us, one eyebrow pressed down in the consternation that would soon be sullen resistance if she thought she was being left out of anything.

I pulled them both out onto the porch and I held them by the shoulders. "Your daddy is a good man and he works very hard. But he hasn't been himself lately, you both know that." I took a deep breath. "Right now, we've got to make sure he doesn't get kicked by any more horses. We need to help him and the best way to do that is to take him away for a little while." The conviction in my voice surprised me. The truth of what I'd said calmed me.

They frowned, nodding. I didn't have them yet, but I was uncertain how much I needed to say. I didn't want to tell them where we were going, but I had to say more if I wanted their cooperation. "The doctors who saw your daddy want me to take him back to the hospital. They've come here twice already, looking for him. I don't know if they can take him away and do things to him without his consent. But we can't afford to wait here to find out." Both of them stared in alarm. Rosie shook her head. I drew them closer. "I know he doesn't need to be in a hospital, girls. He just needs a little rest and a little time away from all of this. This isn't going to be just a vacation. It's something we must do. Now. You shouldn't tell anyone what I just told you—even Lil and Sarah. I don't want to upset them. You understand? Can I count on you?"

They both nodded. They were with me.

"We're on the lam," Rosie announced.

Gracie laughed nervously and tried to blink her tears away.

"Yes, that's one way to look at it," I admitted. Then I lightened my voice. "But we're not criminals and your daddy will be fine. We're helping him. We're on the lam from everything that's happened to all of us in the last year. We *all* could use a little vacation, don't you think? I know I need one. I'll take you to a beautiful little lake where your daddy and I went swimming a long time ago when I was pregnant with you." I pointed to Gracie.

She nodded again, solemnly, and wiped at her cheek.

"Okay then, girls, let's get the food ready for the road."

Rosie gave me a sharp, salutary nod.

Sarah opened the back door and popped her head out. "Y'all stop talking! Let's go! Let's get Daddy and go on vacation!" Behind her, Lil twirled through the kitchen. Then the two of them bolted away and down the hall.

Within an hour, we were ready. Gracie, Lil, and Sarah settled into the front seat while Rosie and I walked Adam out to the car. Groggy but cooperative, he carried most of his own weight and leaned on us for balance.

We waved to Wallace, then pulled away, I and three girls squeezed into the front seat to give Adam and Rosie as much room as possible in the back. With his head in her lap, he fell asleep again before we passed the city limits sign.

Clarion was its normal self, unchanged as it receded behind us. No one would miss us until tomorrow, when the girls didn't show at school and I failed to bring Adam back to the hospital. Still, I expected to see the police behind us, or the shiny black car. I resisted the urge to speed.

We would be taking the old highways, not the new interstate. Florida was at least a twelve-hour drive away. Every nerve in my body seemed to vibrate. I didn't know if I could last that long. We had been on the road for only a couple of hours when darkness fell. We passed around the sandwiches and jars of tea and kept going. Eating seemed to break the quiet. Even Adam woke up. I saw only part of his face in the rearview mirror. He looked okay, just sleepy.

"Where're we going?" he asked.

"A little recuperation getaway. A second honeymoon."

"Second honeymoon? Pauline's?"

I nodded. "We'll lie low for at least a few days first. See how things go, then visit her?"

"Good idea." He tipped his head forward so the girls could reach it. They giggled as they ran their hands over the brown stubble. He drank some water and ate half of Rosie's sandwich—his first food since the accident. Then he lay back down.

Gracie turned and asked, "Is he going back to sleep?"

"Uh-huh," Rosie replied and began to sing "Hush Little Baby." Sarah sang to him next. Then Lil took her turn singing her favorite song to him. We were silent a moment, then Gracie began her lullaby, "Amazing Grace," and I joined her. I pushed on past the first verse on my own. By the time I came to the final verse, Sarah, Lil, and Rosie were asleep.

In the darkness beyond the yellow pool of our headlights, the ghostly shape of that X-ray kept appearing, unchanged by the miles we passed and the subtle shifts I sensed in the landscape around us. What, I wondered, did our daughters have of him? What had I silenced and what lay nestled under their breastbones? I reached over and patted Gracie's arm.

Her face looked older, somber in the light of the dashboard. "Is Daddy going to be okay?"

Anxiety thickened in my throat. I was less certain than I wanted to be. I nodded, unable to lie out loud. I wanted to, needed to offer her something true. "Our honeymoon was the first trip we ever took with just the two of us. Our only trip to Florida. It'll be good for him to go back. The change will help him."

"That's the pretty lake you said you're taking us to?"

"Yes."

She gave me a sly sideways glance. "Your honeymoon? And the place you swam when you were pregnant with me?"

"Oh, shit! Another thing you need to keep under your hat!"

She smiled at me, her first since we'd been on the road, and opened her mouth to speak.

I interrupted, "We didn't have to get married. Once we were engaged . . . We loved each other so much we couldn't wait."

Gracie laughed. "Oh, Momma!"

"Our secret?"

"Of course."

That accidental, inadvertent truth delighted me, lightening the hours of driving.

Gracie was still awake at about midnight when I pulled over at a motel. I checked in as Addie Nell Hardin and dished out more than we normally spent on a week's groceries for a room with two double beds and an extra roll-away bed.

Adam slept beside me, having awakened enough to put his arms around me. Sarah slept in the little bed at our feet. The three other girls were safe in the next bed. My back ached from the hours of sitting cramped behind the wheel. Exhausted, I fell asleep listening to the five of them breathing. We were in Georgia, just outside of Jessup. I slept fitfully, dreaming of men in white coats armed with blue pens, who came to take Adam.

EIGHT

RENEWAL

Our first morning after leaving Clarion, I woke and dressed in the unfamiliar shadows of the motel room while my family snored around me. Adam slept on his side, one arm across Sarah, who had joined us in the middle of the night. In the dim light, the bandages on his chest and head shone against his skin.

Outside, the freshness of oncoming spring and the familiarity of moist red clay mingled with the unfamiliar odors of highway fumes. Trucks hissed by on Highway 301 in the predawn darkness. We could have been anywhere. I imagined the doctor's pink hands removing someone else's internal organs in a hospital far away from us. I unlocked the car and took out the clothes we would need for that day, then went inside to wake my family.

We ate breakfast in a small local restaurant. Adam wolfed down an enormous omelet and grazed off my plate.

"What kind of eggs are these?" he asked the girls, starting the game.

"Fried eggs!" Sarah volunteered.

Gracie shrugged, but grinned. "Good eggs?"

Rosie said, "Good fried eggs from a Geooorgia hen!"

Lil rolled her eyes at the blandness of her sisters' answers. They finally won Adam's approval with good fried eggs from a Georgia hen for a hungry, horse-whacked, napping Daddy. Rosie beat the rhythm on her plate with her fork. Lil and Sarah lapsed into a church-worthy giggling fit. Adam finished the toast and sopped up the last morsel on every plate. The waitress appeared very happy to bring the check.

It was eight thirty in the morning.

The girls raced to the car, laughing and arguing about who would get which seat. I watched Adam as we strolled across the narrow parking lot. My eyes went obsessively to his bald head and the bright bandage. I thought I could still see some trace of blue lines.

He stopped and pressed his finger to my chin, lowering my gaze to his eyes. "I'm going to be okay," he said and squeezed my hand.

Rosie leaned out of the front-seat window. "Momma, Daddy, it's getting hot in here!"

As I drove away from the restaurant, my fears nattered at me. I was sure I'd done the right thing for Adam. But everything else was uncertain. What had seemed like a reasonable, inevitable decision the day before, now, in the morning light, seemed crazy. I turned my mind to the task at hand: keeping Adam safe, the girls distracted, and all of us moving until we could decide what to do next.

We'd driven through northern Georgia at night. Now, as the morning sun glared off the cars of people on their way to work and shopping, I realized how flat the land had become. The soil changed from familiar iron-red to alien shades of gray and black. The road relaxed into distant, straight horizons. Palm trees dotted the landscape. Small towns interrupted stretches of dense forests that crowded the highway and open fields. I had made the same journey with Adam sixteen years before, but nothing looked familiar.

When we crossed the state line, the girls exploded into cheers. "We're in Florida! We're in Florida!"

Adam startled from his post-breakfast doze, rubbed his head, and squinted at the brilliant sunlight. "This was a good idea, Ev." He winked at me.

Beside me, Lil fiddled with the radio dial, unable to find what she wanted. Sarah and Gracie unfolded the Florida map and entertained us with a recitation of Florida towns. "Apopka, Frostproof, Panasoffkee, Plant City, Kissimmee," Sarah giggled, stumbling over the Indian names.

I tried to ignore my watch.

Gracie navigated us straight toward the beach. Adam and the girls hung out the windows, gawking at the marshy landscape. Thick, briny air filled the car.

Claiming a sudden, irrepressible whimsy, I insisted that we stop at the first little souvenir shop for sunglasses and hats. Adam's bare head needed protection and I wanted us to fit in at the beach, not draw any attention to ourselves. Next to the cash register was a rack of Magic Sea Monkeys, stiff little packets accompanied by a jar. Colorful, vaguely crustacean-looking cartoon characters grinned from the illustration. Normally, both Adam and I were immune to the girls' pleas for impulse purchases, especially at the cash register. But after Sarah read the package—"Just add water and your Magic Monkeys spring to life!"—Adam set two of them on the counter. Sarah and Lil beamed with surprise.

"We really are on vacation!" Gracie exclaimed.

Those simple purchases seemed to release something in the girls and Adam. Outside, Lil twirled in the shop parking lot, admiring her new, flamingo-studded sunglasses. Her hair, fluffed by wind and humidity, sprang out in bright corkscrews. "Neat-o, neat-o, neat-o!" she chanted her new favorite word.

Rosie mugged at me, her cat-eye sunglasses low on her nose. "Not neat-o. We are incognito, right, Momma?"

Adam lifted his new hat off his head, laughing. "Five pale, freckled, redheaded gals, a bald guy with a bandaged head, in a loaded car with out-of-state plates? Noncognito is as close as we get."

I cracked up. By the time we got to the beach, I wasn't sure if I was laughing or crying, but I got us to the water safely. Adam and the girls tumbled out of the car, whooping, and bolted for the waves as soon as I shifted into park. I dried my eyes and blinked at the bright expanse of the Atlantic.

I followed them across the blazing powder-white sand to the wet hard pack and managed to get my feet wet before allowing myself to look at my watch. Twelve fifteen. A quarter-hour past the time I said I'd return Adam to the hospital. Whatever was going to happen had begun. The tightness in my chest returned. I could see the doctor and the sheriff knocking on our front door.

That evening, using Addie's name again, I checked us into a moldy little dive of a hotel on A1A just north of St. Augustine. After showering the crispy saltiness from our skin and hair, we all collapsed, exhausted. When everyone else was asleep, I left the room and pulled the car around, to the side of the motel, and backed into the shadows so the North Carolina tag wasn't visible from the road.

I'd registered the girls and Adam's excitement earlier in the evening when they watered the little granules of sea-monkey magic. As I'd rinsed out our wet bathing suits and reorganized the food in the cooler, my mind had been on the next day's route, busy with the strange calculus of our situation. I'd only smiled at the jar Lil, her face livid with amazement, held up for me to examine. But when I returned to the bed, I saw the jars lined up on the desk by the window. A sliver of street light illuminated one of them. Pale, tiny ghosts of creatures fluttered busily back and forth in the water. For a long time, I watched them, unable to decide if they resembled shrimp or tiny spiders. I understood my family's reaction. I fell asleep watching those inexplicable little creatures, my own mental monkeys calmed.

The next day we toured St. Augustine. The dissonance of those old, sleepy Spanish streets and my constant, tensed vigilance nauseated me. But no police officers questioned us, no doctors appeared.

Adam and the girls indulged in ice cream and fried shrimp. They dawdled endlessly over the offering of tourist trinkets in the shops and the placards of history trivia.

That night, when we pulled into a motel in Daytona, Adam held up two fingers and grinned. "Two rooms."

After we were sure the girls were asleep, Adam and I went to our room.

Slowly, tenderly, we made love. As his lips parted and I heard the familiar "ahh," I pulled his face to mine and kissed him. His voice poured into me, muted and absorbed by my mouth and chest. An almost unbearable tenderness.

He was back.

The next morning, while the girls and Adam had breakfast, I fed quarters into the pay phone outside and made my first call home. I would have preferred to speak to Joe, but no one picked up at his house, so I called Bertie.

"Evelyn, where the hell are y'all? The sheriff came to Daddy's looking for Adam! What did he do?" she yelled so loud I had to hold the receiver out away from my ear. Panic constricted my throat.

When I tried to explain, she interrupted, "The sheriff doesn't come after people just for leaving a hospital. Adam must've done something. Did he hurt somebody?"

"He didn't hurt anybody. They just thought he was sick and didn't want me to take him home."

"You weren't with him all the time. Who knows what he could have done."

Silence filled the line for a moment.

Then Bertie sighed. "I think you're nuts, but I won't tell them where you are." Suspicion of official inquiries was native to her character; she would be good on her word. "Well, where are you? When are y'all coming back?"

"We're traveling—on vacation. I don't know when we'll be back. I just wanted to let everybody know we're okay," I said.

She snorted. "Traveling? You should have let the doctors do what they needed to do to Adam. He needs something. I hope you're right and getting him out of town for a while is the answer. One of us will go by and check on your place. Give the girls my love," she said before she hung up.

We continued south, to Titusville and Cape Kennedy, then Melbourne Beach. Each day was a different beach. Every night a different motel. We'd only been to the beach a few times before and now the ocean fascinated the girls and Adam. While they swam, scoured the sand for interesting shells, or scanned the water for dolphin pods, I huddled under a big umbrella, avoiding more sunburn. My gaze kept drifting toward the road and north. We'd made no more calls home. The postcards the girls collected were not mailed.

I knew Adam was relieved to be away from the doctors, and he agreed that it was best not to let anyone know where we were and to keep contact to a minimum for a while, but I sensed in him a calm I could not share. He was absorbed rather than anxious. His only concern was the welfare of the horses. At night in our hotel room, when he laid his hand on my belly, just below my ribs, where my tension knotted, I was grateful for his comparative serenity.

We'd been gone a week by the time we made it to Fort Pierce. I was tired of motels, tired of the salty grit that coated everything I touched, and desperate to know if the sheriff was still looking for us.

I fed a pile of quarters into a pay phone and called Bertie. "Somebody in Atlanta and a doctor at some college" had called again but, she assured me, hadn't gotten anything out of anyone. Then Adam called Wallace for his first update on the farm. The horses were fine and Joe was picking up mail and depositing boarding fees. The phone in the house rang constantly, Wallace reported. The sheriff and doctors had sent Harley Brown around looking for us a couple of times, but that was in the first two days. He hadn't seen or heard a thing from them since then. I celebrated by calling my cousin Pauline in Micanopy to tell her we were on our way.

The following morning, we rolled through the mid-state citrus groves with the windows down. The distinct, exquisite odor of orange blossom blasted through the car. My eyes were still drawn continuously to the rearview mirror. In the backseat behind me, Lil closed her eyes and tilted her face to the fragrant breeze. I was certain that she was thinking of Jennie at that moment. Her lips curved into a small, firm smile. For the first time since we left, I considered that we were going *to* something new as much as we were fleeing the past. For the first time, I realized that the girls, in their own way, might have needed rescuing as much as Adam.

For our last stop before Pauline's, we visited Weeki Wachee Springs. The silly-sounding name and promise of live mermaids was irresistible. In the underground theater that looked out onto the depths of the spring, Adam and our four girls sat beside me. As the sparkling mermaids floated before us on the other side of the thick plate glass, I gazed down the row of my family's rapt faces and felt something akin to hope. The open smile on Adam's face reminded me of Addie in her first days. The sunlight through the blue undulation of water stained our faces an unnatural hue.

Sarah took my hand, her face suddenly sober. "We have to stay here, Momma. It's so beautiful. I don't want to be a mountain girl anymore. I want to be a mermaid."

Later that afternoon, we pulled into Pauline's dusty, pale driveway. She emerged from her house with her poofy hair, cigarette, and coffee cup. "Curiosity got me, I just had to leave work and be here when y'all got in." She hugged all the girls except Sarah, who didn't remember her and held back. She turned to Adam, whose hair was now a thick stubble, the bandages completely gone. "Good Lord, Adam, look at you. You look fine! Let me see those awful wounds the doctors got so excited about," Pauline said.

Adam bent deeply in front of her, showing the scar on the back of his head.

"I love it when men bow to me like that," she cackled. "Lord, this looks like nothing. This doesn't deserve surgery!"

Adam grinned at me sideways and upside down from his bow. I laughed but repressed a shiver as I ran my hand over his prickly scalp and the little pink scar. Those blue lines and the X-ray star still haunted me.

Later that day, after we settled the girls down for the night in the spare bedroom, I leaned against the hall door and listened to Adam singing to them. He hadn't sung their bedtime songs to them since Jennie died. "A tisket, a tasket, a brown and yellow basket . . ."

Since Jennie's death, I'd seen something new in his face. Some freshness or innocence had left him then and that departure had resonated in his features in a subtle way. Now a familiar kind of lightness was returning to him. I heard it in his voice, too. The simple songs he sang to our daughters flooded me with relief.

In the kitchen, Pauline poured herself a beer. She lit a cigarette and patted the table. "Sit down." She studied me.

I caught the beer she slid toward me.

"Now," she said, lifting her penciled eyebrows, "what's really going on? You're jumpy. Vacation, my ass."

The happy mask I'd tried to wear collapsed. I told her more or less what I had told Gracie and Rosie about the accident and hospital. "I just couldn't take it anymore. Too much has happened. I couldn't let them operate on him. He just needs to rest."

She took my hand. "You look like you could use some rest, too, Eve-lyn. Y'all have been through so much. You can all stay as long as you like and for whatever reason, you know that." She reached back to the counter, picked up a box of Kleenex, and handed it to me. "The girls look great. Adam, too! Hell, maybe he's better off. A good kick can do wonders for some men. Though he's always struck me as one who didn't need it."

"I wish the horse knew that." I laughed and blew my nose.

The next morning, Adam rose early and made breakfast for every-one. Perfect scrambled eggs from a Florida hen. In a single meal, we exhausted Pauline's supply of milk, eggs, and bread. As she headed out for work, Adam and I left the girls, still in their pajamas, to lollygag in front of Pauline's TV and went to buy groceries.

I was grateful for the time alone with him and assumed we'd use the opportunity to discuss what we should do next. Instead, we were quiet. We passed a school. We didn't know any of the children in the school or the people driving to work.

I motioned for Adam to pull over at a little park. "I don't like how people were treating you in Clarion. They won't forget it. They won't say anything to your face, but they're thinking about it just the same. It's been so hard to be there since Jennie . . ."

Adam took a deep breath and shifted into park. "I lost control. I didn't know that could happen."

"I know you didn't mean to hurt anyone. But things are different for us in Clarion now." I touched his face and he relaxed into my touch. "I missed hearing you laugh. I missed hearing the girls laugh with you. So much has changed—too much."

He opened his mouth to protest, but I held out my hand to hush him.

"There's something I haven't told you about." Choking on the first sentences, I began my recitation of everything Momma had told me.

He listened.

The words tumbling out, I began to cry. But with each detail of

Momma's story, his face grew lighter, more amazed. As soon as I got to the part about Momma sneaking into the hotel to meet Ben Mullins, Adam smiled. "Your daddy's a carpenter from Raleigh? Lilly Mae McMurrough fell in love and couldn't wait?"

I nodded.

He laughed, throwing his head back in that deep belly laugh.

"Oh, I love Momma," he said. "As Addie, I must've been a constant reminder. She was so certain my momma had lied to me, too." He pounded the steering wheel and said, "I knew there was some other reason Momma was always so sweet to me!" Then he laughed again.

"She fell in love and couldn't wait," I repeated.

"Fell in love and couldn't wait," he echoed. His simple direct statement of Momma's youthful, impatient love seemed happy and I laughed, too. Then we laughed more, each time we looked at each other, hysterical, face-aching laughter. I couldn't see for the tears. Finally, I caught my breath and focused.

"Oh, I miss Momma." Adam blew out his breath. "I guess that makes you and me more alike than we ever knew. All the unanswerable questions about where and who we came from."

Now I was amazed. I shook my head. That had not occurred to me.

He put his hand over mine. "We are both here now, Evelyn. And that is all I need to know." He paused before he reached for the ignition, his face earnest and grave. "She loved you, Evelyn. However she got you, she wanted you."

The warmth of his hand and those simple words felt like a gift. An absolution I hadn't known I wanted. Or needed.

We drove on to the supermarket.

When we called home a couple of days later, both Wallace and Bertie told us the calls and sheriff's visits had stopped. By the end of the first week at Pauline's, we had not yet discussed returning to North Carolina. I could sense the girls' energies turning from celebratory distraction to restlessness. Vague answers satisfied Sarah and Lil, but Gracie and Rosie were another story. I told them firmly that their father and I would decide soon.

On the next Saturday, Pauline took us for a long walk in the woods. Huge, inert alligators draped the opposite bank of the river near our path. For dinner, we ate fried gator tail at a little restaurant near a dark, cypress-shaded creek. That evening, after the girls were in bed, Adam and I sat in the kitchen, talking. Pauline puttered at the kitchen counter. The three of us had just finished discussing the places we had visited that day when Adam said, "This seems like a good place—the springs, the little hills, the lakes, and good pasture land. What brought you here, Pauline?"

"I followed a man down here and then got my heart broke. He left. I stayed. I had a good job by then and I liked it here. No snow, no Momma calling me up wanting to know what I'm doing. Somebody has to die or be born before she'll make a long-distance call." She shrugged. "So here I am. Happy as a clam and not, thank God, married and working in the cotton mill."

Adam turned to me. "We have to decide what we're doing. Soon. The girls should be in school. Financially, we're fine for a while, but we're spending money and not making it. Wallace needs help or fewer horses. The feed crops should go in soon if they're going."

I nodded.

The phone rang. Pauline picked it up and, stretching the cord out to its full length, winked at me as she disappeared into her bedroom. We were cramping her style. We couldn't stay much longer.

We strolled out to her screened porch. She lived on one of the hills near Micanopy. I turned off the light so its glare would not obscure the view. I looked out at the trunks of tall oaks and the hollow of a dry creek bed. "This neighborhood reminds me of North Carolina a little. I feel more at home here than any part of Florida we've seen so far," I said.

Adam studied the trees and yard a moment. "I can see that. But it feels very different to me. Very different." He bounced up and down on his heels. "The ground is lighter. More—buoyant?" He glanced at me for confirmation, then leaned against the frame of the door and stared out into Pauline's moonlit backyard. "Every time I looked out our back door at the farm, I saw where Jennie lay by the tractor." He paused at her name, his voice sliding down. "And if Frank ever showed up again, I don't know." He took my hands, his voice was unsteady, but then he pulled himself together and went on. "I don't know if I could trust myself around him again."

We both turned toward a noise from the living room. Rosie stood at the kitchen door, tears in her eyes. "Daddy," she cried. "What about the horses? What about Beau?" Beau was her favorite, a big, sweet gelding.

Adam returned to the table and pulled Rosie into his lap as he sat down. "Wallace is doing a good job, Rosie. I talk to him every day. Tomorrow, you can talk to him yourself and ask him about Beau. Do you know anyone who'd be good to help Wallace? It's a lot for one man to handle. Think about it and see if you can come up with some names."

Rosie let me lead her back to the bedroom and her pallet on the floor. "We're not going back home, are we, Momma?"

"We're figuring that out, Rosie. Good night, now. You go to sleep." I kissed her and returned to Adam.

He stood at the back door again. "The crickets are already out down here," he said. And we stood listening for a while. "When we stopped on the side of the road to look at that farm near Micanopy and I saw those horses grazing on beautiful green slopes in March, I thought to myself, 'This is not a bad place. I could live here.'" He put his arm around me and drew me closer. "And then I saw the springs, so blue and pretty they looked like the source of sky. You know there might be a river underground, right below us, now, where we're standing? A river that bubbles up into a spring miles from here. Isn't that something?"

The interest I heard in his voice then, the precursor of love, was all I needed to convince me, but he continued. "I feel different. I like the smell of the air here and the ground feels good under my feet."

I felt the evidence of his words as I leaned against his chest. The tightness that had thrummed through him for months had quieted.

"We will miss the farm," I said.

"Just thinking about it feels a little like being unfaithful to the farm, doesn't it?" Adam whispered. "That land has been like a good woman to me."

We listened to the night sounds. An owl bellowed in the distance. "I think maybe Florida could want me—all of me," Adam said.

"She's calling your name, huh?"

He waved his hand. "What kind of place is this?"

"A warm place?" I offered. He raised his eyebrows. "Hot place?" He sighed and rolled his eyes. "A place with horses and rolling green hills?" He gave me his broad smile. Finally, I got it: "A good woman calling your name?"

He nodded. "Call my name." He kissed me, my reward, and I said his name.

"Tomorrow, I'll go look," he said, his voice sober again. "See what work there is. And whether this is the kind of place where my wife can grow beans, tomatoes, and flowers."

"Have you looked at the dirt here? I don't know. We'll have to see if Florida calls my name, too."

"Been a while since you had a good woman, huh?" He pressed his hips against me.

"Yes, it has been, but the last one sent me a wonderful substitute." I kissed him. "Take Rosie with you tomorrow. She needs it. She misses the horses."

Dew fell and the odor of the earth rose up, different from the smell of North Carolina red clay—musky and less metallic. I remembered

Addie, misshapen and lying on her side like a bear in the mud. "Let's not sell any more land. Not just yet, okay?" I couldn't sever that tie.

"No, we shouldn't have to. If I get work, we'll be okay. We need to find someone willing to take care of the farm and the horses."

I immediately thought of Joe's son, Bud. He was grown now and recently married. His wife, Wanda, had been a farm girl until she married him.

With that we decided to try living in Florida. We went to bed and I did not stay awake listening to crickets, mockingbirds, and my husband's breathing. I slept deep and hard and woke to Adam bending over me to kiss me good-bye as he left to look for work.

Adam found a job quickly—a job with a house. Randy and Edith Warren needed a groom and trainer. They hired him on the spot. The job came with a small house if we wanted to live on the property.

The wood-frame house needed paint, and had three small bedrooms instead of four, but its windows looked out on those rolling hills and grazing horses that Adam found so appealing. The Warrens' ranch was pretty, especially in that early part of the year before the summer sun dulled the green of the pastures.

As we dusted, bleached, and cleaned our new home, wolf spiders skittered out of sight. What furniture there was in the house smelled of unfamiliar molds. We quickly discovered how far Florida roaches can fly and which shade of red hair they prefer for a landing. But Pauline helped us, and her presence defused the girls' whining. She and the Warrens loaned us furniture, so each of us had a place to sit during the day and a place to lie down at night. We enrolled the girls in school as soon as possible.

At the end of their first week in school, I made a trip back to North Carolina, alone. A lightning raid to check on the farm and pick up essentials.

The Florida flatlands receded and the sun rose to my right as I drove north. The solitary drive took all day. Through the monotony of southern

Georgia back roads, I waffled between anxiety and anticipation. I reminded myself that the authorities wanted Adam—not me, not our land. I imagined all my familiar things in our Florida kitchen. No more paper plates or cheap, new coffee cups.

By late afternoon, the first of the familiar red clay hills rose around me, a bittersweet, almost sexual pleasure. An hour after sunset, I was on the farm. My motherland. The place my children were born.

In the moonlight, I could see little had changed in the weeks we'd been gone. Wallace had even kept up the parts of the garden already planted. The tea roses needed pruning.

I unlocked the back door, swung it open, and stepped into my kitchen as if into a lover's arms. But before my hand reached the light switch, I felt the emptiness of the house as a tangible, shocking thing. My hand faltered. Then light burst through the kitchen. Everything *looked* the same. Exactly as we'd left it. The only difference was a neat pile of mail in the middle of the table, right where I'd asked Joe to leave it. Numbly, I fanned the envelopes, searching them as if the key to our changed lives resided there. Bills. Letters from the girls' schools. A letter from the Centers for Disease Control. I dumped them all, unopened, in a paper bag, and ran out to the car, away from the oppressive quiet of the house.

Outside, the air seemed brittle and strange, deeply familiar and distant, unattainable as the dead. I wanted to call the names into the air: Jennie. Momma. I wanted to go down on my knees and scream their names into the dirt. But I held my tongue on those fruitless syllables. I walked the perimeter of the hay field. In the garden, I dug my hand into the soil and felt the residue of the day's warmth. The ground rendered nothing of the sweat we'd put into the farm, nothing of the generous bowls of beans, corn, and squash we had passed, hand to hand, at the supper table.

In the empty barn, I methodically scanned every surface with the flashlight beam. The chickens, hog, and remaining cow had gone to

Wallace's and Cole's families. The walls and rafters seemed skeletal, oddly intimate in their solitary exposed planes.

I opened the stable door and listened to the breath of the remaining horses in the close darkness, then went back into the house. At last, I packed. Kitchen, first, then bedrooms. I tried not to look at things, not to think. Just get the job done.

By four in the morning, the car bulged. Luggage and more boxes were tied on top. I knew I wouldn't be able to sleep. I left more money for Wallace and a glowing letter of recommendation Adam had written. Then I fled, again.

As I made my final turn out of Clarion before dawn, I thought I saw a row of police lights atop an approaching car. I pressed the brakes suddenly. Boxes groaned and shifted in the backseat. My heart hammered. I turned in the opposite direction and took the longer route out of Clarion, heading back to Florida as quickly as I could, fleeing what I had, just the day before, looked forward to embracing.

The sun began to rise.

I drove south and turned my heart toward my girls, to consoling and protecting them, as much as possible, from the sorrow of leaving the only home they'd ever known. I wanted to make them understand, to tell them: it will work out. No one will look at your father as people in Clarion had. No one will take him from us. He can return to himself in our new home.

When I pulled into the yard that evening, they eagerly surrounded the car, immediately unpacking and exclaiming over all our old familiar stuff as if I'd returned long-lost treasures to them. My solicitous tenderness found no purchase. They dashed into their bedrooms, unloading clothes and books. Their decorating and organizing decisions seemed endless. The only hesitation I saw was in Rosie. She sat in the dining room, staring pensively at her collection of horse figurines lined up on the table. "I miss Beau." She sighed.

"Soon," I said, relieved that I would be able to provide what she was missing. "Your horse will be here."

The next night at the dinner table I asked my normal questions about school. Lil, who usually just said "Okay," announced, "No one here knows I'm missing anything."

"Yeah," Sarah added. "Here, we're just an ordinary family."

"Cool." Gracie's new favorite word.

Rosie rolled her eyes, her favored reaction to her little sisters.

"You girls will have to set them straight. You are not ordinary." Adam leaned back in his chair and grinned at us. The girls regarded their father with surprise.

"I want to be ordinary." Lil scowled. "I don't want everybody to know."

"Ordinary's good," Sarah echoed.

Rosie nodded.

Adam reached across the table and touched Lil's hand as he touched Sarah's back with his other hand. "You're right. Here we can be as ordinary as we want to be. And we get to decide how we are ordinary, no one else decides."

Lil smiled back at her father.

They managed their mutual goal of being ordinary and fitting in very well. All their conversations now were sprinkled with the names of classmates I didn't know, teachers I'd met only once, if that. With four girls, the phone was ringing constantly. Even Sarah's second-grade pals called. I didn't recognize any of the voices, and the deep, unfamiliar voices of boys asking for Gracie or Rosie always surprised me. The freedom of driving, a necessity since we lived so far out of town, also widened Gracie's social circle. Rosie still came straight home from school each day, changed into dungarees, and joined her father in the stables.

Three months later, I returned to the farm once more, via Greyhound bus, for the truck and some of the furniture. The horses we'd boarded and cared for had all been sent to other stables. Only our two remained. Darling, now docile with age, and Beau, Rosie's favorite, waited for me to bring them to their new home. I braced myself against the shrill vacancy of the farm.

We'd arranged for Joe's son, Bud, and his wife, Wanda, to rent the house. Despite the scattered cardboard boxes of their things, neatly labeled and sealed in anticipation of moving in, the house felt even more abandoned. I walked from room to room, touching boxes and the doors of empty closets. The violent shock of my earlier visit devolved into forlorn sorrow. I tried to imagine the clear spaciousness of when I'd lived there alone before Addie. But I couldn't see past the deserted rooms.

The top shelf of the bureau I'd shared with Adam still bulged with old single gloves, the odd scarf, and a few stray photographs that I kept separate from the photo albums and the shoe box of family snapshots. A wide, white envelope held the photo of the burned Japanese woman that Frank had left years before. With it was the photo of me and Addie that Momma had been looking at when she told me about my father. I recalled A.'s face in those few short days after I found her when she was not yet Addie. The mixture of horror and empathy that had bloomed across her face as she held the picture of the Japanese woman that day was one of the things that led me to trust her so. That quality was still there in Adam; I still trusted him deeply, intuitively. He had changed so much, yet remained the same. But I knew no more about him after almost twenty years. I had no idea what changes twenty more years would bring, but I sensed in him something new since we'd moved to Florida. Good, but slightly different, as if his voice held new frequencies just over the edge of my ability to hear.

I put the two photographs back in the envelope and packed them.

The next day warmed unseasonably. I would have preferred to do all of the moving alone, but knew I couldn't manage the furniture on my own and so had asked Joe to help. I hadn't told anyone else about my trip back to the farm. I didn't want to take any chances, even though Joe assured me there had been no more phone calls or visits from the sheriff.

It wasn't that difficult to withhold information, even about where, exactly, we were living, and Joe didn't press. Without Momma, our family had no center. Except for the day we cleaned Momma's closets, I'd hardly seen Bertie or Rita. As Joe and I sweated, cramming headboard, tables, and chairs into the back of the truck, he told me about Rita's move to Hickory, where her new boyfriend lived. She worked at a store there and rented a little apartment.

Like Daddy, Joe had somehow become middle-aged while still in his thirties. Since Momma's death, he'd even taken up pipe-smoking and now smelled of the same sweet tobacco Daddy smoked. When we'd finished with the furniture and hitched the horse trailer to the truck, Joe hugged me, a rare thing for him. "Come back when you can." His voice thickened. Of all of them, I felt he was the most likely to forgive Adam, the most likely to find a way to treat him like an ordinary man.

"Thank you, Joe. I will," I whispered as he released me. I felt I should say more, but I didn't trust myself. As I watched his car pull away and his hand sweep out the window in a final wave, I knew that I—we—would not be coming back.

As night fell, I leaned against the porch, surveying the pastures and star-filled sky above the stables. A stone of sorrow grew in my stomach. The cooling night air smelled of spring.

Only one task remained. For years, Adam and I had measured the height of our daughters each year in the dining-room doorway. Dozens of horizontal pencil marks, dates, and initials marked the door frame. The lowest mark was Jennie and Lil in early 1959, when they were toddlers. The highest was marked "Dad." I was about three inches below him.

The nails that held the board to the door frame, hammered home long before I had been born, groaned as I pried them loose with a crow-bar. I worked up one side and then down the other. By fractions of an inch, the nails released. Finally, the board clattered to the floor, its dual row of nails jutting up. By the back-porch light, I banged all the nails out except a center stubborn one, then wedged the board into the tight press of the furniture strapped into the truck bed.

After I made a final sweep of each room, I stood in the hall and sang, as steady as I could, for those empty, echoing rooms and all that had happened in them: "Don't sit under the apple tree with anyone else but me." Then the last stanzas of "Amazing Grace," and my own voice dis-appeared into the house.

I made myself a pallet on the bare floor of the bedroom where our bed had once been. I waited for peace, but I felt only the weight of sor-row. Finally, I fell asleep. In the ballet of my dreams, Bud and Wanda's furniture settled into the corners.

The next morning, after I loaded the horses in the trailer, I took a fresh jelly jar from the cellar shelf and filled it with clay from the spot where I had found Addie. I hesitated before screwing the lid on, then I went to the spot where Jennie had bled into the ground and added an-other fistful.

For the last time, I locked the door to a house that I owned but that was no longer mine. The footstool I had sat on as a girl when I pumped the butter churn for Aunt Eva was pressed against the back window of the truck, filling the rearview mirror as I drove away. A few moments later, I parked at the edge of the graveyard. The graves were neat, re-cently mown. The remains of water-stained, wilted pictures of flowers Sarah and Lil had torn out of magazines drooped against Jennie's tomb-stone. I left a little yellow cup with a lamb embossed on the side, Jennie's favorite when she'd been a baby.

Then I drove away to my husband and daughters.

MONTHS PASSED before I stopped expecting a knock at the door. The escape from the hospital and those first days in Florida had burned a new kind of anxiety into my nerve cells. Gradually, the sense of constant vigilance slipped away. While I had no illusions that Clarion would ever be a safe or happy place for Adam again, I began to feel that we were safe where we were.

It was 1966 and the sorrow and loss of our family seemed to be reflected all around us. Kennedy had been assassinated, blacks marched for civil rights, and Vietnam splattered across the TV and newspapers every day. The world smoldered and soon would catch fire, fire of a very different sort than in my youth—the fire of protest and rebellion.

But we had found our refuge.

The change of place began the thaw of grief for all of us. If death had chilled our hearts, the heat of that first summer quickened our pulses. Much of what I felt was the exhilaration of relief at being away from all the problems of Clarion. The rest was sheer physical newness. I perceived the same new lightness in the girls and Adam. But I felt a new grief that was not reflected in their faces.

The first few months in the house on the Warren ranch, everything seemed an affront to my expectations, to everything I knew. Our dirty clothes stained in grays and blacks instead of red Carolina clay. The strange view out the windows. The damp, odd odors of the house. I kept expecting the low, gentle slopes, the house, even the horses to be taken down and carried away like cardboard props so we could all stop the pretense. So we could go home. Then I would remember the empty rooms of the farm, Jennie bleeding in the truck, the faces of everyone I knew as we left her funeral, and it would hit me: this strange, surreal place *was* my home. My heart stumbled from the blow.

While Adam and the girls fell quickly into their daily routines of school and job, I now had nothing to do but housework, and that was finished by noon each day. There was no bookkeeping to be done. There were no hogs, chickens, or cows, no garden to tend.

On the farm, the stable had been within shouting distance. Now Adam spent his days in stables that were rectangles on the horizon, far past the sound of my voice. Gracie and Rosie, both in high school, had begun gathering up their small privacies for the life they would have when they left home. Boys collected around them, calling and dropping by the house, practicing nonchalance in their new men's bodies, their voices as deep as Adam's. Lil and Sarah studied their sisters for clues of what was to come.

What should have been a time of leisure and solitude for me lay heavy, solid as a blanket over my face, and I had no energy to throw it off. Nights, I lay awake next to Adam in the un-air-conditioned house, the mid-spring air already thick with moisture. As spring turned to the full heat of summer, it seemed we slept in the mouth of God, the air already breathed by some huge being. I tossed in the heat, listened for the relief of rain. I thought of everyone in North Carolina: Joe and the rest of my family, Marge and Freddie, and Wallace. I longed to see their faces, but my longing for the land surpassed all other desires. I ached for the sunrise view down the hill. In the swelling heat of Florida, I lusted for the crunch of fall leaves underfoot, the hard grip of the cold under my nightgown as I went out to milk in the morning. I hungered to take that curve where the road dipped to the mill-village houses and Momma's. I would have given almost anything then to press myself into the farm's embrace, to match my contours to hers.

I tried to turn my heart to the living, to the place I was, but putting seed in land not owned by me or my family seemed alien. The sandy, gray-white soil looked like dirty beach sand, not fit for growing anything. It smelled like dust. Yet weeds and trees and wildflowers grew along the roads. When we drove into town, we passed dense, impenetrable woods and fields of corn, peas, and peppers. Such new combinations of seemingly poor soil and happy flora puzzled me. Everywhere I went, I picked up the dirt, examining it for clues. Bringing anything out of such soil would require a whole new language on my part. I imagined that there must be something richer and darker under the gray sand, or some trick the farmers all knew. Trick or no trick, what I had always been able to do well now seemed inaccessible. Still, I searched the yard around our house for the best spot to plant my fall garden.

Meanwhile, with my hands and a good part of my days literally empty, I found myself turning again to Momma's revelation. I circled the question of how could she have kept such a secret from me for so long. Often a second, unbidden, question followed: How could *I*? My daughters did not know their father's origin. A dark, tender anxiety filled me.

One Saturday morning, I found Sarah sleeping next to a family portrait she'd drawn, a stair-step line of bright dresses and toothy smiles. Her nightmares were rare now and she could go to sleep without a light on, but she still slept with her art supplies and drew each night. In this newest drawing, I counted six of us girls and assumed she'd included Jennie. Since our move, the bloodiness had disappeared from her drawings, but so had Jennie, though Lil sometimes appeared outlined in ways that suggested a shadowy figure behind her. I was relieved to see Jennie whole and smiling among us. But I wondered why Sarah had left her father out. Then I saw penciled in below the two largest figures "Momma" and "Daddy."

My gasp must have awakened her, for she stretched, then sat up to peer over at the portrait. Pointing to the tallest figure, she said, "This one is Daddy when he used to be a girl." She regarded my startled face, then made a face at her drawing. "Should he have brown hair?"

I hadn't heard Adam in the hall, but there he was, listening. He came over, searched her blankets, and held up the orange crayon. "This is what I remember having, Sarah. Orange hair, like yours and Momma's, when I was a girl."

"I remember, too, Daddy." She nodded solemnly at him. "I like your hair now. I like you being a boy." She took his hand. "Can I have oatmeal this morning with syrup?"

They both looked at me.

"Sure, oatmeal." I felt dizzy as she rushed past me down the hall.

All children, when they are very young, confuse the male and female. Joe's son had once asked me if I'd liked fishing when I was a boy. But Sarah was seven years old now, past the age for such confusions. She was correct, not confused.

In ways I could not pinpoint, she'd always seemed the one most like Adam, or rather Addie. She often seemed to know things she had no discernible way of knowing.

One evening, not long after we saw Sarah's drawing, I asked Adam if he had ever told the girls—particularly Sarah—anything about himself and Addie. Adam had just returned from his shower. "No, I haven't tried to explain anything to them." He shrugged. "I can't answer *your* questions. How would I answer theirs?"

He stepped into his boxers and climbed into bed with me.

"What should we tell them?" I asked.

"You could tell them about finding me, since you remember it better than me. And I guess I could tell them something about becoming who I am now. But not everything."

"What did you do with Roy Hope in that hotel for two weeks?"

"Everything a body can do to know another body." We both thought about that a moment.

"No." I laughed. "You wouldn't want to tell them about that. But what should we tell them and when?"

"Not now. They're all too young. And they should all be told at the same time so they have company. You would be the best judge of when.

When do you think Momma should have told you about your father?"

I had no answer.

☙

ADAM'S HAIR HAD GROWN OUT QUICKLY, covering the scar on his head. The wound on his chest provided the smile for the happy face Sarah drew on him with a permanent marker. Each night, as he undressed, I saw that the circle and two dots had grown fainter, nearly vanishing, until she redrew them and the process began again.

While I puzzled over the soil and flat pastures, Adam was buoyant. He threw himself at Florida as if it was the Second Coming and redemption was at hand. For him, it *was* a kind of redemption, and his contagious enthusiasm pulled us all in. Even Gracie, who had begun dating, willingly joined in on her father's explorations of Florida.

Adam studied Florida as he had my body when we first met. His interest quickly shifted from tourist attractions to geography and state parks. He familiarized himself with the local bookstores and libraries. On Saturday nights, he scattered the dining room and bedroom with books, maps, and pamphlets, covering every surface as he planned the next day's outing. Somewhere, he found a huge geographical map of Florida and taped it to the dining-room wall. A changing constellation of bright red destination tacks dotted it. "Karst," he said to me one night as he read at the dining-room table. He repeated the new word happily, savoring it. "Karst. That's the name for this place. Limestone and water. That's why the land feels so different here."

With luck, he could be finished at the Warrens' by ten on Sunday mornings and we would take off for a day's excursion as soon as he walked in the door.

"Beats church," Rosie said one Sunday morning as she helped me pack our picnic lunch.

"But won't we go to hell for missing church and going off to do other stuff?" Sarah asked as she poured more cereal into her bowl. She was very interested in rules and the consequences of their violation.

"Not if we sing hymns while we're on our way to the parks. That makes it the Church of Florida," Rosie retorted.

"The Church of Florida" sounded good to all of us. So, on the way to beaches, caves, springs, parks, swamps, rivers—anywhere we could get to and back home in one day—we sang our way through every hymn we knew and saved our souls. We collected Steinhatchee scallops, canoed the Sewanee, and fished at Cedar Key. All the girls learned to snorkel. Adam and Rosie even learned to scuba-dive. Late Sunday nights, we drove home, the girls asleep around us, Adam and I alone in the lights of the dashboard.

Cool water obsessed us those first long, hot months. There were the dark, tannin-stained rivers and cold, crystal-clear rivers, their waters originating in swamps or from deep underground. Unlike the rivers of the Appalachian Mountains, these brooked no boulders, few rocks, no white-water rapids, no muddied rust-colored rise of spring thaw. Florida's rivers were at peace with gravity, sliding along its belly instead of tumbling down into its embrace.

One river in particular excited Adam, the Santa Fe. The first Sunday after school let out for the summer, we drove out to O'Leno State Park and cooled ourselves in orange-brown water near the swimming dock. Then Adam announced that he had a surprise for all of us and led us down the trail that paralleled the bank.

When we reached an observation deck, he laughed and, holding his arms out, proudly announced, "A trickster river."

Below us, the now-black river disappeared into the ground. Heat-stunned, the six of us watched a log crowded with three large turtles pivot in a slow, broad circle on the river surface. The river turned unnaturally and vanished, swallowed by the earth. Above the vortex, the air hung still and peculiarly leaden, almost reverent.

"It's like a big toilet!" Sarah said in a hushed voice.

"Not quite. It resurfaces about two miles from here." Adam pointed to our right.

"Must be some surprised fish and gators popping up there," Rosie observed.

We continued on the path and circled the river's end. Returning to our car, we crossed a swampy area of black soil almost impassable for the clusters of cypress knees. The ground rustled with tiny dark toads that hopped away from our feet, clearing a path for us.

The disappearing river unnerved me. Rivers are supposed to lead us to the sea, not underground. I preferred the spring-fed rivers and pools to the blind waters of the dark rivers. We visited all of the area springs— Blue, Poe, Ichetucknee, Ginnie, Devil's, Fanning—their cold waters so clear we could see the white sandy bottom. At Poe Springs, I stood, chin-deep in the chilling water, and edged along the spring's lip, knowing from the intensity and purity of the blue generally where the drop-off would be but unable to be certain because of the glare of the sun and the water's distortion. Then, suddenly, there was no toehold, and I trod, suspended, almost breathless, above the bottomless place where the water comes out, thousands of gallons per second. That first glance down past my own feet into the dark turquoise mouth of the earth echoed the moment I saw the pulse in Jennie's neck stop, and the first time I saw death on my mother's face. I had stepped off the edge of the earth, over an abyss that could have drowned me, yet I continued to breathe.

Adam wanted me to learn to snorkel. But every time I put my face in the water, I fought an instinctive panic. Unable to convince my body that I could breathe with my face underwater, I heaved and sucked air until I hyperventilated. Though I was a good enough swimmer and eventually learned to relax and enjoy snorkeling, the fear of having my face underwater never left me completely. Adam saw my panic, but he persisted, asking me to learn to scuba-dive and go cave-exploring with him. I could use Rosie's equipment and everything would be fine, he kept telling me, but I refused each time. Going underground seemed too much for him to ask of me. When Adam and Rosie disappeared into the blue, the river and earth gulping them, I turned down the other girls' invitations to play or swim. I sat on the shore, within sight of the guide rope tied to the roots on the bank, checking to see if it had been pulled taut, a sign that they were lost, blinded by kicked-up silt, or hurt and using the rope to find their way back.

At times, I felt left out, unable to share Adam's love of this new place. I would have been jealous, but his enthusiasm for Florida was paralleled by his renewed desire for me at night. The jarring, fierce quality of grief lost its grip on our intimacy. The returning tenderness made it easier for me to forgive Florida its flat unfamiliarity, its alien, sandy soil, its odd weeds and grasses, and its endless wet heat.

The days thickened into full summer heat, and the rain came daily. Suddenly the girls were home all day and we were trapped inside by the oppressive heat and rain. The rain began in July and did not stop. Thunder rattled our little wood-frame house that stood like a lightning rod in the flat pasture. North Carolina had its summer storms, but they were a whisper to the shout and sudden fury of the Florida storms. Thick, heavy drops spat down from the sky onto hot sand. Everything sizzled, then steamed. We draped damp laundry over doors and chairs, anywhere we could fit it. The floors and beds were gritty with sand tracked in on wet shoes and boots.

The newspaper featured pictures of sandbagged houses and the top of a child's swing set half-visible in a flooded backyard. I found little consolation in knowing the weather that summer was not the norm and I was not alone in my amazement under such a relentless sky.

IN EARLY SEPTEMBER, soon after the girls had started school, Adam had a rare weekday afternoon off and asked me to join him on a trip to the springs. We left a note for the girls, in case they got home from school before we returned.

We drove out near High Springs and down a sandy road. Then we parked beside another car in a clearing. A mother and two small children picnicking on a blanket nodded their hellos. The children's wet hair clung to their heads. Otherwise, we were alone. There were no paved roads near the Devil's Springs then, no concession stands or bathrooms, just a path, woods, and the water.

I followed Adam to the back of the truck to help unload his diving gear. I didn't see a snorkel, but there were two scuba tanks.

"Where is my snorkel?" I asked, my hands on my hips.

He picked up the tanks. "It's not much different from snorkeling. And I know you listened to everything I taught Rosie. Come on." He strode off toward the water, tanks and belts in hand.

"Only in the shallow parts," I warned, as I followed him with the masks and fins.

Adam shot me one quick glance, but no response, as he plunged into the chest-deep water.

"Only in the places where I would snorkel. Nothing deep," I added.

He stopped rinsing the tanks and stepped over to the bank where I sat. He touched my cheek very softly, his cool, wet fingers sliding up to my temple. "Only the shallow? But you like it deep." He grinned.

I rolled my eyes at him but returned his smile. "Not in the water."

I slipped into the cold water next to him and let him hoist the tank onto my back. He showed me how to breathe, how to check the air, and how to share one mouthpiece if one of us ran out of air or got into trouble, repeating the lessons he'd given Rosie. The gear felt awkward, and heavier than I would have thought.

Scuba-diving in the chest-high river was pleasant. I had to admit Adam was right. Except for the change in buoyancy with the tank, it wasn't all that different from snorkeling. Sunlight still warmed my back and shimmered silver-blue through the water. As I gazed down at the grasses, I knew I could surface in seconds. I was happy diving a few feet under to get a closer look at a rock or log, pleased with myself for having made my compromise with Adam's enthusiasm for the river. Adam dived lower, glided along the bottom, and circled the small lagoon that surrounded the cobalt mouth of the spring.

When he surfaced and removed his tank and flippers, I assumed he was ready to go home, and began to take mine off, too. He held up his hand. "No, don't. Not yet. I'm just going to the car."

He came back with a light and a thick coil of rope. He had bought a new underwater flashlight recently. Seeing the expensive, shiny new light in his hand reminded me of how comparatively well off we'd been since selling that little corner of the farm before we left Clarion. But I was glad he had the new light. The old one had been secondhand and rusty. I hated to think of him suddenly without light, deep underground.

I leaned on the bank, watching him work his feet back into the flippers. I'd taken my tank off. It lay sleeping on the bank. I was done, I could relax. Adam smiled his happiest, most seductive smile as he adjusted his tank and checked the light. Sunshine streamed down through the trees, speckling the water.

He tied the rope to a tall, thick cypress knee, picked up my tank, and walked out into the water—I thought to rinse it. Instead he turned, holding it up toward me. "You just hold on to me. I'll do the work."

"Oh, no." Panic tightened my chest. "You go on. I'll wait here." I was ashamed of my fear, even with him, and tried to keep my voice casual. But I had shrunk back, certain that he heard the unsteady jerk of my diaphragm in my words.

"It is no different from doing it right here. All you have to do is hold on to me and breathe."

Tree roots and limestone dug into my back. I pressed my hands into the gritty, slick sand on either side of me.

"It is so beautiful, Evelyn. I just want to show you what I see when I'm down there." He looked straight at me, not smiling anymore but waiting, holding one hand out.

I shook my head again. I wanted to say yes, yes for him, but my fear held like iron.

Adam spoke softly, his face resolved and patient. "I want to show you what I see. I want you to feel what I feel. Come on. For me."

I curled my hands, digging my fingertips into the bank behind me. Suddenly I remembered how he had done the same, the nights after Jennie and Momma, when he lay under me, arms outstretched, shaking his head but letting me take him all the same. Letting me have him. I had felt the dense coil of pain in him then. But in the end he came with me.

I owed him the same.

I let go of the bank and took his hand. Without a word, he helped me into my tank and fastened the weight belt around my waist. We moved carefully and slowly. He adjusted my mask, smoothed my hair, and pulled me close. "Just relax. I have you. Hold on. Keep a good grip on my belt and swim behind me. Keep your head down behind my tank while we're in the current. Once we're in the first room and get out of the current, move your fins as little as possible."

I nodded, but my heart pounded, and my skin felt numb and hard. Then we went under, into the silence of water and my staccato breathing.

Over the brilliant mouth of the spring, he handed me the light. He gave a few powerful kicks and we entered the current of the spring. Like a strong, silent wind, it pressed at the top of my head. I kicked hard and could feel Adam using his hands to pull us into the mouth of the cave. The rough rope coiling out from his belt slid against my hip. Beyond our feet was the silver surface of the air. I tightened my grip on his belt. Then there was darkness, and I closed my eyes.

The walls of the spring mouth scraped my arm and the top of my tank. In jerks, Adam pulled us in, gripping the walls of the opening and pulling us down. Down, down, down. I tried to make myself as light and small as I could, forced myself to think of nothing but my breath, my hands on his belt, and my kicking legs.

Adam turned right abruptly and reached back to me with one hand to pull me up beside him. We were weightless, outside the press of the current, released. Adam took the light from my hand. Above us, the cavern wall exploded in light, a wide band of yellow cutting through the silver-gray of limestone. He touched my leg, reminding me to soften the movement of my fins, then, taking my hand, swam us up close to the top of the cave. He held his arms out as if to say, "See, it's beautiful." And it was. More mysterious than beautiful in its mobile shadows, golden light, and silver-flecked silt.

To our right, the cave opened farther into a black hole. We swam once around the cave, our movements liquid and slow. The only sound was my breath, ragged, uneven. I was still frightened and stiff against Adam. I could not tell which way was up or down. But the beauty seeped around my fear.

Holding me tighter with one arm, Adam did something to my tank that I could not see, and unbuckled my weight belt, then he loosed his hold on me, opening his arms a little, and I began to float away from him up, up toward the ceiling of the room, or what I thought of as the ceiling. I pulled at him and shook my head. He took my arm and held his other hand up for patience. I held tight to him, digging my fingers into his sides.

Still weighted, he bent over me to keep me from moving and adjusted the light on the floor of the cave. Then he unbuckled his own belt and it slid awkwardly down in a smoky puff of silt as we began to rise.

Adam twisted, turning so that he was perpendicular to me and held me across his chest as if I were his bride. He adjusted the guide rope still tied to his waist. Nearly blind with panic, I clawed at him. He grabbed my hands with his and clutched them firmly to calm me. His feet hit the cave surface in a small jolt and a sprinkle of sparkling flint. He stood on the roof of the cave, upside down, balanced between gravity, the water's pressure, and our own natural buoyancy. From his arms, I looked up into his face side-lit by the light beaming from below us. At his feet, beyond the roof of the cave, was the surface of the earth. Had the earth's skin been transparent, I would have been able to see past his feet to tree roots and, beyond them, the sky.

He spat his air hose out and smiled at me, a smile that cut through my fear. He opened his mouth and I reached out and put his mouthpiece back for him. He walked us, holding me in his arms around the ceiling of the cave, our shadows changing as we moved. Flecks dislodged by his feet drifted between us, tiny silvery flashes. We were, for a few moments, lovers in some alien airless underground world. All I could see were his eyes, almost black in the shadows, and the changing background of the cave, otherworldly umbers, golds, grays, and whites. I forgot my breath, my panic.

Then he knelt and loosened his arms as if to let go of me. I shook my head and he pulled his arm away to point to our belts on the cave floor. Slowly, he lowered me to the roof and I tilted there, propped against my tank, my legs sticking out awkwardly. The moment he let go of me, my breath lurched in my chest again. I sucked deeply on the oxygen, trying to breathe evenly, but the fear in my diaphragm hardened as I watched him return to the floor and put his belt on then, swim, light in hand, to bring me mine.

He pointed toward the dark end of the cave to another vein that led farther, deeper into the earth's body. I pointed to the surface.

He nodded his head in agreement, but held his hand up asking me to wait. Then he cupped his right ear and cocked his head sideways as if listening. His forehead wrinkled above his mask as his eyebrows shot up in an exaggerated question.

I shook my head. I didn't hear a thing except the jagged rhythm of my own breathing.

Patiently, he repeated the same gesture. Except this time, as he held his ear with one hand, he held his other hand out like a choir director, sweeping it in a slow, steady rhythm up and down. Clearly, what he wanted me to hear rose and fell in a slow, steady rhythm.

I concentrated on softening my breath and listening while I kept myself upright with as little motion as possible.

Still, nothing. I shook my head again.

Adam took my hand and flattened my palm against his chest. I felt his voice reverberate gently through my fingers and up my arm. His other hand rose and fell again. Gradually, I realized that the modulation of his voice matched the up-and-down movements of his hand. His eyes brightened with a question once more as his hand circled to include the whole cave. Then he tapped me on my breastbone.

I felt his voice, but nothing beyond that. I shook my head so emphatically that I suddenly had to use both arms to balance myself in the water. My heart pounded with frustration.

Then I saw the water move between us. From his chest outward, the water seemed to ripple in tiny bubbles. We stared down at his chest. The size of the ripples varied. The variation, I realized, matched the rhythm of the thing Adam wanted me to hear.

Then he opened his arms as if to say "See?" His eyes crinkled into a smile. Before his chest, the water seemed to change again, shimmering. For a moment, I thought he had changed the color of the water, and then I realized what was happening. His voice had loosened little sparkles of sand from the roof of the cave and they were raining down on us.

He beamed. The silt thickened. Too thick. My panic returned. I grabbed his arm.

Adam startled, his face suddenly changed. He swiveled, glancing around the cave in alarm. He jabbed his finger, pointing to the surface as he guided my hand to his belt.

Yes! I nodded. The beam of light danced crazily as we swam through the thick glitter of silt. Adam followed the guide rope, pulling us into the swift exiting current.

The spring spat us out. We shot through the rough tunnel to the undulant blue surface. Then we burst through into air, into sound.

We dropped our mouthpieces, pushed back our masks, and whooped. Adam slapped the water's surface and howled like a dog. I gulped deep breaths.

"Amazing!" He laughed. "Did you hear it? Did you feel it?" He held my shoulders as we tread the water.

I shook my head.

He beamed, undaunted. "I've felt it before here—in Florida—but never this strong. Maybe the water makes it stronger." He held his hand out, sweeping it up and down again in a slow rhythm. "It's like a breath, a vibration. I felt it on the farm, too, Evelyn, if I was very, very still. And in the mountains, always in the mountains. But here!" He pivoted in the water, his head back and his arms spread. "In Florida! It's music! This place is a different note. It is to the farm like a B is to a G. That's the difference. That's it. That's what I've been feeling." His eyes widened as we paddled toward the bank. His hair stuck up in spikes around the mask pushed up to his forehead.

I laughed in spite of my disappointment at not being able to hear what he heard. I flattened my palm on his chest and then let my hand trail down to his waist. "I don't know about that, but I felt you." I licked the smiling scar on his sternum.

"You did feel me, didn't you?" He gathered me in, hugging me close against his chest. "Hurry! Let's get out."

We stripped off our gear and clambered out of the water. Adam ran to the truck with the tanks. I gathered the rest of our stuff and followed. He met me, grabbed everything out of my hands, threw it in the truck, and snatched a blanket. The lone family of picnickers had left.

He cupped my face in his hands, kissed me quickly, deeply, and took my hand. We ran out of the clearing, laughing, like kids. His tented shorts wagged in front of him. In the woods, we slowed to a breathless walk.

Several dozen feet into the woods, we found a few square feet free of cypress knees and threw the blanket down. We peeled our wet swimsuits off in a frenzy and made love under the green canopy and blue sky. The sheer sweetness almost broke me, waves washing over me in a rhythmic baptism over and over until I was undone. Adam's sweet voice rising through and above us like a prayer.

He fell down against my chest. Turning my head to kiss his neck, I saw high in the boughs of cypress a single snowy egret break through and spread herself against the blue sky. I was humbled, grateful for the language of underground rivers, for lovemaking, for the single white uplift of a bird. Grief, for that moment, was only a watcher, a mute child who asks nothing from us and takes nothing, not even pleasure or joy. A presence among us, rather than our essence.

Later, as we drove home under the mid-afternoon sun, we were quiet, soft and liquid in our joints. Adam grinned into the air that rushed through the truck windows.

"I feel different here," he said.

"I know. I see it."

As we pulled into the driveway, the sky shifted into the darker shades of an approaching thunderstorm.

Adam did not open his door when he shut the truck off. He swept his gaze across the pastures of the Warren ranch, our house, and the small fresh patch beside the house, which I had turned over recently for a fall garden.

"Both places have their own music, but Florida seems less dramatic. No hills. No fall colors. But it has its ways. If the farm and the mountains laughed, Florida's land grins a long, sly grin."

Then he laughed and grinned, long and sly.

So I came to live in Florida, to begin to call it home. For the first time since Jennie died, I felt a true hope. He was right to take me there, to baptize me into the new with the familiarity of his touch and his voice.

I hope he felt the same gratitude and knew that when, in his grief, I took his hand and forced my body on him I was trying to do the same thing, to keep him with me—with us—to keep him from floating away.

I never went back inside the caves. I snorkeled a lot, scuba-dived in shallow waters off the coasts with Adam, and teased myself by diving outside the soft, mossy mouths of other springs, but I never went into one again. It was mostly fear that kept me away from the caves. But also, I didn't want to lose the purity of that day, did not want the memory diminished by anything that followed.

Our lovemaking from that point on was as strong and as sharp as when we first met, but it also encompassed a bitter sweetness. A largeness. Early on, we'd been young and bare, our souls and hearts slender with innocence, but now we came to each other robust, fat with grief and joy. When we first were lovers, we did not know we could drift from each other. Our earlier lovemaking had been just us in the bedroom or under the sky. Now we brought with us old scars, a cacophony of experience, and the knowledge that we could part. It made our passion deeper and sweeter.

❧

THE WINTER AFTER ADAM took me diving in the springs, I turned forty. In those first months in Florida, with plenty of time on my hands, I'd scrutinized my face in mirrors, noting the first signs of age. Since Momma and Jennie died, my skin had begun to recall all those days working in the fields. Lines appeared around my eyes and mouth. My hair paled at my temples, the red fading in strands to sandy-gray and white.

One evening, I stood on the back steps, surveying my garden of lettuce, broccoli, and sugar peas. For me, it was an act of faith to put seeds in the ground at that time of year. The garden seemed puny by my standards, but I was growing food again and determined to do better in the spring.

Behind me, Adam straddled his workbench on the porch as he repaired a saddle. His grace of movement and his beauty were still arresting. For a moment, I saw Addie in the look of concentration on his face as he forced the needle through the leather. The sun shone in his eyes when he glanced up at me. The fine lines of his squint disappeared when he returned to his work.

I'd always admired his good skin. Unlike me, he and the girls tanned a golden brown in the sun. Yet his skin had none of the leathery quality I saw on men who spent a lot of time outdoors. I'd noticed many men seemed to age more slowly than their wives. But as I studied him, I saw that he really did not look a day older than when he set foot on my porch with the face of Roy Hope.

He'd arrived with no past, and had lived in an endless present before Jennie died. That innocence had left his life and his face, but its absence did not show as age. His skin reflected only the subtle changes of maturity. He'd settled into his features, but he still appeared to be a man in his late twenties.

How could I not have seen it before? His clock ticked more slowly. I sat down in the chair on the opposite side of the porch. From that angle, the smoothness of his hands and arms was more obvious. My own hands were freckled, the skin on the backs of them not yet lined but loosened.

He stopped at his work and looked up. His eyes were their most golden-brown in the direct afternoon sun. "What?" he asked.

"Nothing."

"You're lying." He laughed.

I went over to him, straddled the bench behind him, and pulled up close, my arms around his waist. "Yes, I am."

He began humming, a song I'd heard on the radio.

"Later," I said. "We can talk later. Finish your work now."

He held up the saddle for me to see his repair.

"I think I need reading glasses," I said as I admired his work.

After that, I studied men my age for their differences and compared them to Adam. Some looked thoroughly middle-aged, worn and beginning to gray. Others had held on to a kind of youthful bearing, their faces lived-in and beginning to slacken with age but not yet showing actual lines or wrinkles. A few had remarkably good skin, like Adam's.

✿

BY MID-SPRING, OUR COUNTRY DRIVES focused on a single new purpose: buying our own land and business. Bud and Wanda were still on the farm and expecting their first child, but not farming. The fields were fallow. When we got a second, even more impressive offer on all the farm acreage along the highway, we sold a few more acres farthest from the house, where the highways intersected, and went to take a closer look at the Mahoney ranch we'd visited several times. The land was perfect: good pasture, a good well, a small pond, a line of deep, wide oaks shading the house, an eight-stall stable in good repair, and a sprinkling of early phlox along State Road 441. The house had four bedrooms, modern walk-in closets, and more than one bathroom. Still, I felt it wasn't wise to take the first thing we saw. We had more money than I'd ever dreamed of having and it was hard for me to let go of it on the basis of what seemed more like luck than serious research. We considered other places but we kept going back to the Mahoney ranch.

Old Mr. Mahoney wanted to sell us the ranch, but he had begun losing patience. One day Adam walked in from work, sat down at the kitchen table, and frowned. "Evelyn, it's okay if we buy the first thing we saw. You were what I saw when I opened my eyes for the first time on the floor of the farmhouse. I didn't look for better when there was no need. There's no need now. We've scoured three counties."

I got the truck keys and we drove to the Mahoneys' to make an offer. That summer, we moved to our own ranch.

The first thing I did by way of decorating the new house was hang the photo of me and Addie that Momma had shown me when she told me about my father, the only photo I had of the two of us together. In Florida, it was the sole proof that Addie had ever existed. No one there had ever met her, not even Pauline. For the girls, Addie was just a relation who had disappeared before they were born, someone who looked a lot like their momma. The picture revealed nothing of the link between Addie and Adam. I bought it a beautiful wood frame and hung it in the hall.

As I adjusted it on the hook, I could almost smell the innocence, the wide-open simplicity of that time. Grief shot through me, then a spasm of regret. I veered away from the sudden memory of the funeral and the girls' faces afterward, when I silenced their father and pled with them to sing only in their normal voices.

They showed no sign of his vocal abilities. No sign of changing as Addie had. But recently I'd noticed how much the girls were becoming like him in other ways. It wasn't just the enthusiasm for Florida that they shared with Adam. They'd begun to smell like him, first Gracie, now Rosie. Lately, when Gracie finished her shower, the bathroom smelled of fresh, newly mown grass, strong as the first time I'd bathed A., that cold winter morning so long ago. Once or twice recently, Rosie had smelled the same after a long day in the stables, the tart greenness underlying the odors of the horses and leather.

The girls had never seen the photo of me and Addie. They gathered around it when they came home from school.

Gracie peered over Sarah's head. "How could the two of you look so much alike?"

Lil turned to me for an explanation, but I had none to give.

At that moment, Addie seemed so far removed from their world of school and the ranch, so unbelievable. I wanted suddenly, desperately, to have them understand everything. I wanted the riddle of their father's origin to unfold like an exotic flower bearing its own explanation, a flower I could hold out in my palm. A mother's offering: I know who your father is. I know *what* your father is.

I shrugged. "Cousins. We were cousins."

"More like twins," Lil said, not taking her eyes from the picture.

I herded them away from the photo. I couldn't fit the story of their father into their world. Yet Adam's identity was as close to them as their own skin. They carried him in their bones and their blood cells, too.

But not in their faces. They looked like me, not Adam or Roy Hope.

"Look what else I put up today while you were in school." I showed them the measuring board from the farmhouse, now mounted in the doorway between the dining room and hall. "Who's first? Sarah? Lil?" I pulled a pencil stub out of my pocket.

The girls knelt on either side of the doorway, reciting dates and names. Lil tapped the highest mark that indicated her and Jennie's height. We froze for a moment as her finger inched up the empty space above that line. No measurements had been added since Jennie's death.

Gracie recovered first, leaping up to grab a ruler from the desk. She balanced it on her head as she pressed her back against the door frame. "Measure us, Mom."

She squared her shoulders and stood very straight and still as I held the ruler level and measured her. Rose was next, smirking with satisfaction to see that she had gained on Gracie, who was now only a fraction of an inch below the line marked "Momma—June 1953."

Adam walked in, wiping his face on a handkerchief as the back door swung shut behind him.

"You're next!" Gracie called to him.

"Stop cheating, Lil." Rosie perched the ruler on Lil's head.

Lil lowered her heels to the floor, then turned to look at the mark Gracie made.

Adam joined us and ran his finger from Jennie's name up to the line of Lil's new height. "Look how much you've grown."

Lil bit her lip. Her eyes went back and forth between the two marks. "She would be this tall now, too," she whispered.

"Yes, she would be," Adam replied. He massaged her shoulders. "Your turn." He touched Sara's back.

Sarah stepped up. She'd grown the most, almost three inches.

Gracie waved the ruler impatiently. "Mom and Dad, you two haven't been measured in years. Come on!"

"We won't have grown, we're already grown up," I protested.

But Adam stepped up and Gracie reached, leveling the ruler over his head.

"Wow! You've grown," Rosie boomed. "Look!"

I pointed to his feet. "Your boots."

Sarah helped him pull them off while he balanced on one foot.

In his stocking feet, he still stood taller than his original height. His feet were flat on the floor. I measured him again. Six foot three and a half. A little more than an inch between the first and second measurement.

He stepped away from the door frame, unimpressed with his growth. I took his place.

Gracie squinted at the line of her father's height above my head. "That is weird. He has grown!"

I was slightly shorter than my first measurement. Adam marked my height right over the new line for Gracie.

Within minutes, all of them had dispersed, intent on phone calls, TV, homework, or chores. My eyes kept returning to the new, darker mark above all the others. He had grown. Only an inch or so in the fourteen years we'd been recording the girls' heights there. We were literally going in opposite directions. But what did it mean about him? About us? Every time I walked through that doorway, I felt I passed through those questions.

⁓

WE PUT UP A SIMPLE SIGN—THE HOPE RANCH, A. & E. HOPE—and built a second, larger stable. Adam began boarding, training, buying, and selling horses as he had in North Carolina. He quickly filled the stables. They were farther from the house than they had been on the farm. But I could hear Adam as he worked, his whistle and calls to the horses, and on the days he gave his horsemanship lessons, his admonitions to the riders to "balance. True yourself."

My garden lay between the house and the stables, and I kept some chickens. Having my own land felt like a wondrous, luxurious relief, endearing me to the place I'd recently found so strange. I still missed the farm. I missed the Clarion hills. I missed Joe, Cole, the Sunday picking parties at Marge and Freddie's, quiet Rita, and even cranky Bertie, but I no longer ached for them.

Lil and Sarah helped me plant persimmon, fig, and pecan trees in the afternoons, when they came home from school. Rosie nearly lived in the stables when she and Gracie were not picking at their guitars or listening to Joan Baez or Beatles albums. In fact, all four girls took up some kind of instrument. Lil joined the marching band at her school and played the flute. Sarah began lessons on violin Tuesdays after school and impromptu fiddle lessons from Adam in the evenings. He found some local picking parties and often took all the girls. I was the only nonmusical one in the family.

∽

THE NEXT YEAR, Gracie turned eighteen and was on a date almost every Friday and Saturday night. Sometimes, Rosie would go out with her—a double date. Ranch life started early in the morning and we were all usually in bed by ten. They complained of their early curfew, but when we stood firm, they relented without much protest.

One Friday night, Adam shook me awake soon after I'd gone to sleep. He pressed his finger to his lips. His other hand covered my mouth. "Gracie and Rosie have just left. Let's surprise them and go with them."

"What?"

He led me out of bed to the front porch. "See, we'll have to hurry." He pointed down the driveway. In the light of a full moon, I could make out Gracie and Rosie hurrying toward the highway. The clock glowed eleven o'clock. I started for the front door, pissed.

"Not yet. Go get dressed first. I'll get Lil and Sarah ready," Adam said. "We need to see where they are going—all of us."

As I changed clothes, I heard Lil's and Sarah's voices.

"Don't," Adam whispered to them. "It'll spoil the surprise if you turn on the lights."

Moments later, as the four of us walked silently down the driveway, we could see Gracie and Rosie clearly in silhouette under the big oak by the highway, their guitar cases propped beside them. They were sneaking out to play music? My anger began to slip. Adam grinned next to me. It had been a long time since we had all been outside at night together. Sarah squeezed my hand and tried not to giggle. A cool wind lifted my skirt. We marched side by side, holding hands.

"Shit!" Rosie hissed when she looked over her shoulder and spotted us.

Gracie, who'd picked up her guitar and stepped closer to the road to peer north toward town, whirled around, her mouth a dark O of surprise.

"We're going out with you!" Sarah ran ahead to hug Rosie.

"We're not going anywhere. We were just out for a walk." Rosie swatted Sarah away.

"Walking your guitars, that's a good one!" Adam laughed.

Lil joined Sarah in a little jig and chorus of "We're going out! We're going out!"

An old, battered station wagon with wooden panels pulled up slowly, its lights out. The driver, a blond boy in a white shirt, got out and stared wordlessly at the six of us. "Daddy, please!" Gracie whispered as Adam stepped up to the boy and held out his hand.

"Thank you, it's so nice that you're letting us come along. We don't get out much," Adam said.

The boy stared at Adam's outstretched hand, baffled. Adam had the advantage of about five inches and at least fifty pounds on him.

"It's okay, Keith." Rosie's voice was flat with resignation.

Keith looked at all of us. The moon shone so bright I could see every hair on his head. He gave us a determined grimace of a smile and then shook Adam's hand.

We piled in. Rosie and Gracie slipped their guitars in the back of the station wagon, then climbed into the front seat with Keith. Adam and I got in, pulling the younger ones onto our laps. The young man next to us in the backseat reached quickly behind the seat and put something away. "This is Andy. Be nice," Rosie said to me and Adam.

"I will," Andy croaked and pressed himself closer to the window.

"Lights, son."

"Thank you, sir." Keith turned on his lights and we were off.

I dared not look at Adam. I bit my lip all the way into town to keep from laughing.

Skinny Andy beside me cleared his throat and adjusted his glasses every mile or so. Rosie turned several times to mutter and slap at Lil, who squirmed and kicked her seat. Otherwise, we were silent until we reached the first streetlights of Gainesville.

"We were going to this place in town where people get together and play music. We're playing there tonight," Gracie said with flat, offended dignity. "If we don't sign up early enough, all we can get is the later time slot."

We pulled up outside what looked like an ordinary house. A few dozen cars lined the street. Gracie led us down a short, dark hall with random squiggled psychedelic colors painted on the black walls, and into a large, dimly lit room. The place smelled of smoke and beer and another, unfamiliar sweetness. Small tables crowded the room of about forty people. No one there looked over the age of thirty. This was nothing like a Clarion picking party.

We were obviously Ma and Pa Yoakum with our gang of young'uns, but after a few quick glances of interest, everyone returned to their drinks and cigarettes. Keith and Andy scooted off to get extra chairs. We sat crowded around a single little table near the back.

A man with a goatee played banjo on a small stage, a familiar but jazzed-up tune. Adam leaned over toward me. "Not bad." Sarah wiggled off my lap and returned to the hall to trace the colored swirls. Keith, obviously deciding that servility would be the best approach to the situation, brought us each a cup of coffee. I thanked him with pointed warmth. Lil, who had recently learned to wink, gave him one.

He stood uncertainly for a moment, then sat down beside us. Rosie and Gracie ignored everything but the banjo onstage.

Then the girls were on.

Gracie leaned over the mic. "We're the Hope Sisters." After the pale banjo player, they were exotic flowers. A few people waved and nodded from the audience. I realized, with a shock, they had been there before. They knew these people, this place. Adam took my hand. To my ears, they did Bob Dylan better than Bob Dylan. A woman in a long skirt brought cookies for Lil and Sarah, who stopped fidgeting long enough to thank her.

After the next song, Gracie covered her mic and said something to Rosie, who first shook her head then nodded. Gracie peered past the lights into the audience and pointed, "Those are our parents in the back."

"Obviously!" someone shouted from near the stage. Gracie smiled, pulled her hair out to her shoulders, and dipped her head in a little curtsey.

"They hitched a ride with us tonight. They don't get out much," Rosie dead-panned.

Adam pulled me to my feet for the quick splatter of applause. Everyone turned to look. It was my turn to be mortified. I blushed.

"And our two little sisters." Gracie motioned them to the stage.

Sarah bolted from behind us. Lil hung back. "Go on, Lil, go to your sisters." Adam pushed her gently. Sarah and Lil blinked at the lights as they stepped up to the stage. Their sisters, who whispered away from the mics, positioned them. Then the four of them sang "Where Have All the Flowers Gone?"

I stood behind Adam's chair to get a better view. He leaned his head back against me. The last time I'd heard them all sing together in public had been at Momma's funeral. I recalled how, when they held some notes, there seemed to be an extra voice, five rather than four daughters.

I listened now, sure that I heard a fifth voice entwined. I closed my eyes and slid my hand down Adam's chest to feel the barely perceptible hum of his breastbone under my palm. When I opened my eyes, Adam gazed up at me. We were submerged in our daughters' voices. Then their harmony seemed to expand, then unravel and move closer, rising from behind me and on each side. With a small jolt, I realized there were, in fact, many extra voices. At the table near us, several women sang along with the girls. Scanning the crowd, I saw others singing. A song I did not know, sung by a room full of people who did not look or think like the people of Clarion, people my daughters might know for many years to come. This place—the house and the town we were in—were not what I had expected for our future. But here the girls would have more options. If there was ever a knock on the door, if anyone came for their father again or for them, they would have options and multiple paths. My world may have contracted, but our daughters' had expanded.

They finished the song. Warm applause erupted. A few people whistled and called for more. Our daughters bowed. Beautiful, innocent, harmonious daughters.

We'd never grounded them before, but we did the next weekend. They also had to muck the stable every day and do the dishes each night for the next two weeks. But we moved their curfew to one A.M. on the nights they played at the Bent Card. Adam stayed up reading until he heard them return.

That fall, Gracie started college at the University of Florida but continued to live at home. On the weekends, the house filled up with young people. They were polite and respectful but they did not call us ma'am and sir, as the Clarion kids would have. They dressed differently, too, and they smelled sweet, like flowers or incense, and, eventually I realized, like marijuana. The boys, at first, wore Beatles haircuts, but soon it seemed they all had shoulder-length hair. All of them, boys and girls alike, wore beads and bell-bottom jeans with patches. Often, I had to take a few discreet glances at their chests or wait until one spoke before I could tell if I was speaking to a boy or a girl. A few of them were black, their full afros bobbing softly. They all carried large macramé bags, backpacks, or guitars.

Their ideas about life were very different from when I had been a teenager. Whatever we thought of our leaders in the forties, we knew the enemy and he wasn't us. But in the sixties, the enemy was closer at hand—white adults spitting on little black girls going to school, assassins, and the advocates of the Vietnam War. The world seemed to be on fire. More than once, the girls sat rapt in front of the TV news, tears of outrage on their faces.

Unlike me, the girls were ready to step into the world they saw on TV. They were young and could not ignore the fire. Flyers announcing protests and rallies, album covers, books, and newspapers littered the house. For hours at a time, Gracie's friends gathered, talking about music, the Vietnam War, or the latest protest on campus.

But for Adam and me, the ranch was an oasis. We were happy to share it, to have all the girls' friends visit. I remembered what a refuge the farm had been for me during the last war and hoped we were providing similar solace.

Today, we'd be arrested for contributing to the delinquency of minors for what went on at the ranch then. Adam and I were uneasy at times. We were also naive. In small-town North Carolina in the forties, there had been only booze and sex, no drugs, no protests. No curfews, because there were no places to go after nine or ten o'clock at night.

Once I saw a friend of Gracie's step out of the back of a van parked in the driveway. As the girl bent to tie her fringed boots, I saw, through the open van door, a boy buttoning his shirt. I knew the girl was only seventeen, a high school senior. A sweet, bright kid. I felt I should do something. But I wasn't sure what I should or could do. At their age, I had the responsibility of a farm. I had first Cole, then Addie, in my bed.

Most of the girls, Gracie told me, could get birth control pills at the local clinics. Many of the boys who crowded our porches faced the bane of chastity: the draft. So, after I'd gone over the facts of life once again with Gracie, I could think of nothing more to say than "be careful and don't get pregnant."

One evening, Adam found a hand-rolled cigarette on the stable floor and a lighter nearby. "It sure doesn't smell like tobacco." He sniffed the twisted end.

We'd both read about marijuana, and the Woodstock festival of muddy, stoned hippies had been all over the news the weeks before. Neither of us was easy with the idea of the girls or their friends doing drugs. But the lighter concerned us as much, maybe more, than the pot. We knew what a burned-down stable would cost.

"I want to know what it's like before we talk to the girls about it," Adam said. "Let's try it."

I held back, reluctant. But Pauline had tried it and proclaimed it "no big deal." She preferred Jack Daniel's, she said.

So we strolled out past the stables and lit up the cigarette, passing it back and forth between coughing fits. A cool puff of wind wafted the smoke farther into the pasture.

Not much happened. Adam seemed a little more talkative. I felt relaxed and a little weird, but not elated or particularly high. It seemed as if the world, not me, had gotten oddly and thoughtfully drunk. An experience far short of the dire warnings I'd read in magazines and newspapers. I scorched the spaghetti sauce for dinner that night, but we both ate a lot and thought it particularly good. Then we went to bed without ill effect.

But we did have some new rules after Adam found the marijuana. No visitors in the stables unless Adam or Rosie was with them. No matches or lighters anywhere near the stables. No one could offer or give Lil and Sarah anything stronger than chocolate milk. And because the number of visitors on the weekends had increased, and a few parents of Rosie's high school friends had called looking for their sons and daughters, everyone had to come through the house and introduce themselves to us.

As the boys would troop by on their way to gather in the fields, Adam would shake their hands firmly and look them in the eye. Then, with uncharacteristic paternal sternness, he'd announce his rules: "Stay away from the stable and horses. Take care of the girls. And have a good time, boys."

"Sure, Mr. Hope, it's cool." The boys always nodded. Rosie and Gracie would roll their eyes at Adam and pull the boys through the house and out the back door.

ON A MAY SATURDAY IN 1970, Gracie and Rosie prepared for a big party they'd be having out in the pasture. Sarah and Lil left earlier that morning with Pauline for the beach. All afternoon, the older girls bustled around in the kitchen and house, driving firewood, tables, and baskets of food out to the spot where they usually gathered, under one of the large live oaks. Adam cleared an area in the pasture we never used for riding. They would be allowed to have a bonfire there. They'd be far enough away to dim their music and debates, but close enough to run back to the house for the bathroom or any emergency.

I spent the day in the garden, mulching, trying to keep the water in and the weeds out. Adam mended the far corral and worked with a young mare, a pretty, gold thing whose love bite had left a bruise on my behind the week before. By sunset, we were beat. We sat inside at the kitchen table, drinking iced tea and watching each other sweat.

After dinner, Adam and I relaxed on the front porch, greeting a steady stream of arriving kids. The yard filled with cars and vans. It looked like it was going be one of their bigger parties.

Finally, the mosquitoes chased us inside. There was no more iced tea in the refrigerator, so we each poured ourselves a glass from a pitcher of bright red Kool-Aid. Adam finished his quickly and poured himself a second glass. I settled down on the couch with a novel while he gave the stables a final check for the evening.

It was well past ten o'clock, my normal bedtime. I didn't feel sleepy but the words on the page blurred toward the margins. I set my book aside. I was back in the kitchen, trying to decide if the Kool-Aid tasted like strawberry or cherry—maybe raspberry—when Adam joined me and a batch of kids shuffled through. We rose to greet them. They were a brightly dressed group, all so sweet and beautiful. I felt a great tenderness toward them.

When they left, the salt shaker on the table undulated slowly to some music I couldn't quite hear. One of the boys had been carrying a mandolin. "That boy must be a very good musician," I said and pointed to the dancing salt shaker.

Adam gave the table a long, quizzical look. We both sat down again.

"The flowers are beautiful," he said. I'd cut some zinnias and lantana and put them in a bottle. They danced, too. The bright pink, gold, and orange petals trembled delicately, keeping time with the salt shaker. They were the most beautiful flowers I'd ever seen. Their hairy emerald leaves curled gently, waving in a breeze. I bent and inhaled the simplicity of tart chlorophyll and sunshine. When I opened my eyes, the room glowed.

Adam, fluctuating between the definite and indefinite, watched me. I held my arms out to him in an invitation. He was surprised, but game. I tapped time on his shoulder as we waltzed around the table. He was the most beautiful and exquisite man. So right and so good.

The whole world was right and good and sweet and we danced. The breeze swirled around us, cooling our skin. I smelled horse, marigold, leather, dirt, and sweat on us. I heard the birds outside, an infinity of calls. The stabled horses breathed and shuffled. Farther out in the pasture, more animals and the voices of the kids, a faint echo of chirps. A car rattled down the road. Our home hummed around us. The room spun slowly and glowed as we danced. We kissed and got lost in the dark forest of kissing; I slowly sank to the floor, pulling Adam with me.

A wave of sound washed down the tube of the hall and curled itself into and out of footsteps, then giggles. There seemed to be a million of them in the hall, thousands of young people, staring down at us. Their faces looked more beautiful and funnier than any I'd ever seen.

"Excuse us, Mr., Mrs. Hope," someone said in a high, tinny voice. It was the funniest thing I'd ever heard. I was gone, rolling on the floor and giggling. The joke was contagious. Every time Adam looked at me, he laughed, too. Wires of hilarity coursed through my face and stomach until I ached.

Then, gradually, we quieted, the wires of laughter loosened. Limp, we watched the undulant ceiling form and reform itself, the skin of the room. We breathed and held hands, lying on the floor, and listened as the house breathed around us. The birdsong brimmed on and on.

The ceiling and the birds were too active, and I turned to Adam.

He grinned. "Why are we still on the floor?"

"Because we can be." I held his face in my hands and got closer. He hummed his sweet bell tone, a lilting spring-green sound. His face began to come apart, disintegrating into its individual features, but the change did not disturb me. I moved into his changing face, closer, until I could see nothing but the dark, bright black of his pupils, the endlessness of him. His features dissembled then reassembled into another complete face. A man, his mouth open in rage and pain. Then he was an Asian woman, large-eyed, expectant. Then a calm, fair child. On and on. Face after face. Each face distinct and whole, historied. Faster and faster, the changes came. Face after face. Like a current sucking me out of myself.

I cried out, jerked away, and shut my eyes.

Then there was just light and breath, the music of him, his essential beautiful alienness. He rose and rose and rose all around. He touched my face. The whisper of his fingertips on my cheek surged down my body and out my feet. A cry jolted me and I realized that the cry had come from me, my own voice of pleasure. I sank back onto my kitchen floor and lay beside my ordinary husband, the father of my children.

Children. Daughters. There was a knife, dark and solid in that thought, but I could not identify it.

I told Adam about the knife. He told me that the Kool-Aid must have something in it. He felt a little funny.

"I'll say," I agreed.

In a single fluid move, he got off the floor and took a sip.

I angled myself up and drained my glass. To me, it tasted like too many things I could not name. "What kind of Kool-Aid is this?"

"Exactly." Adam peered at the glass in his hand. "This is the kind of Kool-Aid we need to ask questions about. I've read about kids putting LSD in Kool-Aid as a kind of test to see how 'cool' someone is." I followed him to the sink and watched him rinse his glass. The swirl of pink water laughed down the drain.

Adam picked up the pitcher and sniffed the Kool-Aid. "There must have been eight or ten gallons of this in the coolers I saw some kids lug into the kitchen earlier." He scowled, somehow both comic and paternal. "How do you feel?"

I rubbed his shoulder, my warmth for him erupting in my chest, radiating down my arm.

"Wonderful." I giggled. "Go! Go find out what it is. I want to know." I pulled him toward the back door and pushed the screen open. "I should go lie down again. I'll wait for you in bed."

He kissed me softly, then obediently set off into the darkness, an inch of brilliant candy-red sloshing in the pitcher he still held. He weaved his graceful way between the cars and vans parked behind the house. His mobility amazed me.

I was no longer sure I had feet, but I stepped outside and looked up. The night sky shimmered with points and streaks of pinks, lavenders, and oranges. Birdcalls slid through. The dark knife remained unnamed, solemn and quiet in the press of sound and color. Odors of hay and horses and wood and young people wafted by. Days or minutes may have passed since I'd sat on the couch reading. Time had turned to rubber. I was happy, very happy until the ground went red—first the rust-red of Carolina clay then blood-red. Then, the dark knife ripped the world in two and everything came in. An animal howl filled me. Jennie! Jennie! Jennie! But I could not bring her face before me. Just darkness. The dark immenseness. Hated, hated darkness. In me, on me.

Then I was inside on the bathroom floor, tearing my shirt off. Sorrow sparking through my clothes as I threw them down. My face was like wax in the heat, my bones too close to the surface. I had to turn from my own reflection in the mirror. I sat with my knees pulled up to my chest, afraid of the sorrow and darkness that breathed through me, faster and faster, until a large hand reached around from behind me. The hand told me that I was alone, that it was my own breath I heard. Those words spread a calm through me. I uncoiled in the thick, warm air and listened. I heard that everything was okay. Good. There was just *is*. Is-ness.

Is filled the bathroom. In all directions it continued. Endless.

After a while, I ran a bath, filling the tub with water. And the water was like water all over the earth. Iridescent. Alive.

Naked, I saw that everything about me was good. In the moonlight through the window, the slackness of my lower belly and my breasts, the silvery stain of old pregnancy stretch marks, the little veins on my legs and ankles, the darker freckling on the backs of my hands and my arms, the colors of my hair dulling toward gray were no longer signs of age but beauty, simple and present as the joints in my wrist, as the crickets outside and the sparkle of the bath water through my hands. All was right and wondrous, sweet, infinite.

I eased down into the cool bath. My body loosened into the water and I knew again without any doubt that the world was well and beautiful. Not all the time and not for everyone, but for the All which the individual and the singular is a part of. I had first known this, beyond any reason, when I was a child alone in the woods, and I knew it again. I breathed deeply and calmly. Stunned.

The pale, half-drawn shower curtain, the bathroom walls, and the small square of the bathroom window seemed to breathe with me. I was in a room in a house on a ranch in a state in a nation in a world that turned.

Then a young man appeared at the toilet. It seemed right that he should be there, peeing with his back to me, but I also sensed there was something unusual about the two of us being in the bathroom together. He sang a few bars of a jumpy little tune. He jigged his shoulders like a gnome. Then he turned and let out a yelp as he zipped up. "Mrs. Hope!" He rubbed his face and eyes. There was still something I couldn't understand. I didn't bother to cover myself as we stared at each other. My inability to comprehend what was going on struck me as hysterically funny and I burst out laughing. He bumbled out the door, calling, "Everything's cool! I'll get help! Rosie's right on the front porch!"

Moments later, Gracie and Rosie exploded into the bathroom, upset over something, turning on blinding lights. They spouted a chorus. "It's two in the morning. What are you doing in the bathtub in the dark? What happened? Are you okay?" To appease them, I let them dry me and dress me. They kept asking if I was okay. They moved too much, they talked too much, and there was too much I did not understand. Funny, sweet girls. They glowed like daughters, but finally I told them to shut up.

They led me to the bed. I propped myself up on the pillows. The sheets glittered white around me. Then Gracie and Rosie sat in the dark on either side of me like sentinels. A good way to go to bed.

I sighed. My body relaxed against the headboard. When I closed my eyes, I could see all my nerves swept clean. Sweet and new as the moment after sexual climax.

"What are we waiting for?" I asked. "Adam?"

"Where is Daddy?" Rosie started to rise from the bed. "I'll go—"

I touched her warm shoulder. "No, wait here with me. He's coming back."

She leaned closer again. "Okay, Momma. We're both here with you. Now, how much of it did you drink?"

"I drank this much." I laughed and spread my arms. But the sentinels did not laugh. Gradually, I stopped giggling, cowed by their solemnity.

"Jennie," I said. "She was a knife."

"Oh, Momma!" Gracie choked.

"She's okay now, Momma. We're all okay," Rosie took my hand.

Gracie began to cry, softly. I reached over and rubbed her back until she stopped. Then she slept, slumped against my shoulder. Rosie fell asleep, too.

Gradually, something like sleep moved through me. I dozed in waves of bright, dense dreams, surfacing long enough to awaken the girls and send them to their rooms. Several times, I had to assure them that I was okay. They murmured apologetically as they stumbled in the darkness toward the door.

Then I slept, a true, deep sleep.

When I next awoke, the brilliance of noon light washed through the bedroom and Adam lay next to me, propped up on his elbow. "Are you okay?"

I nodded, though I had no idea how okay I was. "And you?"

"Oh, I'm fine. But I'm sorry I didn't get back before you fell asleep."

I shook my head. "It's all right. I sent you out to . . ." I had a sudden vivid recollection of his face changing. I rubbed my eyes and pulled my head back a little to focus. His features held. In fact, his face seemed a little sharper, more distinct than normal. His eyes glowed. His skin was clear and ageless. I caught my breath.

He placed his hand gently on my diaphragm. "It was LSD." He studied my face. "You look a little rough."

"Adam, it felt a thousand times stronger than the marijuana we smoked." Slowly, in lumpy, halting sentences, I told him what it had been like for me. He listened intently, not once interrupting with questions. His eyebrows shot up at my recitation of his strange metamorphoses.

When I got to the part about Jennie, he closed his eyes, turned his head away, and moaned. "I'm glad the girls were with you after that. I should have come right back after I found out what was in the Kool-Aid instead of trying to find them. I searched everywhere. All those cars and vans. Even the stables. Then I came back here and found all three of you sleeping peacefully. Are you sure you're all right?" He slipped his hand around mine.

I managed to nod convincingly.

He kissed my forehead. "I wanted to find the girls so badly because I heard something."

I felt myself smile, my face involuntarily reflecting his. "What? Why are you so happy? What did you hear?"

"I heard one of the girls, Evelyn."

"What do you mean? Heard?"

"My voice from one of them." He pressed my hand to his breastbone. "I was on my way out to the fire circle with the Kool-Aid when suddenly I felt it." He opened his arm and his hand swept a graceful curve above me. "So beautiful!" He laughed.

I sat up. "What?"

"Evelyn, I've never heard that except when the sound was coming out of me!" His face shone.

I blinked.

"It had to be one of the girls. I know what I heard. I felt it here." He beat his chest softly.

"Gracie? Rosie?"

"I don't know, but I wanted to find out. I dropped the pitcher and ran. There must have been a hundred kids around the fire. Faces, light, music. I couldn't find Gracie or Rosie. But it had to be one of them." He slipped off the bed. "I couldn't sleep. I've been up all night. We need to talk to them about all of this, now. I called Pauline and asked her to keep Lil and Sarah at her place for the rest of the afternoon. But first let me make you some breakfast. You'll feel better when you've eaten."

I pulled on my robe and followed him into the kitchen.

I distinctly remembered him drinking his first glass of Kool-Aid, then at least one other after that. How could he be so normal?

He pulled out a chair for me and set a cup of coffee on the table.

I sat down and rubbed my eyes. The sun glared through the windows. My brain felt like the transparent, crispy edges of the fried eggs he sat before me a few minutes later. I pushed the plate away and asked for dry toast and water.

"I'll wake up Gracie and Rosie," Adam said as soon as I'd finished eating.

While he went to wake the girls, I watched the salt and pepper shakers on the table and stroked the scratchy leaves of the now well-behaved zinnias. I tried to muster some idea of how we should deal with Gracie and Rosie. Adam had drunk as much of the Kool-Aid as me, maybe more. Had he been hallucinating, hearing what he wanted to hear? Suddenly, the effect of the LSD seemed to return. For a moment, I saw Adam not as a man but as a raw bundle of intentions that could shimmer off into any direction at any moment.

"Momma? You okay?" Rosie and Gracie stood in the doorway, their faces and pajamas rumpled.

I nodded and pointed at the chairs across the table from me.

"Sit." Adam glared sternly at them. "We need to talk."

They wilted under his gaze. Gracie hunched at the table. Rosie poked at some crumbs left on a saucer.

Adam paced behind them, shaking his head. "Leaving that Kool-Aid in the fridge was a stupid, stupid thing to do. Do you know what you put your mother through? Were we the only ones who didn't know what was in the Kool-Aid?" With each pass back and forth behind them, Adam seemed larger. For a few crazed seconds, I thought he might actually be growing.

Gracie twisted around in her chair to look up at Adam, a bare apology on her face. "It was a mistake, Daddy. Everybody else knew! A friend brought all the Kool-Aid. Someone was supposed to bring the last pitchers out to the pasture."

Gracie turned to me. "I'm so sorry, Momma. We didn't mean to . . ."

"Your face, Momma." Rosie held her hands up to her face and then swept them back from her cheekbones. "You didn't look like yourself." She reached across the table for my hand. "Are you okay, now?"

Adam paused for my reply.

"I'll be okay. But it was really rough at one point."

Adam leaned down between the two of them. "If you ever think your mother is in trouble, come get me." His voice was low and dark. "After we realized there was something in the Kool-Aid, I left your mother alone while I went out to the fire to find out what we'd drunk. Then I stayed out there trying to track down the two of you."

Both their heads jerked up.

"You had some, too?" Rosie said.

"Yes, we both had a couple glasses. Not much happened to me, but it was very different for your mother."

They exchanged quick glances then stared up at Adam.

"Your mother and I will discuss this and decide what to do." He began to pace again. The only sound in the room was the rhythm of his footsteps.

Speechless, I just shook my head. I was still stuck at his claim that "not much" had happened to him.

For a long, withering moment, the girls sat, frozen, staring at the table.

He came to a stop and exhaled loudly. "I have one more question." His voice was brighter, his face softer.

The girls' posture relaxed a fraction.

He tapped them each high on their breastbones. "Now tell me which of you did I hear last night at the fire?" He turned an expectant, almost tender smile from one to the other. I understood how badly he wanted them to be like him.

They glanced quickly at each other.

Rosie swallowed. "What are you talking about? We weren't out there at the fire when you and Momma . . . I was on the front porch. That's where I was when I heard Momma laughing and Jerrod came running out."

Adam turned a confident face to Gracie and touched her back. She looked over her shoulder, her eyes darting up toward him. Her gaze held his for a second, then she returned her attention to the table, scanning its surface. "I wasn't at the fire then, either."

"She was with me," Rosie said.

Adam stood motionless, squinting at the top of Gracie's head. He rubbed his chest. A quick smile crossed his lips and I thought he might laugh as he usually did when he caught one of them in a lie. Instead, his eyes narrowed. He slapped his hand on the table. "The Kool-Aid was a stupid thing to do. You didn't tell us what was in it. Now one of you is not telling us where you were and what you did last night. I was not hallucinating. One of you is lying!"

Gracie opened her mouth. Before she could speak, Rosie touched her arm. She flushed and pressed her lips together. I tried to recall when I'd seen that odd spasm of confusion and guilt that crossed her face.

"Go!" I waved them away. "Now. Go get dressed."

I could almost smell their relief as they scrambled out of the chairs and down the hall.

Adam came around the table and knelt beside my chair. "I know I heard her." The certainty in his words belied his puzzled frown.

I held his face in my hands. "It's not like Gracie to lie, especially to you. You drank the Kool-Aid, too. Maybe you imagined it."

He shook his head. "Time sped up. Things were a little brighter and funnier, the volume turned up. But I didn't see or hear anything that wasn't there. I know what I heard, Evelyn! I don't understand why she won't admit it." He pulled me closer. His face looked no older than it had when we'd married.

"Don't cry, Evelyn. Everything will be okay."

"I'm not crying," I muttered into his collar.

He laughed at my lie.

We kissed. He tasted different. Like water. But what resonated softly from his mouth and chest, pouring into me, felt ancient. Older than Addie.

Overwhelmed, I spent the rest of the day in a stupor, napping while the girls moved softly up and down the hall, taking care of the day's chores. Adam brought me soup and crackers for supper.

After I'd eaten a second time, I finally felt coherent enough to discuss what we should do about the girls and the drugs. The power of the LSD awed me, and our daughters were so young and so delicate. I wanted to ban everything like it from the property.

But Adam disagreed. "If it is happening, we should know what's going on. For me it wasn't any stronger than marijuana, Evelyn."

That shocked me into a momentary silence. The drug had hit me like a sledgehammer.

"No. No, Adam, we have to do something! We can't just let them take these drugs. And they did something careless and stupid." I felt my panic rise higher each time I said no.

"Evelyn, did you see their faces when I said the drug had little effect on me? I think it's the same for them. I don't think we can assume that any drug will affect them like it does their friends. Or you."

I remembered what the doctor had said about the uniqueness of Adam's brain and hoped they were like him in this. "Yes, Adam, they may be like you but their friends are not. And even if you think it's fine for all of them to experiment, they should not have disguised drugs lying around. Plus, it's against the law!"

He nodded his concession and sighed. "We need some rules. Still, we can't control what our daughters do every minute of every day. And we've never tried to. We've always trusted them. Gracie is twenty and Rosie is seventeen. If we jerk the reins, especially now, Gracie will pull away and Rosie will run in the opposite direction. And Lil and Sarah will see them do it."

"They are not horses, Adam."

"They are horses. You're a horse and I am a horse. We need to lead them, not take the responsibility from them." Then, with a tender exasperation, he added, "Evelyn, trust me. I once trusted you with what the girls should do. Trust me now."

A nauseating wave swept through me. I suddenly understood what I'd seen on Gracie's face earlier that day—the same dissonance of shame and confusion I'd seen there after Jennie's funeral, when I'd stilled her father's voice.

My resistance collapsed. "Okay," I whispered. "We won't jerk the reins."

THE NEXT NIGHT AT DINNER, Adam rapped his knife on his glass of iced tea. All four girls were immediately silent. Adam looked around the table at each of them, his gaze stopping at Gracie. "Girls, your mother and I trust you. We know you trust us to take care of you. We all have to take the responsibility for ourselves and for others. This is what your mother and I want from you." He glanced at me and his voice grew firmer. "You will never have anything in this house again that does not look like what it is. No disguises. No more Kool-Aid and no funny brownies. Hallucinogens can be very powerful. If you are going to take them, you must do it at home and only rarely. Nowhere else. You must tell us if you or one of your friends is tripping. And if you get caught with anything illegal, we will not mortgage our home and livelihood to bail you out and pay a lawyer's fees. Is that clear?"

There was a round of nods and "Yes, sir."

"Gracie and Rosie, we have more to say to you after dinner." Then Adam raised his glass as if for a toast. "Daughters, you have to know what a thing is and respect its power. You don't fly the *Apollo* spacecraft to the corner store. That is waste, ignorance, disrespect. Respect the vessel you are in. And we will respect you. Evelyn?"

The tension in the girls' faces had already softened to gratitude as they turned to me for my response. I had nothing more to add, but I vowed to myself that I would keep a much closer eye on all of the girls.

After dinner, Gracie and Rosie were contrite. Without complaint, they accepted our list of extra chores and restrictions.

❧

A COUPLE OF DAYS LATER, while Adam was out on horseback, I approached Gracie as she folded clothes in the laundry room. All the girls had been more attentive to the housework since my accidental trip.

"Almost everybody else had some of the Kool-Aid that night," she confirmed. "But I didn't. Rosie either. We didn't bother." She shrugged.

"I've tripped before. But I just felt good. The world was very pretty. And louder. That was all. It's overrated if you ask me. I agree with Daddy."

"Obviously it doesn't affect everyone the same way. Your father wasn't hallucinating. So what did he hear the night of the party?"

Gracie slowly picked up a big towel and folded it. For a long moment, she did not reply. Since the LSD, she and Rosie had treated me with an unnerving self-consciousness, as if they thought I might burst into flame at any moment. She squatted to retrieve more clothes from the dryer. "Momma, you remember when you told us the facts of life?"

"Yes, of course." I frowned at her obvious attempt to change the subject.

"Well, you told us we could ask you anything about sex. I want you to know that I've always appreciated that. I know girls whose mothers never told them anything." She paused to fold another towel. "But you also said that we all have a right to privacy and some things should remain private. We could ask you anything about sex as long as it wasn't about what you had done, personally. And you promised not to ask us the same sort of questions, right?"

I nodded, curious.

She continued only after she saw me agree. "You said it was your duty to make sure we were using protection and you had a right to ask us about that, but the rest was our private lives. You also said you wanted us to tell you if any man ever hurt us."

"Yes, that's exactly what I said. You called it 'limited disclosure.'"

She smiled when I quoted her. "That was the deal." She studied my face as she closed the dryer. "So the night you and Daddy drank the Kool-Aid, I was well protected and nobody was hurting me. But, like you with Daddy, I probably wasn't as quiet as I should have been." She glanced away and I heard the slight challenge in her tone.

"Oh." I recalled the perfect, long-resonating sound of her father's climax with me the night before and understood why she'd blushed when Adam confronted her. I also realized, with relief, that I had been wrong. Her denial had nothing to do with me or what happened after Jennie's funeral.

Gracie ignored my red face and squeezed past me with her basket of folded laundry. "Mom, I'm going to be a junior next year. I really need my own apartment. I think I've found a good place, cheap. Close to campus."

That night, Adam came in late from the stables. He'd been checking on a mare who would foal soon. He undressed in the dark, and spooned up close behind me.

I repeated everything Gracie had said earlier.

He laughed, flipped on the bedside lamp, and sat up. "Of course, that's why she lied! Sex is the one time it's so difficult not to . . . Evelyn, I heard a burst of pure joy from her. As if something enormous swam past me in a flash. Something powerful and beautiful whipping by. Then a long bubbling wake of warmth. I could almost see it." He shivered and wiped his eyes. "What's his name?"

"You really think I'd ask for details at the end of that conversation?"

"Well, no, but that's okay. We'll hear more about him, I'm sure. He made her very happy."

I'd expected at least a little paternal bluster about his daughter having sex. He was, after all, a man. Instead, he placed my hand on his chest and drew me into his arms.

"You're not surprised, are you?" I asked.

"Oh, she surprised the hell out of me that night." He turned his face sideways to look down into my face, smiling at the memory of her voice. "But I've always felt it was a possibility."

I nodded against his chest.

"I've heard other things," he said. "Once in the middle of the night when she was dreaming, Sarah muttered something—funny, almost like a warble of surprise, but she wasn't speaking, her mouth was shut. And Rosie with the horses—there's something going on with her since we moved to Florida. She uses a voice with them. But I've never heard anything close to what I heard the other night."

All these years, I'd been listening and heard nothing. "Why didn't you tell me?"

He didn't answer, but I saw the response on his face, the memory of Jennie's funeral. Again, I felt the crushing weight of that day and what I had asked of him.

Regret choked me.

"Evelyn, it's okay. You were right. It is a powerful thing. For a long time I thought they were not vocal like me. But I decided to let them discover it in their own way if they were—*I* have to respect the vessel they are in. I'm happy to let them come to it in their own way. And they will. We don't have to push anything. We can leave Gracie with her privacy." He searched my face. "You've never heard anything from Rosie?"

I shook my head dumbly.

"Hers may be too high-pitched for you to hear. It's like a whistle. But if you watch closely, you'll know. The dogs and horses turn to her a split second before she speaks and sometimes they respond when she's given no obvious signal."

"This has been going on and I didn't know?"

"No one's been keeping anything from you, Evelyn. I think there are times Rosie's not even aware of what she's doing."

All this time I'd spent with him and I still did not know him. One thing I was certain of: he was without guile and incapable of deception.

It saddened me to think of how he must long for company in his unique gifts. I understood that desire and its insidious burdens, for I had so often craved company in my longing to share what I knew of him. I wondered how much a similar desire had motivated him to take on my form so many years ago.

THE WORLD OF MY DAUGHTERS seemed so different. Or rather, I had begun to feel my difference from them more keenly. All mothers feel that way to some degree as their children become adults, but I harbored those other questions about who they were and what they were capable of. But I began to realize Adam was right. The answers to those questions would be *theirs,* not mine, and they might carry the gifts of their father privately.

For the rest of that summer, all the girls spent more time at home. They sang together in the evenings. Their voices, carrying through the house or across the back porch to the garden, always filled me with a calm tenderness.

In the fall, Gracie moved into her own apartment, a large wood-frame house near downtown that she shared with a menagerie of hippies. Within months, Rosie was accepted at the University of Florida, in pre-vet studies. She followed Gracie, the center of her world shifting away from the ranch.

Sarah painted and Lil read her fantasy novels. Soon enough, they also had parties with their friends in the pasture. They both decided not to wear bras or shave their legs. But they were there for supper every weeknight. Their grades were good, their eyes clear, and their friends respectful.

Lil turned fifteen the following spring. Her birthday seemed to incite a restlessness in her. A new name began to pop out any time she discussed school: Bryce. I recognized the cadences of infatuation in her voice, but there was something else, something not said. I asked Sarah about the boy, but she'd never met him. He was a new kid at school.

Sarah and I were in the living room when Lil and the boy pulled into the driveway. She peered out the side of the window. "Incest," she hissed just as the front door opened and they strolled in.

Not exactly identical, Lil and the boy were certainly strikingly similar. The same shade of red curly hair, Lil's shorter by only an inch or two. The same green eyes, the same tall lankness. His nose was larger, his eyes closer together. Adam, who had joined us, recovered first and offered his hand. The boy's gaze darted past our surprised faces, and then swept the room as Lil introduced him.

Moments later, Adam and I stood in the kitchen and watched the two of them saunter to the stable to meet Rosie and the horses. Adam leaned against the sink, hunched forward for a better view. "I don't like him," he said. "He looked away every time I spoke to him."

Lil laughed and leaned toward the boy, letting her hair sweep toward him.

"There's nothing we can do," I said.

"Sarah's right. It looks incestuous."

"She lost her twin. She likes him because he looks like Jennie and a lot of the people on my momma's side of the family. Every red-headed, freckled one of us," I said.

"He reminds me of Roy Hope. He wants her, but he doesn't see who she is."

"You got your skin and face off of Roy Hope. And other parts." I patted his crotch.

"Your point?"

"She's getting something off of this boy that she needs now. That's all she sees—what she needs. I'll bet she's not seeing him any more than he sees her," I said.

Adam glanced quickly at me, as if to speak, but said nothing, then turned his attention back to Lil and the boy.

I continued. "I know she's vulnerable, but I trust her heart—her eventual heart. If we take the offense now, she'll take the defense." I realized that this was exactly the argument he had made after we drank the LSD Kool-Aid. "She's infatuated and working through something.

Let's just keep our eye on it—on her. We can do that. She still lives here."

"Okay. But I don't want him hurting her."

Before they reached the stable door, Lil took the boy by the shoulders, turned him to face her, and kissed him. I recognized that certainty and directness.

"Shit," I said. "She's in love."

Adam nodded and turned away from the window.

Within a few months, Bryce took up with another girl and avoided all contact with Lil. She sequestered herself in her room to write poetry, refusing to come out even for meals. With only two daughters at home, her withdrawal shifted the balance of the house.

"Let her be," Adam told me when I insisted she come to the supper table.

But he stopped by her room each night on his way to the table.

"I'm not hungry, Daddy," she told him.

After days of this, Sarah arrived home from visiting one of her middle-school pals and announced, "I have had enough of Lil's broken-hearted moping. Time for a cure." Ceremoniously, she set a large, obviously heavy box on the floor. Gleaming gold satin with geometric designs covered the box and lid. "A surprise for later. Don't ask."

Gracie and Rosie showed up for dinner that night. Still, with all five of us at the table, Lil declined to come out of her room.

With a nod to Sarah, Adam said, "Let's go." He scooped up the pot of chili and tilted his head in the direction of Lil's bedroom. Rosie, Gracie, and I loaded up, taking the rest of dinner with us. Sarah followed with the mysterious box.

Lil remained sullen and quiet as we set up the meal on the floor of her bedroom. No protest, no acknowledgment. But she couldn't resist all three sisters. By the end of the meal, she joined in the conversation, asking Rosie about vet school, telling us about her new math teacher.

After we'd eaten, we pushed the dishes out of the way and Sarah sat the box in the middle of our circle. She took out three objects, each nestled inside a larger one, and carefully unwrapped them.

"Singing bowls!" she announced with a flourish of her hand. But they were not like bowls for serving food. They were cylindrical, their sides straight and high, the largest about eighteen inches in diameter. They were made from opaque glass, each one a slightly different creamy shade. Light from the hall shone through them, leaving one side shadowed. Carefully, she arranged them in a triangle on the floor.

Gracie smiled up at Lil. "You have to be near them." She patted the floor next to her. Lil shrugged and obliged.

Sarah took out two mallets. She held on against the rim of the largest bowl and moved it slowly around the inside edge. A tone reverberated, vibrant and soothing, through the room. I almost jumped from the shock; I'd never heard anything so similar to Adam's voice. I glanced quickly at Adam, who sat across from me, between Rosie and Sarah. But his eyes were closed, his head rolled back. The girls leaned in closer as Sarah picked up a second mallet and swirled it gently in the smallest bowl. The timbre and volume changed. Adam's hand moved up his chest. Lil smiled, open-mouthed in surprise. The first interest I'd seen on her face in days.

Adam sighed and shivered, his eyes still closed. The girls inched closer to the bowls. Sarah concentrated. Her breathing was deep and measured as she pressed the mallets slowly, around and around, deeper then higher in the bowl, varying the tone and resonance. Without looking up, she motioned to a third mallet sitting next to her and said, "Gracie, yours."

When the third mallet touched the middle bowl, I heard the sharp intake of breath around me. I felt the harmony in my solar plexus, a sweetness that made me smile. The tone of the three bowls seemed to mingle into a peak, then separate in a broad pattern. As it changed, rising and falling, my family moaned around me. Lil had slumped back against the footboard of her bed. Rosie stared, unfocused, at the bowls, her hand on her belly. Lil blinked, and her eyes rolled back in her head as her back arched slightly, then dropped again. Her face softened. Adam exhaled sharply. Gracie lurched forward in a small spasm and clutched her chest with her free hand. Something I could not see or feel moved through them like a wave, orgasmic.

Sarah moved the mallets lower in the bowl, Gracie followed, and the sound sobered, changed rhythm. She looked around at us. "More?"

"Yes," Adam whispered.

I nodded.

Sarah looked at Lil, who mumbled, "Please. Yes, more."

Sarah picked up the tempo again. "Stay there and a little faster," she said to Gracie. And the sound moved from somber to ticklishly pleasing. Then the room exploded. Adam, Lil, and then Rosie burst into guffaws and rolled on the floor. Sarah bit her lip in concentration. I went limp and happy, leaning back against Lil's closet door, my head warm. But Adam and each of the girls suddenly sucked in their breath, then exhaled explosively, wiggling as if being violently tickled. Tears streaked their faces. Lil pounded the floor and clutched her father's arm. Rosie tried to stand to do God knows what, but couldn't make it up off the floor. Gracie kept her mallet moving, but held one hand over her mouth as if to stifle her laughter. A tear slid down her face and into her bowl. Sarah stared down, mouth open, eyes big, and her pupils dilated.

The sound filled the room, and the strange St. Vitus dance of giggles, guffaws, and snorts continued around me. My head and chest hummed with a tender, amazing joy. But what I felt was clearly not the fantastic joke they all seemed to hear.

Then, abruptly, part of it cut out. I opened my eyes. Gracie, a wide, foolish grin on her face, held both hands up in the air.

The sound dropped and stopped. Sarah put the mallets down gently and rubbed her arms. Their laughter bubbled down to whimpers, then exhausted sighs.

"Wow," one of them moaned thickly.

Gradually, the girls begin to move around me.

"Oh, and to think I used to spend money on drugs," Rosie said.

Adam snored. Gracie stretched beside him and closed her eyes.

Sarah, Rosie, Lil, and I slowly gathered up the dirty dishes and leftovers and wandered back into the kitchen. They washed the dishes while I sat at the table. I watched them jostling shoulder to shoulder in the kitchen. Bright-haired, slim young women. Lil now as tall as Rosie. So like me when I had been a girl. And so like their father when they rolled on the floor laughing earlier.

I thought of Momma. For a moment, I saw her face drawn with illness, the appeal for forgiveness in her voice when she told me about my father. How could I explain to them what I did not understand? Adam was, and always had been, vast and strange, beyond my vocabulary. I glanced down the hall at the photograph of Addie and me hanging there. How could I explain that to our daughters?

Lil put her dish towel down, came over to me, and laid her hand on my back. "Thanks for the sisters, Mom," she said.

"You're welcome."

She looked down at me. "You didn't like the bowls as much as we did, did you?"

"Oh, I like them. But it was different for me."

Sarah joined us at the table. "When I was a little girl, I worried about that."

Lil sat down next to her sister. "Worried about what?"

"That I perceived—saw—things differently from everyone else," Sarah said. "What if, when I look at a pumpkin, I see the color orange. But when you look at it, Momma, you see the color purple and when Lil looks at it she sees yellow. But if we all call the color we see 'orange,' then we would never know that we were actually each seeing different colors, would we?"

Lil nodded. "I thought the same thing, but I had backup when I was a kid. I always knew Jennie saw the same thing I did. I was sure of it." She pressed her lips together the way she always did after uttering her sister's name.

I thought of Adam, solitary, the only one of his kind. "There are things we'll never know. But you're not alone. None of you will ever be alone." My words fell heavier than I intended.

A short silence followed. Then Rosie volunteered: "I have the same problem with sounds. I'm pretty sure there are times I hear things that other people don't." She held up the pot lid she had been drying and tapped it on the edge with a big spoon. *Ting!* The sound reverberated. Rosie swept the spoon through the air as if following the sound. The arc of the spoon continued long after I heard only silence punctuated by Adam's snores from Lil's bedroom. Rosie banged the pot again softly and whispered in mock drama, "And sometimes, ladies, I hear that sound when there is no pot or spoon around!"

Beside me, Lil pinched her thumb and forefinger together and sucked air between them. Sarah snickered.

"No. No," Rosie protested. "Nothing to do with smoking. It started when I was a little girl. Weird droning sounds. Stuff like those bowls."

I wondered what else Rosie might hear that I did not. I shooed Lil away and stood up.

"Well, I have heard enough. I want to hear the dishes getting finished. Go! All of you."

They raced for the kitchen door. Once again, I felt myself to be the solitary one. They heard things I could not hear. They had potential out of my range, possibilities that would ferry them into a future blind to me. They were so young. All of them. Even Adam.

Not long after she returned the borrowed singing bowls, Sarah began the first of her "anatomy" drawings, strange distortions of the human body morphing into animals. She turned Gracie and Rosie's old bedroom into an ever-changing gallery. My favorite was a portrait of Adam as a centaur. She had followed him around the stables for days, stopping him at his work, asking him to take his shirt off.

I caught her sketching me one day as I bent over in the garden. "I'm not taking any of my clothes off," I told her and waved her away.

"Oh, I really wouldn't want you to for this one." She grinned as her hand swept over the paper.

The next day she had a new sketch up, a horse shown from the rear, turning to look back in surprise over its shoulder. The face peering over the broad, heart-shaped rump was an elongated, horsy version of my own.

"She got you!" Adam laughed when he saw it.

"Really?" I asked. "Is my butt that big?"

Adam wisely just grinned and scooted out the door.

Since their births, I'd wondered how different my girls were. As they matured, I couldn't help but ask how it was that they didn't seem to recognize the difference between themselves and others, even as they gave voice—literal and metaphoric voice—to that difference. How could they not know what was in their own blood? In their genes? But, I told myself, we are all stuck in our own skin. Limited to the singular certainty of our individual selves. Each of us knows the world only from a single perspective.

Then the thought jolted me: not Adam. He was not limited to his own perspective, he had not always been stuck in one skin. He'd had mine and Roy Hope's.

I laughed.

Again, he surpassed my understanding.

How would they, his daughters, follow his lead?

❧

THE YEAR THAT SARAH HAD STARTED her periods, I'd begun skipping mine. By the time she was in high school, I had gone through menopause. I had a relatively easy time of it, but I did notice I no longer had the single-minded drive toward sex, and desired it less frequently. Sexual desire had been a part of me since I had become a woman; I was uncertain of how to be a woman without it. Who would I be if it fell away completely?

And even though I had not wanted a child for years, the final impossibility of it made the act less consequential in some way. But its meaning had changed rather than diminished. Lovemaking became a distillation of the bond between Adam and me. Now it was pure touch, pure connection without the tincture of other possibilities.

When I entered the room of Adam's body, everything else fell away. There was only him, his body, his mouth, his hands. Then the moment of sweet, bright harmonics bound us. That remained unchanged.

During the days, Adam seemed a normal man. A normal, *young* man. I could feel, almost smell, the stallion on him.

One day, as I weeded the garden, the tall, blond girl who had come home from school with Sarah wandered out our back door and toward the stables. She had wide hips and a full figure, what people would have once called voluptuous, and a kind of brightness surrounded her. Her youth was heavy on her, like sweat. She walked into the open stable door. I heard the swish of Adam's rasp stop. Then his voice, followed by hers.

I walked past the stable a few minutes later, with a bushel basket of spent basil stems and roots for the compost pile, when Sarah rushed the girl out of the stable and toward the house, hissing, "Jesus, he's my father!" She shook her head at the girl, whose voice rose defensively as the back door shut behind them.

Adam stood inside the stable, wiping his hands and watching their retreat. I tried to read his face. We looked at each other. I walked up to him, pushed his hair up out of his eyes, and studied his face. Not a day over thirty he looked. I was fifty-two. He could easily have passed for my son. I thought of how other women must see him. For a moment, I imagined him in the world without me, outliving me.

He touched my hair, ran his hand down my cheek. He took my hand and pressed it to his breastbone. "Don't leave," he said.

Keeping my fingertips on his chest, I bent to put down my basket and pretended that he wanted me to stay with him in the stable. I did not want to think of what he saw—my graying hair and the lines on my face that told him I was far closer to my end than he to his.

I unbuttoned and opened his shirt. The skin on his bare chest did not have the slight crepe-like quality of age. There was no sinking of the pectorals that I saw on other men my age, no gray hair. But the horse-kick scar remained. I traced it, wanting to press my tongue to it and feel its smoothness. I closed my eyes for a second and saw the pale star in the X-ray of his chest as the doctor had held it up for me to see.

I licked my finger and added the dots and circle that would make a smiling face. "Remember those first months in Florida when Sarah drew that? It took days to wear off. You came to bed each night with it fainter and fainter. Then she would redraw it and the vanishing process would start again. She did that for months."

He nodded and looked down at himself, tapping his sternum with his fingertips, a gesture as old as Addie. "I think of it as a U."

"U for unknown."

We kissed and the odor of his sweat blended with the basil resin on me. He smelled different lately.

"U for what I don't know," he said.

I heard something new in his voice, a lack of ease.

"Will you age at all? Will you change that way?" Then the question I did not say out loud, because I knew the answer: "Will I have to grow old alone while you remain young?"

He looked down at his chest again, then past me, his eyes scanning the house and the land behind me. "I don't know, Evelyn. I changed myself to be this." He ran his hand over his youthful face. "But I don't know how to become a middle-aged Roy Hope."

Anxiety rippled up my chest. I pulled him closer and lay my head against his neck.

"Don't go away," he whispered.

"No one is going away." I looked over my shoulder out the door of the stable. My eyes followed the path of the girl. "Have you ever been with another woman?"

"Evelyn. Evelyn." He took my hand and led me out into the yard. Gripping my shoulders, he turned me suddenly to face away from him. "Look at the sky, Evelyn. Look at the pastures. And the trees. I love that sky, those trees and fields and every horse there. I love all the faces I see in town. I love the way the roads curve or go straight. All these things give something to me. I love all this. It is so beautiful. *So* beautiful." His voice broke and fell lower.

I did look at those green pastures, at the soft undulation of the distant, tree-dotted fields. The depths of cumulus towered in the distance. Through my tears, I saw the beauty he saw.

He tightened his hold on my arms. He whispered again, hard and fast against my ear. "All those things and everyone else is outside of me. But you, Evelyn. You pulled me out of the ground. And I know how your tongue rests against the roof of your mouth, how the sweat gathers under your breasts in summer, how your narrow wrists ache after hours of hoeing, how you take your pleasure from a man. And I know all this not through empathy or imagination. Not even love. But because I have been *you*."

His last sentence was an unexpected turn. He had found the perfect pitch. As soon as he said those words, I knew them to be true. He belonged to me as no other had. And I to him. And he would, in some ways, never belong to me. I did not know his parameters. That was the source of my anxieties. It wasn't the threat of infidelity. It was him.

For months afterward, I thought of Dorian Gray. Every time I saw Adam shaving and my eyes tracked the skim of the razor over his ageless skin, I imagined a middle-aged Roy Hope. Like me, he would have reading glasses on the nightstand by his bed, a tube of Ben-Gay lotion on hand for his aching joints. Several times, when Adam thought he was alone, I saw him scrutinize his reflection, frowning as he leaned in close, turning his head side to side or pushing his hair up to expose a perfect hairline.

Like all other questions about him, the question of his age dogged me, patient and loyal. But unlike other questions about him, time would inevitably make this question public, progressively more public.

∽

BEFORE THE YEAR WAS OUT, Gracie announced her engagement to Hans, the Dutch student she had been dating, the man she had been with the night Adam and I drank the Kool-Aid. They wanted to get married soon, they explained. Then Hans would be able to legally work in the United States while he completed his doctoral degree. Their engagement was no surprise, as Adam had predicted; we'd seen a lot of Hans since that night. But their shy addendum to the engagement announcement was completely unexpected: Gracie was pregnant—a happy accident, they explained.

I should have been disappointed that she had not been more careful with birth control, but all I felt was relief in knowing she could have children. Her pregnancy was the final proof that the girls, despite their sexually ambiguous beginnings, were normal. Not mules but fertile women!

Gracie insisted on a wedding at the ranch. She and I strolled out of the kitchen so she could show me where she wanted to stand with Hans as they made their vows. As she pivoted, surveying the land around her, her long red braid swung out behind her and she shielded her eyes from the afternoon sun. "Yep, this is the spot. And in about a month, the sun will be setting right over there." She pointed.

I realized that we were standing where all the vans and cars had parked the night Adam heard her voice ring out sweet, joyful. I understood why she was choosing to commemorate the spot, and I smiled. She reminded me so much of my younger self at that moment.

The guest list was effusive and rambling, a menagerie of our past and present. Gracie wanted an informal wedding not much different from their parties, except that it included North Carolina relations and friends, as well as Florida horsemen, Hans's family, and, of course, a varied pool of the girls' friends—hippies, academics, campus activists, and a few Florida cracker cowboys.

As we all gathered just before the ceremony, I watched my sister, Bertie, who'd recently found the Lord, bless the non-Baptist masses with a fixed scowl of restrained piety. My brother, Joe, and his wife, Mary, struggled politely through a conversation with a local philosophy professor. Freddie and Marge showed up with banjo, guitar, and regrets from Cole—his wife, Eloise, was ill. The two of them were the most at ease, settling in among the long-haired musicians.

After a few years living in Florida, we'd resumed contact with our Clarion relations, a few of whom had even come to visit. But now I could see the shock that registered in their eyes when they saw Adam's face, so much younger than theirs and mine. Those sideways, assessing gazes reminded me of what we had endured in our last year in North Carolina. I appreciated how much the move had spared us and opened up the girls' lives. But I could see our Florida neighbors and friends making the same comparison now. If they had assumed I was simply aging prematurely, meeting my middle-aged siblings corrected that notion. I did not want to lie again. I did not want to be shunned again. When their eyes lingered a moment longer than normal on Adam's face, I looked away, ignored the smolder of anxiety under my ribs, and turned my attention to other guests.

The wedding ceremony was flawless. The girls were all beautiful, especially Gracie in a long, white, cotton lace dress. Rosie set aside her overalls and donned a long dress to be the maid of honor. Lil and Sarah sang. In his dark suit, Hans looked a fetching combination of shocked and proud. He was clearly a good and reliable man. Adam and I had no qualms about him, and Hans's family seemed to adore Gracie, but we cried at the wedding all the same.

After the short outdoor ceremony, we all ate dinner on long tables set up in the pasture. Hans, normally a rather reserved person, got drunk enough to serenade us in Dutch, then hug and kiss us all, proclaiming his love for everyone. Sarah, the official wedding photographer, captured all our goofy, happy grins. But there were no other surprises. No tainted Kool-Aid. Though I did detect the smoke of marijuana on a few of the guests.

The music went on until early in the morning. We made strong coffee and breakfast for the motley gang of stragglers who had camped all night. Then the honeymooners left for a month in Utrecht.

When they returned, Gracie was almost four months along and beginning to show. They continued living in Gracie's small apartment, where they would stay until the lease ran out or the baby was born, whichever came first, then live with us for a few months after the birth while Hans completed his degree. We counted down the weeks.

Several times I had bouts of anxiety about the baby, though no nightmares as I'd had when I was pregnant with Gracie. Once I asked Adam, "What should we tell her? Should we warn her that he might not look right at first?" I was asking only about the baby, but as the words came out of my mouth, I thought of all her questions that would naturally follow.

My question seemed to surprise Adam. "I don't think there's really anything to warn her about. What good would it do? It would just upset her, like you were before she was born. The girls were all fine and our grandchildren will be, too. And that's all that matters."

I recalled my anxious examinations of the girls when they were little. My question suddenly seemed disloyal and overly fearful. But Adam's face, as he answered, was devoid of anxiety, open and free of judgment. Something in his eyes then reminded me of Addie's response, years before, when I'd asked her if it bothered her to have no past, no explanations or stories for herself. "I am," she'd simply asserted. Unlike me, A. had never needed explanations or stories. It also occurred to me then, as it had in those first moments of Gracie's life, that whatever Adam saw in his children or grandchildren, however unusual to anyone else, might seem natural and familiar to him.

I soothed myself with lighthearted warnings to Gracie and Hans about the particularly intense "newborn" look of Hope babies, but did not share my anxieties. In those last months, when Gracie grabbed our hands and pressed them to her swollen belly and asked, "Did you feel that? You feel it?" the thrill of that firm thump against my palm vanquished any residual worry. The ripple of our first grandchild turning in his mother's womb was mortality and continuity. Adam was right. Nothing else mattered.

We loved Baby Adam at first sight. I had expected to love my grandchild, but couldn't imagine it possible to love any other child with the intensity that I felt for the children who came from my own body. Yet, from the first touch, my love for Gracie's son was immediate, so visceral it startled me, and equal to my love for her.

His features lacked the flat, slightly unformed quality our daughters had when they were born, but his skin looked uneven as theirs had. Exhausted from labor, Gracie cried when she first saw him. Hans tilted his new son in his arms so we could take our first good look. Adam lifted the blanket. Swollen testicles propped up a little stiff pod. Definitely a boy.

"At last, another doolywhacker in the family," Adam laughed. Within hours, Baby Adam's features smoothed. There was no discussion of tests or problems.

Baby Adam was only twenty-four hours old when Adam and I returned to the hospital. The two of us sat on the bed, flanking Gracie, while Hans took a much-needed coffee break in the cafeteria. Adam cradled the baby, and the three of us watched in fascination, cooing each time he sucked his fist or blinked or wiggled in his blankets. Round face, blond fuzz. Eyes blue as the waters of a Florida spring. Perfect, beautiful.

Then a nurse walked in. All bustle and efficiency, she whisked Gracie's food tray aside and checked something on the chart. She glanced at Adam, smiled, and said, "You should give the baby back to your wife."

Adam slid off the bed and came around it toward me, holding our grandson. I opened my hands to take the child.

"No." The nurse laughed. "Your wife. It's feeding time and your wife is down for breast-feeding. Grandma can't do that."

Adam flushed, then wordlessly turned and handed the baby to Gracie, who took him hungrily. He gave me one quick, confused glance, muttered something about coffee, and left.

"Some daddies don't like to watch, but he'll get used to it, honey." The nurse fluffed a pillow and slid it under Gracie's arm.

"It's his first grandchild," Gracie volunteered.

This registered on the nurse's face. "Well," she said.

As the nurse left, Lil and Sarah popped their heads in the door of the room. "We saw Daddy in the hall," Sarah said. "Everything okay?"

I nodded and motioned for them to join us.

They sat enraptured on the edge of the bed, watching little Adam grunt as he audibly sucked his mother's breast, his eyes shut tight. Gracie leaned back against the pillows and closed her eyes. I walked over and looked out the hospital window. I kept seeing the look on Adam's face, its rapid change from reverent pride to an expression I could not define. Embarrassment? Surprise? Shame?

"Are you okay, Momma?" Sarah asked.

I nodded and joined them again at the bedside.

"Why have you two always lied about Daddy's age?" Gracie asked, her eyes still shut, her face serene and tired.

Lil looked to me for an answer. Sarah leaned across the bed, cupped the baby's head, and smoothed his hair down.

"He doesn't know how old he is," I said. "We had to make up something for the courthouse when we got married."

"How can he not know?" Lil asked.

"There were no records of his birth, and he didn't really know his mother," I replied.

"Still, how can he not know how old he is? He should at least know what year he was born? Didn't his mother . . . ?" Lil continued.

Sarah put her hand on Lil's. "Daddy's special." She glanced from her sister to me with that expression on her face that always made me wonder how much she knew and how she knew it.

Gracie raised her head and looked at me. "However special Daddy may be you must have come pretty close to actually robbing the cradle. He was weaned when you met him, right?"

"Yes, young lady, but he could barely feed himself." It was true. For a second, I pictured Addie's hand wavering as she reached for her first biscuit and blackberry jam.

Gracie laughed and gazed down at Baby Adam, who made a loud puppy-grunt of satisfaction at her breast. "Momma," she said and patted the bed beside her where she wanted me to sit. She shifted the baby from one breast to the other, and the newly exposed nipple continued to spurt, the stream of milk landing on her knee.

Sarah and Lil leapt back, squealing and giggling.

The baby startled, lost suction, and then sneezed at the second breast now spraying milk into his face.

"I didn't know they could squirt like that!" Gracie laughed.

GRACIE, HANS, AND THE BABY moved out to the ranch. Their apartment lease had expired, but Hans still needed to finish up his doctoral work. Soon, they would leave for the Netherlands to introduce the baby to his Dutch relations. Then they would live in Washington, DC, for Gracie's Foreign Service training. After that, she would receive her first international assignment.

That summer and through the fall, Adam and I spent as much time with our daughter and grandson as we could. Adam postponed his usual trip to the mountains.

He did not say so, but he missed his time of solitude. I sensed a restlessness in him that went beyond the normal energy and distraction that comes with having a newborn and a new mother in the house. His tautness relaxed only when he held his grandson.

Late one night, I found Adam asleep in the recliner. Baby Adam, exquisitely new and tender, slept slack-mouthed, drooling on his grandfather's chest. I knelt next to them and studied Adam's face. I didn't want to wake him then, but longed to touch him, to assure myself of his substance.

He opened his eyes, in that abrupt way he sometimes woke, without movement or speech.

I pressed my palm to his jaw, and then cupped the baby's head with my other hand. "You two remind me so much of all those long nights when Rosie had colic," I whispered. "You look exactly like you did then. You haven't changed at all." I felt an intense longing for the past. He and I would never again be a young couple with children. Yet, I could see on his face, on the very surface of his skin, that he could have all those things again.

He stroked my cheek. "The first time I opened my eyes, I fell in love with you. Before I knew what love was or who you were. Then, at night, I lay beside you absorbing you as a child does the world. I fell into you. And you met me in everything I wanted or did. It was a sweet, complete immersion to take your form. I didn't expect it, or try to make it happen."

I nuzzled his hand as he continued.

"With Roy Hope, I had to literally push myself into him. I stole from him. And it took two weeks." Adam took a deep, slow breath and gazed toward the dark rectangle of windows. Past the reflection of the three of us, moonlight shone on the yard. Beyond our yard and the faint line of the road lay the darker area of gentle slopes and the sky. I could make out one star. I wondered if he saw the same one.

"Evelyn, it's been years since you had to explain anything about me. But that will change soon. I look at men in their fifties and sixties. Older men, men who . . ." He glanced at me and, mentally, I finished his sentence: "Are your age."

"Adam, I can't keep the inevitable from happening." I felt impotent.

"I know. I don't expect you to. But we need a solution." He looked down at our grandson on his chest. "Before he knows me like this. Before more people here mistake me for his—" He hesitated and then recovered. "I'm not sure what to do or what I can do, but give me time."

I pressed my finger to his lips. "He has a perfectly wonderful Grandpa. And you have all the time I can give."

Baby Adam moaned and rocked his head. Adam rubbed the baby's back and his tiny body relaxed immediately. Then he pulled me toward him for a kiss. A tender, sweet kiss. I closed my eyes. His mouth was the world. Hope was a hard, dark seed in my chest.

I reached up, turned off the lamp, and then wedged myself into the recliner next to him. With our arms around each other and our grandson nestled between us, we fell asleep.

During the night, Gracie retrieved the baby and covered us with a blanket. As I woke, dawn light pinked the sky outside the window. My hips ached from being cramped in the recliner.

"Good morning." Adam planted a kiss on my cheek and, in a single fluid motion, pushed down the footrest and stood up.

FOR THE LAST TIME BEFORE GRACIE'S DEPARTURE, the girls performed together in a coffeehouse near campus. They all sang. Gracie and Rosie on guitar, Lil played the fiddle.

When Adam and I, the official baby-sitters, arrived, the café tables were already crowded with the familiar faces. Many, whom I could barely see in the low lights, greeted me and Adam by name. They cleared a center table for us as the women cooed over the baby, who slept in my arms.

The lights above the small, open stage brightened and the room quieted. Hans joined us at our table. Carefully, I slipped Baby Adam into his father's arms. The girls, far more poised than during their first performances years before, began with a pretty song about bringing a baby home.

Through the whole set, the baby slept against his father's chest, oblivious to the music.

For their last song, they put their instruments down and stepped to the edge of the stage, in front of the mics. An expectant hush swept across the tables and through the bar in the back of the room. Sarah, in her sweet, full soprano, sang a short song that ended with the line: "Mother Earth will swallow you. Lay your body down." She was the smallest, only eighteen, and still bone-slender. She started the two-line song again, and, one by one, her sisters joined her. They sang in rounds until Gracie's single voice finished. The girls stepped down off the stage and sang the two lines once more in unison. Their voices mingled and swelled. Again, I had that strange sensation of hearing not four but five voices as they sang. I thought of Jennie as I watched Lil close her mouth on the final syllable of that strange, short song.

In the second of silence that followed their voices, Adam took my hand and squeezed it, a strange blend of sorrow and pride on his face. He brought my hand up to his lips and I felt a tear.

I opened my mouth to speak, but the audience burst into applause and shouts for an encore. Little Adam woke with a start and cried out. Gracie held up Adam's fiddle and leaned over the mic. "We'd like to call our dad up to help us on this one." They started on a song I'd never heard before. The audience began to sing along on the refrain. Hans slipped the baby into my arms, then he dashed off to crouch near the girls and take pictures.

They danced and hugged each other onstage. Their friends in the front of the audience rose to their feet and joined them. Baby Adam wiggled, threatening to fuss. So I stood up and swayed, rocking him back and forth. Despite the volume of music, the baby had calmed again. Gracie spotted us and pressed her arm across her chest to keep her milk from letting down. For a moment, I felt a stillness and quiet amid the music as I sniffed the sweet baby odor and warmth of him, my first grandchild. I thought of the sadness I'd just glimpsed in my husband's eyes, and Time, that cruel, raucous queen of sorrow, passed a hand over my heart.

NINE

SURRENDER

After Gracie, Hans, and the baby left, there were only the two of us in the house. Sarah had her first apartment near campus. Lil and her new Guatemalan sweetheart, Alphonso, also lived in Gainesville, but would soon join Gracie in DC. Rosie had begun graduate veterinary studies at Tallahassee.

Adam's restlessness soon became more obvious in the unfamiliar quiet. He continued waking in the middle of the night as if he still heard our grandson's cries. The horses snuffled noisily, and turned in their stalls, pawing impatiently as he passed. He rode off more on his own, often for hours at a time.

The question of his age remained. Perhaps it was my lack of distraction in such a childless home, or some loss of mental flexibility on my part, but I could not make the current of my daily life flow smoothly past this question as I had so many other questions about Adam. This was not a matter of concocting a new story. It could not be fixed by moving to another state. A new kind of dexterity and resilience was being required of me just as I felt both qualities ebbing.

Adam and I had not discussed his age again, but I felt a new tension in his touch at night, poignant and infectious.

For the first time in years, I began to have difficulty sleeping. In the mornings, I often stationed myself at the kitchen window, where I could watch Adam take the horses through their routines, his body lithe, undaunted by its own history.

When the certainty of the spring thaw hit the Appalachians, Adam began preparations for his first mountain trip in well over a year. We also had a wedding anniversary coming up—a big one, our thirtieth. We normally celebrated with a simple dinner out, but this year he seemed to have something more in mind. His mood had lifted in the last few weeks, his trip preparations were more elaborate than normal and his usual, already-on-the road, distraction was absent. He really piqued my interest when he asked if I had any plans for amusing myself while he was gone. He seemed happy when I told him I had none.

He whistled softly to himself as he trod back and forth from the house to the truck. Then he stopped at the office door. "Come with me?"

"Come with you?"

He beamed. "Yes. I'll make it worth your while. I want to give you an early anniversary present."

Within the hour, we were on the road, heading north.

All day Adam refused to say where we were going. I had joined him a few times for his horse auction trips to Lexington and Louisville, and we seemed to be taking that familiar route. But when we reached Kentucky, we headed east instead of west. By evening, my suspicion of a second, impromptu, honeymoon was confirmed. Adam pulled over at a motel, a row of cabins nestled against a hill several miles outside a little town called Jensen. "Look good to you?" He beamed at me.

The motel was rustic and on its way to being run-down. But the air, as I rolled down my window, smelled of mountain evergreen, sweet and fresh. "Perfect," I said.

The rotund man in the office peered up at us from his low chair when we asked for a single room. His eyes ping-ponged back and forth between our faces, and he snorted at the "Mr. and Mrs." Adam signed in the registry.

My good mood vanished. A current of anger flashed through me. I snatched the key off the desk and strode back to the car for our luggage.

We dropped our bags in the small, dark room that smelled of mountain damp, of wood and stone. "What are we really doing here?" I asked.

Adam went immediately to the thin, yellowed phone book on the nightstand by the bed. He opened it, flipped a few pages triumphantly, then held it up for me to see. By his finger on the page: four listings for Hope. One R. Hope. "My gift to you, first a middle-aged Roy Hope then a middle-aged Adam Hope."

That literally knocked me off my feet. I dropped down on the lumpy bed, my mouth gaping. "He's here! You found him!"

"No, not yet. But I remembered him saying he came from a mining town in west Kentucky. So I went to the library and did some research. Hold your horses." He dug through the duffel bag of his clothes, then unfolded a small Kentucky map with several towns circled. I counted three more north of us.

Adam swept his finger along the zigzag of red circles. "Jensen sounded familiar, so I brought us here first. If we don't find him here, we'll just keep going until we find him or somebody who can tell us where he is."

Such a simple and elegant solution! All my efforts had centered on explanations and understanding while he had sought a direct, practical resolution. "Happy anniversary!" I laughed.

We went to a little café for dinner. The place seemed ebullient and shiny. We held hands at the little Formica booth and ignored the few odd glances from nearby tables. Adam detailed his plans for remodeling the stables. We speculated on how soon our grandson would be walking and how our family would be expanding with more grandchildren.

We returned to the motel and showered. He sat cross-legged on the bed, waiting for me when I came out of the bathroom; I sat behind him and put my arms around him. "Are you afraid?" I asked.

"No, not of changing. But I'm not sure how this works. I don't want to let you down."

I squeezed him tighter in my arms. "Do you think this will change? Will it be different?"

"I don't know. This is as new to me as it is to you." He shifted his position to face me.

"Yes, I've never had me an old man."

Then Adam lay down with me, and his hands poured over me, as they had so many times before, toes to crown, unhurried, silent until his voice washed over us and he filled the room. Time was mute, irrelevant.

He fell asleep before me, while I tried to focus on my novel. Rain pattered down steadily on the roof, persistent, laudatory, a sound that reminded me of the farm. I put my book down and watched Adam sleep beside me, smooth-faced. I tried to imagine him as an old man, but could not. His transition from woman to man had been so overwhelming a feat. I'd seen no change in his character then, none of Roy in him. Would this time be different? Would he *be* different if he became older, like me? After he became a man, there had been times when I missed Addie. What would I miss after this transition?

I held my hand up, flexing it. In the angled light of the bedside lamp, all the fine lines on my hands and forearms were visible. These signs of age in me had made no difference to Adam. His touch at night was the same. Under his hands' long stroke from my shoulder to my hip, I felt as ripe and beautiful as I had ever been.

I made a fist and the lines across the back of my hand disappeared. I remembered staring at my body when I was high on the LSD. I tried to retrieve that same calm acceptance now. My hand seemed to be melting before me, then I realized I was only crying.

Adam's hand slid out from under the covers. Without opening his eyes, he clasped his hand over my fist. "I can't promise you anything. I have no idea what I'm doing. But I am willing to try." He rolled over on his side to face me. Eyes the color of burnished mahogany. Leaning across me, he switched the light off. "Sleep now. It'll be okay." He drew me closer.

❧

IN THE MORNING, we decided we would go first to the R. Hope address, then move down the list if we had no luck there.

"Do you think he remembers being with you?" I asked as we dressed.

"Oh, I'm sure he remembers. He had days alone in that grimy little motel with Addie! I kept him very drunk toward the end. Drunk and, I'm sure, confused."

I realized that what we were planning was a minor reenactment of that transformation, carrying it forth to some logical conclusion in which Adam would at last share a characteristic with both Roy and me. The thought of their strange history overwhelmed my optimism for a moment. I remembered my amazement when A. had returned as Adam. For the first time, I saw us from Roy's point of view. In the mirror above the dresser we looked like mother and son. "He'll think I'm Addie and you're his son."

Adam shrugged his shirt onto his shoulders and considered his reflection. "Yes, I guess you're right. We could say—"

The strangeness of our situation washed through me. The room darkened and tilted.

"Evelyn! Are you okay?"

I took a deep breath and my dizziness passed. "It was so strange when you returned then. I thought my heart would break from sheer strangeness." I righted myself and covered my mouth. "I was so young. Sometimes I could barely make it all fit together. And I couldn't tell anyone, not even Momma."

Adam took my hand. "This is different. I don't want to change in any other way, just look more my age."

Silently, I wondered: what was his age? Out loud, I asked, "What will we do when we find him?"

"We'll have to cross that bridge when we come to it. Let's find him first. A lot will depend on him."

‹⌒›

OUTSIDE, THE MORNING WAS MOUNTAIN-FRESH, crisp, and cool. A faint tang of wood smoke and coffee sweetened the air. A bright stream of birdsong overlay the mutter of the TV from the hotel office.

With the directions from the desk clerk, we found the R. Hope residence, a small, green clapboard house at the end of a short, well-shaded drive off the main road. There was no car in the drive, but we knocked anyway. Woods surrounded the house and the land rose steeply behind it. Water dripped from the eaves onto a tub of blossoming red geraniums. An old hound loped up, barking, then sniffed us without much interest. Adam knocked again, but no one answered.

Farther down the same winding road, we found the second house on our list. An older version of the first. H. HOPE was hand-painted on the mailbox. A tall, old man on the porch pushed himself up from his chair as we pulled off the road. He was stooped and rail-thin, in faded overalls. A halo of wispy, gray hair wafted around his head. Raising one hand to shade his eyes against the morning sun, he glared at us as we walked up the gravel path. Nothing about the old man's narrow, hollow-cheeked face resembled Roy Hope.

Adam paused at the bottom step.

The old man cackled and slapped his leg. "I'll be goddamn. Look who the cat dragged in!"

Adam and I exchanged grins. The old man obviously recognized him. Adam stepped up onto the porch and took the hand the old man offered.

As soon as Adam was within arm's reach, the old man's eyes narrowed and his hand fell away from Adam's. His puzzled glance bounced from Adam to me and back. "Roy?" he whispered.

"No, sir." Adam shook his head and motioned me forward. "I'm Adam and this is Evelyn. We're looking for Roy. Are you related to him?"

The old man's eyes darted back to me, with surprise. "Well, you don't look like yer from around here." Then he pointed at Adam's chest. "But this one sure is. Can tell that just by looking. Dead ringer for Roy. Are you his boy? Don't recall him having a boy." The old man shuffled sideways, tottering so badly that I dashed up behind him to steady him, and Adam grabbed his elbow. The old man folded himself into a rocker and offered me the porch swing.

Adam sat down in the remaining chair across from me. "I'm not his son, but I'd like to find him. Say hello. It's been a long time."

The old man stared past us and offered nothing. He blinked his rheumy eyes rapidly and I noticed one of his hands shook.

I touched his arm. "The 'H' on the mailbox—what's that for?"

"Hoyle. Hoyle Hope. But everybody calls me Toot." He laughed, then slowly bent over, picked up the cup sitting next to Adam's chair, and spat tobacco juice into it. "Not allowed to spit off the porch anymore. Took a tumble last year." He straightened up and looked Adam over. "Roy coulda used a son. Those two daughters don't have a grateful bone between them. Hardly ever visited him in the hospital."

Adam leaned in closer. "Roy's in the hospital?"

Toot's head wobbled on his thin neck. "No. He's past that. Resting down yonder. The cemetery behind the post office. 'Bout two years now. Car accident. So drunk he forgot that mountain roads curve. His brother, Everett, was with him, died on the spot. Roy hung on for weeks. What'd you say your name was?"

Adam and I locked eyes for a moment. An odd expression swept across his face, reminding me of the time the nurse mistook him for Gracie's husband. His hand moved up toward his chest then fell limply at his side. His head bowed. My heart skittered.

We listened politely to the old man's stories about Roy. Twice he looked quizzically at Adam and asked his name again. "Who was your momma?" he asked once. Adam was uncharacteristically unresponsive. The old man seemed to lose interest in his own questions. His gaze drifted back to his spit cup.

After a few moments, we returned to the truck. Adam picked up our list of addresses, slid it into the folds of the Kentucky map, and stuffed both into the glove compartment.

Silently, we drove into town. It didn't take long to find the grave. But the old man was wrong about the date. Roy had been dead ten years.

A decade. I'd been imagining him aging like me, gauging Adam against that image, and all the while, he was gone.

Beside me, Adam exhaled a long, shuddering sigh and leaned against Roy's tombstone. I remembered the X-ray of his chest, the pale spread of the organ that gave him his voice. He blinked up at the surrounding hills. "This is a strange place."

I looked around me at the nondescript little town and recalled what Sarah had said about never knowing what colors others actually saw. What, I wondered, did he hear, what did he see that I missed? Did Roy's death sever some physical tie for him? Did it matter that the mold for his present state was gone, returned to the earth?

"Evelyn, I've been thinking about this for months. I wanted to give you . . ." His voice cracked. He took a deep, gulping breath. "Give you myself. Again. I hoped I could just hang out with him. Couple of long fishing trips. And each time I'd grow a little older-looking. A natural process. Nothing to explain." He ignored the tears running down his face. "It never, ever occurred to me that he might be dead. I just want everything to go on as it is. With us. For you and for the girls. That's all I want."

My own deflated hope was a suffocating weight on my chest. All I could do was take his hand. "Let's go home."

A few moments later, we passed a battered old station wagon as we turned out onto the main road. The elderly woman at the wheel did a double-take. The bald man beside her turned in his seat, his eyes locked on Adam.

Adam appeared not to notice. He sighed deeply again and gripped the steering wheel. "It never occurred to me . . ."

I touched his leg, and he pressed his lips together. There was nothing more to say. The air in the cab of the truck seemed clotted, unbreathable. I rolled my window down. We drove on in silence. Adam, staring ahead, vibrated beside me. Under the noise of the engine and the open window, I thought I heard something darker, a deep, low drone.

Soon he drove off the highway and took us higher into the hills, up progressively narrower tree-lined roads until there were no more homes. When he stopped, the road was a single-lane, weedy rock path.

His face was closed, private. "I'm going to stretch my legs a little." He got out of the truck and walked away.

Quickly, the back of his blue plaid shirt disappeared into the underbrush. I stepped out of the truck cab into the cooler air. Everything was suddenly unnaturally quiet. The birds had stopped singing. Two deer bolted out of the woods from Adam's direction, galloped across the road in front of the truck, then lunged uphill.

A roar billowed behind them: Adam's voice, sharp as his cry at Jennie's coffin. A rumbling boulder of rage. The skin on my arms and face tingled, my pulse kicked. I covered my ears and fought my own urge to run.

In the silence that followed, I slumped against the side of the truck not sure what would happen next. Soon, the birds resumed their chat-

ter, and I climbed back into the truck. I nodded off, and when I woke
from my nap, the shadows of late afternoon stretched across the road.
My neck and shoulders ached from being scrunched up against the passenger door. My disappointment returned in a surge and I looked around
for Adam. I tried to remember exactly where he had walked into the
woods, but the trees all looked alike. It would be dark soon. His thun-
derous, jagged cry echoed in me. I shivered. He'd once said the mountains answered his call. What could the response to such a call be?
What if he was hurt, trapped under some boulder dislodged by his
voice?

I flung my door open, ready to dash into the forest to look for him
when I saw the rhythmic swing of his sleeve.

Seconds later, Adam emerged, his face lighter, his gait looser. He
circled the truck and stopped at the open door on my side. "For your
patience." He held up a few inches of ginseng root. His eyes were as
resolute and calm as when, years before, he'd stood in the bedroom
bare-chested, offering the gift of himself as Addie.

I smiled at the man and the body I'd now loved for so many years.

"Evelyn, I can still do this. It doesn't have to be Roy. I could find
someone else. You could help me. You could choose the man. We'd have
to figure out some way for me to get close to him."

My pulse pounded in my ears. I had to strain to hear him. I tried to
imagine him with a completely new face, not Roy's. A strange older
man, someone else's face looking at me every morning. The fresh stories,
new lies. A sudden dense fatigue overcame me. I felt my age.

"No!" I said. "No, Adam." My words shocked me.

A question registered on his face.

I'd always assumed that I would accept anything to have him with
me. I took his hand, aware of its weight and strength. "Our grandchildren should know the father their mothers had. The man I married."

He shook his head violently.

I persisted. "What would we do? Fake your death? Then you come back as some new old guy and we take up where we left off? And we try to explain everything to the girls? To everybody? More lies and made-up stories? I want us to live as who we *are*."

He stared at me, still shaking his head.

I gripped his shoulder. "Once I asked you what the difference was between being a man and being a woman. You told me that the greatest difference between me and you was not our sex but the fact that you were not fixed, you could change while I had to remain as I was—a woman—for my entire life."

He squinted at me and I felt him tense as if to pull away.

I held tighter. "You were right in that respect, but I'm not without my own changes. I'm not like I was when you looked like me. *I* am the one changing now. My hands ache after a day in the garden. I lift a fifty-pound bag of feed and my back hurts for days. My eyes aren't as good as they used to be. And this is just the beginning. There will be more and more changes for me. I want you to be with me. I want you down to my marrow. But I can't bear the thought of you giving up what you have to feel like I do. And I don't want to tell any more lies or make up any more stories." I touched his face. "You have a gift. You can't turn your back on it. We must bear this the best we can."

He pressed his face into my hand. "Stay, Evelyn. Don't change," he whispered.

I held his wet face and made him look at me. "I can't help but change. As long as I can be, I will be with you. But I will become an old woman and then . . ." I choked. "Will you stay—"

He stopped my words with a hard, fierce kiss. We made love on the seat of the truck. Frenzied. Quick. We devoured each other.

༄

THE SKY WAS THICK WITH STARS by the time we drove out of the mountains, heading south toward the place we'd lived for so many years without lies. I had no idea how we would navigate those waters before us. What if I lived to the age of eighty-five and he still looked twenty-five? I could not keep the inevitable at bay. A helpless, irrational shame saturated me.

As we drove past homes lit against the falling dusk and returned to the highway, I thought of our daughters. I'd always focused on Adam's most obvious gifts, his voice and his physical transitions, when I considered what he may have passed on to our children. But he'd also given them robust health and, it would now seem, a long life. They had matured at a normal rate, but would they age like me or like him? The older they got, the more they seemed like him. I'd never expected to outlive my children, but they might live far longer than I'd ever imagined. How much of their lives would I miss?

As we left the mountains behind us, I sensed a continuing undercurrent of resistance in his silence. He drove all night, staring straight ahead at the road while I dozed beside him. We held hands, but said only what was necessary for the drive. By the time we pulled into the ranch early the next morning, I understood that, though he had wept at my request, he had not yet agreed to it. I knew, too, that his single howl in the mountains had done little to abate his grief.

I touched his arm, stopping him before he got out of the truck. "I left the land I loved to come here, to safety. And when the girls and their friends were experimenting with drugs, I let you handle it your way."

"Evelyn, no."

But I held on to his hand. "I once asked you to hide your voice, to make that power private, so as not to disturb others or our daughters. You honored my request and found your way through. It seems our daughters have, too. They don't seem to be able to transform themselves as you have. I think they will always be women, like me. But in this other way, they may be like you. If they are, they will need you. You should stay as you are, the man they have known as their father, and I'm not saying this just to avoid spinning new lies or to spare you the physical pain of aging. Our daughters will need you here with them. When their husbands are old men, if they still look like thirty-year-olds, they'll need someone who has been through this to guide them. And when their husbands are old men, I won't be here." My jaw clenched on my last words.

His eyes widened. A dark, horrible grief flashed across his face and something in him seemed to collapse. He nodded his agreement as he opened his arms.

We wept, holding each other as all around us dawn broke.

In the months that followed, we made love more frequently, Adam embracing me as if touch could alter what words were powerless to change. At times, I had the impression that he was trying to absorb from me the aging process itself or to literally press his youthfulness into me.

For me, the sorrow came in waves. My heart, at times, awash in loss.

I'd always known there would be an eventual, inevitable parting, but now I understood its approach and the difficulties it would, in time, bring. However extraordinary he was, we were, in this respect, very ordinary.

SOON AFTER WE RETURNED from Kentucky, one of Adam's favorite thoroughbred mares, Rose of Jericho, was ready to breed. Over the years, our business had settled on breeding and boarding, mostly thoroughbreds and quarter horses. Adam still had a special talent for handling disturbed horses and rehabilitating misguided riders, but he'd also developed a strong reputation for matching sire to dam for a good foal. By then, we had two stable hands: Manny, our full-time groomer and trainer, and Bruce, a pre-vet student at the university, who helped us part-time when Adam was out of town.

Jericho's owner, a Jacksonville investment banker and one of our best boarding clients, wanted his most recent purchase, Hurricane, to sire. The stallion, tall and powerful, was broad-hoofed, but a light, swift racer. Jet-black with a startlingly white blaze, he was also temperamental and willful. We did not use artificial insemination. All our horses bred live-cover—a standard practice with some breeds and for some owners who wanted their sire's line guaranteed, but risky if a stallion became aggressive.

One afternoon, I watched from the kitchen window as Adam led Jericho down the stable to the breeding shed. Within minutes, I heard a horse's scream. That alone was not unusual, but more screams followed. I recognized the kick of hooves on wood and men's voices, harsh and alarmed. I started from my chair. Adam appeared at the back door, his shirt bloody. "Call Ray! Now!" he shouted, then dashed back to the stable.

Unnerved by the sight, I dialed Ray Bentley, our veterinarian.

When I hung up, I grabbed gauze, a sheet, scissors, and the extra first-aid kit we kept in the house, then ran to the stable. Bloody footprints led to the first stall, where Jericho lay on her side. Adam and Manny had stripped to the waist. A broad smear of red darkened Adam's chest. Kneeling at Jericho's shoulder, he held bloody, wadded-up shirts, one pressed at the base of her neck, the other at her chest. His cheek was abraded, and a long, shallow cut oozed at his bicep.

The mare lay still. Only her eyes moved, wildly. She breathed in staccato snorts.

I heard nothing else, but when I touched Adam's back, his voice vibrated under my hand. "The vet's on his way," I said.

Manny muttered a soothing stream of Spanish as he grabbed the sheet and began tearing it into strips.

"Never seen anything like it!" Adam winced as I handed him two thick gauze pads. "He bit the crap out of her, then all hell broke loose. Rearing. Over and over. His hooves slashing." He tossed the shirts aside and pressed the gauze firmly to the wounds. "He wanted to kill her. We barely got her out." Blood blossomed through the compress immediately, oozing around his fingers.

"*Loco, loco,*" Manny muttered.

Jericho nickered weakly when the vet arrived. Ray shook his head as he knelt to examine the mare. I gasped when he removed the compress. A fist-sized chunk of flesh slid sideways from her withers, barely attached.

Jericho erupted, kicked, then lifted her head and shoulders as if to heave herself upright. Everyone but Adam backed away. He moved closer, his hand in her mane, soothing her. At his touch, she laid her head down again.

Ray laid a large, dark case on the ground a few feet away and began to unpack syringes and a large vial. "It looks bad. A local, first. She's not going to like it."

"You don't have to stay for this," Adam whispered to me.

Grateful, I walked away from the agonized cries of the horse. For want of anything more constructive to do, I went in the house and prepared sandwiches and coffee. As I loaded the food onto a tray, another sharp neigh rang. I added a flask of whiskey on my way out.

Manny stood at a respectful distance, watching intently. The other horses in the stable were quiet, their ears perked. The odors of blood and the men's sweat dulled the air.

A big utility light clamped to the stall rails shone down on Adam and Ray. Jericho, her legs tied, lay facing away from my view. I was grateful not to see her wounded chest or her terrified eyes.

Adam knelt at her back, stroking her neck. Her foreleg trembled spasmodically. Her hide rippled.

Ray paused, leaning back on his heels. "I didn't expect anything this extensive. I'm out." He held up an empty vial and shook it. "I can't give her a local on these last two wounds. But I've got to close her up before there's any more swelling. Twenty-five, maybe thirty more sutures. It's going to be rough." He glanced at Adam, who nodded.

"Evelyn," Adam said without looking up.

Ray hesitated, the threaded needle poised over Jericho, and shot a questioning glance in my direction.

The cups rattled as I set the tray down. The only other sound was the mare's shallow and rapid breath.

Not certain what Adam wanted, I stepped into the stall and stood next to him. Ray's needle touched near a gapping slash of exposed muscle. Jericho flexed her forelegs and jerked her head sideways in a scream of protest. The two remaining gashes bled anew.

Adam touched my foot. I realized what he was going to do and moved to stand closer to him, giving tacit permission. Then I braced myself. His other hand slid up the taut muscles of Jericho's neck. His lips parted in exhalation. A single, radiant chime rang out, pure and singular. A test, not his full range. Jericho nickered a soft response. Adam and Ray locked eyes for a second. As Adam's voice increased in volume, Ray's face opened in shock. Adam bent to press his chest to the mare's shoulder.

Ray's eyes followed Adam, then darted down the flanks of the horse who now lay completely still.

Adam's monotone rose and flexed through the stable. His hand encircled my ankle. The air pressed into pure sound. But I heard an undercurrent of uncertainty, a falter in the swell of it. I realized with a shock that his goal was not only to soothe but to anesthetize. My head and chest hummed. I opened my mouth to breathe. His grasp on my ankle tightened. A chill ran up my arms as his hesitant tremolo blasted into full harmonic command. Soothing and hypnotic. To the bone. Ray blinked rapidly and shuddered before guiding the needle in. His hand dipped, then rose for the next stitch.

I closed my eyes. I reached out to steady myself. My hand landed on Adam's head, and the resonance changed instantly as if some circuit completed.

His voice filled my skin. My arm and ribs vibrated. It pulsed down into my hips and feet.

I do not know how long Adam's voice rang through me—through the mare and the stable. Slowly, evenly, he drew down to shallow waves. I opened my eyes. Jericho lay softly beside us, breathing regularly, her eyes closed.

Ray's hands shook slightly as he smoothed the last bandage on. "I couldn't completely close her up, but it will granulate in," he whispered, his words slow and thick. His eyes glistened. "There was ligament damage on her chest that will affect her right leg. But it's the best I can do." His dazed face slack, he rubbed his arms as if they were cold, and stared at Adam, who still leaned over Jericho's neck.

An expanse of white bandage covered her chest, her withers, and her upper foreleg. A small bandage glowed on her cheek.

Adam took a deep breath and released my ankle. I dropped to my knees beside him. I must have looked like I was praying.

Manny stepped forward to pull a blanket over the mare and help Ray collect his tools. Then I heard one of them pour coffee. A spoon clinked on a cup. Footsteps. Then Manny's hands appeared in front of me, holding half a sandwich and a cup of coffee.

A small dread bloomed in my chest. I steeled myself against that familiar pang of anger and shame, against what I'd seen in the faces of Clarion.

Manny set the sandwich and coffee down on the floor in front of me.

I looked up.

He regarded me only with somber concern and a brief nod. "Eat," he said.

I picked up the sandwich and pushed myself up off the floor.

Adam didn't move.

The men turned their gaze expectantly from Adam's back to me. I saw with a start of relief: their dazed faces were respectful, almost reverent. No judgment, no fear. "Please help yourselves to the food."

Adam sat, slumped, one hand still resting on Jericho. I held the sandwich out to him.

"I'm okay." He waved it away.

I followed Ray out of the stall. "Let's let them rest," I said and pushed the stall door shut behind us.

The three of us ate quietly, standing up. I was grateful for their silence as the whiskey flask passed from hand to hand.

After we finished the food, Ray squatted beside Adam and, including me with a glance, gave us instructions for Jericho's care and the dates and times he'd be returning to check up on her. He spoke quietly and to the point, his hand resting on Adam's shoulder.

Adam, bleary-eyed, simply nodded; then, when Ray was done, asked me if I was okay. "Good," he muttered when I told him I was fine. Then he returned his attention to Jericho.

I walked Ray outside. I was suddenly reluctant to have him leave and felt I owed him something. He paused at the door of his truck and turned to me as if to speak. But he said nothing, simply opened the door and got into his truck.

I touched his arm propped in the window. "Thank you" was all I could manage.

"I don't know what to say. I'm glad to have—" He blinked away tears, then sighed.

"You don't have to say anything, Ray."

He nodded and drove away.

I returned to the stable to find Manny standing outside the stall as if guarding Jericho and Adam. He startled briefly, then waved his hand indicating the whole stable. "Is so quiet now."

It was unusually quiet in the stable. I heard only the gentle swish of a horse's tail, then, from one of the far stalls, the faint rhythm of chewing. Adam slept beside the mare.

"They'll be okay. You can go now. Go on home. It's been a long day."

He studied Adam's back for a moment. *"Gracias,"* he whispered with a nod. As he walked to his truck, I saw him cross himself.

My chest still hummed and my ankle felt hot. I went outside and took my first deep breath since Adam had touched me. Overhead, the sky was brilliantly clear, the horizon low and softened by the distant tree line. Florida lay gentle and flat in all directions. Miles away, the sea kept rhythm. Under my feet were the tributaries of springs. This land *was* different. The men in the stable were not a bunch of stoned hippies, not a congregation in pain. They'd heard a soothing, powerful command, not the rage of loss.

I returned to the house for a sleeping bag and pillows to make him a pallet. Adam slept the rest of the afternoon by Jericho's side. All day, I could feel the imprint of his hand on my ankle.

Breath, Adam's and the horses', purled through the stable when I visited late that night. He lay beautiful in his sleep, his face placid and firm, one hand on the mare's shoulder. She slept on her opposite side. He must have awakened and gotten her to stand and turn, a good sign. The bandage on her chest was bloody at the center, but the edges were white.

The next day, Manny stopped me on the back porch. He spent his days in the stables and rarely came up to the house. His normal serious, calm demeanor was unchanged. Still, I braced myself.

But there was only kindness and curiosity on his face. "What happened in the stable?" A quiet, almost formal man, he seldom asked me direct questions.

"I don't know. I really don't know how he does it or what it is. He doesn't know either. But it works on the horses."

"Yes, it works." Manny nodded. "It is his talent."

"Thank you, Manny. I appreciate you seeing it that way."

He returned my smile, puzzled as if wondering what other way he might see it, but said nothing more before returning to the stable.

I went inside and wept with gratitude.

INITIALLY, JERICHO MADE SWIFT PROGRESS, but on the third day she burned with a fever. It took days for the new antibiotic to kick in. Adam stayed with her around the clock, sleeping in the stable. Ray was not optimistic about her chances of a full recovery from the damage to her ligaments. Her owner wanted to put her down, but Adam insisted that she could recuperate. He bought her from the owner to ensure that she had a chance.

At Ray's instruction, he cleaned and dressed the wounds three times a day for the first few weeks, then twice daily for months, and finally only once a day. Adam eventually coaxed the mare into a confident, nearly normal gait, but the stallion, still boarding with us even after the attack, became progressively more aggressive, kicking when anyone walked through the stable, often striking and rearing when Adam approached him. Manny, a very capable, calm groom, refused to handle him.

"I don't understand it," Adam complained repeatedly. "One moment, he's a normal horse. The next, it's like there's no horse in there, just rage and fear. Nothing I do reaches him then. Something's not right. I don't know what to do. This has never happened before. I don't know how to fix this." He rubbed his face as if to wake himself.

One afternoon, I heard the stallion's angry neighs and kicks repeatedly interrupt the soothing ring of Adam's voice. That evening, when I took Adam's supper out to him in the stable office, I found him drowsing at his desk. He looked tired, unfocused.

"I feel like a snake ready to shed," he muttered, ignoring the plate I set on his desk. "Things seem veiled, as if there's a caul over my head." He waved his hand in front of his eyes.

I rubbed his arm and felt the firm muscle and his smooth skin. Our trip to Kentucky had taken something out of both of us. A dull, helpless dread nagged me. I could feel it in my bones, and was uncertain if it was a fordable obstacle or the foreshadowing of my body's eventual surrender. In Adam, I sensed resistance, his energies deferred. He'd been willing to become old for me. Instead, he would, in the youthful skin of Roy Hope, escort me into my old age. He would watch my vigor and remaining beauty slip away. Then I would leave him here to grow old at his own unique rate. The bitter bile of sorrow threatened. I pressed it down, pushed it away, and turned my attention to the comforts I could offer him now. "You need more sleep. Come to bed. I'll give you a back rub."

As we settled into bed that evening, he said, "There's a waterfall in the mountains that I always go to. Near the top of the falls there is a place you can walk behind the water. The ledge is deep, the water falls clear as glass. One night, I saw the full moon through it. And if you stick your head through the curtain of water on a clear day, you can see for miles."

"Yes?" I whispered.

"I think of that place when I'm tired or discouraged. The water never stops. No matter what happens to any of us, to anyone, anywhere, water keeps coming off the mountain. It moves. It was. Is. Will be."

I reached back and rubbed his thigh. "Go. As soon as you can, go."

⁓

A FEW DAYS LATER, the stallion's owner, unhappy with Adam's lack of progress, arranged to move the horse to another stable—another first for

Adam. When the new stable came to pick up the stallion, the horse was having one of his better days, his neck and back supple. Adam pressed his face against the horse's shoulder before leading him out of our stable. At the trailer ramp, he stepped back and held his arms open as he released the horse. I remembered him standing in the rain so many years ago, his arms open to Darling the day Cole broke his leg.

The winter sun bounced off the side of the trailer as it turned onto the highway. The earth seemed to exhale mist as the day warmed and the brown-tipped grass of the pastures returned the morning's rain to its source.

Adam radiated thwarted energy.

Later that day, I found him in the hall, standing next to the phone. He stared into space and rubbed his chest. "The waterfall that I told you about. It *has* stopped," he said. "I called the ranger station there. It's frozen. How could I not have thought of that?"

In bed that night, I switched off the light and I pulled him toward me. Wordlessly, as we had countless times, we touched. His hands were certain, his voice strong. But I woke in the middle of the night to find him naked, silhouetted at the bedroom window looking toward the stables.

"You loved the springs when we first got here. What was it you once told me about them? Millions of gallons a day, every day. Endless. You don't have to wait for your waterfall to thaw. Go to the springs. Think of it as the reverse of the mountain. It's moving water. You just go down instead of up."

"Being underwater feels very different. But you're right. I'll go. Tomorrow." He nodded and continued watching the stables.

Soon, I felt his warm, bruised energy spooning up behind me.

In the morning, Adam packed his scuba-diving gear in the back of the truck. Devil's Springs had been developed as a private park by then, but they still allowed diving in the caves. He hadn't dived that cave in years.

We kissed, a slow, soft kiss, then he was off. I noticed again how he smelled different lately, more tart. I waved good-bye, happy to think of him in the spring where we had taken our one cave dive together. Dust rose behind his truck as he waved and passed Manny's little red dented car on the driveway.

Usually, he was gone four or five hours when he went diving. But he still was not back when the little girl with the leg brace came for her riding lesson in the afternoon.

The girl and her mother sat in the stable office waiting for Adam. I took some iced tea out to them.

"When do you expect him back?" the mother asked, wiping the arm of her chair. An impatient beauty, she seemed to think the world owed her something to compensate for the crippled daughter fate had given her.

"He should have been back by now," I said.

She gave me a look that said she knew that kind of husband. I didn't want to wait there with her. Usually, Adam called if he was running late. I assumed a flat tire, a last-minute errand.

After a few minutes, I heard the soft hiss of her car tires as she drove away.

Still Adam did not come home. In the slant of late-afternoon light, Manny closed the stables for the evening.

As I prepared our dinner, I imagined Adam stopping at the tack shop. I set the table. Spaghetti, the sauce made with my own canned tomatoes. A salad with the first lettuce of winter. I would give him until nine o'clock, I told myself, then I would eat.

My dinner tasted like cardboard. After a few bites, I put it in the refrigerator. I left his plate on the table, a fork and spoon beside it.

Midnight was too late for a stray errand or a broken fan belt. I tried to think who Adam might have stopped to visit. Sometimes, Ray came by for a beer at the end of the week. Adam played poker with Randy Warren and some Ocala horse ranchers every few weeks. A tattered list of typed names hung on the bulletin board next to the kitchen phone— people he played music with. I recognized most of the names. Adam had penciled in a few new names. One had been crossed out.

The flutter of anxiety in my chest became a stone. All night, I waited. First, I watched TV, then I turned the TV off and resorted to the silence of reading, so I would be certain to hear him arrive.

At the first blush of light in the windows, I put his unused dishes away and made a pot of coffee. I poured two cups and went out to the stables. My hand shook slightly as I set Adam's steaming cup of coffee on his desk. I shivered in the dawn cold and drew my robe closer.

The horses eyed me politely, sniffing. Stretching their necks over the stall railing, they poked their velvet noses into my pockets, searching for treats.

I went into Jericho's stall and pressed my palms to her flanks to receive her warmth. The bite scar blazed pale on her shoulder. For a moment, it seemed that Adam must be there in the stable, his footsteps lost in the contented sounds of the waking horses.

❧

THE RATTLE OF MANNY'S APPROACHING CAR outside signaled the beginning of the workday.

Adam would have been home by now if he'd spent the night with a woman. The police would have called if there had been an accident. I went back into the house. I surveyed each room, the front yard, and then backyard, with the irrational hope that I had somehow overlooked Adam. The faint slope of the land I had come to love, the familiar geometry of the white rail fencing, the pasture dotted with scattered shade oaks, and the far green horizon of forest, all seemed to wait with a complacency that comforted and unnerved me.

Three times I picked up the phone, then returned it to its cradle.

When I finally dialed the springs, a man with a nasal voice told me he didn't have time to mess with the whereabouts of a husband who had failed to come home. They had camping sites now. Plenty of people parked there overnight.

"My husband isn't camping. He went there to scuba-dive in your caves. You need to find out if he's there." That got his attention. I gave him a description of Adam's truck.

Minutes later, he called me back. "I found his truck. The hood's cold. Hasn't been driven anywhere this morning. No ma'am. No sign of him. He went diving by himself? We always tell people to take a partner."

I sped to the springs, cursing the morning traffic. I bumped along the dirt road leading to the new Devil's Springs Park, catching a glimpse of tents in the woods, sleepy campers emerging from them.

Adam's truck was the only one in the parking lot near the southern spring mouth. His clothes lay draped across the passenger seat over a folded towel. I unlocked the passenger door and flipped the glove compartment open. His wallet fell out. I scooped it up, quickly scanning it. I searched the corner of the truck bed behind the driver's seat. The keys were there, where he usually put them, hidden under his spare tank and a short coil of nylon rope. Adam was the only thing missing.

I marched to the new stone building nearby, wielding his driver's license as if all I had to do was offer proof of his identity and he would appear. I passed a rack of postcards, and a stack of inner tubes for rental, then slapped the license on the glass-top counter next to the cash register. "This is my husband. Have you seen him here this morning?"

Immediately, the young man at the counter looked up from his book. "I'll get my boss."

He returned quickly, a round, middle-aged man smelling of cigars followed.

The older fellow took one quick look at me, frowned at the license in his hand. "A diver," he muttered as if it were a mild curse, then added, "I've met him. Nice guy." He turned to the kid. "Call for a search."

I nodded.

Then time seemed to stop. Or rather I stopped. Someone guided me outside to a covered picnic pavilion. All around me young men began to bustle in various stages of diving preparations. Masks, tanks, bare chests. The squeak of the rubbery wet suits. Ropes, flippers, and lamps piled on the ground.

Two men in full gear strode off toward the spring. One stepped off the limestone lip of the spring and dropped into the water. Then I looked away.

Twice the older fellow approached me and asked if I would like to call anyone. Each time I shook my head. I sat on the picnic bench, staring down at the rough surface of the table. The day began to warm. Curious campers and other divers appeared drawn by the commotion.

For a long time, I sat at the picnic table. If I remained there, everything else would remain as it was. Then I realized I faced the woods where Adam and I had once made love after he took me for my first and only cave dive. Suddenly, it seemed necessary to find the exact spot where we had lain. I walked into the woods along the river bank. There was a trail now where there had been only underbrush. A soda can. A kid's flip-flop. Just ahead was a familiar juxtaposition of cypress knees. I looked back to get my bearings and gauge how far I was from Adam's truck now as I tried to remember where we'd parked that day. A small crowd had gathered by the spring.

I returned my attention to the ground around me, certain I could find the place. Like me, Adam could have wandered off to find this spot. I listened, sure for a moment I would hear his beautiful, sweet voice. In the hush of the woods, a single birdcall erupted, then a shout pierced the quiet. "They've found something!"

"Something" turned out to be a literal dead-end. A newly sealed chamber deep in the cave. A collapse.

When they brought me over to the bank, I looked down at the two young divers treading water above the sky-blue hole and told them, "He's not there. He must have taken a walk." I shook my head. They stared back at me blankly. "He liked to take walks in the woods, to . . ."

I do not recall completing my sentence. I do not recall who drove me home.

❧

THE GIRLS BEGAN TO ARRIVE, first Sarah from her apartment in town, then Rosie, who drove from Tallahassee. The next day, Gracie and Lil flew in from DC with Baby Adam in tow. The four of them filled the house with anxious energy. Their questions ricocheting around me: When did Daddy leave? How long has he been gone? What did they find at the springs?

All, save the baby, had the same stunned look on their faces that flared back and forth from puzzled urgency to vacant surprise. I couldn't help but think of the day Jennie died.

I kept telling them everything would be okay. "He must have gotten confused and wandered off somewhere. He probably never even went into the springs." Each time I said that, I thought about his recent restlessness, and the possibility seemed more likely.

Within hours of Lil and Gracie arriving, they piled into the car, headed for the springs, their faces filled with hope and purpose.

I didn't want to see that gaping mouth of blue again. I stayed behind with Baby Adam. His babbling filled my afternoon. His manic, toddling dashes toward every open cabinet door and every coffee-table corner required constant vigilance.

At sunset, the girls returned—Sarah, Lil, and Gracie in the car,

Rosie close behind at the wheel of Adam's truck. Before they got out, I saw that they had news, but it was not good news.

We gathered around the empty truck. Crossing her arms over her chest, Rosie stared at the ground and blinked away tears. "The collapsed vein is in one of the deepest parts of the caves, one that doesn't get many divers. An offshoot. They loaned me a tank and gear so I could go down and see for myself. They've already put up a grate to block it off. It's not safe to get close. They gave me a good, strong light, but all I could see was a jumble of limestone far away. They've even filtered the nearby silt for evidence . . . Some sign that he was . . ." Her voice cracked, then she added, "Nothing. I'm sorry, Momma." She covered her mouth.

Gracie bounced Baby Adam on her hip and searched my face for a reaction. "The ground over that branch of the cave has sunk quite a bit. The building where they rent the tubes is very close by. They're afraid that if they try any kind of excavation, the building will collapse onto . . . It would be too dangerous . . ." Her voice trailed off as she leaned against me and put her arm around my waist. Little Adam patted my chest and drooled on my shoulder.

Sarah took my hand and looked around at her sisters for confirmation. "Momma, there was no sign of him on the banks. No sign in the woods. They've looked. We combed the woods again. They've extended the search to include more of the river. Just in case. They'll call if they find anything."

Lil bit her lips and, without a word, went inside.

❧

A WAVE OF BOOKS, papers, notebooks, and textbooks arrived with the girls, covering every surface. Even Lil, the only one not officially a student, was researching to find the best graduate programs. Guitars and fiddles migrated room to room. Picks, capos, and baby rattles littered the kitchen counter. The girls' distinctive chlorophyll odor of new-mown grass was overlaid with the scents of patchouli and baby powder.

Visibly, each of them was a variation on Addie and myself as young women. Gracie was now broader in the hips. Rosie had sheared her auburn mane to short spikes. Lil, who resembled us the most, had grown pale since she'd joined Gracie in DC. Sarah, her lithe frame topped by a mass of curls, looked younger than her twenty years.

Little blond Adam dashed up and down the hall, fiddle bow or yellow highlighter marker in hand, chased by one aunt or another. Hearing his name over and over—in the girls' casual references to feeding or bedtime ritual and their attempts to soothe his fussiness—was strangely disorienting. The name "Adam" leapt out of their sentences. It was particularly jolting when Gracie, who wanted to raise her son bilingually, spoke to him, embedding those beloved syllables in Dutch.

Outwardly, everything appeared to be a normal family gathering. Lil resorted to her standard distractions—housekeeping and cooking. Rosie directed all her attention to helping Manny in the stables. Gracie and I took turns fussing with the baby while Sarah sketched us all. Adam might have been in the next room.

But the girls were fragile with anxiety, their bodies taut and somehow quieter, concentrated as if they, too, were listening for their father's footsteps on the back porch. We all jumped in unison each time the phone rang. Sarah abandoned her little apartment "for the duration" and commuted to campus. Her latest paintings, wide, abstract swatches of reds and blues, leaned on the hall table. I thought of blood and water every time I saw one.

Those first days passed in a grainy, surreal numbness, punctuated by flashes of helplessness that left me exhausted. The thin hope I'd seen on the girls' faces soon devolved into sadness or denial. Everything seemed to hinge on small details that might have been, but ultimately were not, revelations—an abandoned snorkel on the other side of the spring, some broken branches in the woods. Continuously, the girls circled the same questions. How could this happen? Why had he gone diving? Why would he go without a guide line?

I knew why he had gone to the springs: he went because I had sent him. Go down into the water, I'd told him. Go find your solace in Florida. But the lack of a guide line made no sense. Therefore, I reasoned, he wasn't in the cave. He'd walked off into the woods as he had on our way home from Kentucky. He'd gone off to find release, to unleash his voice. The locals might already be telling stories of a strange new haint near the springs. Or he'd met some older man in the woods and was undergoing a new metamorphosis. He'd be back. I remained optimistic.

To distract ourselves, we turned to music. Only in those moments when they played—Gracie and Rosie on guitars, Lil on the fiddle, or when the five of us sang—did their faces relax. Though I strained to hear Adam's tenor in the braid of their harmony, I heard only their voices and the chair next to me remained empty.

Their friends began to visit, wandering in at odd hours to offer condolences in low, serious conversations that paused if I walked into the room. If I woke in the middle of the night, the soft mutterings of grief and comfort drifted down the hall. In the mornings, when I sat at the kitchen table nursing my first cup of coffee and surrendering to my insomnia, the house seemed to buzz with their loss.

But I sensed that my placid demeanor frustrated and puzzled the girls. I'd noticed a disconcerted ripple move through them as I continued to refer to their father in the present tense. Once, Gracie moved Adam's coffee mug from the end table in the corner of the living room where he'd left it the morning he disappeared. When I moved it back immediately and found a new spot for her beer, I caught her glance of surprise. I also saw a spark of pity and resistance.

Early on the morning of the fifth day, I got a call that the search was officially called off. When I gathered the girls in the dining room, and I told them, a wordless, leaden grief enveloped the breakfast table. Rosie pushed her coffee cup away, then left to help Manny in the stables. The rest of us sat as if waiting to be released.

Moments later, we all startled when the door opened and Rosie walked back in. She came and stood beside my chair. "Mom, you've been saying he can't be in the cave because no guide line was ever found and he always used one. This is the line we used the last time we went diving. I found it on the top of the office file cabinet." Carefully, she laid a neatly tied bundle of white nylon rope in the middle of the table.

I recognized Adam's method of looping and knotting ropes. A strand of blue ran through the supple cord. A clip dangled heavily from each end.

"He never kept his diving gear in the stable. Never. He must have stopped to check some file before he left for the spring. Then he forgot and left the line." Rosie's chin quivered. "He went in anyway."

Lil stroked the rope tenderly. "He once told me he knew that spring like the back of his hand. He'd explored every 'vein and artery.'"

Sarah rubbed her chest and whispered, "He believed he'd be able to find his way out, by touch or by listening, if anything went wrong."

I shivered. They were eulogizing.

"What do you know about what he might have done?" I snapped. In the sliver of silence that followed, I picked up the rope and moved it to the kitchen counter behind me, out of sight.

"Momma," Rosie cried, "Daddy's not lost in the woods!"

Out of the corner of my eyes, I saw Sarah's quick shake of her head and her warning glance at Rosie.

I took Rosie's hand, and the gesture seemed to calm her. She drew closer and stood next to my chair with her arm around my shoulder. But I could not bring myself to agree with them.

Gracie wiped her eyes with the heel of her hand. "Shit. Shit. I miss him."

Baby Adam beat the table with his tiny fists. "Shit! Shit!" he chirped. Then he stopped, his hands in the air, and stared, his happy gaze taking in their stricken faces. "Shit?" His grin broke into a wail of alarm, and they all burst into sobs.

Lil laid her head on the table. "I can't believe he's gone." Her arms muffled her voice.

I smoothed her hair over her head, feeling her heat and youth. I longed to reassure them, to offer some hope. I wanted company in my optimism. I yearned to have them understand everything about their father—who he was, how he came to me, and how he might once again return to me—to us. But the story seemed so large then, impossible for one person to unfurl. I'd always imagined the two of us telling them. I could not bring myself to speak of him in the past tense. Such a recitation, however much I owed it to them, seemed delicate, precarious, even dangerous without him there. My heart veered.

While my daughters wept around me, I literally choked on my words. My energies drained out of me. I was helpless against the momentum of their story and their assumption that he was there in the springs, entombed.

I had no intention of becoming my mother. I didn't want to keep them from the truth about their father for decades. But I also had no idea how rare such opportunities to confide in them would become, how infrequently all four of my daughters would be able to visit at the same time as they spread out across their various careers and, later, the globe. Rarer still would be times the five of us would have without husbands, boyfriends, or children.

The next day, they wanted to return to the springs. They spent the morning efficiently and solemnly preparing for what I realized was an informal, impromptu funeral. Pauline and some of their friends would be joining them. They insisted I come, too. But I was equally insistent on staying home, again, with the baby.

That evening, the table was crowded with Adam's favorite dishes: gumbo, collards, corn bread, Key Lime pie, and my canned peaches.

"We need to do something more. Something official. Daddy had lots of friends," they began to say. I understood their need, but each time, I shook my head. "Not yet." A hopeful denial hardened in me. I was quiet any time they discussed their father.

A restlessness trailed their sorrow. They were young. They had the distractions and the promise of new life to contend with.

Lil's boyfriend, Alphonso, had been calling every evening, missing her and hoping to be invited to join us. Sarah confided that Gracie was in danger of losing her first Foreign Service assignment if she missed much more of her intensive Spanish studies. Rosie took the phone out onto the porch when she pleaded with her professors for extensions on her lab assignments.

"There's nothing more you girls can do," I told them one night at supper. "I'll be okay. You can come back when you need to. If there is news." Their exchange of glances told me that they were certain there would be no more news. They regarded me with varying degrees of indulgence and concern.

"You sure, Momma?" Gracie asked.

"Yes, I have to be alone eventually." I looked away from their up-turned faces and imagined Adam walking up to our door in new form, ready to once again be my husband.

༄

AFTER THE GIRLS LEFT, stripping our home of their books, clothes, and guitars, Adam's things emerged as the land does out of a melting snow. His handkerchief, still wadded on the little shelf by the back door, where he always dropped his keys on the way in. His copy of *Bartram's Travels* on the coffee table. His bedroom slippers by the recliner.

I was in limbo. My husband was gone and I was alone, but I did not consider myself a widow. I kept everything as it was before he disappeared. All his clothes hung in the closet. His razor and shaving cream sat beside the sink. Like me, they seemed to be waiting for what would come next.

Two images haunted me: Adam's back as he disappeared into the woods on our way home from finding Roy Hope's grave, and the look of wonder on his face when he was underwater with me and his voice shimmered between us just before the rain of silt sent us scurrying out of the cave. Parallel, twin questions always followed. Why had I sent him to the springs, down into the earth? When and how would he return to me? Over and over, I relived the morning he disappeared, tracing it back through the days and weeks and months before. I combed through every gesture, every word, for significance.

Without acknowledging to myself any contradiction, I vacillated between the conviction that he was in the earth, deep in a watery grave, and my certainty that he walked the earth, seeking a viable path back to me as an old man, as he once wanted to. He would return to me once again and he would be similar to me. Not in the obvious ways Addie had been, but like me in that one, crucial way. He would be enough like me to, once again, be *with* me. And that single similarity would allow him to return to me all that I craved of him—his wondrous, inexplicable strangeness.

ॐ

A FEW DAYS AFTER THE GIRLS LEFT, I got a call from the stallion's owner. The crazy horse had started having seizures and they'd put him down. An autopsy had revealed a brain tumor the size of a ping-pong ball. The banker complained about the cost of the autopsy but wanted to let me know that the problem had been the horse, not my husband. I thanked him for letting me know. Adam would have cherished the comfort of knowing it was not his failure.

Our business phone calls soon fell down to a couple per week. But I did not disconnect the phone in the stable office. Its occasional eruptions, evidence that someone else also expected Adam to be there, soothed me.

The horses comforted me, too. One cool night, I took off my shirt and put on the flannel shirt Adam had left draped over the footboard of our bed. The shirt was well-worn and soft against my bare skin. I smelled his sweat on his hatband as I slipped his hat on my head. Then I turned the horses out under a full moon. Curious, they gathered around me. One by one, they sniffed under Adam's hat, questioning. Their breath steamed my face. I closed my eyes. Their warm flanks slid by me, under my outstretched hands. I cried then. Not for Adam, not for my loss. But for the horses' wordless generosity.

Over the days that followed, their owners moved them to other stables. From the kitchen or the back porch, I watched while Manny led those fine, proud animals into trailers that took them away. I studied their gleaming coats and smooth gaits, the angle and tension of their ears and tails, and I asked myself: What kind of horse is this? What kind of man is my husband? Where is my husband?

Would he appear at my door as he had when he returned as Adam? Would I hear his voice again, feel his touch?

At night, I tossed in my bed, craving him, wanting to enter the room of his body and feel his hands on my face. To taste his mouth and press my chest against his. There were no buffers between the need, the absence, and myself. When I wept, I wept for need, not grief.

If I kept everything ready for him, Adam would return. Years before, my readiness, my ripeness and solitude as a young woman had called him out of the Carolina clay. Surely, my loneliness could now do the same. I waited and waited and waited. I, along with all his clothes, and his horses, and his tools, waited.

The pasture greened up in the first rains of spring, but otherwise, everything remained the same. Weeks, then months crept by.

The girls and Pauline visited as often as they were able, and the emptiness of the house always seemed fresher, stronger, in the wake of their departures. I deflected their requests for a memorial. Some days, I did not answer the phone.

I kept up the house and the garden. The tomatoes came in by the bushel. White acre peas, cucumbers, and corn followed. I made Adam's favorite relish, an old recipe of Momma's. I lined the jars up on the pantry shelf. Gleaming, ready.

By midsummer, the tension of waiting for his arrival had stripped away my passivity. Methodically, I pulled out all of Adam's Florida maps. I worked my way through his bookshelves, reading his books on Florida history, geography, flora, and fauna. I studied his notes in the margins, then visited all the circled destinations on his maps. What I initially told myself would be a tribute to Adam quickly turned into a desperate search. I began to see older men who looked like him everywhere.

His individual physical features that I had savored for so long now seemed common. I raced down a crowded Cedar Key pier to touch the arm of a gray-haired man whose wide back reminded me of Adam's. At the farmer's market, my heart startled and I gawked at a man who laughed like Adam. I drove across the parking lot of a state park to pull up beside an old man who walked like Adam. Each time left me with a dissonant sense of failure, as if my mistaken leaps of recognition were somehow dispersing the very qualities I sought.

Still, I scrutinized every stranger who paid me the slightest attention or kindness. Everywhere I went, I watched and waited, on alert. I was looking for a single straw in a haystack.

Listening for his return seemed to be the only thing that held my muscles to my bones, that kept the supper dishes from sliding off the table, and brought the sun up in the morning. My clothes hung loosely on me. I dug through boxes and closets to pull out smaller clothes the girls had left behind.

I struggled to hold myself open, to remain vigilant for his return to me.

One day, I went to a local nursery for some flowers to plant by the back door. I reached over the flats of four-inch pots, searching for the most robust among the dark orange marigolds, Adam's favorite shade. From behind me a man's voice asked, "Can these take full sun?"

I turned.

He was exactly my height. He appeared to be in his sixties, gray hair, warm hazel eyes, and a thick white mustache. He laughed at my surprise and repeated his question, his broad hand grazing the flower tops. He absently scratched his breastbone and told me how much he liked the color I'd chosen.

As we strolled by the vine section on our way to the checkout counter, he cupped a passion vine blossom and asked, "What kind of flower is this?"

His words whipped through me. Our question game! I searched his face, his pale, intelligent eyes for signs of recognition. All my nerves were poised, ready for Addie's beaming smile or Adam's deep laugh. I touched his arm, squeezing to stop my hand's trembling.

As I opened my mouth to say Adam's name, the man glanced over his shoulder awkwardly and shifted the potted flower he held so that his arm slipped from my touch. "Excuse me, I need to help my mother."

"You have a mother?"

"Um, yes. She's waiting for me over there. Thank you." He nodded toward the cash register and left to join a thin, ancient woman in the checkout line. They had the same forehead, the same square chin.

Suddenly, I realized how I looked to them—a gawking, haggard woman.

I wandered around the back of the nursery near the potted fruit trees until the man and his mother drove away. I left without buying any flowers.

Shame tightened like a crust on my skin.

I gripped the steering wheel at the first light. The world slipped, angling off away from me. The light was green. The driver behind me honked. I went on to the next red light. Stopping at the intersection, I made myself take deep breaths. I looked around at the people. Boys with their loud stereo in the next car. A young woman pushed a stroller across the street. In the noon light, everyone seemed outlined, purposeful, and new. The world overflowed with people. All of them were going to or from the people or places they loved. Just as A. had come to me. I remembered lifting my Aunt Eva's quilt to see his strange face for the first time, before he was Addie, before he was anyone.

Something broke in me. I could feel it, the precise moment of surrender, like a bone snapping. A sudden, terrible miracle. Any one of them could be Adam. Old, young, male, female, black, white.

He was gone. Not forever, not from everything. But from my life. All my questions about him would remain unanswered. Forever.

The car behind me honked. I drove on. I wept, for the first time as a widow.

❧

THE NEXT DAY, I pulled out an old WWI army-issue metal box that one of my uncles had given me when I was a girl. Inside, I placed a lock of A.'s hair, a perfect, glossy, brown C-curve from the seventies, when he let it grow a little longer. Five other locks of differing shades of auburn and red hair nestled in the box. I added copies of my favorite photos of Adam: a snapshot Momma had taken of the seven of us, the girls in their Easter dresses squinted at the spring sun; a black-and-white of Momma and Adam at our wedding, their shoulders touching as they leaned toward each other, smiling; the photo of me and Addie that Momma gave me the day she told me about my father; a shot Sarah took of Adam on horseback, crouched forward gracefully over the horse's withers, mid-jump; and, last, the photo of the burned Japanese woman Frank had left at the farm years before. On top of them, I placed Adam's copy of *Song of Myself* that the girls had given him a few years before. The last thing to go in the box: a jar of Florida's sandy soil.

Then I drove north, straight to the farm.

Bud, Wanda, and their kids weren't home. A privacy hedge now separated the yard from the field, but the decayed stump of the apple tree was still there and I could easily locate the spot where I'd found A. I sank down onto my knees. I kissed the earth that had given him to me and tasted the clay grit on my lips, bringing him into my body one last time.

He was gone.

I dug, and the opened earth exhaled a feral musk. I wrapped the box in plastic, then in an old oilcloth. A gentle rain began to fall as I shoveled, burying the box.

The land, level and empty, seemed to stretch out endlessly in the twilight. Gradually, I realized that the pale lumps in the distance were earth-moving machinery. Then I remembered hearing that the fields had been resold and were being cleared for a new mall. The oaks still buffered the land where it dropped down to the railroad tracks. The Starneses' land was split; the half near the highway was now a subdivision. Cole and his brothers had held on to the house and southern pasture. I took a perverse pleasure in thinking of all those future shoppers coming and going for years near the spot where A. had last come into this world, ignorant as we are in Florida of the rivers that vein the land below us. I imagined Adam watching. The sky seemed to hang directly above me, low and mobile.

The rain began to fall in earnest as I dropped the final handful of red clay.

Car wheels whispered on the driveway behind me. I heard Bud and Wanda get out of their car. I walked around the hedge to greet them.

"Good Lord, Evelyn!" Wanda gasped. She and Bud hurried me out of the rain toward the house.

On the porch, I stared back at them stupidly, then realized how I looked, shovel in hand and dirt on my mouth. My clothes rumpled from the long drive and now muddy, my hair wet.

For the first time in months, I laughed out loud.

Everything in the recently remodeled kitchen shone new and modern. In the brightly tiled bathroom, I washed my hands and face. The iron-red clay swirled away from my dirty hands in the white porcelain sink.

After they fed me a hearty supper, I walked through the stable. The barn had been taken down the year before. Old furniture cluttered one of the far stalls. Dismembered motorcycles, Bud's hobby, filled the stalls closest to the house. The air smelled of engine oil and dust.

When I pushed open the broad door at the far end of the stable, the air moved behind me. Something fluttered at the corner of my eye, and I turned just in time to see an owl, pale against the darkness of the trees, bank off to the left and disappear into the large oak that had been the base of the twins' playhouse. I followed him and listened for a long time. In the last of the light, I heard only the traffic of the highway, distant and oceanic.

Something seemed to release in me, not a wild widow's grief but a sharper, more specific need. All the things I'd never said about A., all my silent months since he'd been gone, everything I might have said at a funeral, beat inside me. I wanted to speak. I lusted for the truth. I wanted to, as Adam had always urged his riders, "true myself."

I went inside to call Cole, the first person I had lied to.

We hadn't seen each other in years, but he readily agreed to meet me the next day at the little pizzeria that had replaced Bun's Café.

I arrived early and kept my eyes on the door. I let myself relish how right it felt to be telling Cole. Like me, he had known both of them. Many times he had sat across the supper table from Addie and then Adam. Now, finally, he would know who they were. He would also understand why I had left him so many years ago.

When I'd finished telling him, I would go straight back to Florida, round up my girls, and tell them. They would understand, I knew, and that rift I'd felt between us since their father went into the cave would be healed.

I felt light-headed, filled with a giddy anticipation. What I wanted to tell Cole felt enormous, but like a great weight poised on the summit of a hill, I had only to give it a gentle push and everything I knew about Adam would roll away from me, no longer mine alone. I squirmed restlessly on the bench seat while I waited. Was this how Adam had felt on the way to his mountain trips, the release of his feral howl waiting in his chest?

As Cole climbed out of his truck and strolled to the restaurant, the slight limp from the bad break so many years ago was barely noticeable. The lines around his mouth and across his forehead had deepened, but something of the boy remained in his smile. His brown hair had thinned. His sixty-plus years of life showed. In his thirties, he'd quit horse-breeding and gone to the mill. One of his sons had died of a drug overdose, and his wife, Eloise, of cancer.

While we ate our pizza, I told him what had happened to Adam, knowing he'd surely already heard. He told me about his wife and son as if I might not have heard. Then he spotted the bouquet of flowers I'd brought lying on the seat next to me. I held the bundled blossoms up for his inspection. "They're for Jennie and Momma. Come with me to visit their graves. Please?" For a second, I was afraid he might refuse and I would have to tell him about A. in a crowded restaurant.

He smiled. A good, ordinary man. I wondered, as I had many times before, what my life would have been like with him. He saw how I studied his face; he touched my hand. "Of course, I'd be honored."

I drove us to the cemetery. Cole chatted about his family's land and the changes at the mill. The cadences of my birthplace ran through his voice. He stretched out his legs beside me and lapsed into a respectful quiet as we pulled into the graveyard. He waved his assent as I motioned that I would be back in a moment.

At their graves, I steeled myself against the weight of sorrow and all I had not said to them. Thankful that they had both heard Adam's voice, I hoped they forgave me my silence. "Listen now if you can to my voice and help me find the right words," I whispered over their graves.

Then I turned my attention to Cole. A relaxed concern filled his face as I returned to the car.

"I have something I need to tell you." My heart pounded as I began to speak. He patted my hand. I started at the beginning, with Aunt Eva's death and my move to the farm.

When I spoke of his first visit and our inexperienced sex, he smiled shyly, as he had then. "I imagine we've both learned a bit since, over the decades."

I understood again my original attraction to him. When I mentioned finding Addie, his face brightened with interest. He listened intently to my brief recitation of her transformation, his head tilted to one side, his gaze resting on the tombstones in front of us, an odd quizzical expression on his face. I wondered for a second if he had a hearing problem. Then he said, "Buried, covered in mud in that storm." His tone was level, a simple summary of what I'd said.

I nodded, encouraged, then stumbled on, uncertain that I could explain the depths of her change. He said nothing, but sat very still, listening, and did not interrupt.

He gave me a wry, sideways smile when I mentioned his broken leg. He adjusted his feet under the dashboard. "I still regret that."

What could he have to regret, I wondered.

"That horse in that storm. I still feel it every winter." He rubbed his leg. "But that's nothing compared to what poor Addie must have been through before you found her."

I couldn't read his head shake—indulgence or dismissal? The inside of the car seemed too dark, too close. I wished we were outside in the full light, where I could see his face better.

I took a deep breath and plunged on. "She's the reason I couldn't be with you. She and I were very close . . . we were . . ." I tripped before the word "lovers."

"Well, that does explain things." For the first time since I'd mentioned Addie, he looked directly at me. "I'm not that surprised. But that was a long time ago. You went on to have a good marriage and all those pretty girls. You did fine. Me, too."

"Cole, Addie wasn't like us. She had an unusual voice. That's why she was so good with the horses."

He pointed his finger in agreement. "You're right about that, she did have an amazing way with them. And a good singing voice, too."

"No. No, I'm not talking about her singing voice." Despite my prayer, I had no words to explain. "She had another way of . . . At night, with me . . ." I felt my face redden. "When she—"

He reached out and took one of my hands, lowering it to the console between us. "This is getting interesting—very interesting. But, Evelyn, you don't owe me any explanations."

"Cole, I want you to know. You have to know. You have to understand." I wiped my face, sat up straighter, and began again.

He leaned back in his seat and listened to me through my description of Roy Hope. He nodded when I told him about finding the note

from Addie and waiting for her to reappear. "Some people just take off
and don't look back." He shook his head.

"But she did come back. That's what I'm trying to tell you."

He was still smiling, as I began to explain Addie's transformation
into Adam. His face registered greater surprise. His smile vanished. A
muscle flinched in his jaw. "Look, I know Adam did something crazy
at Jennie's funeral. God knows, people talked about that for years. But
this is even crazier. You're trying to tell me they were the same person?"

I floundered and my heart pounded. I realized I'd been unconsciously
counting on that one time everyone had heard Adam. He had been
exposed then; everyone who'd heard him would know in their bones
how extraordinary he was, and would be able to understand everything
else about him. But I'd forgotten Cole had left the funeral early.

For one second, I hoped he might still be with me. I began to sweat.
"Yes, that's what I am telling you, Cole." The timbre of a plea clung to
my words.

A grimace flickered across his face, followed by a small, uncomfortable smile.

"Evelyn, honey, I know Addie had a gift with horses, a special way
of talking to them that was . . . was . . ." he waved his hands as if trying to scoop the words out of the air. "Unusual. Lord knows it was
amazing that Adam had the same gift and showed up when he did. But
he came to Clarion because he'd heard of how good she was with the
horses. You said so yourself then. He may have replaced her in your
heart, but . . ."

He looked down at my hands pressed together as if in prayer and
shook his head rapidly. "That doesn't make Addie and Adam the same
person. A woman can't turn herself into a man." He wrapped his hands
around mine and I felt myself shrivel. "Listen to me, Evelyn. You're still

in shock. You can't let the grief get to you. I know when Eloise passed, I thought I would go crazy."

We stared at each other for a long moment.

Shame flooded me. The impotence of not being believed crushed me. I had no recourse. No proof.

He leaned closer, trying to catch my eye. "Evelyn, do your girls know you're here? Do they know you drove up here by yourself?"

I withdrew my hands from his and drove him back to the pizzeria. Then I returned to Florida, my shoulders and neck aching from hours of driving, stunned by the dual loss, by the final glance of pity on Cole's face. My throat closed.

He was the only person I ever tried to tell this story to.

BY THE TIME I WAS IN FLORIDA, I had decided that, if cowardice once again prevented me from attempting the truth, I could, at least, offer my daughters closure. A memorial for their father required no validation beyond what they already believed.

I called Sarah first. "I want you to make something for me, for your father." I described the simple fired-clay plaque I wanted.

"Good. I've been waiting for you to ask," she said gently.

Then I had to go swimming. I needed to cleanse myself of the memory of doubt and pity I'd seen in Cole's eyes. I wanted to wash away my mother's shame and the weakness and fear that made me like her. In the water, I would be with Adam and I would be like him—no past, free of explanations.

Families and small children filled the park surrounding Devil's Spring. The smells of grilling meat and sunscreen hung heavy in the air. In the cold water, families shouted and splashed around me. Bright, inflated toys bounced against me as I waded into the shallows. I put on my mask, snorkel, and fins, glad to have children nearby as counterbalance to the blue void below the surface.

I swam past them and circled the mouth of the spring, peering down on the place where he had taken me. The place that had taken *him*. Bubbles of air escaped from the azure hole and a guide rope disappeared into it. As I dove lower, underwater silence overcame the sounds of playing children. The spring mouth loomed, a vivid, continuously deepening blue. I understood Adam's attraction. The spring seemed placid, not the menace I had imagined there for months.

Then I surfaced.

ॐ

MONTHS LATER, I STOOD near the same spot surrounded by my daughters, our hearts on the same shore again. Holding hands, we waded knee-deep into the water. The girls' long skirts floated around them, except for Rosie, who was in full dive gear. Lil carried her father's fiddle. Little Adam bounced and burbled on his mother's hip as we passed the memorial plaque hand-to-hand, admiring the terra cotta, the color of the Carolina clay, and the pale, crackled blue glaze. Clearly carved into the surface in Sarah's square, neat calligraphy were the words from Lil's and Adam's favorite Whitman poem: "Stout as a horse, affectionate, haughty, electrical, I and this mystery . . . In memory of A. Hope."

Gracie, Lil, Sarah, and I watched Rosie and one of the springs dive crew disappear down into the spring, to place the plaque in the cave, just outside the grate that now barred divers from the vein that led to the collapsed chamber. Lil raised the fiddle and began to play "Amazing Grace."

I remembered the silt glittering around me and Adam when we had been in the cave together, the water vibrant between us as his hand marked a rhythm I could not hear. For the first time, I allowed myself to imagine him there alone underwater, his feral howl radiating, restless and joyful, through the land he loved. And, for the first time, I considered that the land had once again answered him, not with rhythm but with a terrible embrace, their duet now airless and unending.

I kept my eyes on the guide rope, not completely at ease with the thought of Rosie so deep in the earth. I studied the serious, expectant faces of my daughters. For a moment, I had the notion that he was calling to them from underground and they were listening, able to hear him as I never had.

After what seemed far too long, Rosie broke through the water, her thumb up and her short hair clinging to her head. "It is done."

We returned to the ranch for the official memorial. A small stage was set up in the backyard. Beside it stood Sarah's latest painting. Adam filled the large canvas. Pictured from the waist up and nude, his arms stretched out, his fingers spread. He looked directly at all of us. A familiar expression filled his face, relaxed and curious, as if he waited for a reply from someone he knew well. A plate-size asterisk radiated from his chest, white at its edge, cobalt in the center. The likeness was strikingly realistic in all respects but his hair. She had given him auburn hair.

When the girls sang, I found I could no longer pull their individual voices loose from the braid of their harmonies. Only when one of them took the lead could I tell who or how many were singing. There might have been five voices, there could have been six.

One by one, neighbors, cowboys, musicians, divers, hippies, and horsemen stepped up to the microphone with some story or song for Adam. People whom Adam had touched surrounded me. Their voices buoyed me. Neither Ray the veterinarian, nor Manny had ever again mentioned what they'd heard from Adam the day the stallion attacked the mare, but Ray paused during his praise of Adam's horsemanship and his eyes sought mine in the crowd. Then, with a nod, he seemed to find the word he was seeking: uncanny.

I did not speak. The single, unique story I could have told was a weight in my chest. A star of dark matter, a thing that held its own gravity, enthralling my heart.

Things were not good after that, but they were better. Grief's gutting blade was preferable to obsession. The questions of what I might have done to prevent or foresee what had happened still seduced me at times, but they never dominated me as they once had.

From that point on, to be reminded of my husband, I could look at any stranger's face. To honor him, I had only to treat every stranger as if he or she might have been my lover and the parent of my children. I hung Sarah's portrait of him in the living room. I gave his clothes away. I sold all our horses except for Rosie's favorite and Jericho.

༄

NOT LONG AFTER THE MEMORIAL, I sold the ranch and moved into town. I became, at last, a herd animal, at home in the casual company of a neighborhood, pleased by the crowds at the markets and art fairs downtown. My home is now a short walk to a creek, a park, the public library, a supermarket, a funeral home, a birthing center, a theater, and the courthouse. You can do anything here. And there are plenty of folks to do it among—lots of families, a few oldies like me, a drunk guy, and one friendly transvestite laundress who strolls by every day after the local dry cleaner closes. There are also possum, armadillo, raccoons, a few snakes, and some ducks. A curious otter, a wild turkey, and a black bear have wandered into the neighborhood—not all at the same time. The only thing missing is the sky. Aged water oaks tower over the houses, shading the yards.

It seems I will not be wandering off into the woods, as I did as a girl, but will take my leave here among my own kind.

I lived alone until a couple of years ago. Then Lil discovered that Alphonso, her college sweetheart and husband for almost twenty years, was not what she thought him to be. After the divorce, she came home to Florida and decided to live with me. I'm old enough now that all the girls thought it was a good idea that one of them be around to keep an eye on me.

They are not so young themselves. Gracie will turn fifty within days. But, like their father, they all seem to be aging at their own special rates. The curve of their earlobes, how they lift their faces when their own children speak to them, how their hips and breasts have filled and shrunk with the changes of maturity and childbirth, continue to fascinate me—not as frequently, but no less intensely than their perfect bodies did when they were new and fresh. I still feel flashes of tenderness toward them, amazed that they are here in the world and are mine. They are profoundly, cellularly familiar to me, and they are, in the distances and privacies of their adult lives, a series of mysteries.

Adam may be responsible for the youthfulness of their faces, but I claim responsibility for the gene that sent them to the edge of their tribes for a mate. The same gene that sang in me as I dragged A. in out of the cold rain. Our daughters are now scattered across four continents. Mayan, Chinese, Dutch, and African blood runs through the veins of my grandchildren. In their careers and their choice of husbands, they've covered the globe. Gracie lives in the Netherlands. Still married to Hans, she now has a diplomatic appointment at The Hague. Their sons are mild, witty Dutchmen like their father. Vet school led Rosie to research in genetics and species-hopping viruses. She married Mussa, a fellow geneticist, and they commute between California and Africa on a seasonal basis. Her boys all have their daddy's beautiful tropical skin and big hands. Sarah lives and paints in China with her husband, Jian, and their son. She has just been authorized to return to the United States. Lil lives down the hall. The mother of two grown sons, she left the Library of Congress last year and took a position at the UF library as a digital preservation specialist. Eventually, she ceased being the twin left behind, one half of a whole, and became her singular self. Seeing her become a mother separated her, at last, in my heart, from Jennie, who remains nine years old.

About a month ago, I woke from a deep sleep to a sound I had not heard in twenty years: the reverberations of Adam's sexual climax. Instinctively, I reached across my empty bed for him. Still half-asleep, I got out of bed and followed the rising voice, then realized I was outside Lil's bedroom door. Gently, I pressed my palm flat on the door as the cry peaked then vanished.

A man's voice boomed, "Wow!" Lil's new lover.

Lil's laughter followed—surprised, joyful laughter.

Only then did I realize who I'd been listening to. I stepped back into my bedroom and quietly shut the door. I wanted Adam. I wanted the beautiful harmonic of him, wanted to pour myself over him.

Down the hall, their voices continued, indistinct, muffled.

Eventually, the house became quiet again. Then I heard Lil's footsteps in the hall. I found her sitting at the kitchen table, just outside the pool of light from the stove hood, her features relaxed and soft. She shook her head when I sat down at the table across from her. "Momma, just when I think I'm on an even keel and I understand how things are and what I'm capable of . . ." She sighed.

"I know. I heard."

"Yes, I guess you would've." The corner of her mouth lifted in an apologetic half-smile. "We always knew with you and Daddy. There would be the click of your bedroom door closing, then after a while . . ." She paused and glanced at me a little sheepishly.

"Yes?"

"Then you'd make that sound you always made. The walls hummed, then Daddy laughed."

"The sound *I* made?"

Her face reflected my surprise.

I touched her hand. "Lil, that was your daddy you heard, not me. It was never me."

"Daddy? Really?" Her mouth hung open and she stared at me.

I nodded.

She snapped her mouth shut. "Wow . . . I thought it was something only women did. Sarah does it when she's with Jian. Remember, I stayed about a week with them when they lived in Chicago. The walls were so thin. And I've heard Rosie . . . So that was Daddy?" She rubbed her chest. "And that time after Jennie's funeral when you stopped Daddy, I thought it was because he was doing something only women did. I thought you were upset because he was acting like a woman."

I wiped my eyes and tried to smile at her. "Do you remember the time in the mountains with all of us?"

She squinted in the effort to remember, then her expression changed. "Oh, when the rocks sang? That was amazing. You were right there when I opened my eyes. Are you saying that was Daddy, too?"

I nodded.

After a moment, her face slowly broke into a wide smile. "Momma, a while ago in bed, when I . . . it was like my chest opened up in a new way. Wonderful and scary." She paused and sighed. "So, you are telling me that, at forty-four, my body has learned a new trick and it's unique to us?"

Not to "us," I thought—to you, the daughters of Adam. But I just nodded.

Lil's revelation stunned me. It had never crossed my mind that the girls would attribute his voice to me or their unique voice as a gift from me.

But I know how secrets and assumptions grow larger over the years, fed by the tensions and yearnings of their keepers. They also diffuse as they settle, like a strange pollen, spreading invisibly over the fields of our daily lives. Simultaneously everywhere and nowhere. What we do not say never ceases being. It waits. Robust. Elemental.

The day after my conversation with Lil, I received a brief letter from Sarah:

> *Momma, I'm including this picture to prepare you—all of you. It's the latest picture of me. I haven't done anything to myself or the photograph, I swear. I probably should be alarmed, but I'm not. It feels natural. I'm okay. I'm happy. And I am pregnant again! Three months by the time I see you! A daughter is coming, I'm sure. Oh, and there's a canyon here that reminds me so much of Daddy. Looking forward to seeing all of you soon.*

> *Love, S.*

In the photograph, Sarah squats beside her young son, Michael. He grins up at the camera, a happy little Chinese boy sporting the cheekbones of the McMurrough clan and a purple shirt. Sarah looks directly at the camera, her face is serious, her chin thrust out as if offering her features to the world. She is still quite distinctly Sarah. Same chin, same forehead. But her once-curly auburn hair is black and straight, her pale irises are now dark brown. Her eyelids are Asian. She has become a Chinese woman. The daughter of A.

I stared at the photo until my eyes burned, then teared. I had it finally: proof.

I began to write.

Recently, I found out that the "magical sea monkeys" we purchased for the girls when we first moved to Florida are a species of tiny shrimplike animals, triops, which survive in the hidden pools that are the carved afterthoughts of desert flash-floods. When the pool dries completely, the dehydrated creatures, lifeless by all human measures, can wait decades for the next flood, when they will once again spring into life and swim.

I find a humbling, comic comfort in triops. In their company, Adam seems normal, or at least natural. In the last decade, I have gotten tired of questions and of questioning.

What is simply *is.*

My hope is that my daughters will forgive me my innocence, my ignorance, and my fears. All I know is this: A. was and is. He walks this earth, whole and unrecognizable. He is here among us, somewhere. Beside you, perhaps. And on this December day in the year 2000, I know that the Florida air is warm, the windows are open. My grandsons run down the hall. Gracie's plane is touching down. Sarah and her family are flying over the Pacific. The odors of baking bread fill my home. In the kitchen, Lil and Rosie sling Christmas carols around like cabaret songs. "God Rest Ye Merry Gentlemen," indeed.

Within hours, my youngest daughter will come through the door bearing in her body her second child and undeniable proof of A.

I will hand my daughters all that I have written here.

I will, at last, be true.

I HAVE OFTEN FOUND myself thinking of that day long ago at the springs when I lay on my back under A., looking past his shoulder into that one-bird-filled sky, lying like a girl, naked under my husband in the woods. I felt the shadow of his disappearance then. Faint in that spring brightness, but not undetectable. I chose not to look at it then, not to pull the thread of that individual loss and sorrow out of the tapestry, but I knew it was there. I've wondered if he intentionally brought me to the place where he would take his leave, the deep blue mouth of the earth that would be his door out of this life. Probably not. I don't think he knew any more than I did at the time. He was simply and eventually true to his own nature. He left my life as he entered it, through elegant and elemental forces. He left me to listen after him to this new land.

Now he is of this land and this water. The water here, like him, is of no discernible origin. Pulled by the sun's endless energy, it rises from far-off shores to fall on Florida soil. It makes its way through the dense, fragrant darkness of mulch, tannin-drenched sand, and the limestone. In dark, underground silence, droplets form trickles then brooks. Brooks join to become small rivers beneath this thin skin of earth. Small rivers join to make larger rivers, increasing exponentially in force, power, and volume until millions of gallons spring from the earth into the lazy flow of the Suwannee, the Withlacoochee, the Itchetucknee, the Santa Fe. From there, the water flows to the sea, or it makes its way into the bellies of alligators and snakes, or inches up through dense cellulose of cypress. Or it rises as singular molecules again toward the sun to fall once more on other faraway forests.

Countless times, I have imagined A. rising through the rivers of this land, to the surface of Florida to be found again, pulled into the air by new hands. The possibilities are endless, but most often I imagine him found by children. Above him, the sky shimmers and undulates blue through transparent springwater. Then four small brown hands break the surface and pull him into the air and into their excited and frightened vocabularies. The delicate bones of their arms and ribs absorb his voice, shattering their knowledge of what is possible.

Acknowledgments

Three women were crucial in this novel's journey to your hands. Though my dear friend Peg Libertus did not live to see its publication, her early and highly enthusiastic support for the idea of A. Hope kept me going as I slogged through the earliest versions. I am very grateful to my agent, Mollie Glick, for saying yes to me and the story of Adam Hope. Her professionalism and warmth made the process of finding publication astoundingly smooth. Lee Boudreaux's reassuring cheer, lucid edits, and trust in my creativity invigorated the final revisions, opening up solutions I wouldn't have thought of on my own. I am very fortunate to have these three on my team.

I am thankful for the many friends and fellow writers who patiently read this book in manuscript form and gave me the impetus and the tools to push on. Special acknowledgment must be given to those who read the awful first drafts in part or full, without laughing or trying to smack some sense into me: Susan Mickelberry, Susan Gildersleeve, Julie Robitaille, David O'Gorman, Manuel Martinez, Margaret Luongo, Richard Nuñez, Naana

Horne, Kathy DeWitt, Sidney Bertisch, Peggy Payne, and Flo Turcotte. Pat Rowe and June Edelstein read earlier drafts and offered unbridled encouragement throughout the process. My fellow Writers' Alliance of Gainesville members Frank Fiordalisi, Robin Ecker, Shari King, Persis Granger, and Art Crummer spent many a Thursday afternoon poring over *The Enchanted Life of Adam Hope.* Their supportive critiques were invaluable to me.

Robin Ecker and Deb Jennings generously gave me the benefit of their years of experience with horses. Other friends and family have provided research, support, ideas, or observations: Roxanne Colwell, Dot and Kit Martin, and the Gainesville group of Like-Minded Women.

I am personally grateful to my children, Daniel and Rachel, who suffered, with very little complaint, the deprivations of a tiny rental house so I could afford a sabbatical to write. I thank Doran for years of friendship that have nourished my imagination and my heart.

The final revisions were written with the support of an Individual Artist Fellowship from the State of Florida Division of Cultural Affairs.

My appreciation for the writing of Michael Ondaatje, Terry Tempest Williams, and Craig Childs has informed this novel. My humble thanks to them for how well they have done their jobs.

I would also like to acknowledge the efforts of all who seek to protect and conserve Nature, particularly those who work to preserve the purity and plenty of Florida's amazing and endangered waterways. If this novel has sparked your interest in the springs of Florida, please visit http://floridaconservationcoalition.org/ or http://www.floridastateparks.org/